Over My Wed Body

EXCERPT

Bailey sat on a stool at the kitchen's island counter in front of a platter of fried chicken, scrolling through her phone. Good chance she was shopping for supplies. I'd rarely seen her not working since I'd arrived in Bride.

"You'll ruin your appetite for dinner."

Bailey jolted, dropping a leg of chicken and spinning on the stool. "You scared me. Too hungry to wait another hour."

"Same here." I intercepted the chicken leg as she raised it toward her lips and then I sunk my teeth into it.

Bailey's eye twitched. "Nice manners. I was eating that." She reached for the plate of chicken and chose a wing. I snagged that too, wrestling it from her hand. She slipped off the stool and threw a punch at my bicep. She used to always playfully beat on me.

"You want it?" I smashed the chicken leg on her face, smearing chicken fat around her mouth and coercing her lips apart.

She belly-laughed, throwing punches faster than I could dodge them. "Such a jerk."

Jerk, yes. But she was laughing again. With *me*. I reached for a fresh drumstick and jammed that at her face too, swiping it across her cheek.

She crammed a wing into my nose, mainlining the spices and grease directly into my nostril. Her eyes lit with a familiar mischief before she squished the chicken into my hair.

This was war. And, what the hell, I needed a shower anyway.

I shoved her against the counter, about to stuff the chicken leg down the front of her shirt and froze, my gaze locking onto the creamy swells at her neckline. Her chest rose and fell with each pant and my gaze met hers. She licked her lips, then focused on my mouth.

Not one to let a perfect opportunity pass, I seized the moment and leaned in.

Over My Wed Body

VERONICA BLADE

Gardnerville, Nevada

Over My Wed Body

Crush Publishing, Inc
Gardnerville, NV 89460
www.CrushPublishing.com

Crush Publishing, Inc name and logo are trademarks of Crush Publishing, Inc and are used only with its permission.

The places, characters and events portrayed in this book are fictitious. Any similarity to real persons, living or dead, is coincidental and not intended by author.

ISBN 978-0-9995994-1-9

Cover design and layout by Rose Nomura

Printed in the United States of America

For Zayne and Joceline

I'm grateful every single day for you two

Chapter One

HUNTER

Some hot chick had hijacked my best friend's Silverado.

I saw only her backside as she tossed something into the backseat of the truck—probably making room for me in the front—but her arms were toned and her butt perfection. She wore Daisy Duke shorts with cowboy boots and a purple crop top that teased me with a little bare midriff. Judging by her wild curves and long legs, she invested some serious time keeping that body in wicked condition.

I hauled the crate while dragging my luggage through the double doors of Austin-Bergstrom airport toward the curb, slowing my pace to allow more time to gawk. A thank-you was in order to my best friend Blake for arranging my ride—and providing such a prime piece of eye candy. I predicted my drive to the B & B ranch would be surprisingly pleasant. Even if she already had a boyfriend, I could still enjoy the view.

The crate shifted in my hand and Muffin whined. "Hang on, baby. As soon as my bags are loaded, I'll get you out of there."

My gaze swept the woman's body again as she tossed her waist-length auburn hair over her shoulder and swiveled....

My mouth flapped open, and both handles of the luggage slipped from my grasp. I lowered the crate to the concrete. "Bailey?"

"Hey, Hunter." Her plump pink lips curved up as she spotted me. "Need a ride?"

I wanted a ride from her but the scenario rushing through my brain didn't require a truck. I blinked, trying to purge those kinds of thoughts. This was Bailey, my best friend's little sister. Bails, who I'd watched grow up. Being attracted to her wasn't an option.

"Are you okay?" Bailey aimed her gray eyes at me, her perfectly arched eyebrows drawn.

I hadn't been back to Bride since before I started my vet internship over a year ago. Actually, I hadn't seen Bailey since a few months before that, when a bunch of us had met in Vegas for a friend's wedding. How had she changed so much in so little time?

The Bailey Thayer I'd known most of my life hadn't troubled herself with girly things like curling her hair. She'd always kept it shoulder-length for easier washing after mucking stables, and it was almost always in a ponytail. Aside from prom or an occasional date, I didn't remember her wearing makeup. And I'd rarely seen her out of baggie jeans and a loose t-shirt that hid anything remotely feminine underneath. Who knew she had a body like *that*?

"Of course I'm okay." I laughed once, then poured on the charm, hoping she wouldn't notice how she'd thrown me. "Why wouldn't I be?"

She smirked. "Then get in."

I steeled myself not to take her words in a sexual way as I bent and reached for the luggage handles—and got a glimpse of her inner thighs as she rounded the hood to the driver's side. I grimaced, wishing I could go back in time to when she was ten, and I thought of her as my kid sister. Why did she have to wear such short shorts? How could Blake let his sister leave the house wearing so little?

Before I got to the passenger door, two guys strolled past the truck, their gaze riveted to Bailey's butt. Suddenly in a hurry to get her away from the leering men, I dumped my baggage into the bed of the truck, then climbed into the passenger seat with the crate. If anyone was going to perv on her, it would be *me.*

Bailey tipped her head toward the crate. "Take him out so I can meet him."

"Her." I opened the gate. "C'mon out, Muffin."

She snorted. "Muffin?"

"That wasn't my doing. She already knew her name and I didn't want to confuse her."

Bailey gasped as Muffin poked her face out of the crate. "She's adorable. Black and tan King Charlies are my favorite." She reached toward me and gave Muffin a rub under her chin. "I didn't think you liked small dogs. How did you end up with her?"

"Got a house call to check out a mare about three months ago and the mare's owner asked me to examine her puppy. When I told her Muffin had cherry eye and the surgery may not be permanent, she said she didn't want a defective dog."

"Seriously? That woman has no soul," she muttered, starting the engine.

"Yeah, more worried about her pets maintaining perfection than the animals themselves. It gets worse." I absently rubbed Muffin's ears between my fingers and her lids lowered. "Then she asked me how much to put the dog to sleep. She ended up payin' the fee and signed the necessary papers to murder her puppy."

Bailey scowled as she punched the gas, pulling away from the curb. "So you slipped her the paperwork which signed over ownership and the woman didn't read what she was signin'?"

I grinned and leaned in to kiss Muffin's forehead. "And got myself one cool little girl. Best decision I ever made."

"You've had her for three months, huh?" She gave Muffin a quick pat. "Good thing she's not an actual woman or she would've already been rehomed."

A witty reply stuck in my throat. But what could I say to Bailey when she was absolutely right? I was twenty-six years old and the longest I'd dated any woman was about ten weeks. I couldn't give any human unconditional love, even my own family—not that anyone would blame me for not liking my parents. The one thing I'd really dedicated myself to was vet school but only because it involved animals. They didn't betray you like humans did. "True. When I meet a human who isn't completely flawed, my commitment issues might change."

Bailey scoffed. "Plenty of good women everywhere. You're just not payin' attention."

But I'd learned the hard way that the people I trusted most would let me down the hardest. The only exceptions I'd found to this rule were the Thayers—Blake, Bailey and their parents.

As I repositioned Muffin and settled in for the long drive, I got a whiff of Bailey. Oh man, she smelled like cherries. I swallowed, stifling the urge to touch her and see if the skin on her legs felt as soft as it looked. Instead, I ran a hand through Muffin's fur to keep my fingers occupied.

Bailey rotated, glancing over her shoulder to check the next lane. Her crop top inched up and my gaze stumbled on more exposed skin above her waist. This new side of her would add an interesting dynamic to the next few weeks. At the very least, life at the B & B ranch wouldn't be boring.

When Blake had called two days ago pleading for me to return and stand in for him at the family ranch, my brain searched for any excuse to stay away. But the Thayers had been incredibly generous through my teen years, providing a safe haven for me. Since Blake was wearing a full leg cast, I couldn't abandon him or his family. Ranch chores had to be done.

Plus, the Thayers already knew I'd recently finished my internship with Dr. Mayfield, and that I hadn't decided where to set up my equine veterinarian practice. I was also toying with the idea of going back to school for surgery. Regardless of what I ended up doing, or where, I was in limbo. I had no excuse to avoid my family and friends in Bride, Texas.

This trip wouldn't be all bad though. I truly loved the Thayers and anytime I had come home during college breaks, I always stayed with them. I dropped in on my parents out of obligation. If my parents found out I'd been in town without seeing them—in a town this small, someone would surely sell me out—I would never hear the end of it. Their constant micromanaging was bad enough when I hadn't actually done anything wrong.

I'd left my hometown of Bride for a good reason—to get away from them. I didn't want to undo my hard work by growing roots. Deep down, I'd probably always wish for a normal relationship with them, but I kept my expectations pathetically low. Disappointment stung and I'd had enough of that. Texas and the ranch life would always draw me in, but for my own sanity, I wouldn't stay any longer than necessary and I couldn't let down the emotional walls I'd built. I let the walls down for the Thayers, to a degree. And Muffin. That was it.

My stay in Bride would last until Blake's cast came off and not a second longer. But I wasn't a kid anymore and my adult pride prevented me from being extra baggage to them. I'd get in, help them through this, then get the hell out. I could do this for them. Besides, it's not like I had any other obligations at the moment.

I just had to keep my hands off Bailey.

Conversation. Something needed to distract me from her and my strange new fascination with her body. "How's Blake doing?"

"Not great. He's not used to feelin' worthless." She sneaked another peek at Muffin. "He's been threatenin' to saw off the cast."

"What? That's beyond stupid." I commanded myself to look at the green light ahead and not at her creamy thighs. "His leg won't heal properly without the cast."

She rolled her eyes. "Agreed. But the doctor told him he may never have one-hundred percent use of his leg. So he already knows what to expect there. He figures his odds for a better outcome will be with a different route."

"I can't believe you're related to that guy." I banged my head on the window. "He can't get around on his own yet, right?"

She raised one brow. "They're called crutches."

After replaying the question in my head, I saw how stupid I'd sounded. But when did she become so sarcastic? I preferred the sweet Bailey who used to hang on my every word. "We'll make sure any kind of cutting tool is hidden from the moron until he's no longer insane."

Her soft laugh sent my skin humming. "It's all talk. Blake knows he won't be in a cast forever but he's anxious to have his life back. When he resumes his duties, you'll return to L.A. and everything will be right with the world again."

Did I detect a hint of acid in her tone on the subject of me and my inevitable departure? Now that I thought about it, where was the exuberant hug and adoration Bailey usually lavished on me? I'd been too busy ogling her to notice the lack of warmth in her greeting. She'd been friendly enough not to come across rude, but not sweet like she used to be.

In fact, the last few times Bailey had answered the phone when I'd called to check on Mrs. Thayer, she had barely said a word to me. "Are you mad at me or somethin'? You've been different since the Vegas trip."

Her gaze cut to mine and her mouth straightened, before she returned her attention to the road. "We agreed never to mention Vegas again. What happens in Vegas stays in Vegas, remember? It's in the ad campaign and everything."

I grunted. "It didn't stay in Vegas or you wouldn't be actin' weird."

The tires skidded across the asphalt as she yanked the truck to the side of the road. She pivoted in her seat and glared. "I've been avoidin' you since Vegas and you're just now noticin'? If you gave a crap about anything but yourself, you would've asked what was wrong months ago." She angled her chin up, her eyes hardening. "This conversation is over."

What? I didn't pretend to understand women. Sure, I knew how to get their attention and keep it long enough to get them into my bed. But actually understand them and make a relationship last more than a few weeks? Nope.

Not knowing what to say to make peace, I shut my trap and waited for the storm to subside.

"Other than pet owners devoid of hearts, how's the furry patient business doin'?" she asked after a long stretch of silence.

Did I really want to make small talk with Bailey when something was bothering her? Seemed better than the awkward tension sweeping the cab, and talking might make the trip pass quicker. "I'm lovin' it. I especially like workin' with horses. Tryin' to decide between a surgery residency or settin' up a practice and gettin' straight to work."

She cast me a skeptical glance. "Doesn't your little starlet have guidance for you?"

"Abigail's not *my* starlet." I inwardly groaned, wanting to forget the existence of Abigail. "I met her at a dog park and gave her potty trainin' tips for her puppy. That was it."

Bailey clucked her tongue. "Pictures of you two kissin' were plastered all over the internet."

I cringed, remembering how hurt Abigail had been when I'd stopped calling. In my defense, I always warned girls of my bad dating record in advance. But they rarely listened. Each one believed they'd be the one to change me. Then when I broke things off, they were always shocked. Apparently, I hadn't made my intentions clear enough with Abigail and in the end, she'd accused me of using her.

As much as I wanted to shift the blame to Abigail for not heeding my warning, she was right. I'd used her. I'd used them all. And I hated myself for making them feel weak or doubt themselves, like my parents had done to me. I didn't want to be alone for the rest of my life but a happy or loving relationship wasn't in my future. So I stole pleasure in bits and pieces when I could—and destroyed lives along the way. I sucked. If I had to be celibate the rest of my life, I vowed never to put another girl through that kind of pain. At the very least, I needed to avoid nice girls. "Haven't seen her in a couple months."

"She's been rehomed, huh?" Bailey laughed once before covering her mouth and suppressing a giggle. "Saw that comin'."

Why should I waste my time defending myself when Bailey had already tried and convicted me? Though I couldn't blame her, the hostility was a bit much. She was either hormonal or more pissed off at me than I'd originally thought. This was going to be the longest drive ever.

Either way, she'd get over it. Eventually. Maybe after she saw me day after day over the upcoming weeks, she'd remember why we were friends and warm up.

My gaze drifted beyond the window at my side. As we left Austin behind and hit the main highway toward Bride and the B & B Ranch, the concrete sidewalks and buildings gave way to dirt, burnt orange leaves and tall yellowing grass.

Instinct told me to shut down like Bailey had—show her two could play at that game. But she wasn't the type to be petty or sulk unnecessarily. Whatever I'd done to make her mad, being an even bigger jerk to her and playing mind games wouldn't get me back in her good graces. I needed to behave. Unfortunately, proper behavior had never been one of my super powers. But Blake and his family had been my lifelines since I was ten years old.

For Bailey, I'd try harder.

When my parents had avoided our home to have extramarital affairs—too busy to deal with their wayward son—Mr. or Mrs. T picked me up from football practice. And they always had a place for me at the table. As an only child, I had loved being treated as part of their family, Blake and Bailey's sibling. I'd done Big Brother duties with Blake, watched over Bailey when she went out with her friends and laid down the rules to her loser dates, chasing down any boys who disrespected her in any way.

I would always be connected to my biological mother and father, the little I could tolerate. But the Thayers were my true family. As much as I wanted to let Bailey work out her anger on her own, and as much as I didn't want to talk about my feelings—or listen to any woman talk about hers—I really wanted to get back to normal with her.

"Whatever I did, Bails, I'm sorry. But I can't fix it if you don't tell me what's going on."

Her grip tightened on the steering wheel. "Forget it."

Bailey's attitude made forgetting about her anger kind of difficult. "Bails..."

She eased off the accelerator and sighed as the Silverado slowed. "I'm glad we got an annulment, Hunter, don't get me wrong. People shouldn't be allowed to get married when they're that wasted."

Dread smothered me—the last thing I wanted to revisit was that colossal mistake. I'd never been more wasted than that night. Except for flashes of images, I didn't remember much. I could almost pretend it never happened. And the more often either of us were reminded of our drunken night in Vegas, or talked about it, the higher the risk Blake might find out. Granted, we hadn't slept together—whew!—but we'd gone far enough to drive Blake to try to kick the crap out of me.

As much as I wanted to avoid the topic, I knew Bailey needed to get it all out so she could move on. "And?"

"The panic in your eyes and how quickly you filed the papers, like you couldn't wait to get rid of me, didn't do much for my ego. You were downright insulting." She ground out the last word, shifting her attention to the stretch of road in the distance.

That's what was eating at her? Piece of cake. "Are you kidding me? Blake is my best friend. We've been practically family forever. We had to reverse it quickly so Blake wouldn't discover I'd violated his little sister in any way." My gaze fell to her naked thighs.

A memory invaded my brain—Bailey lying under my weight, her frantic hands fumbling to take off my shirt as our mouths fused. A tingle ambushed my nether regions and horror filled me. I had to purge all memories of our Vegas adventure, forget it ever happened. I focused on the mile marker ahead, but another memory assaulted me... her heavy-lidded eyes and flushed face as she arched her neck.

Why was this haunting me *now*? We'd had a blast, drank too much, gotten married and I'd passed out before we'd consummated. The next morning while Bailey distracted Blake during breakfast, I'd started the annulment. They'd both returned to Bride and I'd flown back to Los Angeles. And I'd never allowed myself to think of that night again. Done and finished.

Bailey hadn't replied and it had been more than a minute. "I was trying to save us both from Blake's wrath. Why is that so bad?"

"It's not." She tilted her chin. "I don't know why you're still trying to explain. I'm over it."

Yeah, right. She was over the Vegas fiasco like I was over her smokin' legs and sexy-as-hell mouth. But since I didn't know what else to say, I focused on the upcoming mile marker. Twenty more miles to Bride. It would feel like forty.

Spending the remaining drive in uncomfortable silence wasn't what worried me though. I wasn't sure how I'd survive the next few weeks living in the same house with her. First, because I didn't know how to make things right. Second, because even as I vowed not to be attracted to her, I couldn't help but be—all I had to do was look at any part of her. She wasn't just more beautiful than I remembered. She was more confident. Sassier. Smarter.

Intriguing.

Third, it was only a matter of time before Blake noticed something weird was going on between Bailey and me—and the reason. And then he'll want to kill me.

Chapter Two
BAILEY

I wasn't over the Vegas disaster, not by a long shot.

Trying not to dwell on old wounds, I kept my attention on the road ahead and did my best to forget Hunter was sitting in the passenger seat. Not possible. But as my blood boiled, I knew Hunter didn't *try* to hurt people. It just came naturally to him. His parents had created a monster, messed with his head and now his inner wiring was crossed and tangled.

I had watched his face every time they missed a game or when he'd shown up at our house because they were fighting. Any time my family tried to mediate between him and his parents, Hunter had bailed. Resolving things and bonding with his folks would mean making himself vulnerable. After the world of hurt they had inflicted on him, he was afraid to allow himself to truly love anyone.

Unfortunately, women got the brunt of that fear. As soon as a girl got serious, he'd dump her. Although Hunter frequently amazed me for turning out as good as he had, he was still a womanizing sack of horse manure. I'd always known the real Hunter and had fallen for him anyway. I had no one to blame but myself for my damaged ego. Still, his insensitivity and obliviousness toward me made my chest ache.

He hadn't said another word since our little spat minutes ago, and as much as I wanted to believe he was trying to do as I'd asked, more likely he didn't care. Any sadness I felt because he didn't fight for me was quickly replaced by renewed fury because, once again, Hunter's first concern was Hunter—with my mother and Blake tied for second place. I didn't rate.

I reminded myself that he was basically a good guy and he tried to help others when he could—like returning to Bride to help my family.

"How's the ranch doing?" he asked. "Is it much more difficult without Mr. Thayer?"

"Not as easy as it used to be. Between the medical bills and additional staff to cover Dad's workload, my parents emptied their savings account. We sold off a few hundred acres and used the money to pay the last of Dad's medical bills and then his funeral expenses." My body wilted in the driver's seat as the loss of my father hit me all over again. "We couldn't risk having a bad week and not being able to pay our staff, so we laid off some of them. Which means the brunt of the work falls on Blake and me now."

"You guys are catching up though, right?"

Asked the guy with the multimillion-dollar trust fund. For him, money came easy. He had no clue about profits and loss, balance sheets, taxes, insurance and the myriad things needed to breed horses of this caliber or train and sell them. He had no sense of the level of responsibility and determination it took to run a successful ranch, had no idea how my family, our employees and so many others depended upon Blake and me for their survival. That kind of pressure carried a heavy weight.

"No, Hunter, we're not." I leaned forward, resting my forearm on the steering wheel to stretch my lower back, and wondered if I might have a day anytime soon without tired muscles. "We're not pulling the profits Dad did. Mom handles the bookkeeping, orders supplies and various other things, but she's always been too busy raising us and running the house to get involved in the inner workings of the ranch. Blake and I are learning, but we're not there yet."

"How can I help?"

"Your hands will be full doing Blake's chores." I moaned. "I have so much to accomplish over the next few weeks. Iesha and I have *got* to place in Tulsa World Finals."

"I haven't seen Iesha work cattle in a while. You really think she could beat the other cutters?"

"I do." Hunter would be more aware of Iesha's skills if he kept tabs on me at all. He would know Iesha already had several wins under her saddle and her winnings have been decent. Too bad all the money had gone to paying old bills. "Even if she only gets second or third place, we might be fine. If not, we have to sell an awful lot in stud fees or we won't make the mortgage payment. We can't keep selling land or we'll be out of business with no place for the horses."

Hunter scratched his scruffy chin. "You have some fantastic brood mares. If you breed all of them that you possibly can and sell the foals, wouldn't you get a little extra?"

"Gestation period is eleven months, remember? We've got several foals, but they aren't ready for sale. Some of them aren't even weaned yet." I sighed, not wanting to think about how much less money we had now and how much longer before I'd see a share of the ranch profits. How I would've loved a new dress or two. We could be paying on our debts for years before we're able to funnel any of it back into savings. At least we always had wholesome food on the table, mama made certain of it. "We're at the end of breeding season. I have about two weeks, three tops, to breed the last broodmare. Then my window is gone."

"Serenity Ranch has some beautiful Arabians. I'm wondering if you could buy a couple of their older foals closer to training age. The sooner you can work with a horse and show its potential, the sooner you can make some money and pay off the debt. Right?"

I knew how it worked, geez. Had I not just spelled out our financial situation? I exhaled loudly as irritation crept up my spine and out through my mouth. "I'm confident Serenity has some great stock, but they don't come cheap. We're barely paying the help and feeding the horses as it is."

As the highway lengthened behind my brother's Silverado, the occasional building was replaced by fields, fences and cattle. Fall was my favorite time in Texas when the cedar elm's glossy green leaves turned a glorious shade of orange and the late aster blooms exploded into lavender. But with Hunter sitting inches from me, drinking in all the beauty of autumn in Texas was much more difficult.

Hunter's cluelessness about normal life hardships got me riled up too often. But I loved him anyway. When I'd waited for him at the airport curb and taken one look at his dark brown eyes, shaggy sun-streaked brown hair, those broad shoulders and muscular arms, butterflies fluttered in my stomach so hard, I'd become nauseous.

I hated being a slave to emotions and my body's cravings. I didn't want to love Hunter.

Hunter had always been almost too perfect. And he exuded confidence, making him seem more ruggedly sexy. Watching his biceps flex as he'd loaded his luggage into the back of the truck hadn't helped suppress the longing igniting in the pit of my belly. Seeing his face soften and his eyes light up as he beamed at Muffin had nearly killed me with envy.

He would never look at me that way.

The dashboard clock read nine a.m. and after we passed the picturesque little town of Bride, we would have another five minutes before cruising into the driveway of the B & B ranch. My fingers twitched on the steering wheel. "Mind if we stop by Two Cups? I rushed to the airport this morning without getting my caffeine fix."

"Sounds great. I'd love some coffee." He stroked Muffin's fur and I wished, for his sake, that one day he could lavish that level of tenderness on a human—even if it wasn't me.

"Excellent," I said, hoping we wouldn't run into Noelle. She frequented the little cupcake shop, usually finishing appraisal reports while sipping a cappuccino. I didn't want to be reminded of how she'd dated Hunter in high school and had gotten further with him as a girlfriend than I'd gotten with him as his wife. Even after a rough divorce, she was prettier than she'd been as a teen.

I couldn't control which women Hunter interacted with, but I didn't want to witness it with Noelle. Again.

Hunter lapsed into silence as the *Welcome to Bride, Texas* sign approached. My eyes landed on Two Cups in the distance, which sold the tastiest lattes for miles. Not to mention their fabulous cupcakes. At the sight of the white painted brick exterior, my mouth salivated. I accelerated the gas, anxious to satisfy my addiction.

On the other side of the parking lot stood the fire station. Across the street, the American flag waved from the post office and on the corner, rows of gas pumps lined the lot of a convenience store. And, as always, the bronze statue of Bride's founding bride, Ellora Shepherd, stood forlornly, destined to wear that old fashioned dress for all eternity. The faraway look in her eyes made me think of my own love life—except she'd probably had better luck than I had.

I eased off the accelerator and swerved, pulling alongside the curb. Without glancing at Hunter, I hopped out of the Silverado and sprinted into the cupcake bakery. Hunter managed to grab Muffin and arrive at the entrance to open the door with his free hand. I thanked him, wishing he wouldn't make an effort to be nice, and immediately spotted Noelle on a stool facing the wide front window. I instantly deflated when she swiveled to beam at Hunter, then she hopped off the stool and made a beeline directly for him.

Hunter met Noelle halfway, weaving past the full tables and across the brown-and-cream-checkered floor. He slung his free arm around her waist then kissed both her cheeks. Wishing we hadn't stopped for coffee, I averted my gaze to the pastries and cookies displayed on the other side of the glass.

Noelle had always been naturally beautiful with no need for makeup. Her sunny-blond hair flowed in thick waves and her flawless skin pinkened as she smiled at Hunter. Between her petite frame and trim figure, she was the exact opposite of me. I understood why Hunter had dated her on and off. But if he couldn't last with someone like Noelle, I didn't stand a chance.

She could take a portion of the blame for her relationship failures though, since her picker was obviously broken. I'd never been privy to the details of her multiple breakups with Hunter, but no doubt he was the start of all her bad luck. My guess was if he were given the opportunity, he'd take advantage of her again.

As much as I wanted to dislike her, however, I couldn't. Though she and I hadn't been close, she'd never been anything but nice to me. Since she'd been the one to land the boy I'd been crazy about for years, a little distance was fine by me.

"The usual, doll?" the cashier asked. I could never remember her name, but I always easily spotted the spiky pink hair.

"Yes, please." I scooted closer to the counter. If I didn't ask Hunter if he wanted anything, I'd come across rude and I thought it wiser to avoid that. I forced my eyes back to him and Noelle who were busy doting on Muffin. "Hunter, did you want something?" I called out loud enough to carry over the din of voices.

"Red eye," he mouthed, then circled to face Noelle again, essentially ditching me for her. As usual.

After ordering, I waited for my latte, facing in the opposite direction of Noelle and Hunter, to the pink walls displaying decorated cakes. When our drinks appeared on the counter, I flipped around to locate Hunter. Had he been staring at me? Whatever. I pointed toward the exit, grabbed our cups and dashed out. By the time I climbed into the truck, he was sprinting toward the passenger side, Muffin's ears flopping with each bounce of his foot.

Muffin was freaking adorable. And Hunter was so sweet to her. Warm and fuzzies clouded my brain.

He got in and shut the door. "I need to visit my parents."

Of course he did. "Why? You could see them tomorrow or the next day."

For some reason I couldn't fathom, Hunter made a real effort to stay in touch with those awful people.

Blake and I always referred to them as freezer folk due to their icy stares and lack of emotion. Any time Hunter had invited Blake over, they dragged me along as a buffer. Blake and I always attempted to get out of it and accepted only as a last resort.

"Bails, they're my *parents*. I haven't seen them in over a year."

A call couldn't suffice? I shrugged, knowing that his parents could be even colder and Hunter would still do what was expected of him. "I'm sure Blake won't mind you borrowing the truck by yourself. Not like he's using it."

He shifted in his seat to watch me. "Want to come? You probably haven't seen them in ages."

I gave a harsh laugh. "Right, because they're scary. And I'm not going to sacrifice myself so you get a break from them."

Hunter slumped against the door, leaning his head on the window. "Can't say I blame you."

"Skip it. Tell them you're busy settlin' in." I huffed. "No matter what you do, it'll be wrong anyway. If they don't bitch about you not coming, they'll complain about something else."

He rubbed his chin. "Hm. I could bring Noelle."

I somehow found the strength to keep my mouth from twisting into a grimace. "The backlash from your parents would keep things interestin'."

Hunter groaned. "C'mon, Bails, help me out. You've always been able to distract them."

"You want me along because you know if I'm there,

they'll try to get rid of me and you'll be obligated to leave with me since I'm your ride."

"Precisely. I need to get in and get out so I can start straight away on ranch business. That helps you and Blake, right?"

"Fine," I growled. "I'll go but under one condition. Before we do anything else, give me my copy of the annulment papers, like you've been promisin' for over a year."

As anxious as Hunter had been to dump his new wife and get an annulment, I couldn't understand why he hadn't already sent me the papers. I hadn't brought it up to him until recently because I didn't want to be reminded of how hurt I'd been when he'd pursued the annulment with such gusto. Knowing Hunter, he'd written an incorrect address and the stamped papers never had a chance to get to me. Either way, didn't matter. We weren't married and in the eyes of the law, never were. Never happened.

Having the papers in my possession wouldn't change my status with Hunter and the physical proof of our non-relationship shouldn't have been important to me. But it was. The papers represented closure and once I had them in my hands, I could let Hunter go and then get on with my life.

"Deal." He rubbed his hands together. "They're much easier to get along with when you're there."

I winced. He'd give me my walking papers, literally, then we'd spend time with the freezer folk. Anxiety coated my palms in sweat.

Chapter Three

HUNTER

Bailey maneuvered the Silverado over the dips, and past the curves of the long dirt driveway of the B & B ranch, then parked in front of the house. After killing the engine, she darted out of the truck and went for my carry-on.

I dropped a kiss on Muffin's forehead before hooking the leash to her collar. We jumped out of the truck, the leash straining as she shot off in all directions at once, eager to explore the new environment. In the distance, a black German shepherd raced toward us.

Muffin barked, wagging her tail. Keeping hold of her leash, I bent to rub my hands all over Chester. He showered my face with saliva. "Chester, you handsome dude. Good to see you."

He shifted his attention to Muffin and while they sniffed each other, I took a moment to breathe in the pungent odor of horse manure, earth and hay. God, I'd missed those smells, even the less pleasant ones. After high school, the urge to get away from my parents had driven me to Texas A & M where I'd studied equine medicine. Then I'd taken the residency in California to add a few more miles between my family and me. I'd met a variety of people and explored their worlds, but the Thayers always drew me back to Bride.

I never stayed long though, because it didn't usually take me long to remember why I'd left. As soon as Blake could work and I completed my mission, I'd be gone again. I wasn't sure yet where I would settle, but it wouldn't be Bride. I didn't want to live my old life and I sure as hell didn't want to be anywhere near my parents.

The B & B ranch hadn't changed much; several structures still surrounded their modest but pretty four-bedroom home. The real time and money had been invested in accommodating their exquisite Arabians—a breeding barn with a laboratory to process the stallions' semen, as well as spaces needed to train champion horses in cutting and reining. The ranch also boasted three stables holding ten stalls each. A washing station stood on the other side of an exercise pen right next to the hay shed. Beyond the tack room with an attached workshop, cattle grazed with a few mares.

I couldn't wait to get my hands on some Arabians, and work with them a little like I used to. But first, I needed to see my parents.

Bud, B & B's long-time ranch foreman, slapped me on the arm. "Good to have you home. Need some help?" He nodded toward Muffin. "I can take her around and introduce her while you settle in."

"I'd appreciate it, man." We knuckle bumped and I watched as Bud led Muffin toward the stables. Chester dogged them all the way.

By the time I'd dragged my two giant suitcases over the dirt, Bailey had already disappeared into the house. When I got through the door, I stumbled on my carry-on. She'd just dumped it in the entryway.

A dull ache began in my chest. I loved Bailey like family but I couldn't compete with the blood ties she and Blake shared. I had to believe I could fix whatever was bothering her and this bump would smooth over. It had to. I'd always felt closer to her and Blake than anyone else. I couldn't lose that.

Maybe her attitude would improve once she got those papers.

My military boots sounded over the old wood floors as I scooped up my bag. I hung it over my shoulder, then started up the stairs with the rest of my luggage. I exercised regularly and kept myself in great shape yet getting everything up the stairs was ridiculous. If I hadn't packed the bags myself I might've suspected someone filled them with bricks.

Navigating the load through the tight passageway, I grunted and took care not to scuff the walls. When I finally reached the top of the stairs, snickering reached my ears.

"You couldn't make two trips? Or wait for me?"

I slowed my ragged breath so she wouldn't see I was winded. "Figured one trip was more efficient and I had no idea you planned to chip in." While I wished

I hadn't brought so much crap with me, I'd be in Bride at least a few weeks and didn't want to take time out for frequent laundry loads or to stop and buy more clothes when I was needed at the ranch. Plus, I hadn't had a chance to search for the annulment papers Bailey had requested before I packed. So I'd snagged a small stack of files, which added to the weight.

"It's just as well. That was quite entertainin' to watch." She bit her lip, suppressing a smile. "Had to check on Blake. You know what a big baby he is when he's sick or hurt."

I'd quit panting and could talk without effort now. "I remember vividly. Mrs. T around?" I was dying to see their mom. My parents could wait. So could the annulment papers.

"No," she said, still talking to me from the bottom of the stairs. "She left early this morning on ranch business. Should be home by lunch."

Which gave me two hours to visit my parents and get back. "I'll stow these and find the papers. Then we can leave, if that works for you."

"Sure. Take your time, unpack. I'll make a round through the ranch until then, check on Muffin." Bailey didn't wait for a reply, striding out the front door.

"I'll be ready to go in five," I called out.

The Thayers had always kept a room for me, though I'd never officially lived with them. Even when I'd gone away to college or after I'd been swallowed by life in Los Angeles, Mrs. T refused to reassign the room.

I pushed the door open, bumping into the doorframe under the weight of my baggage. Everything in the room was the same as I'd left it. The navy rug still lay by my bedside over the oak floors, our team flags hung on the wall and football trophies lined my dresser. None of that had meant anything to my parents, but Mrs. T had always made sure a celebratory dinner was ready after every win. Mr. Thayer had never missed a game.

He'd passed away two years ago and it felt like yesterday. The meanest man in Bride, my grandfather, had made it into his eighties, but the kindest man I'd ever met hadn't reached his fiftieth birthday. My throat swelled and I blinked away the burn in my eyes.

After tossing one of the suitcases on the bed, I unzipped it, moved my medical bag out of my way and pulled out the stack of files. I sifted through them, chose the folder marked "Vegas" and located the thick mustard packet from Las Vegas Municipal Court. I instinctively sought the opening and noticed the envelope was still sealed. I plucked a knife from my dresser top and sliced along the end, then slid out the stack of legal papers and scanned for the one with the official stamp.

After reading through the court's notes, I set the papers aside, swallowing hard. My plans for staying in Texas had just taken a drastic new twist.

Bailey was already angry over the Vegas thing. Would she be even less happy with me when she learned we were still married? That wouldn't be fixed overnight and I couldn't leave Bride without knowing we were good. Not to mention I couldn't risk not seeing the annulment through to the end.

I couldn't take off until I knew the ranch financially sound anyway. Deserting the Thayers when they were in danger of losing more of their land wasn't an option. I'd have to stay in Bride a little longer than I'd thought. A few months maybe?

Threading my fingers through my hair, I paced the wood floor in a panic. Bailey was going to kill me for messing up on the annulment.

I tucked the stack of papers back into the suitcase then bolted into the hallway and leaped down the stairs. "Bailey!"

"Hunter?" she called out from somewhere outside.

I flew out the front door. "Where are you?"

"In here."

I followed her voice to one of the stables to see her running her hands over a foal, touching its mane, tail, hooves. Imprinting, getting the foal used to human contact so she'd be less flighty and manageable as she got older.

After a quick scan of the vicinity to make sure we were alone, I huddled closer to her and whispered, "You never received anything from the Las Vegas court? Anything, like maybe papers notifying you of missin' signatures?"

"No." Her hands balled into fists and she slowly stood to her full height, already glaring in anticipation of what came next. "You better not be sayin' what I think you're sayin'."

"The thing is..." I craned my neck around, checking again for eavesdroppers. "I never opened the envelope. It arrived and I naturally assumed it'd been approved by the judge and stamped. So I never actually looked."

Bailey's nostrils flared and her eyes grew wide and wild. She stepped away from the foal. "Are you tellin' me you did it wrong and we're still married?"

"No. I'm not sayin' that." I backed away so she couldn't take a swing at me. "But only because you already did."

Her cheeks flamed. "Hunter Evermond, I hate you right now. And if you speak a word of this to anyone, I'll feed you to the pigs."

"You guys don't have pigs." I sidestepped, creating a little more distance between Bailey and me. She smelled wicked good and I needed to focus. "Trust me, I don't want anyone finding out about this either."

"Of course you don't." Her lip curled up and she shoved a set of car keys at me. "Have fun visitin' the freezer folk. Alone." She stormed out of the barn.

That could've gone worse, I supposed. I sighed, knowing mending things with Bailey would be twice as hard now. On the upside, I'd be seeing my parents shortly. If my dad honored client-attorney privilege with me, he could give me advice on how to approach the annulment. Maybe he could even do it for me. I'd promised Bailey I wouldn't tell a soul but shouldn't my dad get a pass if he made it his mission to detach me from Bailey? He'd want me to cut all legal ties with her as quickly as possible to ensure she never got her hands on Evermond money.

Evermonds didn't marry people like the Thayers. We were supposed to choose partners of equal breeding and social standing. My family was so full of it. People didn't come any better than the Thayers. Fortunately, my parents' snobbishness could work in my favor and get me out of this mess sooner.

After collecting Muffin and giving Chester another rubdown, I jumped into the Silverado and hightailed it out of the driveway toward the old mansion that had never felt like home, to the people who had never felt like family.

Ten minutes later, I cruised over their smooth paved driveway, past the picturesque garden. The graceful lines of Fletcher Manor and the sweeping landscape always calmed me. Fresh paint covered the clapboard exterior but it remained white, as always. The friendly wraparound porch welcomed me in southern style, yet couldn't fool those who knew the kind of people who lurked inside.

Sunshine beat on the windshield of the truck as I killed the engine, making me grateful for the autumn breeze. I ran a hand over Muffin's silky fur and let my head fall back, stealing a moment for thought. How could I present this situation to my father without appearing like an irresponsible moron? My dad tolerated little nonsense and would guilt me to no end—the main reason why I rarely came to him for help—and even then, he might leave me to handle it on my own.

A movement outside drew my attention. I climbed out of the truck, leaving Muffin on the seat. An enormous straw hat shadowed a smudge of dirt under my mother's eye. Her loose long-sleeved button-down over a T-shirt and loose-fitting jeans told me I'd interrupted her gardening.

"Hi, Mom." I bent to deliver the obligatory kiss on her cheek.

She patted my arm and turned way, waving for me to follow. "What brings you by?"

Did I need a reason? Had she realized I'd been fourteen hundred miles away all of last year? As usual, I felt like an outsider being invited to someone else's home. I scooped up Muffin and raced to catch up to her. "I'm here for a couple months helpin' out the Thayers. Blake was in an accident and can't work the farm."

"Come say hello to your father." She held the screen door open for me, her gaze drifting to Muffin. As if oblivious to Muffin's extreme cute levels, my mom spun around and barreled through the foyer. "He's in his study. Are you stayin' for dinner?"

That would involve staying for lunch. And her words may have formed a question, but it hadn't sounded like an invitation either. I'd never figured out whether my mom was oblivious to how she came across to others or if she intentionally worded things in such a way not to inspire deep bonds. The latter, more likely.

"Thank you, no. Just arrived and came straight here—haven't even unpacked yet. But I'll come by again as soon as I have a chance." Or when I couldn't avoid it any longer without being rude.

We stopped in front of the door leading to my dad's study. My mom eyed Muffin then reached out with two fingers to pat the top of her head. Riveted to the pup, she leaned in to smell her. Apparently satisfied she wouldn't catch a terrible stink, she stroked Muffin's back.

"Dan, Hunter is here," she called out. "I'll leave you two alone." Still petting Muffin, she pushed open the door to his study and ushered me inside. She was about to dart away when she froze, hesitated as she stared at Muffin, then reached for her. "I'll take that."

"You don't have to. I can watch her. She's very well behaved."

She clucked her tongue. "Exactly. She won't be a hassle at all."

Weird. My mother had never been much of a pet person. I'd had to beg for every single animal we'd ever had. The familiar woodsy scent of my dad's cigars tickled my nose and I surrendered Muffin—along with the mysteries surrounding my mother.

"Hey, Dad." I shuffled over the plush cream rug and sat in the chair opposite him.

"Good to see you, son. What's the occasion?" He slid the newspaper aside and set his cigar in the ashtray, tendrils of smoke curling up then dissipating.

I mentally deflated at their lack of warmth, that they would be surprised at my visit. They thoroughly lived up to the nickname Bailey had given them. "Just flew in to give Blake a hand on the ranch for a few weeks. Thought I'd stop by before I got too involved with my duties there." I'd accidentally given myself a segue and I was going to use it. "Not sure how easy it's gonna be to escape or how often I'll be able to visit. They're goin' to keep me pretty busy."

He flicked the end of his cigar into the marble ashtray, his unflinching gaze steady on mine. I tapped my fingertips on the polished surface of his gleaming cherry wood desk, my focus bouncing between the shelves lined with leather bound books, the wide window and the mounted antlers behind my dad.

I had to get out of there.

"Spit it out, son."

I blew out a breath, annoyed at him for assuming I needed something. I mean, I did *now*. However, I'd already planned to visit before discovering the big problem. But once either of my parents set their minds about someone, no one could change it. I resigned myself to them believing I didn't have the decency to come calling to be social. "Can we keep this between us?"

His eyes shot to the ceiling as though he'd already lost patience with *me*. "Yes. What is it this time?"

My jaw clenched. It's not like I asked him to help me every time I saw him. In fact, I only asked them for help as a last resort. "Remember when I went to Pierre and Renee's weddin' in Vegas a year ago last summer?" When he nodded, I forged on. "I partied a bit too much one night and ended up marrying this girl." I laughed once and waved an arm through the air.

He raised one brow, his mouth flat-lining. "You became inebriated and thought it would be a great idea to be totally cliché and get married to some girl you didn't even love?"

"Obviously, I wasn't thinkin' clearly. I immediately went to get an annulment the next mornin'," I added before my dad had a chance to judge me too harshly—which was inevitable and made me wonder why I was trying to save myself.

"That's a relief." He rested his elbows on the table, waiting patiently for me to finish my story. "So what's the problem?"

"Turns out the annulment was never finalized." I waited a beat. "I'm still legally married and I was hopin' you'd help me finish the annulment, make sure it gets done right."

"Since you were married there, the residency requirement may not apply. But I'm not licensed to practice in Nevada and not sure of the laws. Haven't handled an annulment here in years." He expelled air from his lungs and ran a hand over his silver hair. "I believe it may be too late for an annulment in Texas. Well, you could try, but that may require presentin' your case before a judge. You'd have to wait for a court date and it'll take some time."

Oh, crap. Bailey was going to be pissed—more than she already was. I let my forehead fall into my palms as I groaned. "Bailey's gonna to kill me."

"Your wife is a friend of Bailey's?" The leather of his chair creaked as he leaned forward. "Any woman would be entitled to half of everything you've earned since marriage, but you've been in school, then the internship. No real income to speak of. If she gets an unscrupulous attorney, they could argue for spousal support on the grounds of infidelity. Likely since you've undoubtedly been with other women since the marriage. She could receive more as the injured party."

My brain staggered with all the scenarios. "She doesn't want anything except freedom from me. It should be simple."

He scoffed. "All women want something. What's her name?"

I swallowed, bracing myself for his reaction. "Bailey."

A low rumble built in his throat. "You married that Thayer girl?"

I banged my head on his desk. "Relax, dad. She's not a gold digger. It was one night of drunken stupidity and the marriage was never consummated. She wants out as badly as I do."

He stood, signaling he was done with me. "I'll do some research, work out the best way to approach this. In the meantime, be nice to her. Don't do anything to give her the urge to take you for a ride."

I was more worried I'd have to spend extra time with my dad than Bailey ripping me off. The freezer folk weren't what I considered fun. "I'll be careful. And you'll call me when you work out how to handle this?"

"Don't worry, son. I'll figure out a way to make this go away." He relit the cigar which was my cue to leave.

He only smoked alone or with other gentlemen of his social standing. Offspring didn't count.

"Everything else going good? The practice is thrivin'?" I asked, not ready to be discarded. Despite feeling like I'd always been in their way growing up, I couldn't fight the natural desire to be closer to my parents. And since I'd likely be in Bride long after Blake returned to work to see the divorce through, I may as well try to get through to my parents. If that was even possible.

He raised a brow. "Did you come here to talk business, son?"

My mood plummeted. And it was already low after my last conversation with Bailey. "No. I just want to know how you and mom are."

"We're not going to die any time soon, if that's what you're wonderin'."

"Never crossed my mind." Frustration rippled through me. "Give me a break, Dad."

He shot me a narrow-eyed look. "We're fine."

I stared at him a long minute, wondering if I'd ever be able to break through to either of them. Regardless, it wasn't going to happen today. "I'd better get goin'."

He glanced down, then gingerly flipped the page of his newspaper.

I followed the scent of my mother's lavender perfume winding through the house, finding her and Muffin in the kitchen.

My mom held a tiny piece of cheese in one hand, the other on her hip as she towered over the pup. "Sit."

"You're spoiling her. Normal dog treats are sufficient and easier on the digestive track." Muffin's tail wagged at my voice and she scrambled toward me, her rump fishtailing on the slippery marble floor. I plucked her up and planted a kiss on her furry mouth, careful to withdraw quickly. Muffin's tongue could be lightning fast and that wasn't the kind of tongue action I liked. "Also, cheese gives her gas."

Mom tapped her lip. "I'm worried Muffin will get lost on the ranch. And aren't you afraid coyotes will get her?"

"Chester's presence discourages wildlife from the ranch." I tilted my head and wondered why she, of all people, would micromanage me with a pet. She knew how caring I'd always been with animals. My love of animals is what inspired me to go to vet school. "Besides, she's with me most of the time. At night, she sleeps on my bed."

"I don't know." She set the cheese bit on the counter and affected a dire tone. "You'll be busy at the ranch. She won't get the attention she needs."

What angle was my mom working? She had to know I was incapable of abusing an animal in any way and I'd never neglect Muffin. Regardless, Chester and many humans around the ranch would be more than willing to entertain Muffin.

Maybe my mom was trying to steal my dog. I'd prefer her to bond with *me*, but I wasn't sure her having a dog to love was a bad thing at all. "You don't have food or toys here."

My mom's eyes sparkled. "I was about to go to the market and grab a few things. I can make one more stop at the pet store."

Air whooshed out of my lungs in resignation. "Switching food can upset a dog's stomach. Also, she likes squeaky toys. Rope, too, but only if you're going to use it and play with her."

Her face lit up like sunshine as she reached over and removed the dog from my clutches. Without acknowledging me further, my own mother baby-talked to Muffin as she strode away. I stood there until her voice faded. I didn't even get to say goodbye to Muffin.

Had I lost my damn dog?

Chapter Four

HUNTER

I'd grown so used to being with Muffin nearly every hour of every day these past few weeks, I barely remembered how to function without her by my side. But for the first time, possibly ever, I saw warmth and maybe even compassion stir within my mother. Getting married and having a child—me—hadn't softened her. Perhaps Muffin could. Maybe my temporary sacrifice of a beloved pup was for a good cause.

Probably wishful thinking. More likely, my mom needed a quick puppy fix and I'd be reunited with Muffin shortly.

I climbed into the Silverado and texted my mother with the correct type of dog food. I fired up the Silverado and minutes later, I was tooling along the highway, immense relief rolling off me in waves. The initial visit was done and, apparently, they'd had enough of me. I wouldn't be obligated to see them again until I returned for Muffin. If my mother lived up to my expectations, she'd be arranging a puppy transfer soon. I'd give her a couple hours or so.

My thoughts drifted to Bailey, my shoulder muscles tensing again. Maybe she just needed a chance to cool off. If I snuck into the house and went directly to Blake, then later went to my own room to unpack, and only came out to visit with Mrs. T, Bailey might be spared of seeing me the rest of the day.

As soon as I parked in front of the house, I zeroed in on the stables. I immediately located Bailey on Iesha in a pen with some cattle. I observed them, admiring Iesha as she repeatedly blocked a heifer from rejoining her herd. And she did it with style and grace. I'd seen enough horses cutting to know when they stood even half a chance at winning a competition. Bailey had a promising future with Iesha.

After jumping out of the truck, I sprinted into the house and barged into Blake's room. He lay on his bed, looking just as he always had. Brown hair that was cut efficiently short, making it impossible to ever get in his way, and gray eyes a shade deeper than Bailey's. On his other side, Chester took up nearly half the bed. A mangled coat hanger bobbed up and down as Blake inserted one end of the wire between his skin and the leg cast.

"Itchy?" I punched him in the arm, chuckling when he took a swing at me and almost lost his grip on the hanger.

"You're an ass," he muttered.

"Not gonna deny it." I ambled through his room, noting the changes to his knife collection hanging on the wall. "Enjoying your vacation?"

"I spend most of my time worrying about the ranch."

"Micromanaging everyone else doesn't improve your mood?" I snickered.

"Not really." He scowled at the cast. "Can't wait to get the damn thing off. And when I do, you're dead meat."

My head snapped around at the *tap tap*. I was already making my way to the door when Mrs. T popped her head inside. I flung the door open the rest of the way and pulled her into a bear hug, lifting her slight frame off the floor. "Great to see you, Mrs. T."

"Put me down." She giggled. "And how many times have I told you to call me Liz?"

A million times. But calling her by anything other than a proper title seemed disrespectful and she deserved better than bad manners for everything she'd done for me. Besides, I wanted to avoid first names, which seemed more personal. I couldn't risk anything leading us to verbalizing our feelings. I'd never told anyone I loved them. Loving words of any kind were never uttered at Fletcher Manor.

If I was going to tell anyone I loved them though, it would be Mrs. Thayer. I'd gotten more warmth from her in the last few seconds than a lifetime with my parents.

I gave her another squeeze before lowering her to the floor. She looked amazing. Her dark brown hair had enough slivers of gray to shimmer from the light above. A buddy had once told me if you weren't sure about dating a girl, check out her mother. If the mother was a MILF, the daughter had a good chance of aging well too. I didn't have to look at Mrs. T though to know that Bailey would be beautiful at any age. Not a bad deal for her future husband, whoever he would be.

"How's everything?" I asked.

"We're managing. How is your family?"

My smile dulled but I determined to hold it steady. "Same."

"Where's that puppy I heard so much about?" Mrs. T leaned past me, scouring the room for my missing dog.

"I got tricked into leavin' her with my mom."

Mrs. T's brows flew up. "I'd be interested in seein' how that works out."

I nodded briskly. "Me too."

When my phone dinged, I fished it out of my pocket and checked the screen. I laughed and faced it toward Mrs. T. "So far so good."

Mrs. T snickered at the image of Muffin lounging on my parents' priceless antique couch, tummy exposed and tongue lolling.

"Animals can be powerful medicine." Mrs. T peered over at me adoringly, cupping her palm against my face. "Glad to have you back. Thank you for comin' to help out."

I covered her hand with mine, trying to remember why I'd resisted coming to Bride. Now that I was seeing loved ones, being here felt like the most natural thing in the world. "It's the least I could do."

"I need to get started on dinner." She patted my cheek then slipped out the door.

"I can hardly wait," I called out. The thought of how much I'd missed her southern cooking made me grin. Except Bailey would be eating too and I'd vowed to avoid her, for her sake. I twisted to face Blake. "I remembered this thing I have to do, some L.A. stuff I promised to finish. And I still need to unpack. You think your mom would mind if I ate in my room?"

Seconds lengthened as he scrutinized me. "Bailey made a lame excuse earlier, sounded awfully similar to yours. Something goin' on between you two?"

I huffed. "What? No. Why would you think that?"

"She's been acting weird since she found out you were comin' back." Blake cast me a glance full of suspicion. "Now I'm *sure* somethin' is up. What gives?"

I opened my mouth with no clue what to say. How could I explain to him that I'd married his little sister in a drunken frenzy, failed epically on the annulment, and now most likely would have to go through an actual divorce to make things right? Worse, Bailey would already be divorced at age twenty-four. "Nothin'. I'm just trying to navigate her mood swings."

"What did you do?" His eyes narrowed.

I threw my hands in the air and moaned. "How am I supposed to know? I've never been able to figure out women."

"Then I'll ask *her*." Blake folded his arms over his chest but didn't look any tougher, not with the bum leg. "You're hidin' somethin' and I'm gonna find out what it is."

Before I became aware of what I was doing, I had crept toward his window and was searching the grounds below. I immediately spotted Bailey walking a stallion. "Good. And when you find out what's agitatin' her, be sure to tell me."

Blake seemed to buy my innocent act. But if I avoided the dinner table, everyone else might become suspicious too. Damn. My fingernails tapped the window sill and I veered away from the distraction below. "I'll hurry and get my work done now, so I can eat with you guys." I swiveled to leave, but stopped at his voice.

"Thanks for being here, man. Don't know what I would've done if you hadn't stepped up."

I smirked. "You would've driven everyone nuts with all your whinin'."

"Screw you." He turned a pillow into a missile, hitting me in the shoulder.

"See you at dinner." I tossed the pillow at him and crossed the hallway to my room, not looking forward to unpacking. My phone rang and solved my dilemma. I checked the screen and considered rejecting the call. I'd rather color sort my shirts than talk to my dad again. But he didn't waste time making unnecessary calls. I swiped the screen. "Hey, Dad."

"Two things working against you. First, it's been over a year since you got married. Second, you'd have to prove that one or both of you were under the influence when the ceremony took place. In your favor, however, you've been residin' in separate states. Also, you did attempt the annulment immediately after the unfortunate event. That said, the lack of follow-through could be construed as a lack of desire by one or both parties to reverse the marriage. Not to mention you're currently livin' together at the B & B ranch, which could be considered cohabitatin'. Disqualifies you from getting an annulment."

Wow, no hello or anything. Just straight to the point. But what else was new? "So what should I do?"

Papers shuffled. "Get started right away on the divorce. I'm sure you want to be free of her as soon as possible."

Maybe return to the scene of the crime. Vegas would be faster, and since we got married there, seemed logical we could divorce there. I'd need to research that, of course, before I made the trip. Regardless, an out-of-state excursion wasn't going to happen in the next few weeks since the ranch couldn't do without both Bailey and me for several days. And how would we explain to everyone why we needed to fly to Vegas together? "Is there any way to petition the court here to proceed with the original annulment, maybe with a judge you know?"

"I play golf with someone who may be willin' to do me a favor. But not for something that was started in another state. Your situation is murky at best and he won't risk his reputation to bend the law for you." He paused and I waited, hoping he'd come up with a brilliant idea. "As much as I pity you for being saddled with a Thayer, I think a divorce here in Texas is your only option. My best advice is to avoid doing anythin' that might set her off so when it comes time to dividin' assets, she doesn't try to take advantage of you."

I bristled at the stream of insults on Bailey and her family, but stifled the irritation. The least I could do was be gracious since he was doing me a favor. "Thanks, dad. Appreciate the advice."

"Goodbye, son."

I hit the end button, fury clouding my vision and muddling my head. He pitied me for being tied to a Thayer? He thought so little of Bailey that he believed her to be capable of trying to screw me over? If my dad had any ability to see into people, if he'd been capable of any kind of an emotional connection to humans, he would view Bailey like I did—as a sweet, beautiful, kind and generous woman. She wasn't rich like us, but any guy—and it wouldn't be me—would be lucky to have a girl like her. And whoever he was, he'd definitely be marrying up.

I yanked my other suitcase from the floor and set it on the bed, then rummaged through the contents for my speaker. I cranked up the play list from my phone and an instant later Waylon Jenning's *Just to Satisfy You* came on, promising someone was gonna get hurt before I was through.

Reaching down, I skipped that song. I didn't need to be reminded of the mess I'd made with Bailey or how long she'd be furious with me for keeping her married against her will.

After rifling through my bag for my laptop, I booted it up to search for more information on getting a divorce in Texas. Next time I spoke with my dad about filing for the divorce, I didn't want to sound like an idiot. But the more I read, the punier I felt.

Banging from the other side of my door made me jolt. A split second later, Bailey barged in, her mouth set in a hard line, her hands at her hips. "Well? Did you ask your dad about it?"

"Shh. I thought you didn't want anyone to know," I whispered, motioning for her to shut the door.

"I don't." She closed the door, and crossed the room toward me. "But you must have spoken to your dad about gettin' an annulment. What did he say?"

The scent of cherries floated the short distance to my nose. And, damn, when did she get so pretty? I mean, she'd always been pretty but she'd also been like my little sister. Why couldn't I find Big Brother mode that I'd always lived in? I needed to completely slam the door on any intimate thoughts of Bailey. Cleaner thoughts would begin with me not paying any attention to her physical beauty. I vowed not to let my gaze travel below her neck.

"Unlikely we'd qualify for an annulment since it's been over a year. And it'll be more difficult to prove intoxication because it's been so long. I'm thinkin' we should find out if we can return to Vegas, since that's where we got married and maybe they'll finalize a divorce sooner than Texas would." When did she get so curvy? And those legs!

"Up here, Hunter." She pointed at her eyes. "Can you not act like such a guy right now, please?"

Disgust filled me. I hated being lumped in with every other deviant male. But since I'd been caught staring at her legs, I deserved it. "Well, you oughta put those things away. If you don't want anyone gawking, wear some damned clothes."

She frowned, taking a long deep breath then exhaling as if she was expending great effort to keep her cool.

My dad's earlier words popped into my head, reminding me not to piss Bailey off. Not that I thought for even an instant she would try to screw me over. I just needed a smooth annulment to give her what she wanted. "Sorry," I said. "I'll try to be more gentlemanly in the future."

Her face softened. "Where's Muffin?"

"My mom didn't want to give her back."

She blinked once. "Sorry, but I can't imagine your mom being inconvenienced by a human, much less an animal. First time Muffin digs in the garden bed or chews on one of her Manolo Blahniks, your mom will be begging you to pick her up."

As much as I wanted Muffin by my side, I needed my mom to bond unconditionally with some kind of living thing other than plants. But my expectations were extremely low, as always. "No doubt I'll be seeing Muffin very soon."

"On another note, we can't fly to Vegas. Not for at least a couple months and even then, I won't be in a position to leave the ranch. There's no one else to do my work. I want this marriage dissolved *now*," she hissed.

"We can start the process here in Texas right away, but they have this pesky sixty-day waiting period before we submit the particulars on the dissolution, like who gets what."

"Nothing to decide there. Anything that belonged to you before we realized how negligent you'd been in handling the annulment is the same as what you still own. And that applies to anything belonging to me." Her chin jutted out. "Agreed?"

"Absolutely." Especially since I had the trust fund and parents with deep pockets.

"Good. We'll go to the courthouse first thing in the morning. Unless you'd prefer your dad handle it," she said, her tone clipped and formal.

I hated the coldness creeping into her voice. I'd had a lifetime of that from my parents. Maybe she'd get back to the old Bailey, the one who used to rib me in the cutest way or look at me like a hero, after the divorce went through. "I'll get him to do it, make sure it gets done correctly. But we can't get around the sixty day wait."

Her eyes darkened. "Let me know what you need from me." Without another word, she swept out of the room.

Looked like Bailey had pretty much abandoned our friendship, yet I refused to give up on her. I would keep trying until I had exhausted every possibility, and done everything imaginable to bring her back. Writing off my parents as hopeless was one thing. Letting any of the Thayers go was quite another.

But was it really understandable to write off my own parents? Had I done everything in my power to get through to them? All I'd done was lower my expectations and cross my fingers every time I visited them. Very little effort beyond that.

I popped off the bed and went after her. "Bailey."

She stopped before the stairs, pivoting on her heel. "Yes?"

"I was thinking... So long as I get all Blake's work done each day, the hours don't matter much, right? Some of it can be done at night, like mucking the stables. We've always had good lighting out there."

She squinted. "Your point?"

I lifted one shoulder, trying to be casual. She thought my parents were hopeless, but I wasn't ready to abandon them yet. "Figured I'd arrive at my parents' place early when I can and hang out with them, maybe help my mom in the garden."

Her lips pursed. "And if they don't respond the way you want them to?"

I flashed her a grin to hide the twinge of despair. "Then I'll keep trying."

Her mouth softened and her eyes grew shiny. "Do what you have to do. If you can't get to some of your chores, let me know and I'll cover for you." She was about to leave, then swung back around. "I wish you'd let us pay you for your work here."

I gave her a humorless laugh. "If you could afford to pay someone, you wouldn't be short staffed and selling off your land. I can't take your family's money anyway after everything you guys have done for me. And it's not like I'm poor."

"Whatever." She disappeared from my view, her cowboy boots thumping each time she touched a step down the flight of stairs.

My lungs strained to expand for air, my body refusing to function like normal. It was an odd sensation, something I'd never experienced before. Similar to withdrawals, like when I'd quit partying after Vegas. After I'd screwed up so royally and married Bailey, I'd decided that I preferred being in control of my actions. But I'd had to get used to not always having a drink in my hand at parties or other social events, limiting it to only one or two.

Missing the cold smooth glass of a bottle against my palm, the heat of the alcohol as it slid down my throat, was drastically different than the ache in my gut now. I had a powerful urge to spend time with Bailey. Certainly not because I wanted more than friendship with her, but because she'd been a part of me most of my life.

A vision of her flashed before me. Long gorgeous legs, slim waist, perky breasts... and the feel of her mouth against mine. *No, no, no.* Those images were supposed to dull over time, not become more vivid. If I couldn't get my wits in order—and I wasn't sure if I'd be able to anytime soon—I was screwed. I had no clue how to get back to normal with Bailey. I'd just have to work harder at it because the alternative—losing her entirely—was unacceptable.

Chapter Five

Hunter was not a prospect for me and he never would be. But I could look good while being rejected by him. Although I still had work to do in the stables after dinner and would certainly get dirty again, I showered, then dressed in a pair of tight jeans and a snug t-shirt, and then did my hair. Not wanting to give him or anyone else the impression I was going out of my way to impress Hunter, I wore only enough makeup to appear like I wasn't wearing any. My fingers remained crossed that my mother or brother wouldn't blurt out anything during dinner about my appearance.

By the time I descended the stairs and ventured into the dining room, they were already seated. As usual, my mom had claimed the head of the table and Blake had snagged the other end. Which left one chair across from Hunter. Kind of hard to avoid eye contact when he was right in front of me.

"About time," Blake mumbled, scooting the pot of chili my way. "We were about to start without you."

My mom passed me the tray of cornbread. "You look nice, hon. Going somewhere?"

Hadn't planned on it but now that she'd brought attention to the fact that I'd gone out of my way to look decent, I had no choice but to leave the house. "Craving a latte and I still have so much to do. Figured I'd make a trip to Two Cups for a pick-me-up."

"Coffee sounds great. I'll go with you." Hunter avoided my gaze as he dipped a chunk of cornbread into his bowl. As if not making eye contact with me decreased his chances of me saying no.

And why did he want to go with me anyway?

Blake's spoon clanged on the floor tile. "Damn."

"I'll get you a new one." I sprung from my chair, grateful for an excuse to put some distance between Hunter and me. I skirted the table and passed my mom toward the doorway to the kitchen. *Don't look at him*. And, of course, my eyes betrayed me and snuck a peek at Hunter. His gaze had anchored to my butt.

His staring wasn't what sent butterflies in my tummy into hyperdrive, but the intensity of his stare. Whatever his affliction that caused him to study any part of me like that had to be a fluke. Maybe he just happened to look while his mind was on something else. Didn't matter. I couldn't allow my head to be hijacked into believing that any momentary attraction on Hunter's part would ever lead to anything serious.

After sailing into the kitchen to get Blake's spoon, I returned to the table and rushed through my dinner. The sooner we got the coffee trip over with, the sooner

I could get away from Hunter and back to safety. I secretly hoped he'd change his mind and skip the coffee run.

"Anyone else want anything from Two Cups?" Hunter asked as he wiped his mouth with a napkin and tossed it on the table, dashing all my hopes of him forgetting about our little excursion.

"No thanks." My mom rose and began stacking our plates. "You two have fun."

"But not too much fun," Blake said with a straight face.

"Yeah, like that's something you should worry about," I replied wryly, resisting the urge to flare my nostrils in warning. What a jerk. Hoping Hunter would change his mind if I took long enough, I grabbed glasses from the table to help my mom clean up.

"I'll get that, hon." She nudged me away then halted. "On second thought, bring me back a hot chocolate, would you?"

My lip skewed but I smoothed it out, not wanting to protest too much and be obvious about my aversion to Hunter. I didn't want them asking too many questions. "Sure. We'll be back soon."

I headed for the truck, not glancing back to see if Hunter was following. As I got to the driver's side of my Explorer, the front door slammed. He slid into the passenger side just as I was shifting into reverse.

"What's the plan for tomorrow?" Hunter buckled his seat belt.

"Work, work and more work." At the main road, I checked both ways for traffic.

"Care to give specifics or should I run around the ranch guessing at what you want done first?"

Struggling to change out of bitch mode, I sucked in a long breath. "Feed the chickens, horses, cows. Turn out the horses and switch out all the water. Muck the stables. I need to get Malik under a saddle before a potential buyer comes out next week. That will be *my* priority tomorrow."

"Isn't he only three? You sure he's ready?"

I'd been working with Arabians my whole life and Hunter had the nerve to doubt me? "Malik's almost four, actually, and we've been preparing him for months. He's ready."

"I can work with him and still muck the stables. That should free you up a lot."

I clucked my tongue doubtfully. "You can't put in enough time and still get everything else done."

He chuckled. "You worry too much. I'll work with him between other things and still get lots of time with him. Maybe he won't let me ride him after the first day. But if it can be done quickly, I'll make sure it happens. It's all about trust."

With everything else he had to do? I wanted to see that. "Knock yourself out."

Our trip to Two Cups was uneventful. No surprise there since Noelle wasn't anywhere near the place. Apparently, no one else wanted caffeine on a Tuesday night. We were in and out in five minutes and on our way back to the ranch, much to my relief.

Back at the ranch, we parked and Hunter

intercepted the hot chocolate before I could get it. "I'll drop it off to your mom."

"Just as well. I have to finish up some stuff in the stables." Like bring in the horses for the night and make sure they had fresh water.

I started with the closest stall, throwing out the water and filling it up. After dragging the hose to the next stall, I filled that one up too. Footfalls alerted me to Hunter's approach. I'd recognize the sound of his swagger any day.

"Where's Malik?"

I caught a glimpse of a halter and lead rope in Hunter's hand, a blanket in the other. What had to be a carrot protruded from his pocket. "Buying his love, huh?"

"How else?" He grinned and my insides went mushy.

"C'mon." I jerked my head toward the exit, led him to another pen and pointed at a white Arabian. "There he is."

Hunter whistled. "He's handsome as ever."

I had the same thoughts about Hunter. "We have two buyers interested. The easier he is to work with, the more I can demand."

"You've done the hard part, getting him used to a bridle and blanket. I got the rest." Hunter brushed my arm as he passed and I shivered. He draped the blanket over the fence and let himself into the pen, approached Malik slowly then laid both hands flat on Malik's shoulder. "Hey, boy. Remember me?"

The stallion responded immediately, bobbing his head and looking for his treat. Hunter snapped the carrot in half and while Malik chomped on the first part, Hunter slipped on the halter, then attached the rope. The stallion chewed on the rest of the carrot as Hunter walked him around the pen.

Work waited for me but I couldn't tear myself away. Hunter's calming effect around animals had always fascinated me.

Hunter slowed Malik and snatched the blanket off the fence as they passed it, then gingerly laid it on the stallion's back. Malik's front legs lifted and he snorted. Hunter stroked his shoulder and talked to him in a soothing voice. Malik gradually settled down and Hunter began walking him again. He threw me a wide grin over his shoulder and my stomach fluttered.

Why was I still standing there, wishing Hunter would treat me as lovingly as he treated animals? I had work to do. Without a glance or a goodbye, I got as far away from Hunter Evermond as I could get. Which, unfortunately, was only a few yards. At least his wild hair and sexy grin was out of my view. He was way out of my league and not right for me in any way. Plus, he had zero interest. I needed to get a grip.

Chapter Six
BAILEY

I gunned the engine of my Explorer, a driving need pulsing through me to get away from the ranch. Hunter had been in town three days now and I didn't know how much longer I could take the constant anxiety and conflicting emotions his presence induced in me—disgust over his urgency to get the annulment and now the divorce, disappointment at losing him again, wishful thinking that he might fight for me, and fury knowing he would never value me enough to want me like I wanted him.

Worse, irritation at myself for being so pathetic.

I'd been pining over him since I was eight years old, the first time my brother had brought him to our house. Back then, I'd idolized him because he was popular, and he had something I wanted—my brother's respect and loyalty. When I'd come into my tween years, I'd crushed on Hunter as though he were a rock star. Sadly, my hero worship for him had never faded. By the time I'd turned eighteen, as much as I resisted those feelings, I'd fallen hard for Hunter. But when I'd noticed he was still chasing other girls, I'd reconciled myself to never having him.

Just like I had done my whole life, I gravitated to him in Vegas. If he made plans to drink at the bar, that's where I would be. By the time the wedding reception was over, Hunter was already more than halfway drunk. When a high school buddy of his had suggested taking the party to the bar, Hunter had enthusiastically agreed, telling his pal he'd be there in just a few minutes. We found out the next morning that the hotel had two bars.

Hunter polished off his plate of snacks, held out his arm and gallantly escorted me to the bar down the corridor. We ordered a drink and appetizers and then another drink. And another.

I propped my elbow on the bar and supported the side of my head in my palm. "Hey, where are your friends?" I slurred.

He chuckled and shrugged. "No idea."

Moments later, the bartender cut us off and we staggered to the elevator, giggling the whole way. Once he saw me safely into my room, he came inside and sprawled out on my bed.

"The ceiling is spinnin'."

I fell onto the bed, lying next to him like I used to do when we were kids. "That's 'cause you're drunk."

A donkey noise came from his throat and I was pretty sure he was trying to laugh. Then he rolled over. "Funny. I never get tired of you, Bails. Every other girl..." He shook his head and his hand balled then opened to mimic an explosion.

Like an idiot, I said the same thing that my friends would say to each other when I was seven. "If you love me that much, you should marry me." I rolled over, snorting and honking in a fit of laughter. After a couple of minutes, I flipped over to face him, expecting to find him asleep since he'd been so quiet.

He vaulted off the bed, then dragged me off the bed and out the door.

"Where are we going?" I nearly stumbled over the carpet as he tugged me toward the elevator.

"We're getting married."

Infamous playboy Hunter Evermond wanted *me*. My wish had finally come true and I would soon be his wife.

As soon as he'd bolted out of the elevator, he'd declared, "But first, we need to find a bar."

The warm night air of Vegas had done nothing to snap me out of my delusion that Hunter actually loved me. We'd stopped at the nearest bar and each had two more drinks. Hunter's orders were doubles. Outside the bar, he did a search on his phone for the nearest wedding chapel.

He grasped my shoulders and maneuvered me out of the way of pedestrians. His face grew somber. "Listen, Bails. If they think we're unable to make rational decisions, they won't let us get married. Can you hold it together long enough to seem sober?"

I blew out a raspberry and waved a hand, the motion nearly knocking me over. "Of course."

We had found someone stupid enough to marry us—or someone willing to take Hunter's bribe and overlook our condition. My wedding that was supposed to be a once-in-a-lifetime event to be cherished forever was just a blur the next morning. I remembered it now only in fragments—saying "I do" and Hunter slipping a silicone ring on my finger, then delivering a scorching kiss until the minister finally kicked us off the stage. We'd staggered back toward the hotel and when we came to the bar we'd been in just before our wedding, we sprinted inside for shots of tequila.

After downing the contents of a shot glass, Hunter lined it up next to several empties. "Let's go, wifey."

I giggled, letting him take my hand. Just outside, he halted, spun me around, then pressed me against him. "I really love you, Bails."

The last thing I remembered was snuggling up to a passed-out Hunter, already imagining what our children would look like. I woke up the next morning still fully clothed. Hunter was looming over me, his face flushed in panic. I tried to focus on a very official looking piece of paper he was waving. "Wake up."

"What is that?" I croaked.

"It's our marriage certificate. We have to fix this before Blake finds out. Get up. Get dressed. I need you to distract him while I get an annulment." He stalked off and a stream of profanities came from the bathroom as he splashed water on his face.

I glanced at the gray silicone ring on my finger. "What's the rush?"

The water turned off and Hunter reappeared an instant later. Panic had been replaced with irritation and his words were clipped as he searched the room for his belongings. "Really? If Blake finds out about this, I'm dead meat. You know how he is when he thinks a guy is trying to take advantage of you."

But my brother would never be upset about his little sister finding happiness with the man she loved. Hunter's comment said it all—he had no intention of sharing that kind of happiness with me. My eyes stung.

He spun and disappeared into the bathroom again. "Oh, man, I really screwed up this time."

If Hunter genuinely cared about me, I would've woken to a much different conversation. More likely, we would've stayed in bed and skipped making any conversation at all. Instead, Hunter was on damage control.

He didn't love me. Not even close.

And just like that, all my dreams came crashing down like a meteor. Except the scorched crater had been left in my heart, not the ground.

And it still burned.

I had to somehow figure out a way to make peace with the knowledge that Hunter would never change, never want me in the way that mattered.

I parked the Explorer in the post office parking lot, dashed inside and purchased the stamps I needed. Stowing the roll of stamps in my purse, I exited the building, my step faltering at a familiar image leaning against my car. Hunter's father wore a black fedora and matching suit, despite the unseasonably warm day. Probably to appear more intimidating. The chill from the Evermond freezer made me shudder.

"Mr. Evermond, to what do I owe the pleasure?" I vowed not to allow this frigid, poor excuse for a human rattle me. His cold gray eyes stared into me and the back of my neck tingled. I straightened my spine.

"Let's get straight to business, shall we?" One side of his mouth curled up. "You are currently married to my son and I understand divorce has been agreed upon. I'm prepared to pay you ten-thousand now and another ten-thousand on the day your divorce is final, providing you keep only what you came into the marriage with, and fulfill all requirements for a timely divorce. Your family's financial struggles will be eased and Hunter won't have to worry about losing anything that could be considered community property by the court. Everyone wins." He thrust a small piece of paper at me.

I glanced at the zeros on the check, chewed my lip as I gathered my scattered thoughts. "When I give Hunter his divorce, it's because *we* want to end our marriage, and because it's the right thing to do." I took a step forward, lowering my voice to a growl and gritting my teeth. "I'm not surprised a man like you tries to bribe people. What amazes me is you thought I could be bought. Now please move out of my way so I can get into my car."

Clearly, he wasn't expecting me to stand up to him. He hesitated a second or two, then stepped aside, a perplexed look stuck to his face like cling wrap.

After pushing past him and climbing behind the wheel, I revved the engine and peeled out of the parking lot. The nerve of Mr. Evermond! On the bright side, I had the opportunity to be enraged at him instead of his son.

Unless Mr. Evermond's reason for attempting to buy me off was because Hunter had voiced his concerns. I bristled.

I already knew I was wasting my time wishing Hunter would choose a different path. But I couldn't seem to pick the correct path either. Nope, I just kept waiting for Hunter to see that he loved me. Kind of like Hunter wasting his time trying to break through to his parents. One day when he realized there was no hope for them, he would be devastated.

Like what I'd felt that morning after our drunken night in Vegas.

I forced my muscles to relax as I steered into Two Cups. No, I didn't need the additional caffeine when I was trying to calm down. But I couldn't go home yet, not until I had a chance to push past the adrenal rush from my confrontation with Mr. Evermond.

What was my brother's Silverado doing in the parking lot of Two Cups? Hunter was likely there, no doubt flirting with Noelle. Not something I wanted to see. But I wasn't leaving without my latte fix to get me through the rest of the day.

I surveyed the inside of the bakery, but Noelle wasn't there. My eyes found Hunter, though, standing by the register, his gaze sweeping my body. I shivered, suddenly feeling like I hadn't worn enough clothes. Yet I'd dressed in jeans and a light flannel earlier that morning to combat the slight breeze that had since died. Except for my face, neck and hands, my entire body was covered. Nothing to see here.

"Buy you a drink?" He grinned.

What the hell. I needed a coffee, right? It may as well be free. "Sure."

He ordered my latte and another coffee for himself, paid for them then moved out of the way for the next person in line. "Managed to escape the ranch, huh?"

"Errands." In my peripheral vision, his arm muscles flexed as he raised the paper cup to his lips and downed the remainder of its contents. "You?"

"Same. Bankin'. Things like that."

I kept my gaze on his, suspicious of his quick answer. Something was going on with him. His serious face discouraged further questions, so I switched the subject to satisfy my other curiosity. "How did it go at your parents' this morning? Muffin still alive?"

"Muffin's doing great. She might even like it better there than with me. My mom is surprisingly good to her, doting over anything she does. Gives her cheese." Hunter's grin withered. "I helped plant daisies, dug a ditch for a pond. She may have warmed up to me a bit, but it's difficult to tell."

"And your dad?" Although I wanted Hunter to make progress toward his goal, Mr. Evermond wasn't worth the paper his check was written on. Until he could put his son's needs first and not bulldoze innocent people, Mr. Evermond didn't deserve his son's love or respect. He hadn't earned it.

Hunter's eyes dulled. "Nah. He was sucked into work stuff, then had to leave for some meeting."

Yeah, a mystery meeting involving me. Mr. Evermond was probably congratulating himself at being able to corner me while his son was down the street and unable to witness the attempted bribe.

"Has he made any progress on the situation?"

Hunter mumbled what might have been a mild curse. "Uh, yes. Divorce papers are ready. That was one of my stops today, to sign them. He said he was gonna contact you today."

Apparently, Mr. Evermond figured his time was better spent bribing me than taking productive steps toward getting my signature to close the deal. Idiot.

Secretly, I was happy that I didn't have to take that step—not today anyway.

The barista called my name and we moved to the pickup counter. Hunter handed me my drink, then removed the lid from his new cup and poured cream. He drank it black last time. I guess he liked his coffee like his women—an ever-changing variety.

"Your dad being busy gives you the opportunity to spend quality time with your mother." I offered him a sympathetic smile. Sure, I was perpetually resentful toward Hunter but that didn't mean I wanted him to suffer. Ok, I did want him to suffer. A little. But only at *my* hand.

"Hey, what are you doing tonight after work?"

Hunter asked. "It's Friday and you've been working like a slave for days. Thought it might be nice to get out, relax, maybe dance. I haven't been to the Stable in a while."

"Intriguing idea." I sucked my bottom lip into my mouth, not looking forward to the next awkward moment. "Which is why I'm goin' there on my date tonight."

"A date? With whom?" Hunter's jaw tightened before he took a sip from his cup then gestured toward the corner. "Want to get a table?"

He limited his use of who and whom correctly when he was irritated. I hadn't been trying to annoy Hunter when I'd accepted Trevor's invitation. At the time, Blake didn't have a broken leg and Hunter had no plans to return to Bride anytime soon. I considered pointing that out to Hunter, but I seriously doubted he was jealous. He was probably just miffed because now he'd have to make an effort to find someone else to go to the Stable with him. No point in wasting my time explaining something that didn't matter.

"No, I can't stay." I leaned a hip against the counter wall. "Remember Trevor Harris?"

"Tall, skinny guy with black hair and bad skin?" He quirked one brow. "Didn't figure you for the nerd type."

I huffed. "You'd be surprised how different he is since law school and passing the bar." Hunter's eye twitched and I squashed the urge to laugh. "He's filled out a lot. Apparently, all that studying made him antsy, and lifting weights gave him balance. He's coming at six so you can see for yourself." I gulped from my cup, wishing I hadn't stopped for another cup of coffee to get even more jacked up. Dialogue with Hunter wasn't helping my nerves.

Hunter flashed me a gorgeous grin full of mischief. "Be sure to tell him you're married."

"I'd be happy to." I hit him with a syrupy smile. "As soon as you tell everyone *you*'re married, including all your girlfriends in Hollywood."

He sighed. "I don't have any girlfriends in Hollywood. Or here."

"Then there's no reason to keep it a secret. Do you want to tell Blake and the rest of my family or should I?"

Hunter scoffed and shook his head in bewilderment. "When did our friendly banter become chilly sarcasm?"

"When our friendship stopped mattering to you." I reined in the anger, shrugging to come across as indifferent. "And to me," I added as an afterthought.

He flinched. Moments ago, I had fleetingly thought about making him suffer. But in reality, I probably felt worse now than he did. I didn't like who I was around Hunter. If I couldn't contain my impulses, I needed to do a better job avoiding him.

"I don't believe that. You're still mad at me for reasons unknown, but at some point, you're gonna to tell me what I did. Then we'll fix it."

He sounded too sure of himself. When I just stared at him, he blew his long wild hair off of his face. "I'll be here when you're ready," he said. "In the meantime, I want to talk to you about the ranch. We need to get viable again and the quickest way would be to borrow money for some mares with champion blood lines. Then pay off the loan slowly, as they foal. Boom. We're in business again."

I'd already tried borrowing and the banks had said no due to our damaged credit score two years ago when we couldn't pay everything. The only way I could get my hands on that kind of capital was a private loan at a scary high interest rate and the only person crazy enough to lend my family money was Hunter. Investing money into mares would also give him a stake in the ranch. I didn't want anything holding him in Texas. I needed him gone.

"We?" I stalked toward him. "Over my dead body. Listen closely, Hunter Evermond. My brother will be able to work in a few weeks, at which time, you will get on the first plane out of here. You're not staying to oversee an investment or anything else. You're going home to Hollywood so my life can get back to normal."

"What the hell, Bailey?" he rasped, gripping my wrist. "I don't understand what's got you so riled up."

Right, he couldn't comprehend the devastation he'd inflicted on me. "I married you, Hunter. I would've done it drunk or sober, because I *wanted* to. And you tossed me away like a piece of trash. You treated me abominably and you expect me to still respect you? Why would I ever let you in long enough to hurt me again? Sorry, cowboy, but you're just my brother's best friend to me. That's it."

Hunter blinked, hurt blanketing his face as if losing me had sunk in. I knew the feeling all too well.

"I need to finish some work and be cleaned up by six." I shook my wrist free, disgusted with myself for making Hunter as miserable as I'd made myself. Worse, divulging my secret—that he'd broken me.

Nausea rising, I concentrated on putting one foot in front of the other until I'd finally made it to my car and got the hell out of there. At least I'd be out with Trevor later, out of the house and away from Hunter. A much needed break.

Back at the ranch I hustled, checking on Kamilah to see if she was ready to breed, walking the stallions, stacking firewood. Anything I couldn't finish, I delegated. I even asked Hunter to put the chickens in for the night. I wanted enough time to emerge from my room looking fabulous enough to make Hunter's eyes wander below my neck again.

After showering, I took pains with the curling wand to get my overly long hair to stay curled. Then I used ten tons of hair spray. It didn't need to move the rest of the night, right? I grabbed my laciest bra then slipped on a frilly top that dipped in the front. Then I stepped into a mini skirt showing a good portion of my legs. I topped it off with a pair of high-heeled cowboy boots.

Satisfied and slightly smug, I waltzed out of my bedroom and into my brother's. I jumped when I almost crashed into Hunter who'd been hovering by the door. "Just popping in to say good night since Trevor might keep me out late."

Hunter relocated to the chair in tight-lipped silence, avoiding my gaze.

"Have fun," my brother said in a tone that meant the exact opposite. "Do remind Trevor if he touches you inappropriately, I'll beat him to death with this cast."

I snickered. "Of course." I waited an instant for Hunter to say something, then quietly closed the door when what I assumed were knuckles pounded on the front door. I picked up my pace, sprinting to the first floor and flinging open the door. After offering him a smile, I stepped back. He was gorgeous, clad in a button-down shirt, jeans and brown cowboy boots. His black hair had been recently trimmed, making him appear nicely manscaped. A far cry from Hunter's unruly shoulder-length hair. I tossed the image of Hunter out of my mind. "I have to get my purse."

Trevor whistled. "You look amazing, Bailey."

"Thanks." I scooped up my tiny purse I'd set on the couch earlier and grabbed my cowboy hat off the hook by the door. "You're not so bad either."

"You still want to go to the Stable? We could eat somewhere else then go there for dancing." He stuffed his hands into his pockets like he didn't know what to do with them.

"I don't want to miss out on their fries. And I'm starving." I compelled my mouth to curve up before heading out the front door. His fingertips on my lower back guided me to the passenger side of his BMW. He opened the door for me and saw me safely inside. As I finished buckling myself in, he folded his long frame behind the steering wheel. "Besides, they have a live band tonight," I said.

"The Stable it is then." Trevor glided away from the house and I attempted to analyze my emotions, specifically why I wasn't as excited to go out with him as I should've been. Another unwanted image of Hunter assaulted me.

"Pull over." I rolled the window down and aimed my nose toward the soft breeze.

His gaze whipped toward me. "What's wrong? Are you sick?"

The car stopped and I opened the door, but remained in my seat. I inhaled and exhaled several times before closing the door and shifting in my seat to face him.

"I have to tell you something." I squeezed my eyes shut, not wanting to reveal my secret to anyone, but feeling obligated to confess. I couldn't go all evening letting Trevor think I was totally into him. That was Hunter's style, not mine. "I've been fixated on Hunter Evermond most of my life."

"You and every other girl in Bride." He lifted one shoulder then dropped it. "And?"

"Well... when he left town, took me a while to realize he had no plans to return and we weren't going to live happily ever after. Knowin' he wouldn't be around gave me tremendous relief, like I could breathe again."

Trevor's head bobbed up and down, his brows drawn. "And you're telling me this because..."

"I'd finally gotten him out of my system, Trevor. And as if the universe knew I'd finally been emotionally liberated, you came along. So when you asked me out, I said yes. I mean, why not go out with you? You're smart, hot and you have a great future. In theory, you're a great prospect."

He canted his head. "Only in theory?"

"Yes. Unfortunately, I haven't resolved my feelings for Hunter. Since he came back—"

"Wait." He held out a palm to stop me. "*Hunter's in town*? Is he staying at your house, like he used to?"

"Yes. And I'm pretty sore at him right now but it'll pass. To be fair to you though, it's probably better if we don't go out or anything until Hunter leaves. Or until he no longer has an effect on me. Whichever comes first."

"Hm." He studied me a long moment. "The whole town knows you've been half in love with him for years. I figured you'd gotten over it, or I wouldn't have asked you out."

"I'm not in love with him," I lied. But soon it wouldn't be a lie at all. I was determined to kick that love in no time—as soon as he disappeared to Los Angeles. At the rate he was pissing me off, maybe sooner.

Trevor scratched his chin thoughtfully. "I'll tell you what. Let's go out and have fun anyway. After Hunter leaves town and you want to go out again, call me. Tonight, we dance and be merry. Just as friends."

"Seriously?" I squirmed, kind of wishing I'd stayed home.

"Absolutely." He wiggled a couple fingers, indicating my body. "The way you look, I'll be the envy of every guy there. And being seen with you will increase my market value."

I chuckled. "So you're using me to get dates?"

He flashed me a lopsided grin, starting the engine again. "No more than you're using me to get under Hunter's skin."

My hand shot out to grip his shoulder. "Trevor, when I said yes, I had no idea he'd be coming back. I thought he was out of my life."

Trevor patted my knee, then switched his attention to the road. "I know. And I don't expect a second date with you, ever."

Blinking, I struggled to understand his meaning. "Why is that?"

"Because I don't think Hunter is stupid."

Frustration gnawed at me, but I didn't want Trevor's cryptic comments clarified. If Trevor meant Hunter had feelings for me, I might let the concept go to my head. I might become hopeful again and that was the last thing I needed. Hope was dangerous, because it opened you up to a world of hurt. I should know. I refused to give Hunter any kind of power over me again, and keeping my heart intact began with purging him from my thoughts and not allowing hope.

"If I'm not his type, doesn't mean he's stupid." I spied the Stable sign and sighed in relief. Inside would be too noisy for deep conversations.

"You're *every* man's type." He maneuvered the BMW into the parking lot.

I unbuckled my seat belt, more than ready to be finished with this portion of our date. "You're wrong. Hunter couldn't be less interested in me in that way." Except maybe on a temporary basis. Hunter wasn't meant to settle down with one girl. He wasn't built for intimacy or anything involving a true connection or bond. I wasn't stupid enough to think I could change him.

I dashed out of the car toward the Stable. "No more talk of him tonight. Let's dance."

Hours later, Trevor steered the BMW down the B & B ranch driveway. I'd had an amazing time two-stepping to the live band. Trevor was surprisingly smooth on his feet and kept his hands to himself like he'd promised. With the pressure off, I'd relaxed and let myself forget about Blake and his broken leg, the heaps of work to be done at the ranch, the mare likely needing to be bred tomorrow, my unwelcome houseguest and our inconvenient marriage. I'd danced my butt off, laughed too much and worked off the meal we'd eaten.

If only Blake had never gotten injured and Hunter hadn't come back. Trevor was a pretty great guy and in a perfect world, I would've jumped at a second date with him.

After the Stable had closed, we detoured to an all-night diner just outside of Bride. Well fed, again, we hit the road and returned to the real world.

Trevor regarded me an instant before killing the engine. "I'll walk you to the door."

I knew Trevor wasn't going to kiss me good night, but Hunter didn't know that. And once we were in front of the door, Hunter wouldn't be able to see us to know what happened either way. The slightly buzzed side of me reveled in the thought of getting under Hunter's skin. But did I want to stoop to playing mind games with him? Not so much. My relationship with Hunter was messy enough.

Trevor was already out of the car by the time I fished for my purse and opened the door. I glanced over to see a shadow move beyond the living room curtain. Judging by the height and width of the silhouette, Hunter was still awake and lurking. Clearly he wasn't aware of the light behind him.

At the top of the porch stairs, Trevor leaned in and bussed my cheek. "I had a great time."

I smiled, relieved he hadn't aimed for my mouth. "Me too. Thank you so much for dinner. Both of them."

He tipped his hat, then leaped the stairs and jogged the few feet to his car.

I let myself through the front door, fully expecting to see Hunter. But the place was deserted. As I tiptoed up the stairs, I heard a bang coming from the direction of Hunter's room. I wouldn't assume he'd stayed up for me out of jealousy. He'd taken the role of big brother years ago and that kind of mentality probably wasn't easy to shake. Hunter could have pretty much any girl he wanted; I couldn't imagine him setting his sights on me. If he had a moment of insanity, like when we were in Vegas, he'd probably snap out of it soon enough. Just as he had in Vegas.

I didn't know why I was even allowing my mind to ponder the impossibilities. I needed to get Hunter out of my brain.

If only I could.

Chapter Seven

HUNTER

I stood in the hallway with a mug of coffee in hand, staring at Bailey's bedroom door.

If the Stable closed at two a.m. and they were seven minutes away by car, why had Bailey arrived home well after three? When Trevor had brought her back and walked her to the door, did he kiss her? Had Bailey kissed him back?

And, for crying out loud, it was already after nine and she hadn't dragged her ass out of bed yet. I didn't mind helping if they needed it, but I'd thought the Thayers were desperate and shorthanded. I didn't appreciate spending ten or more hours a day slaving so she could party all night and miss half a day's work.

Chastising myself, I remembered she hadn't had a day off in ages. One morning sleeping in was the least she deserved after how hard she worked. And despite the sweat I'd put in these past few days, my time in Bride so far hadn't been as bad as I'd thought it would be; the manual labor meant more because it helped the Thayers. Plus, my parents had been much less unpleasant than the last time I'd visited.

The knob clicked and her door creaked open. She stumbled out of her room, her waist-length auburn hair curling all around her tall, lean body. Her skimpy pajama shorts showed off those gorgeous legs and bright pink toenails. She wore a loose tank with no bra and I could easily tell where her breasts peaked.

She moaned and pointed to her sleepy eyes. "Up here, Hunter. It's too early to be ogled, especially when I probably look like I've been wrestling with my sheets all night."

A visual of her wrestling with *me* all night seized my brain. My stomach pinching, I sped down the stairs. "I'm off to run errands," I called out, scooping up my hat as I neared the front door. "I'll be back to help you in a few hours."

Forty-five minutes later, I arrived in Austin. As I prepared to make a right at the light, a shiny red truck caught my eye. I pulled into the dealership, parked and made a beeline for the Ford F450.

It was a freakin' beast. And I fell instantly in love.

"I can arrange a test drive for you," a voice purred behind me.

I spun to see a pretty blonde. I sized her up quickly—attractive, confident and by the double meaning in her offer of a test drive, she was definitely available.

Strangely, I had zero interest. I was in Texas for specific reasons—mend things with Bailey, which involved giving her the divorce she wanted, try to break through to my parents, and help save the B & B. This beautiful blonde wasn't on my To Do list. Plus, I'd sworn off women for a while. I didn't need the hassle while I was in town.

"No need. I've driven one of these before. Can you have this delivered to Bride?"

I loved paying in full for whatever I wanted. Much less paperwork. I was out of there in less than an hour and on my way again to Serenity Ranch. Unannounced. I wasn't sure how the Angelos felt about doing business on a weekend, especially with no warning. But money talked and I crossed my fingers they'd be willing to listen. Hopefully, my family's connections would get my foot in the door and my knowledge of horses would ensure I got the Thayers what they needed.

The B & B ranch depended on it. Bailey's future depended on it.

I steered the Silverado over the cobblestone driveway, parking behind a monstrous black Hummer. The front door of the mansion opened and a stout woman approached, clad in loose-fitting jeans and a long-sleeved t-shirt. I grabbed my cowboy hat off the seat and jumped out of the car.

She extended a hand. "You're Dan Evermond's boy."

From what I remembered, these were my family's kind of people, the elite. They also had a reputation for fair business dealings. I shook her hand. "Yes, Mrs. Angelo. Nice to see you again. I hope this isn't a bad time for you, but I'm in the market for some quality Arabians."

"On a Saturday?" She cocked her head. "What's the rush?"

"So sorry to arrive unannounced, ma'am." I tipped my hat, really not wanting to waste time again driving to and from Serenity. I didn't want to come across desperate either. "I was in the area and thought I'd give it a shot. If you'd rather do this another day, I understand."

I thought she was about to salute me, and I then realized she was shielding her eyes from the sun. I sidestepped and gave her shade, like any good gentleman.

She smiled. "Well, since you're already here, what do you have in mind?"

I hooked a thumb through my belt loop, so my request would come across more casual. "Your best champion stock. A mare or two, preferably one in foal, a couple three-year olds already training."

"That's a tall order and won't come cheap. But if the price is right, I might be willing to part with one or two I may have otherwise kept and shown." She flicked an index finger toward the first in a row of long red stables with at least twenty stalls. "Let's have a look."

Starving from spending most of my morning negotiating, the urge for a snack before heading back to the B & B almost convinced me to stop at Two Cups. But I'd already used up a huge chunk of my day. Although the Thayer family had always made it their policy not to work weekends, I knew enough about

84

ranches to know the animals needed feeding whether we wanted a day off or not.

Ideally, Bailey's chores had been minimal. Either way, I'd feel like a dog for being gone most of the day. I'd track her down and pitch in, do whatever it took to soften her up. And maybe she wouldn't be as furious with me when she discovered what I'd been up to.

When I arrived at the B & B and killed the engine of the Silverado, I scanned the grounds for Bailey. I spotted her in the training pen, working on the gate. Her legs were fully covered and she wore boots, a flannel shirt and cowboy hat. Her hair was loose with strands flipping around in the breeze, and I couldn't quite tell from this distance, but something dark stained her cheek.

She looked sexy as hell.

She could've acted helpless and waited for me to make the repairs. Instead, she took control. I didn't know if it was the emotional strength Bailey exuded or the fact that she was completely self-reliant.

My heart skipped a beat.

She made another adjustment on the wood fence, although I couldn't quite tell precisely where, then she stood and examined her work. As if satisfied, she slipped the pliers into her pocket and pivoted. After a few steps toward me and the house, her pace faltered. Yep, she'd seen me.

Still several yards away, she veered toward the stables without a hello or wave. Fine, I'd follow her. "It's Saturday. Fence couldn't wait until tomorrow or Monday when I could do it?"

Without glancing up, she began examining one of the horse's hooves. "You're needed for other things on Monday. And we don't take days off anymore, Hunter. If we don't do the work ourselves, then we have to hire someone. We can't afford that right now."

I knew she'd been putting in more hours, but didn't she at least reduce the time on weekends? With my recent acquisitions, the viability of the ranch would improve in the near future. I couldn't do anything to save Bailey from immediate work though. Scratching my chin, I wondered how many more hours she needed to put in before she ended for the day. "Everyone needs a day to decompress. Whatever else you need done, I'll do it. You can relax."

"Won't be today. The unexpected errand earlier put me behind on my chores. Met with your father and signed the papers." She stood and marched down the passageway between the row of stalls. "Kamilah's in season, and I'm late filling orders for one of our stallions."

My stomach bottomed out. She'd signed the divorce papers? That shouldn't have fazed me but it did. A lot. Not because I wanted to stay married to her. Of course not. I didn't want to be married to *anyone*. I just didn't want to feel that Bailey was further out of my reach than she already was. Now I had even less time to find a cure for my strange and irrational feelings.

Maybe I could stretch out the divorce if my dad couldn't make it to the courthouse on Monday.

"Orders for Omari?" I remembered Omari being their most popular stud. "So... you're going to need *my* help using Kamilah to get him excited to get the sample? And then again to get Alcatraz to mount her to get her pregnant? Or were you going to get Alcatraz on the dummy to do his business in the fake vagina?" I twitched thinking about the process.

"Since artificial insemination requires a vet and we've been avoiding the extra costs, Alcatraz will do it live."

She wanted to save money on vet bills, but I was a vet and I could do all those things for her. Except I much preferred letting the horses go at it than being the one to insert the sperm. Dealing with semen was my least favorite part of the horse breeding business. Worse, I'd have to go through two rounds of stallion ejaculation. I surveyed the vicinity in search of anyone else who could help.

She flinched, avoiding my gaze as she stopped at Omari's stall. "All the hands have weekends off, remember?"

"But even if I helped, you still need a third." I resisted the urge to flee. If she knew how much I didn't want to watch horse porn while standing next to her, she'd rub it in my face. "Not worth either of us getting hurt. Or the stallions."

"Alcatraz and Omari know the routine. I work with them each day so they aren't difficult when they need to mount. Alcatraz will perform without fuss. Always does." She stroked Omari's flank and he snorted. "Has to be done today. I can't miss this opportunity."

Breeding the mare in the next few days was no longer life or death. But I couldn't tell her yet about the deal I'd made. "Plenty of people will be around on Monday."

"Too much going on next week." She chewed her bottom lip. "Maybe Blake could help me."

"Forget Blake. He'll probably lose his balance and break his other leg." As long as I'd known the Thayers, they'd sold the semen of their finest studs. Out of curiosity, I had occasionally helped them collect samples. But I had limited my assistance to holding the mare's reins or calming the stallion. I never touched the stallion's male parts and I certainly hadn't been the one to handle them long enough to aim the sample into the artificial vagina. "I'll help. But you'll be pointing him in the right direction, not me."

"You're as bad as Blake." She tapped her foot. "Surgical gloves, ever heard of them? They protect you from direct contact with whatever you're avoiding."

I recoiled. "Direct skin contact or not, I don't want to feel any penis in my hand, Bails."

She stifled a giggle. "You're going to have to get over it if you're going to be a horse vet."

I grimaced. "I know. But not today."

Bailey sighed. "If you want to bring Kamilah to the breeding shed, I'll get the canister and supplies."

Obeying, I tracked down the mare and led her into the enclosure then moments later Bailey brought in Omari. After allowing him to sniff the mare and get excited, we coaxed him onto the phantom mount. Predictably, the stallion finished his business in under fifteen seconds. While Bailey sealed the canister and took the stallion to his stall, I left to get Alcatraz.

I wasn't looking forward to more horse porn at all.

Watching Omari do his business with a fake vagina had been bad enough. Now I'd have to watch the real thing... with Bailey, the girl for whom I'd developed a severe case of lust.

Bailey was patting Kamilah's flank when I came in with Alcatraz. He sniffed her, then nudged her with his muzzle and I tugged on the reins to get him under control. He whinnied and I led him in a circle to steady him.

"He's ready now." Bailey positioned Kamilah and I reeled Alcatraz in, facing him toward the mare. He mounted her but I watched only long enough to make sure he got in. Then I circled away from the horses and Bailey. Witnessing horses in the act had always been awkward for me. Watching it now with Bailey was even worse since it only reminded me what I wanted to do with *her*.

Alcatraz collapsed on Kamilah then slid off. The ten seconds of horse porn had seemed like ten minutes.

"I'll finish in here. You can take Kamilah to her stall." Bailey thrust the reins at me and I complied, getting the hell out of there.

When I arrived back at the breeding barn after settling Kamilah into her stall, Bailey shoved the canister at me. "Do you remember how to process it? Once I take Alcatraz back, I still have to muck the stalls, and... I have a ton of other things to do."

"You process. I'll put Alcatraz away, then muck." No way could I concentrate on processing the goods knowing Bailey was out there doing manual labor. "I'd probably mess up the sample anyway. It's been a while."

She shrugged and snatched the canister. "Whatever."

Mrs. T popped her head through the partially open doorway of the shed. "Bailey?"

"What's going on, Mom?"

"Did you pay the mortgage?" Her brows crinkled in the center. "I tried to pay online and we have nothin' due for the next three months."

Bailey chewed her lip, mulling it over. "Weird. I definitely didn't pay it. Do you need me to call them in the mornin'?"

Mrs. T huffed. "So weird. I'll check the books again and if I can't figure it out, I'll call them myself tomorrow."

I was about to get busted. Although I didn't want Bailey or her mom wasting any more time on this mystery when they could be more productive elsewhere, Bailey would be extremely displeased, to say the least, if she knew I'd forced my money on her family. If I was going to make progress wearing Bailey down into forgiving me, she needed breaks between the storms. I'd track down Mrs. T in a bit and corner her in secret.

"Let me know if you need a second set of eyes on the books," Bailey offered.

"Will do." Mrs. T smiled before slipping out of the shed.

"You didn't do anything, did you?" Bailey asked.

Oh, crap. When in a pinch, answer a question with a question. "Like what?"

Her eyes narrowed to slits. "Like pay our mortgage?"

I wrinkled my nose. "How would I even go about finding out which bank you owe?" Wasn't difficult at all. I knew where the Thayers kept their files.

She sighed. "Ok, fine. Not sure why I'm still standin' here. So much to do."

"I'll skip visiting my parents for a couple days. If I can get ahead of the work, maybe next week you'll have time to take a break. Sleep in and relax all mornin'."

She whistled in relief. "That would be amazing, especially since I'll be out late next Saturday night."

My spine stiffened and I tried to cover the tension by shoving my empty hand into my pocket. "Another date with the nerd?"

She smirked. "Since when are you interested in my love life?"

But she hadn't answered the question. "Since always. How did you think Lorenzo got a black eye after he took you to Homecomin' and copped a feel?"

Her brows flew up and she stepped forward, giving me the stink eye. "How did you know he copped a feel?"

"Boys can be stupid. He bragged to friends and those idiots couldn't keep a secret. Didn't take long for the news to get around to Blake and me."

"I was fifteen," Bailey hissed. "A boy finally came along who was brave enough to ask me to a dance, despite you two, and you made it impossible for anyone else to even glance at me until after you guys graduated. You ruined my life." Canister in tow, she stomped out and disappeared from my view.

"Bailey, geez." I trailed after her, and into the nearby lab. "Something wrong with lookin' out for you? The kid was scum. Nice guys don't brag about their conquests."

"He made a mistake." She set the canister on the desk by the slides and slammed her fists on her hips, glaring. "He shouldn't have talked. But he was one of only a handful of boys who treated me like a normal person. All the other boys were too scared to go near me. And my activities outside this ranch aren't any of your business."

Ouch. The truth hurt. "He only wanted one thing."

"And you were any different with Noelle or the other girls? Please, I can't take the hypocrisy." She pulled the bag from the canister, then removed the filter and poured the liquid into a vial.

I didn't want to watch Bailey process the sample. But she was talking to me—potential progress toward her eventually cooling off. "You're right. I'll try to stay out of your love life." I glanced around the lab, itching to get away. "I'll get started on muckin' the stables."

One more check over my shoulder before slipping away revealed her looking through a microscope. The perfect opportunity for a discreet conversation with Mrs. T.

As I passed the arena, spotting the horses in the mare motel yards beyond, I made my way back to the main house. Once I found Mrs. T in the small office, I stepped inside and shut the door. "It was me," I whispered.

Head tilting down toward the ledgers, her eyes became visible above the black frame of her reading glasses. "Explain."

I tiptoed to her desk and settled into the chair in front of it. "I paid the three months mortgage. It's just... I hate seein' you and Bailey work so hard when I can easily help out."

Her chin trembled. "When we get on our feet, we'll pay you every cent we owe."

"Why should you?" I scowled, ready for a battle. "How many meals have I eaten here? How many times did you drive me around? Helpin' out with your mortgage doesn't even begin to pay you guys for everything you've done for me."

"You were a child. We did what any decent human being would do." She scoffed. "No child should be expected to repay their parents. It's not possible."

"But if they can, what's wrong with tryin'?" I crossed my arms over my chest, leaned back. "I, too, did what any decent human would do."

"We're not children with no one to turn to, Hunter. We're adults. And you shouldn't be bailin' us out."

I shook my head. "If you have a problem with me makin' some mortgage payments vanish for you, you're really not gonna to like what else I did."

Mrs. T set her pencil aside with a snap. "Talk."

I held up one finger. "You can't tell Bailey. Promise me."

"Fine, I promise. For the time bein'." She groaned. "What did you do?"

"I kind of bought you guys some horses. Phenomenal bloodlines. You're gonna love 'em."

Her eyes hardened. "If you bought them, you *own* them."

I scooted my chair away from her desk, preparing to bolt. "I put B & B as registered owners."

Mrs. T's mouth tightened. "While I appreciate the thought, I can't take charity."

I scrubbed my hands over my face, not sure I could handle *both* the Thayer women mad at me.

Chapter Eight

HUNTER

"*It's not charity.* It's more like payback. You guys helped me when I needed it most. Now I'm repayin' the favor."

Mrs. T's nose wrinkled. "I don't know. I'm not sure how comfortable I am with a loan so big."

"Doesn't matter. I don't need to be reimbursed. Even if you made me take it, which you can't, there's no rush."

She tapped the pencil against the register. "If you were an investor, you'd receive a share of the profits."

"Which means I'd have a share in the ranch?" That concept was a little too appealing since my urge to leave Bride had gradually become less intense over the last few days. And I'd get to be around the Thayers more. And Bailey. If I were to be completely honest with myself, I didn't really want leave Bride again. Since I'd been showing up at my parents' house for no other reason but to hang out with them, they seemed slightly less cold, maybe a touch more manageable. We may never be as close as I would've liked, but at least I no longer had the urge to avoid them.

I wanted to stay in Bride and set up my practice here, water the roots I'd already grown in Bride.

Mrs. T grinned. "Why not? You've always been a part of this family. I'll have papers drawn up. I can use some of the money I'd planned to put toward the mortgage on an attorney."

"Can we keep this between us for now? Bailey's perpetually irate with me these days."

"Any particular reason she's unhappy with you?" Mrs. T asked, her brows descending.

Now that Bailey had given me an explanation, I could tell her mother and Blake. But I didn't know how to explain without revealing details of the Vegas disaster. I'd have to be vague.

"She says I was rude to her. Didn't mean to be. I'm working on her, but if she thinks I'm going behind her back, it'll make things worse." I abandoned the chair, the need to get to work weighing on me.

Her eyes twinkled, as if she already had information I wouldn't be privy to. "I'll have a chat with her."

"Whatever you could do to help would be great." I let myself out and sailed off to the stables. Passing the lab, I poked my head in. "Everything all right?"

Bailey set some vials in the fridge. "Almost finished."

"I'll be in the stables." I stopped at the tack room to grab a broom, rake, shovel and manure fork, then chucked them in a barrel. I loved caring for her horses, working with them and healing them. Mucking stalls, not so much. Thankfully, the horses generally spent the majority of time in one of the pastures and their stalls didn't require daily cleaning.

Hours later, I'd cleaned twenty-something stalls and spread out new bedding. I was sweaty and smelled like horse urine, and all I wanted was a cool shower. It wasn't four o'clock yet and I still had more work to do but I couldn't stand my own smell.

I stumbled on my way to the house. The exertion of mucking stables had drained me and my balance was a bit off. Or maybe I was just hungry. Anxious to help Bailey, I'd forgotten to eat lunch when I'd arrived from Serenity Ranch. Yeah, food sounded so good. I returned the barrel and supplies to the tack room then rushed to the house.

Bailey sat on a stool at the kitchen's island counter in front of a platter of fried chicken, scrolling through her phone. Good chance she was shopping for supplies. I'd rarely seen her not working since I'd arrived in Bride.

"You'll ruin your appetite for dinner."

Bailey jolted, dropping a leg of chicken and spinning on the stool. "You scared me. Too hungry to wait another hour."

"Same here." I intercepted the chicken leg as she raised it toward her lips and then I sunk my teeth into it.

Bailey's eye twitched. "Nice manners. I was eating that." She reached for the plate of chicken and chose a wing. I snagged that too, wrestling it from her hand. She slipped off the stool and threw a punch at my bicep. She used to always playfully beat on me.

"You want it?" I smashed the chicken leg on her face, smearing chicken fat around her mouth and coercing her lips apart.

She belly-laughed, throwing punches faster than I could dodge them. "Such a jerk."

Jerk, yes. But she was laughing again. With *me*. I reached for a fresh drumstick and jammed that at her face too, swiping it across her cheek.

She crammed a wing into my nose, mainlining the spices and grease directly into my nostril. Her eyes lit with a familiar mischief before she squished the chicken into my hair.

This was war. And, what the hell, I needed a shower anyway.

I shoved her against the counter, about to stuff the chicken leg down the front of her shirt and froze, my gaze locking onto the creamy swells at her neckline. Her chest rose and fell with each pant and my gaze met hers. She licked her lips, then focused on my mouth.

Not one to let a perfect opportunity pass, I seized the moment and leaned in. She slanted her head to accommodate me. Our lips touched tentatively before her arms slipped over my shoulders and wrapped around my neck, pulling me closer. When our tongues brushed, a flame ignited in my belly.

Bailey pressed closer, the length of her body against mine. I didn't remember her feeling *this* good, this right. My one hand circled her waist, then crept along her spine to anchor my fingers at the nape of her neck. My other arm hooked into the waistband of her jeans, dragging her closer to me.

She slammed a palm into my stomach then ducked, escaping my clutches. "See, this is the kind of thing that led to our little situation last year. From now on, keep your distance, Evermond. Also, you stink." She grimaced, slapped a tainted drumstick into my hand and stormed out.

Okay, but her reaction to my playfulness only proved she didn't hate me and I could still get through to her. Eventually.

And once she was no longer irate with me, then what? Could I go back to playing big brother? After the scorching kiss just now against the counter, no doubt I'd never view her as anything but a real woman. A prospect.

The truth I'd been avoiding hit me full force. I wanted Bailey.

But if I ever got my way with her and we tumbled into bed, our relationship would go nowhere, like any other relationship I'd ever had. When it ended, we'd wind up further apart than before. Trying to imagine forever wasn't any more possible with Bailey than with any other woman. I'd left my comfort zone with her and could no longer see her as a sister, but I didn't love her the way a man should love a woman. I wasn't capable of forming the kind of love that binds one to another for a lifetime. My parents had made sure I could never deliver like I needed to. Bailey deserved nothing less than the whole fairy tale. She deserved better than me.

From now on, I couldn't entertain any thoughts of getting intimate with her. I couldn't ever think of her as any kind of possibility. Period. I'd get my act together, apologize for crossing the line and try to repair any damage I'd done. Hopefully, she wasn't more upset now than before.

After a snack and a shower, I wandered the house looking for Bailey, not finding her anywhere. I strolled outside to the stables, finally locating her in the lab.

"I'm sorry about earlier. Extremely inappropriate."

She jolted, then set the box on the floor and stood. "Would you quit sneaking up on me?"

I frowned. "Not my fault you're as jumpy as a cat, no matter how much noise I make. But I promise to keep my hands to myself." I paused, choosing my words carefully. "Listen, Bailey, I know you've been upset with me. But you have to know I'd never intentionally hurt you. You're my family."

She stretched her shoulders, then picked up the box again. "I know. I'm trying to make peace with the Vegas thing. Honestly, I'm probably madder at myself than you."

Bailey didn't dote on me like she used to. She didn't seem emotionally invested in me at all. So, why she'd be mad at herself, I didn't know. But I wasn't going to pry, because I didn't entirely understand why she'd been so upset with me in the first place. And since I'd finally cracked her armor, I didn't want to lose my momentum. I'd keep my distance, not do anything else to incite her wrath.

By the time she learned how I had weaseled myself into being part of the ranch, we'd already be back to normal and she'd have no reason to be mad at me all over again. Maybe by then we'd be showing some profit, or a glimpse of it anyway, and she'd see my actions had been for the best. She might even appreciate my efforts. Maybe she'd even like me again.

Bailey swiveled to face the Styrofoam and inserted a piece into each box. She dipped into the freezer, withdrew an icepack, then counted how many others were there. Satisfied the boxes were ready to ship out semen tomorrow, she straightened. "Did you need something to do? Because the horses need to be brought in from pasture, then watered and fed."

"I'll help you with all of that, but I've been mucking stables and doing slave labor since I flew in. I've barely had a chance to see the ranch. Mind doing a walk-through with me? I'd love to get your take on whatever you feel needs fixin'."

She chewed the side of her mouth, contemplating. "Sure, after we bring in the horses. And if I take time for a tour, you'll be feeding and watering them."

I'd expected to work a bit longer anyway. "But isn't this kind of early to put the horses in for the night?"

"Yes, but Mom wants it done now." She left the lab and ventured into one of the pastures, me right behind her. "I'm exhausted and too tired to walk them all in." She climbed onto a horse bareback, and herded the others into their paddock.

Her grace and ability to control horses dazzled me. Lots of people rode bareback, including myself, and I shouldn't have been so impressed. But she did it with such style and ease. Why was that so sexy to me now?

I longed for the days when all I required was a nice rack and a great ass to be mesmerized. Bailey had raised the bar.

She slid off a gelding then led him into the stable. I joined in, capturing the bridle of the gelding closest to me and walking him into his stall. As I cornered the last mare and gave her muzzle a rub, I turned to see Bailey on her last horse. "Free now?"

"Still so much to do today. But now's as good a time as any." She strode out of the stable and I followed. "Nothing major has changed since you were last here. Dad had planned to install an eco-friendly draining system in all the stalls, but he never had a chance."

I made a mental note, adding one more thing to my list of upgrades.

She kept a brisk pace along the walkway toward the breeding shed. I steeled myself to not think about breeding with Bailey. If I continued letting myself go there, I was going to totally screw things up with her again.

"You have four empty stalls after selling the mares, right?" When my new acquisitions arrived—or rather when I collected them on Monday—I wanted to make sure they had a place to stay and that Bailey wouldn't be out of sorts over me ruining any plans she had for them.

"More spare stalls than four. Plenty of room at the inn." She pivoted and continued walking the dirt path toward the exercise pen. "Blake and I already agreed to save them for any future horses we add."

"Good." Following her lead, I stopped. "I wanted to talk about the vet visits. No need to hire anyone while I'm here. You may as well take advantage of me and save the money. I can do anything he'd do, unless a horse needs surgery or something."

"Thank you." Bailey's forehead smoothed out, worry fading from her face. "They all need annuals and shots. We're overdue, in fact. Especially Iesha since I'll have to prove she's up to date before taking part in the competition."

"I'll have to wait until the vaccines arrive, but I have everything else needed to start tomorrow."

Her mouth curved up as she cast me a glance. "I'm sorry for being a jerk lately."

I'd finally broken through her anger and even been rewarded with a smile. My heart swelled, filling with her. The sun had lowered, casting a soft shadow across her face and making her prettier than ever. And all I could think about was kissing her.

Do not look at her lips. "What do you say we go to the Stable one of these evenings after work?"

She inched back, her eyes narrowing ever so slightly. "I thought we were going to keep a reasonable amount of distance."

Damn, yes, that had been the final decision. I didn't want her as merely a coworker though, someone I saw in passing throughout the day. I wanted time with her away from the ranch. But she was right. We couldn't put ourselves in a position where we might reenact any part of the Vegas incident. "I meant a bunch of us. Besides, we'll see people we know there. We'll be far from alone."

I convinced my trap to stay shut and not ask about the nerd or anything else too personal which could provoke her. I would be strictly business, and maybe keep the progress I'd made.

"I'll find out who else wants to come and then we'll figure out a day." She flicked a hand toward the chicken coop. "We have some termite damage and a few hens have escaped. We need to renovate the hen house soon."

As we passed the coop, I eyed the structure, noting some wood requiring replacement and other needed reinforcements.

We circled back toward the stables and she sighed as we walked the long passageway between stalls. Heads poked out occasionally, begging for a nose rub. I extended my arm to stroke their soft muzzles.

God, I'd missed this, the smell of horses, hay and leather. I'd missed the feel of their coat, the tickle of their mouths as they looked for treats, their kisses. Hell, I almost missed mucking the stables. I halted, spotting the most gorgeous chestnut mare ever to be foaled. I'd only caught glimpses of her since I'd returned to Bride and hadn't had time to give her the attention she deserved. "Hey, beautiful. I've missed you the most." I rubbed her jaw, mussed her mane.

She whinnied and puckered her lips, earning a chuckle from me. "What a charmer."

"Don't let Liza fool you." Bailey brushed my shoulder with hers as she reached out to pat the beauty. "She escaped the other day and showed a couple others the way out, practically starting a mutiny."

Bailey was close. Too close. I unconsciously shifted toward her and ended up with our faces inches apart. My gaze instantly went to her full mouth.

Her eyes darkened, that gorgeous pouty mouth turning down. "Tour's over and I have to shower. You're feeding and watering the horses, right?" Without waiting for a reply, she took off toward the house at a brisk pace as though she couldn't get away from me fast enough. Seconds later, the front door slammed.

Damn, I may have just lost all the progress I'd made earlier. If only I hadn't gotten distracted by my hormones. Again. If only she hadn't accidentally touched me. If only those lips weren't so sexy.

Which made the whole thing *her* fault.

Except she probably hadn't expected me to act like such a guy. Why couldn't I hold it together around her? What the hell was wrong with me? Why couldn't I manage to prevent an image of her naked in the shower from invading my head? If I was going to repair the damage between Bailey and me for real, I needed to do much better than ogle her and unwittingly act like a hormone-crazed teenager.

I trudged back into the house and flopped onto the recliner across from the sofa where Blake lay.

Chester was hogging the other half of the sofa, his head resting on Blake. By the smell in the kitchen and a couple dirty plates on the counter, they'd had an early dinner.

He regarded me curiously, absently rubbing Chester's ears. "How did you piss her off this time?"

Bailey and I had obviously been talking too loud outside. Sometimes, I missed the freeway noise and traffic of Los Angeles to muffle private conversations yards away. And after she'd slammed the front door, she had probably stamped through the house in a huff.

I shuffled to the fridge and opened it, then glanced at him. "I looked at her wrong. Hey, I thought you were going to find out for me what's buggin' her."

As soon as the words had hit the air, I regretted them. The last thing I wanted was for Blake to find out anything about Vegas.

"Tried. She insisted everything's fine." Blake rolled his eyes. "Load of crap, I know."

I'd dodged a bullet with Blake this time. But what if I never fully fixed this with Bailey? What if we never went back to cute banter and playful wrestling? My stomach twisted.

"How's it going with your parents?" he called out, sounding farther away now. "Bailey says you're trying to get them on defrost. Any luck?"

I scoffed, making my way to the living room with an apple. "Hard to tell. My dad is harder to melt, but I'll have a chance when we build the gazebo together."

"At their age, you think they'll change, that they're

capable of bonding like normal people?" Blake cast me a skeptical glance.

"Maybe not." I leaned against a wall, then bit into the apple. "But I have to try."

Blake nodded several times, then snatched the remote. "Great. Good. Are we done with the girl talk? Because the game's about to start."

I laughed and slogged outside to feed and water the horses.

◊ ◊ ◊

After I finished in the stables and all the animals had been fed and watered, I trudged through the front door and lodged myself on the couch near the recliner currently occupied by Blake. His attention was glued to the football game.

A moment later, Bailey waltzed by. I'd finally stopped thinking about her and now I had to start from scratch all over again. Worse, she was showered, wearing snug jeans and a skimpy blue top. Her compact purse hung from her shoulder and I squinted at the screen on my phone, noting it was just after five.

"Where are you going? It's too early for dancing at the Stable." I assumed she wasn't going out to dinner since she'd eaten not too long ago.

Her gaze locked onto mine and one side of her mouth curved up. "Out."

"With Trevor?" As soon as the question passed through my lips, I regretted it. Sure, I had no right to ask about her love life. But technically, she was still my wife. A married woman should have the decency to stay home. With her husband.

I inwardly groaned at the thought. Clearly, I needed to sort out and resolve my feelings for Bailey. I longed for the old days. But viewing her as anything remotely similar to a sibling had proved impossible. She was a beautiful, independent woman and, as much as I didn't want to be, I was insanely attracted to her.

Blake decreased the volume on the TV and set aside the remote, his attention riveted to Bailey and me.

Bailey's perfectly arched brow lifted. "And risk anyone getting a black eye? News flash. You're not my brother. Even if you were, I still wouldn't have to tell you a thing."

Damn it, she had me there. My nostrils flared involuntarily as I stared at Blake. "Don't you have anything to say to her?"

Blake's gaze bounced between Bailey and me. "Bailey doesn't like it when I hover. But she knows if she needs help, I'll be there."

She grinned, then bent and delivered a kiss on the top of his head. Without even a glance my way, she disappeared out the door.

He studied me, tapping his lip. "If I didn't know better, I'd say you have thing for my sister."

I made a guttural sound in disgust, then realized I probably shouldn't protest too loudly. "It's not what you think. I'm extra frustrated because even if things got better with her, I still wouldn't know why she's been mad at me. All this is messin' with my head."

"We've been friends a long time and I've seen how you operate." He stared hard at me. "If you hurt my sister, none of our history matters. I'll pound you into a pulp."

I grunted. "First, you'd never win a fight with me. Second, I'd never intentionally hurt your sister. Trust me, there's nothin' going on between us." And there wouldn't be, especially since she made it impossible. And though I'd been freakishly drawn to her, I knew the pull wouldn't last. Once my weird obsession with her faded, we'd be friends again and all this would be nothing but a bad memory.

"Good." Blake's focus drifted back to the TV screen.

As soon as I relaxed, I began to wonder again where Bailey had gone. Out with friends? Trevor? Or was she dating a different guy? I wanted to ask Blake what he thought of Trevor but that would raise red flags.

I did my best to get lost in the football game but I wasn't a big fan of the teams and the occasional noises from the kitchen distracted me. A snack seemed like a great idea, but I didn't want to move again. To keep my mind off Bailey, I dug out my phone from my pocket and checked my email.

"Darlin', would you help me in the kitchen?"

I flinched, knowing this "help" wouldn't involve cooking, since they'd already had dinner. Anything was better than obsessing on Bailey and who might be pawing her. "Be right there, Mrs. T."

Blake snickered as I crossed the living room.

When I got to the threshold, Mrs. T was already pointing at a cabinet above the stove. "Would you get me that vase?"

"Sure." Even though I was knowingly walking into a trap, I adjusted the step stool she nudged toward me, and prepared to take whatever lecture she dished out. I reached into the cupboard and pulled out the only vase there. "This one?"

"Yes, thank you."

I descended, handed her the vase then folded the step stool and leaned on the counter. "I'm bettin' you could've fetched the vase yourself. So why am I really here?"

"Don't be silly. My ankle is misbehavin'." She ran water into the vase. For having an injured ankle, she sure had been busy creating a fancy food spread. Trays lined the counters, some stacked on the stove, ranging from vegetable platters to fruit salad. Serving bowls held a variety of chips and dip. I didn't have to wonder why she'd been making so much noise earlier.

"Expectin' us to be unusually hungry later?"

One side of her mouth lifted. "I've arranged a gathering this evenin' and I'll need your help with the guests. Since they're here to celebrate your return to Bride, you should stick around."

She had to be kidding. I'd been slaving all week and these last hours mucking stalls had finished me off. I hadn't done this kind of manual labor since graduating high school. Sure, I hit the gym at least a couple times a week, but that was a totally different kind of activity which used different muscles. And the rest of my time had been spent studying or treating animals. Exhaustion threatened almost every cell in my body. But for Mrs. T, I'd tough it out. Besides, might be good to talk to folks I hadn't seen in a while. And her sentiment warmed me.

I grinned, rounding the counter to gather her into a bear hug. "You're the best. Thank you."

She giggled, patting me on the back. "Put me down, silly."

I obeyed, lowering her to the ground and dropping a kiss on the top of her head, then claimed a stool. If I hung around long enough, I'd find out what Mrs. T wanted. "Need help with anything else?"

"Not now, since I'm finished. But I could use the company." She smiled as she inserted one flower at a time. At that rate, she'd be at it a while.

Knowing her, she had lured me into the kitchen for conversation. Probably about my feelings—never a topic I liked. But for Mrs. T, I'd do anything. Settling in, I planted my elbows on the counter, resting my temple against my knuckles. "Other than daily ranch worries, things been okay while I was away?"

She gave a subtle shake of her head, whistling out a breath. "Mostly, yes. Bailey's been a pill ever since y'all went to Las Vegas last year. Do you know why?"

And there it was, the reason she'd called me for help. But I refused to divulge the secret Bailey had sworn me to.

My palms flew up, like they were pressed against glass in front of me. "I'd give you the details if I could." Because, other than the marriage and inevitable divorce, I genuinely didn't know what was bothering Bailey. Sure, I'd been callous and she'd been wounded. But beyond that, I couldn't fathom what had sparked such bitter resentment toward me. I had nothing to give Mrs. T.

"Something is going on between you and my daughter." She glanced at me from her flower arrangement, long enough to make me fidget, then she plunged another stem into the vase.

"I'll admit, it's been a little weird, but it's not for lack of trying on my part. She's not cooperatin'." My mind drifted to Bailey. What was she doing now? Who was she with?

"I see." She removed two flowers, mixed the others around again, then put the two back that she'd taken out. The flower arrangement looked exactly as it did moments ago.

"When you figure out what's goin' on, do let me know. I could use some help with your daughter."

She eyed the flowers once more, then her expression softened as she slid the vase aside. "I'll do what I can, sugar."

I meandered into the living room to find Blake conked out on the sofa, his cast propped up on the coffee table and Chester wallowing all over him. A movement beyond the front window caught my eye. Bailey hopped out of her white Explorer, then sprinted to the back and opened the hatch. After a minute, she became visible again, carrying a case of water bottles. Oh, hell.

Bolting out the front door, I left it open. "Let me help you with that."

She brushed past me, shifting the case of water aside as though unwilling to relinquish the heavy load. "There's more to bring in."

A pang of sadness blanketed me. If she wouldn't let me do a little slave labor for her, I still had a ways to go to mending her wounds.

I saw case after case of every beverage I could imagine, from beer to soda. Mrs. T must have invited the whole town. The depression faded, replaced by joy—Bailey had been running errands, not hanging out with another guy. Specifically, Trevor. At least, not that I knew of. The depth of my relief worried me. As much as I wanted to feel brotherly toward Bailey and watch out for her, and make sure she didn't date any losers who might take advantage of her, I could no longer avoid the truth.

I didn't like Bailey dating Trevor because I wanted her for myself. She had been crystal clear about not wanting me anywhere near her. Probably for the best since I couldn't guarantee how long before any interest in her faded. Best not to start anything that could end worse than our Vegas fiasco and cause even more damage to our friendship. So I would control myself. I had to.

Irritation crept in and blindsided me. But what

had I done to warrant this kind of anger? I hadn't been as considerate as I should've been in Vegas. But it was unintentional and I'd apologized. What was I supposed to do, bend over backwards and suck up to her for the rest of my life?

Between being on the defensive and dodging my wild attraction to her, I was mentally fried. And nothing would change anytime soon because she was still mad and I still wanted to drag her to my bed. How the hell was I going to endure her mom's party without going a little nuts, much less survive the next few weeks?

Chapter Nine

BAILEY

"*I need you* and Hunter to load drinks into those big coolers from the shed, then fill them up with ice. While you're at it, have him help you bring out the long table and move it into the livin' room. And the extra chairs."

Getting ready for the party meant I'd spend the next hour, minimally, with Hunter. Five minutes at a time was difficult enough. I swallowed, butterflies doing somersaults in my belly at the memory of our earlier kiss. I'd slipped and got caught up in him, his sexy smile and rock hard stomach. A renewed craving for his touch overwhelmed me. I ached for him now more than ever.

He wouldn't get another chance to be close enough to kiss me again. If I had to be over-the-top bitchy to accomplish that, so be it. "Sure, mom."

After storming into the living room, I stood in front of the TV. "Mom is requestin' you help me get the drinks and tables and everything ready. Even though I could probably do it by myself," I muttered, slamming my fists onto my hip and letting my bottom lip jut. He probably thought I was acting like a spoiled five-year-old. But so what? I wasn't trying to impress him.

Unless I had a date. Then he needed to know what he was missing, regret trying to dump me so soon after our night in Vegas. But wishing for remorse from Hunter was like trying to get affection from the freezer folk. Wasn't going to happen, ever.

Hunter leaped off the couch and I wished he wasn't so eager to help. It made me remember so many things I loved about him. Like when he'd taught me how to ride a horse. I'd been a big chicken and he was so patient. Or when I'd lost my favorite teddy bear and he'd searched the house until he found it—under the sofa. I would rather believe he was a prick but his distress over my anger and his efforts to put things to right made it harder for me to hate him.

But I needed to hold onto some semblance of hostility, because otherwise my hideous and grotesquely inconvenient infatuation for him was impossible to tamp down. And the more time I spent with him, the more difficult for me to control my emotions. Breaks from Hunter were vital to my emotional state of mind. This task for my mom needed to be done quickly.

I tilted my head toward the back door, then hiked out to the shed, knowing he'd follow. Just because I had to work with him didn't mean we had to talk. Talking and other interaction was bad, as we'd proved all evening. Talking also opened us up to feelings, the very thing I wanted to avoid.

In silence, I directed him to the table. He gripped one end and I got the other. We hauled it into the living room and set it along the side by the front door, then I made my way to the shed to locate the coolers. Hunter shadowed me, of course.

"How long are you going to keep this going, Bails?" He gripped the handle of the cooler and waited for me to get the other end.

"Keep what going?" I asked, my eyes wide and innocent.

"Really?" He cocked his head, casting me a doubtful glance. When I didn't volunteer anything else, he stopped, then lowered the ice chest which compelled me to do the same. "We've been practically family forever and now you're throwing it all away."

"Practically family, huh? Seemed more like a dictatorship to me," I hissed. "Let's see...You bullied any boys who dared to look at me. You teased me mercilessly. Ruined my love life. And then acted like I had some kind of disease in Vegas. Tell me again how close we were?"

He stomped toward me and I took a step back, bumping into a wall. He hulked over me, his eyes dark. "I'm not going to let you do this."

"Wow," I said sarcastically, keeping my voice monotone. "Proving my point by actin' like a bully. Next thing I know, you're going to try to whitewash everything by tellin' me you care."

"Damn it, Bails, I do care. But I'm not a mind reader so unless you tell me what I did wrong, I can't change anything. And don't blame the Vegas thing. You know I had to get the annulment quickly so Blake wouldn't find out. I may have rushed it, but I wasn't rude. So that's not your problem or this would've already resolved."

Part of me wanted to yell at him, inform him how much he'd hurt me. But lashing out wouldn't help. His only crime was not loving me. If I even attempted to give him a story, he'd sense I wasn't being truthful and he'd press for more. Our talk would probably end with me in tears confessing my undying love for him. And as ragey as I was, I didn't actually want to hurt him.

I just wanted to stop feeling.

"I'm sorry." I sighed, wilting against the wall. "I promise to make an effort to be nicer."

"I don't want you to *try* to be nicer. I want you to *want* to be nicer." He growled. "Like things used to be."

"We've both changed, Hunter. We're not kids anymore and it'll never be like that again."

He rocked back on the balls of his feet. "You're deflecting."

"No, I want to get this little chat done so I can get on with the preparations, and be presentable before guests arrive." I raised my chin. "Are you finished?"

"Not even close. We'll talk later." He mumbled something else, then grabbed the handle of the chest.

An hour and a half later, I descended the stairs dressed and ready for the party. I'd opted for a silky short-sleeved top with a plunging neckline, a mini skirt and a pair of strappy sandals. I'd spent so much time helping my mom prepare for the party that I didn't have a chance to curl my hair. Instead, I pinned my long bangs in a clip and did full makeup. Staying in or not, it was still a party. I had to look good.

As I reached the last step, the doorbell rang. Our first guest. Anxious to focus on hosting and ignoring Hunter, I made a beeline for the door. And... Noelle. Knowing her, she'd monopolize Hunter all night and I cringed at the thought. On the upside, she'd keep him occupied and away from me.

"Welcome." I reminded myself she wasn't at fault for liking Hunter and she wasn't a bad person. I offered a friendly smile and waved her in, noting her fabulous outfit. "Love the dress."

I guided her to the drink table, then busied myself putting final touches on the snack platters. As I was setting the playlist on Blake's phone and raising the speaker volume, the doorbell rang again. I pulled it open to see Trevor, and grinned. "Hey."

He leaned in to brush my cheek, whispering, "Your mom invited me when I saw her at the bank. Thought it would be fun to come and irritate Hunter."

I laughed, grabbing his hand and yanking him inside. "You're the best."

"I know. I've been here a matter of seconds and already making progress."

I felt my brows crinkling. "What do you mean?"

"Hunter's glaring," he said softly, slinging an arm around my waist. "Why don't you give me a tour of the house?"

As Trevor and I swung in a circle through the living room and into the kitchen, I caught a glimpse of Hunter. Yep, a scowl creased his forehead. But if I were anything more to him than a friend, he wouldn't have been so desperate for the annulment. I could allow that he found me attractive, like Trevor hinted. But any feelings Hunter may have had for me weren't serious. I'd turned eighteen six years ago and was free to date whomever I chose. Except for one night in Vegas, Hunter hadn't wanted to date me since then. Why would anything change now?

I wouldn't allow Trevor to make me believe the impossible.

"I was right about last night," Trevor said, snagging a beer from the cooler.

The doorbell rang again and Blake hobbled to the door and let several people in. Returning my attention to Trevor, I steered him to the dining area and to the snack spread. "Which part?"

"Bein' seen with a beautiful woman ups your market value."

The living room was getting cramped and someone had raised the volume on the music. We didn't have to be quiet anymore because the noise was muffling our conversation. I bumped hips with him as I dipped a tortilla chip into the salsa. "Did you get a date?"

"No. But only because I didn't want word to get to Hunter." He popped an olive into his mouth. "She was all over me though. Extremely pretty."

I chuckled. "I'm happy for you."

"Man, look at that guy. No, don't look. Take my word for it though, he's got it bad for you."

My pulse jackrabbited. I didn't want to know who he was talking about, not if the guy was Hunter. "If you're talking about *him*, please don't."

He glanced at Hunter on the sly. "Yeah, I could be reading him wrong anyway. Could have nothing to do with you at all. Maybe he just really dislikes me."

I ribbed him with my elbow. "That must be it. Besides, I think he still likes Noelle."

"That would be a shame." Trevor snorted.

"Why?" I dipped another chip into the salsa and bit it in half.

"Because she's had a thing for Blake since high school."

I choked on my chip and scooped up a glass of punch to wash the shards of chip down. "Why would you think she likes him?"

"Not think." He flashed me a smug grin. "Know."

"What makes you so sure?" I shifted to scan the living room, and located her. Following the path of her eyes took me to Blake. Interesting.

"I wasn't properly socialized in school, due to being such a nerd. So I spent most of my time observing other kids, learning about them. And because I was considered innocuous, half the time people passed by, not even realizing I was there. You wouldn't believe some of the crap I overheard."

I blinked, stunned and intrigued. "Tell me more."

"Like the reason she broke up with Hunter. She—"

My fingers clamped onto his wrist. "Wait. I thought he was the one who dumped her. At least twice."

"Wrong." He shook his head. "Remember Heather? Noelle told her that she wasn't interested in college or a career. She wanted to get married and start a family, be a stay-at-home mom. And Hunter wasn't a good candidate to father her children."

"The Evermond fortune and social standing wasn't good enough for her?"

"Being with someone who could truly love her was priority number one." He lifted one shoulder and gulped from the beer bottle. "She refused to invest in him emotionally because he couldn't give back. And because of those inadequacies, she felt he shouldn't reproduce."

"Wow. Good memory." In a way, Noelle was correct about Hunter. But saying he shouldn't reproduce? Harsh. I wasn't sure I agreed with her. Sometimes having a child changed a person. Another glance at Noelle revealed she was still watching Blake, but on the sly. "I wonder why Blake doesn't go for it. She's freakin' gorgeous and smart too."

He shook his head. "It's like you don't know your brother at all." When I stared blankly, he took mercy on me. "Blake is incredibly loyal. He's never gone out with any girls Hunter dated seriously—or as serious as Hunter was capable of. That goes double for an on-again off-again girl who dumped him at least twice."

I pursed my lips, studying Trevor. "You're quite insightful."

"I had to be. Being at the bottom of the food chain inspired me to work harder to get to the top and I did that by paying attention. Which came in handy learning law. I'm like a human lie detector." He shot me a lopsided grin. "You have stupid love for Hunter."

Should I deny it? "Whatever my feelings, I'm fighting them. I'll win, I swear."

"Hunter's not the marrying kind and you're smart to dodge him. But he cares much more for you than you give him credit for."

I clucked my tongue. "We've already established he's incapable of giving back."

Trevor shrugged. "People change. I did."

Pondering his assessment on Hunter, I bit my lip. Hunter's feelings were irrelevant. Only his capacity to love and to commit mattered. In that area, he was an epic failure. Not the guy for me. I'd have to get over it and move on.

I spent the majority of the evening with Trevor and as much as I tried to ignore Hunter, I couldn't. While I didn't have to worry about him reconciling with Noelle, he was always with some gooey-eyed girl who was sidling up to him and batting her lashes. *Gag.* I'd never seen anything like it. As if he held some magical command over anyone with a vagina. Sadly, I was included in that group.

Chapter Ten

HUNTER

In school, I was king. Literally, crown and everything. I may have seemed good on the outside, but I had no real value. But like tractor beams, Noelle and nearly every other girl couldn't resist the initial pull. For my sake, I let them go before they saw through the façade and discovered how worthless I was. Except in Noelle's case. She'd dumped me multiple times—but she'd kept coming back for more.

As a kindness to the other girls I'd dated, I always dumped them before they fell too hard. Some of them fell for me anyway, completely blind to my flaws, with no encouragement or participation on my part. Not much I could do about that.

I used to think Bailey was one of them, the forever devoted. She'd proved me right in Vegas—or so I'd thought. Or maybe she'd just learned the hard way that loving me was pointless. Since I was unlovable, as my parents demonstrated daily, this didn't surprise me. Bailey would probably never care about me again. She could do way better than me anyway, a guy who would never give her his whole heart.

Still, I couldn't stop thinking about her. I wanted to punch Trevor in his holier-than-thou face. What happened to him anyway? I liked him better when he was a lanky geeky invisible dork. Now he was formidable competition. No wonder Bailey wanted nothing to do with me.

Through the entire night, one girl or another dogged me practically every second. I'd shake one and another would appear. Some were older who'd been off to college while I'd been in high school. And others who'd been in middle school when I graduated. They all seemed to think they might have their day with me. Flattering, but none of them interested me.

While I dodged girls, I was forced to watch the guy who was better than me in every way flirt with the girl I could never have.

But I was home again in Bride, with the people I cared for most, in the town I'd missed. I'd done well while studying at Texas A & M, and I'd been too busy to get into much trouble. When your parents come from old money, and tons of it, and they threaten to cut you off if your grades fall below 4.0, you somehow find the will to keep your priorities straight. After college, I'd gone directly to L.A. and thrown myself into a completely different world where people passed you on the street without even so much as a glance.

Everyone knew me here, some judged me for my past and some didn't. But these people were real and they were mine. I would stay in Bride permanently, have my own practice here. I'd eventually get over my weird thing with Bailey and play uncle to Blake or Bailey's future children.

This revelation, realizing Bride was my forever home, made me kind of dizzy, but in a good way. Sure, my parents were frustrating and maybe they would never love me like they should. But at the very least, if I visited often enough, they'd see I didn't only want them when I needed a favor.

I'd probably always be a bachelor. And that was okay because I had never set my expectations higher.

At that moment, Trevor and Bailey laughed at something he said. They'd hung out by the snack table, but had left for a while. And now they were back, picking at the chips and dip, poking at the crackers and cheese. The way she looked at him between bites, so free and easy, set my teeth on edge. Trevor ogled Bailey like she was one of the snacks. And by her frequent smiles, he was pouring on the charm.

So he thought he could come into our home and flirt with *my* wife?

"I have to visit the ladies' room," said the girl hanging on my arm.

"Good. I have someone I need to talk to." I waved off whatever-her-name-was, possibly Adele. Suddenly, I had an urge for food. Careful not to make eye contact with Trevor or Bailey—didn't want to give the impression they were being targeted—I waltzed to the snack spread. Making a show of examining the goodies, I rounded the table. Just as I was about to butt into their conversation, Bailey whirled past me into the kitchen.

"So... Hunter."

I hated his smug grin. I smothered the urge to wipe it off his face. "Trevor. Good to see you. Heard you passed the bar."

He folded his arms over his chest. "Heard you finished a vet internship."

Raising my chin, I crossed my arms over my chest too. "Yep."

A ghost of a smile played on his mouth. "Staying a while or going back to Cali?"

"Staying. Longer than a while." Maybe that would discourage him from putting the moves on *my* wife.

After a slow, thoughtful nod, he said, "Does Bailey know?"

"Nope."

Trevor pressed his lips together in amusement and I wondered what the hell was so funny. "Well..." He plucked his beer off the table and took a chug. "Good luck with that."

As if he knew Bailey better than I did. He didn't own her and he didn't have inside information into her head. He was an outsider who was way out of her league. My hands balled into fists with the need to punch him. If Trevor knew what was good for him, he'd back off.

"There you are." Silky fingers curled around my biceps and flowery perfume wafted up my nose. Had to be Adele, finished in the restroom way too soon. Young, pretty bottle-blonde—exactly the type of girl I usually liked. Not tonight.

I could feel Bailey's gaze on me from wherever she was. I wanted her to see I wasn't interested in Adele, not even a little bit. But what good would it do? Bailey would still be distant and she'd still choose Trevor.

For the first time in my life, I wanted someone who didn't want me. I wasn't going to get the girl. Not because wooing Bailey would be impossible but because once I'd gotten my curiosity satisfied, I'd lose interest. Or I'd stumble on another way to screw up, like I always did. An imaginary weight bore down on me and my lungs stretched and shrunk like a sponge. I needed to get out and away from the crowd, go someplace I could breathe again. "I have to go."

After disengaging from the blonde, I weaved through guests and hit the steps. Upstairs in my room, I rummaged for a paper bag. No luck. I slid the window open and stuck my head outside, then slowly exhaled.

What the hell was wrong with me? So many girls to choose from and I couldn't control the impulse to pursue the *one* girl who wanted nothing to do with me. What an idiot. This infatuation with her would pass though. It always did. I just had to be patient.

A few more deep inhales, slow exhales and my pulse steadied.

I didn't love Bailey in the normal way. I was just going mental at the idea of losing her friendship.

Once we squared things away and returned to the way things used to be, I'd get over this strange... whatever it was.

One thing I knew for sure, I couldn't let Bailey go. I couldn't. To ensure she stayed in my life, I'd keep my cool and not get weird on her. I'd stay focused, think of anything but the fact that I could *never* have her. I would not obsess.

I could do this.

Sprinting out of my room and down the stairs, I spotted Bailey beyond the landing.

Stay cool. Act normal.

She stomped toward me, her eyes on fire. "You told Trevor you were staying in Bride, that you weren't leaving."

The rat bastard couldn't keep his mouth shut. I wanted to pummel him. But not yet. Right now, I had to find out why my staying would make her go ballistic. "Bails, I grew up here. This is my home."

"Your plan was to come back and stand in for Blake. And then leave." Bailey's gray eyes grew charcoal as she closed the distance. "Once Blake can do the work, you need to go."

Closer was better, so we could keep our voices low and not make a scene. "You're telling me where I can and can't live?"

Bailey smirked. "Don't pretend like Bride is big enough for you and your ego. It can never give you the excitement you need."

I gritted my teeth while I mustered up calm. "Don't

pretend to know anything about me or what I need."

Her cheeks flamed, her ramrod-straight spine lengthening her body. "You'll stay in this house over my dead body."

I shrugged, trying to appear casual even though I felt as if my foot had slipped from the stirrup. "Fine. I'll leave as soon as Mrs. Thayer asks me to."

Her gray eyes blazed, her nostrils flaring. "Then I'll demand she make you leave."

I raised one brow in defiance. "And what reason will you give her? Will you tell her about our adventure and how we're still married?"

Her chin tilted up. "You're not staying, Hunter. You can't."

And... splat. I'd metaphorically fallen from the horse. Because although I didn't want to go anywhere, I was getting further and further from ever fixing things with Bailey. "Why are you freaking out about where I live?"

"You've spent all your life pushing everyone away and now you're surprised it worked?" She edged closer. "I've watched you from afar since I was eight, Hunter. Aside from my parents and Blake, you care about *you*. The rest of us get scraps. So ask me again why I mind if you stay in Bride."

"You've never gotten scraps." My jaw muscle cramped from clenching. "You're going to be annoyed at me no matter how hard I try to mend things between us."

Her mouth hardened. "Looks like it."

"Well..." If whatever I did made no difference... "You should know I bought into the B & B. For all intents and purposes, we're business partners now."

Chapter Eleven

BAILEY

"Can I speak with you?"

My mom blinked then slung an arm around my shoulder. Yep, she knew I knew. She smiled at Mr. Weathers from the local hardware store. "Would you excuse me?"

After he agreed, she steered me outside. I went blindly, not caring where she took me, so long as I didn't have to see Hunter again anytime soon.

Beyond the stables, well out of earshot of guests or anyone else, she stopped and gazed up at the stars. "It's a beautiful night."

"You didn't have to take his money, Mom. We could've done it on our own." A sob slipped out and I cringed. "The sale of Malik would have bailed us out."

"And what if the Smiths decided not to buy Malik? Omari's stud fees only go so far."

"A couple of other colts are coming along and should meet my asking price."

Her head swung slowly side to side. "Too many variables."

"We'd figure out a way. Or we'd hold off paying some of the bills and handle them when Iesha wins at Nationals. I've seen some of the other cutters. They don't stand a chance against her."

"Even if Iesha has a strong chance, what if she gets injured or has a bad day? What if she doesn't place at all?" She patted my hand. "You haven't been able to put the time into training her that you need to. Haven't you been warned against putting all your eggs in one basket?"

Tugging out of her grasp, I angled away from her. "When did you become so negative?"

"When did you stop seeing our situation for what it was?" Her voice took on a firm, motherly tone.

"I don't want us owing Hunter anything." I couldn't ask her to make him leave the ranch though. She'd ask more questions.

"Sweetheart." She sighed and glanced at the dark sky. "I've always loved Hunter as my own. Seems fittin' he should have a stake in the ranch. Besides, he's bringin' a lot to the table."

I didn't want to know what else Hunter was doing. That he was here to stay was plenty.

"Love hurts and I can't help you heal faster. But he's saving the ranch, honey. We're not riding on a wish and a prayer anymore. We won't have to stress that everything your father worked so hard to build will slowly die."

Yes, he was saving our ranch and my family. I believed he was sincerely trying to do the right thing.

A tear snaked down my cheek and I gave her my hand, squeezed hers. "You did what you needed to do. I'll figure it out."

She turned and faced me again. "He's different now."

"Maybe. Maybe not." No one changed that much, and any improvements didn't apply to his attitude about love or his habits with women. Hunter wasn't wired correctly and as he matured and learned, the wiring inside would stay the same.

"When you're ready to talk about whatever happened in Las Vegas, my ears are always willin'." She leaned in to brush a kiss on my forehead, then patted my arm and strode into the house.

I'd have to be a dumbass to be surprised my mom knew I was in love with Hunter and that something had happened in Vegas. But I didn't want to talk about how he'd stolen my heart long ago, massaged it, spoken pretty words to it, then tossed it into the garbage. I couldn't share the humiliating details of the attempted annulment with her or how we were still married but he didn't want me.

Taking pains to avoid Hunter, I stole inside the house, and searched for Trevor. He was talking to the blonde, Adele, who'd been monopolizing Hunter earlier. Unless I was reading Trevor and Adele wrong, they were totally into each other. I said my good nights to both, then quietly slunk away to my room.

I woke extra early the next morning, hoping to get most of my Sunday work finished then escape to my room and avoid Hunter. But when I tiptoed into the kitchen and peered outside, the Silverado was already gone.

After putting the horses out to pasture and feeding them, I made a round on the property to make sure everything looked good. I didn't want any distractions the next few hours. My mother had been right about one thing; I needed to put more time in with Iesha if I wanted to ensure we placed top at world finals.

For years I'd scrimped and saved to buy Iesha, planning to use most of any prize money on the B & B and give back to my family. Now that Hunter was a part of the business, I would need my independence and a separate income. Placing at Nationals would raise Iesha's value and increase the fee for her future foals.

The money would put me one step closer to getting my own apartment. The idea of staying and seeing Hunter everyday made me want to trash all thoughts of moving away. But the idea of seeing Hunter every day reinforced what I knew—that I had to escape as quickly as I could. Deep down, I knew Hunter was capable of being a loving husband. But *he* didn't know that. Even if he had some kind of epiphany, that love would never be lavished on me and most certainly not long term.

The rest of my Sunday would be spent working with Iesha. Her placing at the horse show was essential to my freedom.

As I glided the brush over her white coat along her flank to remove any particles that might irritate her under the saddle, a gentle roar tickled my ear. I set aside the brush to see who had arrived. A huge, red F450 idled in the driveway. Iesha would keep for a moment.

I'd put that particular truck on my list of dream cars I might buy one day, not only because it was gorgeous and spectacularly badass but because it would tow multiple horses. This one had a tow package, bed liner, custom wheels, tinted windows, and everything else I could wish for. Whoever owned this truck meant business. Maybe he'd come to shop for a horse.

The engine died and a thin man with a white beard and baseball cap hopped out. He glanced around, clipboard in hand.

"Can I help you?" I asked.

He tipped the bill of his cap. "Yes, ma'am. Lookin' for Hunter Evermond."

My stomach pinched thinking of him, which only reminded me that I may have been successful in driving him away. Just because his disappearance was for the best didn't mean I had to like it. "He didn't say when he'd be back. Anything I can do?"

"Depends if you're Bailey Thayer and authorized to sign for this truck."

Lucky me. I had the privilege of helping Mr. Botched-Annulment's life easier. On the upside, he had his own vehicle now, so he could leave the ranch more often. I signed the sheet on the clipboard, then the man passed me the keys and sprinted down the driveway to his waiting ride.

I hoped Hunter could find a home as quickly as he bought a truck. On the other hand, he deserved to be stuck with the freezer folk for a while.

Envy kicked in when I pivoted and came face to face with the red beauty. The ruby paint shimmered and the leather seats looked so buttery they almost glowed. I craved a long whiff of the inside.

I had a key now, didn't I?

Taking great care not to scratch or scuff any part of the truck, I climbed in and slipped behind the wheel. I let my head rest against the seat and my lids drooped. I gave up and let my eyes shut completely, inhaling the scent of new car. I shifted to get even more comfortable, then muscle by muscle, tension evaporated. Temptation to take a quick nap consumed me.

Why was I wasting time on a truck and torturing myself when I wouldn't have one for a long time? And I still had a ton to accomplish today. Scolding myself for getting caught up in the sexy red dream, I scrambled out of the truck—and crashed into Hunter. Both my left feet tangled and I nearly toppled but Hunter's arms circled my waist and I fell against his chest.

His musky scent assaulted me as his thighs brushed mine. I reeled when his thumbs pressed into my side to steady me. Butterflies did flips in my tummy and my breath caught. I persuaded myself to avert my gaze since eye contact would likely lead to me melting against him. Permanently.

"Thanks." I pulled away and sidestepped out of his reach.

"You can take it for a spin, if you want." He flashed me a one-sided grin.

"I have to train, but thank you. Nationals is a couple weeks away." My freedom and sanity were at stake. There would be time for pretty trucks later.

Hunter backed away, putting more distance between us. "I'll find my bag and see Iesha in a few minutes."

Right, he was going to give all the horses annuals today. "You have everything you need, supplies and whatever?"

"Other than vaccines, yes. Medical records are still in the filing cabinet in the lab?"

"Yes." Why wasn't he giving me attitude? Worse, he was being thoroughly agreeable. Already the desire to snuggle with him crept in on me. After I tried to rehome him last night, he had stormed off and now he was back to being his old cute self. None of the current sweetness erased the Vegas fiasco though and I'd never forgive him. But when he was charming, the sting of his years of rejection faded.

I needed him to be a douche bag.

I swiveled around to bolt, but when I lifted my foot he cleared his throat and uttered my name. I glanced at him over my shoulder, wishing he'd be quick. "Yes?"

Hunter stuffed his hands in his pockets and rearranged his leg to redistribute his weight. "I know you think I'm a tool. But no matter your opinion of me, you can't believe I'd intentionally hurt you or your family."

I knew he wanted to be in my good graces again, but some things couldn't be fixed. "I trust you with my mother and Blake, to do right by them." I inhaled sharply, struggling to get the rest of my thoughts onto my tongue and out of my mouth. "Things will never be good again between you and me. Let's do the best we can and try to work together the next few weeks."

"Only a few weeks?" He squinted, brows lowering. "Going somewhere?"

Not at the moment since he was holding me captive. "The B & B won't die without me, not with your resources. Whatever Iesha wins, I'll put toward an apartment closer to Austin. I have a friend who'll board Iesha in exchange for helping her in the stables. I hear Serenity needs a good trainer. Thought I'd try for a job there."

He flinched. "Fair enough. You'll be happy to know my dad's filing the papers tomorrow. Then we wait the required sixty days."

"Great." Finally, the annulment—or divorce—would happen. Real steps toward severing my legal ties to Hunter. Soon, he'd be my ex-husband. Nausea rose from my gut, threatening to make me hurl. "Blake can help you with the horses, match each one with their medical history and update you on anything new with them."

"Great." He stared at the ground.

"Great," I echoed. I pivoted, straining to put one leg in front of the other, getting farther and farther from him. I returned to Iesha and walked her to her stall. As calmly as my wobbly legs could manage, I strolled inside the house and straight to my room. After locking the door, I plucked the ear buds off the dresser on my way to the bed. Curling into the fetal position, I opened the playlist on my phone and let the first song explode in my ears. Sturgill Simpson sang about living a little, but I didn't think I could. Not for a long time.

Chapter Twelve

HUNTER

Before Bailey stirred in her room across the hall, before the sun came up Monday morning, I prepared one of the pens with food and water, and hitched the 4-horse trailer to my F450.

I swung onto the main highway toward Austin and Serenity Ranch. Work had been hectic since almost the moment I'd arrived at the airport, so the down time was kind of nice. I would make a quick stop at Two Cups and grab a coffee to make sure my trip was at maximum enjoyment. And I vowed to keep my mind off *her* to guarantee a relaxing trip.

Whether Bailey liked it or not, she was stuck with me. At the rate I was making everything worse with her, I'd need the next few weeks to reverse it. I had to hope that in the end she wouldn't move out.

Either way, I would feel the burn. I had a financial stake in the ranch now, which required busting my ass and skipping visits with my parents—and Muffin. Not that the traitor who greeted me with a wagging tail would even notice. After a round of licks, she eagerly crawled into my mother's lap. As if I no longer existed.

Once Blake could work again, I would be more likely to squeak out a little more time to win back Muffin's loyalty. And I so badly wanted a breakthrough with my mom and dad. I'd keep trying when I could. For now, every spare minute would be dedicated to helping the family I was indebted to. As a side benefit, the return on my investment might make my father stop treating me like a thug.

Get the ranch viable and thriving, then what? By the time the B & B ranch showed a healthy profit, Bailey would be gone. Bailey... I couldn't look at her without my chest aching and my tongue tying up and rolling over itself. I'd apologized to her every way I knew how, tried to be extra nice and I was still in the dog house—probably a life sentence.

She was almost all I'd thought about in days. Each morning, I woke more sleep-deprived than the night before and each time I saw her, fear of losing her closed in on me. Could we ever find that easy camaraderie again? What if I'd lost her forever?

I'd grudgingly come to Bride, expecting Blake's speedy recovery and a quick escape for myself. Now I couldn't imagine myself living anywhere else. Excitement coursed through me at the idea of applying my vet skills to the B & B horses, being a part of the legacy Mr. T had created and building on it, helping them expand and become more successful than ever. Mostly, I loved the thought of being an essential part of a life I'd always envied.

Spending time at the B & B would also give me the

opportunity for months or years to come—however long it took—to get through to Bailey. She wouldn't cut off her mother and brother, and since they'd all be at the ranch most of the time, she couldn't avoid me forever.

I navigated into the parking lot of Two Cups and dashed inside. Noelle waved me over as soon as I bellied up to the counter. I collected my coffee and complied, claiming a chair across from her. I could spare a couple minutes. "Hey."

"Good morning." She beamed and shoved her laptop aside. "Things good at the ranch?"

"Not bad." She didn't need all the details. "Picking up some new acquisitions. I'll probably stop for coffee again on the way back."

"I might still be here. Finishing an appraisal report on a big house I did yesterday." Noelle flashed me a sweet smile, making me wish she could find her soul mate. She deserved someone amazing. "Blake healing and on schedule to relieve you?" she asked.

Something about the way her voice changed when speaking of Blake gave me the impression she was fishing. Did she want insight as to when I was leaving town? Even when dumping me, she'd always been generous and kind. And I'd never felt any hint of animosity from her at my failings. Her fishing couldn't be about me.

I chugged some coffee, set the cup down and donned my poker face. "Are you in love with Blake?"

Noelle gasped and went pale. "W-why do you ask?"

I chuckled, proud of myself for nailing it. "All this

time, I thought you dumped your husband because you couldn't get over me. You've had a thing for my best friend this whole time."

She went another shade whiter, her eyes shifting like a meth head. "You're way off. And you'd better not mention your theory to him."

I shook my head in mock disapproval. "How horrible to deprive him of the most beautiful girl in town."

Her eyes narrowed. "You mean *second* most beautiful."

An image of Bailey invaded my head, taunting me. I opened my mouth to disagree with Noelle but that would be lying. "Yeah, I think Bailey's gorgeous. So what?"

"You're the one with the secret love." Her gaze riveted to mine, like each of us were waiting for the other to crack.

But I was pretty good at poker. "Seems a little incestuous to me."

"Bull. Your *best friend's* sister, not yours." Noelle gave me a smug smile. "How do you think Blake will take it when he realizes you want to violate his sister?"

I groaned. "This is all in your imagination."

"Maybe." She bit her lip, studying me. "Don't give Blake any ideas about me and I won't tell him about Bailey."

"Nothing to tell." I scoffed. "I'm not in love with her."

"You're the one mentioning love, not me." She tilted her head condescendingly. "You're always staring at her. You look like hell so I'm thinking you're not sleeping much. I'd wager you can't stop thinking about *her*." When I opened my mouth to object, to tell her that not being blind around a gorgeous woman didn't necessarily mean much, she held out one vertical finger to stop me. "You and I split because—"

"You mean you dumped me because," I interrupted.

"Quiet." She gave me the stink-eye. "I accused you of having commitment issues, said I wanted to start a family soon after high school and I didn't see you as the fatherly type."

Irritation clawed at me. "Why are you rehashing this? I was there. I remember why you dumped me."

"That was the reason I gave you, with enough facts to ring true to you. But I always suspected you had a deeper connection with Bailey than you ever would with me."

"Doesn't mean I'm in love with her."

"Again, you mentioned being in love, not me." She observed me a moment. "It's why you made an excuse to punch any guy who went near her. It's why you never date any girls when you're here in town, why you keep coming back and why you dislike Trevor so much. She's your forever, Hunter, the one who will always love you no matter what. And whether you admit it or not, you love her the same way."

My smile faded and I rose. Without another word to Noelle, or even a glance her way, I strode through the exit, jumped into the F450, and peeled out of the parking lot.

Ridiculous. Noelle was so full of it. She would always be special to me, but she had overstepped. Of course I loved Bailey. But *in love*? No way. If I were in love with Bailey, I'd know it. Yes, I probably ogled her too much, but no sane man could blame me. Long-time family friend or not, I was still a guy.

And, anyway, most of my staring was spent trying to figure out a way to patch things between us — same reason she was constantly on my mind. And *of course* when we were teenagers, I'd punched those creeps who were taking advantage of her. I knew firsthand what teenage boys were like and my job was to do the brotherly thing and protect her. No more, no less. Noelle was out of her mind to believe anything else.

I had to think of something other than Noelle and her grossly inaccurate assessment of my feelings for Bailey. The ranch... I made a mental list of things to be done after the new horses settled in: upgrade the stables to eco-friendly naturally draining floors and purchase screens to easily sift through the shavings. We could cut the mucking time to a fraction of what we currently spent. The huge upside would be less torture for me when I got stuck mucking. Repair the hen house and possibly build one more pasture. And then get Bailey anything else she wanted.

I flinched at the last thought. I shouldn't want to get Bailey her heart's desire. I should want the ranch to be known worldwide for its top quality Egyptian Arabians. That's it. And I refused to entertain any other reason for me to have Bailey's interests foremost than me possessing simple decency. Naturally I'd be concerned and thoughtful of any human being. That was all there was to it.

Before giving Serenity Ranch the final payment, I briefly examined each horse to make sure they were sound, then loaded them into the trailer. I didn't want to stop by Two Cups on my way back. With my luck, I'd run into someone else who wanted to lecture me on my love life and tell me how I really felt. As if their opinions were more valid than my own firsthand knowledge. And right now, the only opinion I cared about was Bailey's.

But I wanted some coffee. I could check the lot for Noelle's car before going into Two Cups to make sure I didn't run into her again. As I neared the cupcake bakery, I verified that her car wasn't around. I parked and leaped out of the truck then sprinted inside, coming face to face with Nancy Redd, the town matchmaker. The very last person I wanted see right now. She was nice and everything but with my luck, she'd try to set me up with Bailey.

Too late. She'd spotted me. Before she crossed the room, I held up a finger. "I just remembered I have an appointment." And I bolted out of the bakery like lightning.

"How's that sweet Thayer girl?" she called out.

"Great," I answered, then raced to my truck. The whole town was conspiring against me.

My old high school friend, Everett Jeffries, cruised into the parking lot just as I was pulling out. I wanted to catch up with him and ask him how his dad was doing, but I couldn't risk Nancy cornering me. Instead, I waved and kept driving.

As the red beast roared over the B & B driveway, I spied Bailey standing by one of the stables. As if completely unaware of my arrival, she knelt, beaming at our ranch hand Finn's three-year-old daughter. Bailey stood up, then entwined her fingers with the girl's and walked with her toward the stable.

Bailey had always been sweet to the staff's family, inviting them to roam the grounds and even ride the horses. Didn't matter how busy she was; she always made time for others. I sat in my truck, trying to think of a time when I'd seen Bailey be anything other than kind to everyone. She was generous to a fault—unless she was dealing with me.

I climbed out of the truck. The horses in the trailer whinnied and, despite my irritation and frustration with Bailey, a thrill shot through me. What would she think of our new acquisitions?

"Finn, want to give me a hand?" I unlatched the door and pulled out the ramp.

Finn dashed into the trailer ahead of me and I shadowed him to witness his reaction. He stroked the pregnant chestnut mare. "Beautiful." He moved to the black mare, cooing and stroking her muzzle, then mumbled similar compliments to the colt and filly.

"We'll need to quarantine them until I have a chance to get blood samples and run tests." They had checked out okay during my visual examination and likely all Serenity's stock were clean. Still, they needed to be kept separate and gradually introduced to the other horses.

"The east paddock?" Finn asked.

"Yes." We led them to the recently stocked enclosure, one horse at a time since I couldn't risk leading multiple horses and losing control of one of them. As I walked the last horse to the paddock, I caught sight of Bailey who was showing the little girl one of the youngest foals.

While I was settling in the ebony mare, Blake hobbled over. He leaned a crutch against the fence and hung his elbows over the top rail. "She's stunning." His gaze switched to the chestnut mare Finn led in. "Wow."

My eyes automatically sought Bailey again, locating her outside the tack room. Her glossy auburn hair hung loose and she'd shed the flannel, exposing all that creamy skin around her shoulders, neck and the swells of her breasts. Slinging the three-year-old on her hip, Bailey's face lit up and my breath hitched. The familiar ache in my chest wormed its way to my gut.

I needed to concentrate on work, not her. I had to get a grip.

"Thanks, Finn." I waved him off, knowing he had plenty of work to do.

"You got some beauties here, Hunter." Blake adjusted his cowboy hat. "I'm impressed you pulled this off."

"Just some minor negotiating and dipping into my trust fund. Not like I had to work for the money."

"Still, I appreciate it." Blake knuckle bumped with me.

"Not a big deal, man. I kinda owe your mom. All of you, actually. Not sure what I would've done if you guys hadn't been there for me growing up. Probably would've been even more screwed."

Bailey walked by the pen toward Finn's wife. "It was so nice seeing you again." The rest of her words were muffled by the distance. Two minutes later, the mother drove off with the child and Bailey hiked across the dirt road to the stables.

"Grateful or not, Hunter, some things are deal breakers."

I snapped around, this-close to giving myself whiplash. Blake's tone had changed so drastically, I braced myself.

He gripped the fence hard enough to whiten his knuckles. "On our friendship, Hunter, tell me you didn't sleep with my sister."

My stomach bottomed out. "What?"

"The way you keep staring at her—and don't insult my intelligence by denying it—anyone would think you guys have something going on. If you slept with her—"

Both of my palms flew out as a white flag, and I shook my head briskly. "I didn't sleep with her, I swear."

"Well, *something* happened." Blake scowled and tipped his head. "You know that saying about a woman scorned?"

"Uh." I blinked. "I guess."

"You think any woman would be that pissed if she never cared about the guy?"

"Don't know." I already didn't like where this conversation was heading. Out of respect for my childhood friend—not to mention I *did* make out with and then marry his sister—I'd hear him out. But inside, I cringed.

"How do you act when you don't care either way about a girl?" His brows lifted expectantly. "You shrug it off. Move on and never think of her again. Anyone else would too. But Bailey isn't."

"You couldn't be more wrong. She hates me these days." If I had to have another conversation about Bailey or me and who loved who, I might vomit.

"C'mon, Hunter. You're not stupid. Women don't act like that unless they're hurt. And they only get hurt if they cared. The more they care, the more they hurt."

How could I get out of this conversation? "I don't know what to tell you, Blake. Maybe it's less complicated than you think. Or she's simply learned to hate me."

"Don't be a dumbass. She's always been in love with you, Hunter, and nobody can flip the switch like that." His fingers curled into my shoulder. "I don't know what's going on in your head, but dating my sister is off limits."

I rubbed my temples, anxious to be finished with this conversation. "Obviously."

"Get square with Bailey." He let go of my shoulder. "Without sleeping with her."

Frustration welled in me. "Don't you see I'm trying?

Have I not been busting my ass to help out here and make nice with her?"

The worry lines around Blake's eyes vanished. "Be careful with Bailey." He placed the crutch under his arm and hobbled along the fence. "Tell me more about the new horses."

Blake studied each horse as I gave him background on each one's lineage and accomplishments. He relaxed as if the earlier conversation was forgotten. And since we'd covered my love life, seemed fair we cover his as well.

We watched the filly do laps around the pen, occasionally nipping at the colt. I leaned my forearms on the fence, and Blake mimicked my move. "Question. Why didn't you ever date Noelle?"

Blake shot me a cautious look. "Your ex?"

"Right." When he put it that way, yes, Blake dating someone I'd slept with might feel weird at first. But I could easily get past it if he could. "What if she was the perfect woman for you?"

"You don't date your best friend's ex." He stared ahead, watching the newcomers munch on hay. "Ever."

"What if your best friend was totally cool with it?" I asked, trying to keep a casual tone.

"Are you?" Blake spared me a glance.

I faced him. "She's a nice girl. I think she deserves a good guy for a change. She's paid her dues. And why should you be deprived of a great girl just because I suck?"

He raised one brow. "Even if I wanted to date Noelle,

this isn't a trade-off. Bailey is still taboo for you."

I sighed, hating that he thought so little of me to warrant having a cow if I went for Bailey. On the other hand, with my history, I couldn't blame him. "Dude, it'll never happen. Trust me."

But a part of me wanted it to happen. And that scared me. Because as hot as Bailey was, and as much as I wouldn't mind kissing her again, what I really wanted was for us to laugh together again. I missed the hell out of her. I loved the hell out of her. Always had. Add in my new attraction for her and it was a dangerous combination. I'd never had both a deep physical attraction for a girl and such a strong desire just to be around her.

And I couldn't do a damn thing about either of those feelings. Not only had I been forbidden to go near Bailey but I'd made a promise to my best friend. Plus, no matter what Blake said about Bailey loving me, I found it difficult to believe.

If I couldn't date her—not that I would put her through unnecessary contact with me—how the hell was I going to get her out of my system?

Chapter Thirteen

BAILEY

Finn held back the small herd of cattle while letting one young bull through. I maneuvered Iesha side-to-side to keep the lonely bull from returning to his herd. Though I sensed Hunter observing our training session, I convinced myself to stay on point and not make eye contact with him.

After letting Iesha do her job, I signaled for her to let the bull go then I waited for Finn to reorganize the herd and send a heifer our way.

As though I had no control over my own body, my eyeballs cut straight to Hunter. He flipped his thumb up and grinned. "Looking good, Thayer!"

And now I had to answer in some way or I'd be plain rude. I returned the thumbs-up and let Iesha do her job with the heifer.

I'd successfully avoided Hunter for a full week, giving him only a casual nod as we passed each other. He now knew what to do on the ranch and didn't need me directing him. Even if he hit a snag, he could ask Blake. When a task came up I was unable to handle, a note taped to his bedroom door always solved my problem.

Part of me felt bad for giving him the icy shoulder. But this was survival and my sanity was at stake. If that meant Hunter's feelings would get hurt, then so be it. He'd get over it soon enough, like he always did. I mean, seriously, was there any woman out there who could make a lasting difference in his life? Doubtful.

I just had to get through the next few weeks. The Tulsa competition was two weeks away and Iesha needed to nail it.

She held the heifer off until Finn gave the signal. "Fantastic," he called out.

I patted Iesha's neck. "Good girl. Let's go clean up." I steered her to the edge of the corral. Hunter was already waiting for us and opened the gate. I twitched, hoping he didn't try to talk to me. The withdrawals had been fierce these past few days, but I was sure the misery would be ending soon. I didn't need him messing with my head and throwing away all my progress. If you could call it progress.

Giving him a slight wave, I directed Iesha to the tack room, threw a leg over her back and slid to the ground. I loosened the cinch but as I reached for the horn to drag the saddle off, Hunter got there first and effortlessly lifted it.

I rounded on him, coaching my tone to show maximum irritation. "What's up, Hunter?"

My annoyance wasn't genuine. But I needed him convinced it was. In truth, I ached to reenact the kitchen kiss, desperately, and would've done almost anything to sniff his hand like Iesha was currently doing.

"Well..." He stared at the dirt around his feet and Iesha mouthed his shoulder. "At some point, we're going to have to prioritize upgrades. I'd like to get started as soon as possible on whatever's most important."

My gaze shot to the tack room ceiling and I shook my head. I switched out Iesha's bridle for a nylon halter that could get wet, then pivoted and led her outside to the washing station. "Why talk to me? We both know you can go through the list with Blake. Or my mom. I won't be here in a couple months anyway."

"So what I'm hearing is that you don't care what happens to the ranch or your family, even the animals."

Whether Hunter intended to or not, he always managed to push the right buttons. Ignoring him, I parked Iesha at the washing station. I silently thanked my dad for building the structure with no walls. I'd have felt too hemmed in with Hunter so near. The problem, though, was stepping off the rubber mat. My boots always got muddy. Maybe Hunter could figure a solution and add it to his list of ranch upgrades.

"Fine. What did you have in mind?" I tied Iesha's lead rope to the railing, thankful I could concentrate on her the next few minutes and not Hunter's gorgeous brown eyes. I checked the washing supplies in the bin, then yanked on the overhead hose and turned on the water.

He reached into his pocket and his hand came up empty. "I forgot my notes. I'll be back in a minute."

I loathed the tightening of my chest as he got farther way.

After a slight adjustment to the water temperature, I sprayed Iesha's legs, then worked the water up and over her back. When I'd finished hosing her down, I ran the sweat scraper over her body. As I was patting her dry with a towel, Hunter reappeared.

I wondered if he'd waited on purpose so he'd have more of my attention. I inwardly growled at the prospect of not having a distraction and being required to look at him when he spoke. We were behind the stables and I couldn't see any of the ranch hands, but it was broad daylight. What was the worst that could happen?

"Couldn't find my list so I made a new one." He brandished a small piece of paper.

"What's on it?" I refocused on Iesha's legs, wiping them with the towel, then tossed the wet thing in the bin. I twisted around to face Hunter, but both my feet slid in the mud and I flailed in a desperate attempt to get a grip on anything other than Hunter.

Hunter reached out to catch me but I came at him too fast, the momentum of my fall propelling him backward. I landed on top of him, my breasts coming into contact with his chest. Electricity ping-ponged through my body. In horror, I flattened my muddy palms against his shoulders to shove off of him as he shifted his hands to my waist. My hands slipped and I slammed into him again, my breasts fused against his chest. Tingles shot from my stomach to my toes and I froze.

I may have even whimpered.

"Bails," he whispered, his gaze locked onto my mouth. His fingertips pressed into my hip bone and I became aware of his thigh brushing mine.

I had to disentangle myself and get out of there.

"Breathtaking." He reached out to touch my hair, lingered a moment before cupping the nape of my neck. He pulled me down, slowly, closer and closer toward his full sexy mouth. And I let him. Now we were a hair away. "I can't stop thinking about you," he said.

I didn't want to move. I wanted those words, this moment, to last forever. I wanted to believe he desired me, that I really was that beautiful to him. I wanted to give in to the need, the ache. My lips parted and I held my breath. His mouth met mine but barely touched, just teasing me into inviting him in. I angled my head and edged closer, savoring the sweet taste of him, and the subtle scratch of his stubble on my chin.

I wanted to stay like this with him forever.

His one hand gripped my hip while his other secured my body against him. Then he ravaged my lips a little more.

"Hunter, what the hell?" Blake shouted.

I vaulted into the air and Hunter scrambled to his feet. If only I'd been paying attention to my surroundings and had heard Blake approach. Mashing my lips together, I avoided his gaze, like a guilty school girl caught smoking in the bathroom. A vein pulsed at Blake's neck and his hands balled into fists as he glared at Hunter. "I need a private word with Hunter."

"Don't be mad at him, Blake. It's not his fault. I could've moved any time but I didn't. If anything, he was kinda trapped." I'd been angry with Hunter for months, but that didn't mean my brother needed to defend my honor when Hunter wasn't to blame.

Blake ignored me, his shoulder aimed at Hunter. "This is between Hunter and me. Go."

"Absolutely not. You're not going to fight with your best friend over something I did. I'm not going to let my mistake come between you two." I dug in my heels, bracing myself for a battle as I focused on my brother. "Besides, what I do with Hunter is none of your business."

"Blake is right, Bailey. His reason for being furious with me has nothing to do with you. Only Blake and I can fix this."

I'd expected Hunter to return fire at Blake, but his tone was resigned, like he'd expected this and knew he deserved it. I wasn't sure I agreed in this particular instance. But since they both clearly wanted me gone, I'd let them have at each other and pray it didn't come to fists.

"Whatever." I spun and led Iesha to the stables.

I wished this latest kissing incident had made me more hostile toward Hunter. Instead, my sadness had grown more profound. Hunter's capacity for warmth and tenderness blew me away.

But it wasn't enough for me. I'd never loved him more than I did today, but he would never give all of himself to me. Rather than have part of his heart, I'd choose none.

The only man I'd ever truly loved could never give me what I needed.

Chapter Fourteen

HUNTER

"*You swore to* me nothing was going on with you two." Blake's knuckles turned white from fisting his hands.

"And that was the truth when I said it. Kissing her wasn't part of some diabolical plan. But she fell on top of me and..."

"Spare me the details. You broke your promise, my trust." He squeezed his eyes shut, pressed his lips together. "You could have any other girl but you kiss Bailey who's been desperately in love with you since she was eight. And you're too self-absorbed and oblivious to understand why this is so bad."

I shook my head, taking a step away. I didn't want to get punched and if he swung at me, I probably wouldn't hit back. "She's not in love with me."

"You're an idiot if you believe that." Blake kicked the mud, sending chunks into the air. "If you're stupid enough to believe your mistakes don't have devastating consequences for her, you can't be in her life. At all."

"Wait. Hold on. You act like I'm the worst person in the world, as if I'd hurt her on purpose. I know she's your sister, but would it be so bad if I dated her?" Because I was dying to. I wanted Bailey like I'd never wanted any other woman.

"This isn't about you dating my sister. Hell, someone's going to marry her eventually. Actually, you two being a real couple would be a dream come true for me and Mom. Except you'd destroy her because you can't give her the love she needs."

I blinked, knowing he was right. I married Bailey and had somehow messed up so badly she barely spoke to me.

"You can't stay here anymore."

I wasn't willing to surrender my place at the ranch. If I gave in, I might never have another chance to make amends to them. "Kind of hard to get rid of me now that I'm part of the B & B."

"Not hard at all." Blake ground his teeth. "You're an investor, silent partner if you will. I read the documents you and my mom signed, every word. You have no say in ranch business. None. Any help you provide, outside of capital, is allowed at our discretion." His eyes narrowed. "You're no longer welcome here."

This couldn't be happening. I sucked in a long, deep breath as I swallowed his words. They were the only true family I'd ever had. Losing them wasn't an option. "You need help on the ranch."

He rocked back on his heels. "Yes, we do. Now that

the mortgage is paid ahead of time, we have a little extra money to hire a temporary hand."

My tongue dried and stuck to the roof of my mouth. I tried to think of something clever to save myself but I had nothing. By helping them financially, I'd completely screwed myself. Even if I schemed my way into the ranch again, I couldn't bear to stay knowing they wanted me gone.

I thought I'd finally found a place where I belonged, but I was wrong. I had no value at the B & B, no worth. They didn't need me.

I pinched the bridge of my nose as my throat thickened. "I'll pack my things and be gone in no time."

Without another word, Blake took off toward the house.

I don't know how long I stood there, staring at the mud and remembering what it had been like being with Bailey, the plump of her mouth, her silky hair between my fingers, and the length of her body against mine.

Still sitting in my truck outside Fletcher manor, I frantically tried to think of a solution, a way to get the Thayers back into my life. But I didn't know how to make up for breaking a promise to my best friend, crossing the line of friendship. I wanted to get out of my truck and unload my things then stumble to my room and fall into my bed. And do what? Obsess on Bailey and how I wished I could travel back in time and do things differently? And what must Mrs. T think of me? Did she feel betrayed? Did Bailey hate me more than ever for taking advantage of her?

Lethargy blanketed me and I shrunk in the seat, then jolted at the tap on the driver's side window. I hit the button and the glass lowered. "Mom. You scared me."

"Muffin will be glad to see you." My mom scanned my face, her perfectly made-up eyes studying me.

Muffin would be glad to see me. What about my mother? Was I destined to live my life as a loner, never truly loving anyone or being loved back? I'd already reconciled myself to being single the rest of my life, never having kids. But to have no one, no one at all who truly cared whether I came home at night? Even Muffin had abandoned me.

"Come in and I'll make you some tea." She marched into the house.

I could get my luggage later. After dragging my ass out of the truck and into the kitchen, I slumped on a stool at the counter and stared at the floor while she put a pot on to boil. She leaned over and planted her elbows on the counter across from me. "Tell me what's bothering you."

Now she was going to play parent? Fine, I'd tell her the truth and watch her panic when she realized she was the worst advice giver ever. Either that or she'd tell me everything was all my fault. But what the hell. At this point, I had nothing to lose. "I got caught making out with Bailey. Blake flipped out and banished me from the ranch."

She pursed her lips in thought. "What part of this troubles you, that you've lost your place at the ranch or that you might get bored?"

Irritation chipped away my patience. Why did she have to be so blunt, so cold? "It's not about boredom."

"You care about the Thayers and you're feeling the loss." It wasn't a question. I probably should've given her credit for some life experience.

"Yep. It sucks."

"And Bailey? Was giving in to temptation worth losing them?"

I cringed. "Way to comfort me, Mom."

She shrugged. "I know you care about her, but do you love her?"

I huffed, not sure if I wanted my mom to know how deeply losing Bailey had cut me. "She's always been like a sister to me. Sure, I love her."

My mom cocked her head. "Most people don't make out with their siblings."

I recoiled at the truth in her words. "I'm attracted to Bailey. Who wouldn't be? And the intensity of that threw me. But I'm not in love with her or anything."

"Are you sure about that?" Her eyes stared into mine, as if willing the truth from me. "You did marry her."

I winced and slid off the stool. "I have to get my bags from the truck."

Once I'd lugged all my things into my room, I rifled through my suitcase, located my laptop and booted it up. I wasn't allowed on their property which prevented me from apologizing in person. But I could email Mrs. T, let her know how sorry I was.

Dear Mrs. T,

You don't know how angry I am with myself. But I can't imagine you guys not being in my life and I have no idea how to make things right again. Please tell me what to do.

Love always, Hunter

Yes, it was lame. But although Mrs. T would always nail me when I was out of line, she could always tell when I was sincere. I clicked the send button.

I wanted to find Muffin, maybe steal her and snuggle with her the rest of the day. But she'd already chosen my mother. She'd deserted me, just like everyone else I loved.

Two days and I hadn't heard a peep from Blake or Bailey. Granted, I hadn't reached out to them, but they were the ones who had banned me from the ranch. Bailey knew it wasn't my fault and I'd already explained the situation to Blake. I should've been vindicated. Thankfully, Mrs. T had taken mercy on me and replied to my email, even if she'd been completely stingy regarding information on Blake or Bailey.

The gazebo still needed to be built and the pond hadn't progressed since I'd dug the ditch days ago. Plenty to do around Fletcher manor, but I'd barely left my room in two days. Why be productive when I could wallow in my misery? Why do something that might distract me from my insane thoughts when I could dwell on my misfortunes and let the raw emotions fester?

My yet-to-be fully unpacked suitcases sat ready to trip me and two days of dirty clothes lay scattered across the floor.

I disgusted myself.

I opened my laptop, accessed my email and clicked on the compose button.

Bails, I'm so very sorry. You've probably given up on me and I wouldn't blame you. I want you to know that I never meant to hurt you. You're the last person in the world I'd want to hurt.

The last person? What was that phrase supposed to mean anyway? Of all the millions of people out there in the world, she'd be my very last choice to harm? Logically, the last person would be the one I cared for most. Did I love her more than anyone else in the world?

I kind of did.

She was the first person I thought of each morning and the last each night. And every moment in between. If I had to pick one Thayer to reconcile with, as much as I loved Mrs. T and Blake, I'd choose Bailey. No question.

But could I see myself with her twenty or forty years from now? Hell, I'd already known her for sixteen years and not once did my affection for her waver. But *in love?*

My head spun and I closed my laptop, leaving the email to Bailey unsent.

I had to admit, at least to myself, that I loved Bailey the way a man should love a woman. I didn't know if I was built to make the relationship last though. And I'd already hurt Bailey enough. She deserved the best and that sure as hell wasn't me.

My bedroom door rattled from the pounding from the hallway. "Son, are you done feeling sorry for yourself?" my dad called out from the other side of the door.

What an insensitive dog. "Not quite yet, Dad, but thanks for asking," I replied sarcastically.

"Your mother needs help with Muffin." The footfalls on the rug gradually faded.

I shuffled out of my room and down the stairs where my mom and dad waited for me.

"Take your dog for a walk, preferably all the way to the bark park if you're not too atrophied from doing so little lately," my mother ordered, scanning the list in her hand." I'm sure she'd love to play with her friends. I have errands to run."

"And when you come back, time to get to work on the gazebo you've been promising me. If you're staying, you'd better earn your keep." Without waiting for a reply, my dad wandered away.

The freezer folk struck again. Time to face reality that I was never going to get anywhere with them. They were old dogs. No new tricks in their future. I should be contacting a real estate agent to begin searching for my own home. But as worthless as my parents were, they were all I had and I didn't want to be alone.

Muffin slathered me with kisses and my limbs lightened. At least she still loved me, even if I wasn't her first choice.

I had to keep trying with my dad. With Muffin in tow, I raced after him, arriving just before he closed the door to his office. He studied me, holding the door ajar but not moving out of the way so I could come in. "Been seeing a lot of you lately," he said.

I tipped my head to one side, marveling at how he could question extra time with his son. "It gets worse than that, Dad. I'll probably still be here next week too."

"And rarely leaving the house, it seems. Is there a reason?"

A reason for what? He excelled at acting like I was unwanted. I suspected he was fishing for information though. But what kind? "You think I'm spending more time here because I need something from you? Wrong. I..."

"Spit it out, son."

I rolled my eyes, knowing that he rarely saw the good in me. That said, his prior assumption had been correct, so I couldn't really blame him.

"Okay." I straightened, pulled my shoulders back and rearranged my hold on Muffin. "I've lived here most of my life and you guys are my parents, yet when I'm here, you treat me like a stranger. I shouldn't feel like an outsider, yet I do. I want to change that. So I won't be looking for my own place any time soon."

He recoiled. "You're not going to start hugging us all the time, are you?"

"It depends." Muffin wiggled in my arms and I repositioned her. "Why haven't we smoked cigars together?"

"Had no idea you enjoyed cigars." He shrugged.

I didn't like cigars, or cigarettes or anything that required inhaling—aside from air. And maybe the cherry scent on Bailey. "I don't. But it's the principle involved."

"I'll keep that in mind," he said in a monotone voice.

Unlikely. I could see less of his office through the crack now than seconds ago, like he was gradually shutting me out. "Really? Because you're still holding the door, as if you want to prevent me from coming into your office."

He sighed, pushed the door open to reveal... several plants in pots. "Your mother's been looking for these but the nursery has been out of stock. I special ordered them and was planning to surprise her with them in the morning."

While I appreciated getting a glimpse into their relationship and seeing him do something nice for my mother, his thoughtfulness apparently didn't extend to me. I'd already seen what he was hiding, yet he made no move to invite Muffin and me into his office. I had a long way to go still to thaw him out. Deflated, I left in search of Muffin's leash.

"Our next competitor is Bailey Thayer who splits her time between working with Arabians and breeding them. She's riding Iesha, bred by the B & B Ranch in Bride, Texas and owned by Bailey. Iesha is a talented Arabian who's already garnered over thirty thousand. Younger than others in the competition and less experienced than your average cutter but from what I've seen of previous competition, I'm looking forward to her scoring well."

The buzzer went off and the timer started. Bailey and Iesha separated a steer from the others then Bailey let the rein go slack, signaling to the horse that the rest was up to her. I tuned out the commentator and got lost in Iesha, her nose pointing toward the calf as she cut side to side to block the steer.

After about thirty seconds, Bailey pulled back and the calf scurried away to rejoin the herd.

"Nice run," another voice from the speaker declared.

After two more runs, the timer ran out and Bailey walked the horse along the outside of the arena. "Some really nice cuts." The commentator paused a beat. "Waiting for the scoreboard."

I chewed the inside of my mouth in anticipation of the score. I'd never been the patient type and couldn't handle suspense at all.

"And Bailey goes to the lead with two twenty-nine."

At the opposite end of the arena, Blake grinned and used his hat to wave at Bailey. With only two more contestants, Bailey was sure to place well. If the last two didn't beat her score, she'd stay in first place. I would've loved to seek any of them out and make the

Tulsa trip worth the flight. But I knew when I wasn't wanted. Careful not to be seen by any of the Thayers, I vacated my seat in the back and slipped out.

Chapter Fifteen

BAILEY

I stared at the card that read simply *Congratulations.* No signature and I didn't recognize the handwriting.

"Stunning orchids." My mom came the rest of the way into the foyer and peeked over my shoulder. "Who are they from?"

I stared at the beautiful bouquet trying to think of anyone else who would send me flowers. Certainly not Blake. He had been happy for me, but he'd been more interested in Iesha's improved market value and potential foals after garnering second place in cutting. Trevor? No, he would've signed his name to drive Hunter mad with jealousy. Doubtful he even knew my favorite flower. Hunter did.

Hunter may have been wrong for me in the way that mattered most but he always knew how to make me feel special in other ways. The flowers had to be from him. I shook my head, more to purge him from my thoughts than to answer my mom's question. "No clue. Whoever it was didn't write their name."

"I've been thinking, sweetie. I want you to keep all your winnings."

I shot her a threatening squint. "I spent an awful lot of time cutting with Iesha when I should've been doing other ranch work. No, Mom, the money belongs to the ranch."

She nodded. "I figured you'd say that. At least keep a chunk for yourself. Go shopping. Take a few spa days."

I could finally buy a new outfit and I had no special guy to see me in it. Why make the effort to shop? I wasn't in the mood for going out or being social anyway.

"Sweetie." She stroked my back. "You have to let him go."

My breath caught as she exited the kitchen. Was I that obvious?

Three weeks ago, Hunter moved out and I hadn't heard a peep from him since—until the flowers moments ago. If they were even from him. And if he'd meant them in a grand gesture of love, he would've signed his name.

His occasional visits to Bride before Blake's accident had kept my hope alive. It was time to squash the hope like a bug and make sure I left no signs of life. He would never love me like I loved him. My mom was right, as usual. I shuddered and embraced the reality I'd battled for years. The battle was finished. I'd lost.

I didn't have to wait the remainder of the sixty days before the next step in the divorce. Now that the horse show was over, and we had a couple extra hands on the ranch, I could take time off and go to Vegas for the divorce—redirecting some of the money my mother insisted I keep.

Whatever Hunter was up to or if he was still in Texas, I had no idea. Doing the divorce without him would require having him served and would take more time. He'd have to meet me in Vegas. Besides, I needed to see him one more time and close this chapter of my life, say goodbye. Nausea churned my stomach and a gnawing ache burned deep inside me. I gripped the table that held the vase and steadied myself. I'd get through this. I had to.

Chapter Sixteen
HUNTER

After slamming in another nail, I set the hammer on a slab of wood and swigged half my bottle of water. My pocket dinged. Ignoring the text alert, I stepped away to view my work, satisfied my dad would approve of my progress on the gazebo. Almost finished.

I swiped the screen of my phone and punched in my password to see who had texted me.

Bailey. *Are you free next weekend for a Vegas trip? No point in waiting the full 60 days when we can get it done sooner.*

My legs gave out and I dropped to my knees into the grass. I didn't want anything to do with a Vegas divorce. Not because I preferred to stay married to Bailey, of course, but because divorce meant we no longer had any ties and she was lost to me forever. I needed a chance to figure out how to get the Thayers back in my life and handling the divorce in Texas would give me that extra time.

I had to do as she asked though. I owed her that much.

Except that I'd forgotten to check the residency requirements for Nevada. The whole thing could be a wasted trip. But I'd have Bailey all to myself, both of us in a city where we didn't know another soul. Maybe after not seeing me for a while, she missed me. She might even seek my company. This was my last chance to get through to her.

I'm free anytime. The least I could do is make it easy for her, especially since I had no other obligations. *Doubt the courts are open on the weekend tho.*

Oh, right. Maybe arrive Wed night so we can be at the courthouse first thing Thurs? If we run into any snags, we'll still have Fri.

Wednesday? That was only four days from now. I couldn't wait to see her. *Sure. I'll let you know when I've booked the flight and hotel.*

Same, she texted.

What if she'd done the research, gotten a lawyer and they'd figured out how to skip the divorce and do the annulment the right way? Had I just made a huge mistake by helping her get rid of me so efficiently?

I leaned back and sank into the grass, the phone slipping through my fingers as my arm flopped listlessly to my side. Muffin seized the moment and bathed my face in saliva. Normally, Muffin made everything better, but not this time.

I'd had low times in my life, like when I was eleven years old and realized my parents weren't ever going to change. Or when Blake had demanded I leave the B & B. Or the silence from Bailey since I left the ranch.

Knowing she was anxious for the divorce and I would probably fail at my last chance to get her back into my life was a brand new low point for me.

Maybe someone else could take my mind off her. I could stay in Vegas after we finished at the courthouse, mingle with girls who weren't Bailey. But the thought of pursuing a relationship with anyone but her didn't interest me in the least. I wanted Bailey. Just Bailey.

God, I missed her.

All this was payback for royally screwing up—exactly what I deserved. But as much as I hated the mere thought of losing Bailey, she needed freedom to move on to someone better for her.

An overwhelming sadness devoured me.

"C'mon, Muffin. Let's go inside." If I had to book a flight, I would do it while being horizontal and out of the sun. I hadn't slept well in more than a month. Maybe I'd sneak in a quick nap and put off the inevitable a bit longer.

I dragged myself up and Muffin followed me into the house, her little paws pattering behind me on the wood floor. After trudging to the living room, I plopped onto the first piece of furniture I came to. It was one of those chaises that looked elegant but unfortunately couldn't meet minimum expectations for comfort. Despite the too-firm stuffing and oddly angled back, fatigue willed my muscles into dissolving into the fabric.

Muffin hopped onto the chaise and snuggled into the crook of my arm. Just when I thought I might catch up on some much needed rest, a shadow compelled me to open one eye and see who could be cruel enough to interrupt my wallowing.

"It's nice having you home again."

I searched for a hidden meaning in my mom's words. If she had any feelings, she was never one to express them. "What?"

"We're happy to have you around." She wasn't frowning in sarcasm, and her mouth might have been curved up a smidgen.

"Thanks. It's nice to be here." Maybe...

She waited a beat and I wondered what was going on with her. I didn't have to wonder long. "Are you in love with that Thayer girl?"

"Of course not," I denied too quickly. With renewed energy, I popped off the couch and stood so she couldn't tower over me. "And would you please call her Bailey?"

She rested a palm on one hip. "If you love her, you should tell her."

After the beating I'd taken from Bailey the weeks leading up to my unexpected departure and then her most recent frigid texts, I had no plans of revisiting the topic of love anytime soon. Certainly not with Bailey and especially not with one of the freezer folk. "I don't want to talk about this, Mom."

"I'll be right back." For several blissful moments, she was gone. I collapsed onto the chaise again and Muffin jumped into my lap. All I wanted to do was forget every detail about this time in my life, and I wished my mom would cooperate. But that was not to be. My mom reappeared, her petite frame bent toward me as she held her palm open.

"What is it?" I stared at the pretty diamond ring in the old fashioned setting, pondering what about it was so familiar to me.

"It's your grandmother Irene's wedding ring."

Yeah... I'd never paid much attention to women's jewelry but I remembered seeing the ring years ago and had made note of its size. "Why are you showing it to me?"

"For Bailey."

"What? Why? I'm not staying married to her." I shook my head and inched away. "And Dad won't appreciate you giving away his mother's ring."

In a completely uncharacteristic gesture, she rolled her eyes. "This was *his* idea."

"Why would he want me to have it?" She must have misunderstood him.

She blinked, hard. "Because you're his son?"

I scoffed. "Like that's ever mattered."

Her brows shot up. "He insisted I give it to you for Bailey."

"That makes no sense." I grunted and stood again, ready to bolt. Was nothing sacred? Why couldn't they let me be? And why was everyone thinking I was in love with Bailey? "I can't imagine Dad letting go of a family heirloom, especially one belonging to his mom."

"His mother, *your* grandmother. She's gone and you have every right to her ring." A pained looked flashed across her face. "Sit."

I obeyed, surprised when she sat close to me. I nearly jumped out of my skin from shock when she placed a hand on my knee.

"Believe it or not, your father has great respect for Bailey." She bit her lip, like she was mulling over what to say next. Her eyes darted in the direction of my dad's study just a few yards away then she lowered her voice. "He'll kill me for telling you this... A few weeks ago, he tried to bribe Bailey into divorcing you quickly. Despite how badly their ranch needed the money, she refused to accept his offer. She said if she divorced you, it wouldn't be because she was being paid."

I wanted to be outraged at my dad for insulting Bailey with a bribe. But I was too elated that she'd refused it.

My mom lifted one shoulder. "I think your father likes Bailey. And... I do too." My mouth dropped open, but I had no words. She cleared her throat, forging on. "Were you aware your father and I separated years ago?"

"No." In fact, I couldn't believe they were still together. "What happened?"

"I'll start at the beginning, so you understand." She patted my knee. "Although our families pushed us together to combine and preserve our wealth, essentially arranging our marriage, your father and I always loved each other deeply."

"No kidding?" I had never been convinced they even liked each other.

"Neither of us have been accustomed to displaying emotion... as you know." She licked her lips, pausing. "Your father and I... we each believed our love wasn't returned. That led to frustration, anger and eventually extramarital affairs. Wasn't until we were ready to file with the court that we had an open and honest conversation, and then we realized we had it all wrong. It took the *end* of our marriage for us to begin our life together and finally act like husband and wife."

Holy crap. "Why are you telling me this?"

She sighed. "Just because we haven't shown you love—which I see now has been as destructive for you as it was for our marriage—doesn't mean our love doesn't exist. Why do you think I borrowed Muffin from you?"

All I had for her was a blank face. "No clue."

"I wanted to make sure you came back. I could guarantee your visits if I had possession of your dog."

I suddenly became unable to make my tongue do anything I wanted it to. Not that I had anything to say.

She laid a palm on my cheek. "You, Hunter Sage Evermond, are *our life.*"

To my horror, my eyes stung and watered. Oh, man, I needed a good night's sleep or I might break down and cry like a girl.

A door slammed and my father strode over the fancy rug toward us. "What are you two whispering about?"

"We weren't whispering." Not for all of the conversation anyway. "Mom's trying to give me your mother's ring." Now we would get to the truth. Just because my mother had turned out to have a heart after all didn't mean my father did.

"Which is exactly what your mother and I decided, yes. What's the problem?" His gaze bounced between my mom and me.

"You're giving me the ring *for Bailey*? Why? I thought Evermonds didn't marry into families like the Thayers." My eye twitched having to utter such vile words.

"Why wouldn't I want it passed on to my own son?" my dad growled.

I didn't want to voice my thoughts because saying it out loud made it too real. But I needed to. I folded my arms over my chest, tucked in my chin. "Because you think I'm a loser and you don't like Bailey."

His mouth pinched, brows puckering. When I didn't retract my statement, he rubbed his temples. After threading his hands through his hair, his gaze bounced around the room. "You got into a lot of trouble and cost me a mint. I had other things I should've been doing instead of bailing you out of jail. Twice." He held up two fingers. "You were supposed to pass the bar and join my practice but you chose a path I didn't want for you. I'm not going to lie, that was incredibly disappointing."

My own father confirming what I'd known my entire life. Numbness set in. I wanted to walk away but imaginary weights held me immobile.

"You chose *your* path, not mine." He shrugged. "In the end, you needed to go through all the bad behavior to learn from it and become the man you are today. Every parent's dream is to have their child live a better life than they did. I'm lucky enough to see you doing what makes you happy, a life that you're proud of. The only loser here is *me* for not telling you how impressed I am with the man you've become."

I swallowed, not sure if I'd ever heard my father say so many words in a single stream that didn't involve cussing—directed at me.

"Bailey's a good girl and she's got guts. If you love her, that's enough for me." By his flushed face, pressuring him to talk so long about his feelings had cost him. "I'd be proud to call her family."

Mom opened my hand, placed the ring onto my palm, then curled my fingers around it. "Don't do to Bailey what your father and I did to each other, what we've done to *you*. Make sure she knows you love her and then never let her forget it."

A lot of good an engagement ring did me for a girl I'd *already* married and had no intention of staying with. Except that I *did* want to stay married to Bailey. I couldn't think of anything in this life I wanted more than to be her husband. For life. But I couldn't imagine her wanting me after all I'd put her through. Even if I worked up the nerve to ask her to forget about the divorce, she'd never say yes.

I had to try though.

Chapter Seventeen

BAILEY

The chicken fried steak smelled heavenly. My mother, Blake and I had sat together for dinner only a handful of times since Blake had broken his leg. We'd been too overworked and I'd been too busy avoiding Hunter.

I'd be seeing him in four days though. My stomach fluttered, nearly killing my appetite. "I've decided to take your advice." I laid the napkin in my lap and waited for my mom to take the first serving.

My mom beamed. "A little mini vacation?"

I did my best to match her enthusiasm, though a trip to officially end a marriage with the love of my life wasn't something to celebrate. "Yes. I already booked my flight. Leaving Wednesday for Vegas."

Blake cut a bite from the steak. "With who?"

"Whom," my mother corrected.

"She's right." I told him, determined to get them both off subject. "Whom. What did the doctor say today?"

He shoveled a huge portion of mashed potatoes into his mouth. "I've got at least two more weeks."

"Not bad." I studied my brother as he piled another forkful into his face, chewed quickly and then reloaded. "In a hurry?"

He froze. "I'm going out tonight and if I don't leave soon, I'll be late."

Blake always took his time. If he rushed, he usually had a girl waiting for him.

"Hot date?" my mom asked, clearly on the same line of thought as me. I watched for his reaction.

"Going to hang out with a friend." He'd continued eating but had slowed. Maybe too slow, like he didn't want to come off as too eager.

Which meant he was eager.

Jealousy hit me like a slap in the face. I would've loved to get out of the house, work off some steam. But what if I ran into Hunter? Nope, I'd be staying home until Vegas, even knowing I may never learn the identity of Blake's date. "The Stable?"

His fork hovered in front of his mouth as he peered over at me. "Why, so you can spy on me?"

"I wouldn't need to spy if you spilled it." I suppressed a grin, knowing I was about to corner him. "What's the big secret?"

My mom's eyes twinkled. "Good question. If you weren't hiding something, you'd have no problem telling us who you're seeing."

"Fine. I give up." Blake muttered a curse word. "Noelle is meeting me at the Stable."

Warmth gently cloaked me and I grinned. "It's about time."

Blake flashed us a dazzling smile. "Agreed."

And I'd escaped the question of who I was going to Las Vegas with. "We won't wait up for you."

"Oh, c'mon. It's a first date."

I smirked. "With a girl you've known most of your life."

"We'll see." His smile faded. "I don't have to worry anymore about her being my best friend's ex."

Because Hunter was no longer his best friend. "Do you think you could ever forgive Hunter?" I asked.

"We all love Hunter, baby. We always will." My mom glanced away. "I think he'll figure out a way to get in our good graces again. Eventually."

Blake nodded. "Yeah, he'll work it out."

My poor pathetic family. Hunter was a part of us and we couldn't let go. But I'd watched him waste people left and right, especially girls. Throwing people away was his specialty. Why should we be any different? I'd let my family keep their hope though. But after my Vegas trip, I was done. I had to move on. My future and my happiness depended on it.

◊ ◊ ◊

After I checked into my hotel room and unpacked, I texted Hunter. *I'm here. I'll meet you in the lobby in the morning as planned.*

Knowing I'd be seeing Hunter had my nerves worked raw and my adrenals drained. Not even noon and I already needed a nap. But once I woke, then what? Why had I flown in so early? I could go to the hotel bar or hit a show. But what if I ran into Hunter?

I arrived early this morning. I was about to grab a bite. What are you doing for lunch?

Take a nap or meet Hunter? I hadn't laid eyes on him in nearly a month. I was supposed to be avoiding him, which should've resulted in him fading from my thoughts and I should've been well on my way to getting on with my life.

Oh, hell. Now that I knew he was somewhere in the hotel, he would be all I thought about until I saw him in the morning. Wasn't seeing him one last time supposed to be part of the trip? I was in a town where I didn't know anyone else. What could be so bad about hanging out with Hunter to see if I was still as crazy about him as ever? I could be in for a pleasant surprise, maybe wonder what I ever saw in him. *Meet you in the lobby in 15.*

Who was I kidding? All these years and my love had never died. I was hopeless. I dropped the phone on the bed and stared at it. Crap. I should text him again and call it off, tell him I decided to order room service.

But wasn't facing ones fears a good start to conquering them?

After leaping off the bed, I rummaged through the closet for a blouse. I grunted and put it back, opting for a t-shirt and jeans. I didn't want Hunter to think I'd dressed up for him. I dashed into the bathroom and retouched my makeup, then fluffed my hair. He'd seen me straight out of bed a thousand times, so this was a step up.

I gulped several long, deep breaths then grabbed my purse and headed to the elevator. Conscious of each sound in the shaft, and each ding as I moved through the floors, my pulse raced.

I should cancel and give myself the rest of the night to calm the hell down. But would I be any better tomorrow? This was Hunter, the man I'd loved for sixteen years—who I was about to cut all ties with. I'd never be okay with this. All I could do now was savor what little time we had left together.

The floor quaked beneath my feet and then the elevator door opened. My eyes scanned the lobby, finding Hunter about three yards away in front of the registration desk. Damn, he was gorgeous. His wild hair cascaded over his shoulders as he leaned against the wall, hands in his pocket. Just seeing him and being in the same room with him, my anxiety vanished, replaced with a rush of adrenaline. I couldn't wait to talk to him.

I wished I didn't have to waste these precious moments with the man I loved. I didn't want to hide my joy at being near him. I wanted to crash into him and throw my arms around his neck. Our trip together would end way before I wanted it to.

But I couldn't let him into my heart again. While trying not to appear too eager, I kept an even pace.

He dipped toward me and landed a kiss on my cheek. "You look great."

"Thanks." I took a step back, knowing I should limit our physical contact. We couldn't have a repeat of our last trip to Vegas, or the make-out session in my kitchen at home or our dirty encounter in the mud. Not that he acted remotely inclined. "How've you been?"

"Uh..." His gaze fixed to the tile floor of the lobby and he laughed once, but not as if it was actually funny. "Been a rough few weeks."

I had no words of comfort since I'd been in the same boat and probably twice as miserable as he'd been. Highly doubtful his source of stress stemmed from his lack of time with me. My best guess was that he missed Blake and my mom.

In silence, we strolled toward the restaurant, passing by a gift shop and conference rooms. Once we were seated in the curved booth, my nerves flared again. I discreetly scooted away and placed my purse between us.

"Can I get you something to drink?" asked the thin, blond waiter.

No alcohol for me, that was for damn sure. Not with Hunter nearby. "Iced tea, please."

"Same," Hunter said. The waiter vanished and Hunter stared at the condiments rack, tapping his fingers. "How are the new hands working out?"

"Good. They free me up so I can get more training in with the horses." As I snuck a peek at Hunter, I wondered why he'd bothered inviting me to lunch when he couldn't even look at me. Maybe he didn't want to eat alone and didn't want to take the time to woo some chick. "How are things at Fletcher Manor?"

He scratched his chin. "Interesting."

Could he be any more vague? On the bright side, he wasn't complaining. "So you've made progress with your parents?"

His head rocked up and down as if he was contemplating it. "Sort of. They're no different than before. I just understand them better."

I wanted to know the details, yet I didn't want to engage too much with Hunter. But I heard "better" and that was good enough for now. "Still hoping to escape?"

"I'm already working with a realtor." He used his butter knife as a pointer. "But I'm waiting to see how other things turn out before I make an appointment to see inside any of the houses."

To see how other things turned out? With what? Was I supposed to ask or was it a secret? Irritation welled within me. If Hunter didn't want to elaborate anything, I wasn't going to beg him for the details.

The waiter delivered our drinks. "Have you decided what you want?" he asked.

Not even close. I only knew I should get something light in case I got too stressed over Hunter and became nauseous. "A bowl of chicken noodle soup, please."

Hunter studied the menu another moment then glanced at the waiter. "Chicken sandwich on rye, hold the mustard, please."

After the waiter left, we made small talk until the food came. Only about half of the soup made it into my stomach. Hunter gobbled all his fries and most of the sandwich. Apparently, nothing ruined his appetite.

As he gobbled the last bite, his eyes veered to a woman strutting down the aisle. She wore a snug black dress that barely covered the important parts, exposing gorgeous legs. Her fake boobs were shoved so high and the neckline so low, they looked like they were about to pop out and go rogue. When she sat two tables away, Hunter managed to keep from ogling her. Impressive.

But his short answers and lack of conversation didn't inspire me to talk. I peered over at Hunter from under my lashes. He wiped his palms on his jeans and licked his lips. Was he nervous?

"Is something on your mind?"

"Um." He scowled. "What if we didn't get a divorce this trip? What if we just hit some shows and enjoyed ourselves?"

Because he didn't want to make the effort? I didn't want to ask if his version of this trip would involve alcohol and falling into bed. I wish I hadn't agreed to lunch. Though I'd justified spending time with him by lying to myself about seeing him one last time, I wished Hunter would realize I was the perfect girl for him. But he was the same old Hunter who would never change.

I despised myself for wanting him, for needing him to see me as a woman. I hated that I'd convinced myself he wasn't worth my time, yet I still craved his approval. I wished for him to want me, though I'd vowed to never get involved with him no matter what.

Hunter would always have a piece of my soul. But I couldn't let him own it all. And yet I still held the hope that one day, he'd declare his love for me and we'd live happily ever after.

My vulnerability made it impossible for me to be around him.

I plucked my wallet from my purse, chose the right amount of cash and tossed it on the table. "I have to go. See you in the morning."

He jolted, his eyes squinting. "What's the rush?"

"I finished eating." I scooted out of the booth.

"Wait." He tossed a wad of cash on the table and slid off the seat. "I thought we'd spend more time together."

To give him someone to sit with while he put off our divorce and prolonged my misery? Someone to have a conversation filled with vague answers? No, thanks. Unless he wanted to stay married to me for other reasons.

I steeled my heart, reminding myself that a future with him simply wasn't going to happen. I had no business harboring any kind of fantasy where Hunter was concerned. End of story.

"This isn't a vacation for me." Well, it was supposed to be. But clearly I wasn't going to have any fun. "We're here for one thing. That's it."

Hunter sidestepped to avoid a waitress and for an instant, he was out of my line of vision. I seized the moment, scurrying down the aisle and out of the restaurant. The elevator ahead dinged and the door opened with the arrow above pointing up. I darted inside and the doors closed as I spotted Hunter racing toward me and calling my name.

Why was he chasing me? I commanded my brain not to let in the tiny shred of hope of him being in love with me. He was never going to declare his undying love. He was lost to me forever and I had to accept it.

The floor jolted beneath me then the elevator climbed up. After a couple of stops, it finally arrived on my floor and I sprinted to my room. Once safely inside, I checked in with my mom, composing a text so she wouldn't worry. I clicked the send button and my phone dinged.

We need to talk. What is your room number?

If he had something that important, he should've covered it over lunch instead of looking at everything but me. Better yet, he should've talked to me instead of giving me curt replies. *We can talk in the morning. I'm switching off my phone now.*

And then I silenced my phone and tossed it into my purse. I didn't want to know if he called or texted again. I'd always been a sucker for Hunter and I didn't want to be tempted to give in.

I crashed onto the bed. Exhaustion permeated every muscle and depression brought on more lethargy. I closed my eyes and dreamed of a world where I didn't compare all guys to Hunter. Where he'd never been born and I could love another.

But the thought of him no longer being in my life spiraled me further into apathy. All I wanted to do was sleep.

◊ ◊ ◊

My lids scraped against my eyes like sandpaper. Dragging my feet off the bed and onto the floor, I shuffled to the dresser where I'd set my purse. Finding my phone, I checked the screen for the time. I'd done the dance of the dead, sleeping for two hours.

Not nearly long enough.

Four texts from Hunter? Vowing not to let him distract me from my goal, I left the messages unread and hurled the phone onto the bed.

I wanted a soda but getting one required leaving my room. Hunter didn't know which floor I was on, much less my room number. The chances of running into him were slim.

I grabbed a glass from the counter and my room key, stuffed my phone and a few bucks into my pocket, then slipped into the hallway. I smiled at the cute brunette whose t-shirt sported the hotel emblem. I craved that soda and she knew how to get it. "Where's the ice machine? Praying you have a vending machine too."

"Across from the exit sign." She pointed behind me, then glanced over her shoulder. "Is your name Bailey?"

"Yes." I froze, suddenly suspicious. "Why?"

"Someone had your picture on his phone and was asking people if they'd seen you."

I grimaced. "That's creepy. Can you describe him?" Judging by the light in her eyes, I was pretty sure I already knew the answer.

"Long hair." She touched her shoulder, right about where the ends of Hunter's hair would stop. "Extremely hot."

Why couldn't Hunter let me suffer in silence? Why did he ruin my perfectly good resolution to forget him? "I know him. And I'd rather he not have my room number."

"Of course. Everything all right? He was pretty desperate to find you." She bit into her bottom lip. "Should I call security?"

Desperate, huh? Maybe he had an emergency. Something could have happened to one of his parents and he needed to rush home. Guilt smothered me. "No. He's harmless, but thank you."

Harmless physically anyway. I fished my phone from my pocket and turned on the sound. It rang immediately. Seeing Hunter's name on the screen, I swiped. "Hunter?"

"Bails, where have you been? I've been trying to reach you for hours." The urgency in his voice told me something was off.

My pulse hammered as fear gripped me. "What happened? Is everything all right at home?"

"What? Sure, everyone's fine." His harsh exhale blew into the phone. "I was worried about you."

While I appreciated his concern, his odd persistence sent me into a panic. He was being too sweet which made me more likely to give in to him. I had to get him off the phone. Because whatever he was about to ask me for, I was this-close to saying yes.

A security guard hovered at the other end of the hallway talking to a female bellhop. A door opened ahead of me and a woman with two children filed out, all clad in swimsuits and toting towels. A housekeeping cart rounded a corner, pushed by a maid in a gray uniform.

No privacy.

"Uh..." I huddled close to the wall and cupped my free hand around my mouth and the phone. "I'm good, but I have to get back to my room. Um, see you tomorrow." I compelled myself to hit the red button to end the call.

Nausea swirled and rose into my throat. I'd hung up on the man I loved. Tears welled in my eyes, but I knew if I compromised now, if I let down my guard, I'd be dealing with more than a few tears in the future.

I was about to carry on with my mission and froze instead, the skin on the back of my neck tingling.

"Bailey."

Hunter, live and in person. How was I going to avoid him now?

Chapter Eighteen

BAILEY

I shouldn't have come out of my room. Could I get away with pretending I hadn't heard Hunter and that I didn't know he was behind me? The exit sign loomed in front of me. I stuck the phone in my pocket and tore off to the ice machine.

"Bails, you can't run forever."

"I'm not running, Hunter," I said, trying to sound bored. I kept the pace and entered the tiny room which consisted of the ice and soda machines. He appeared in the doorway as I set the cup under the spout. "I don't understand what you want and why it can't wait. Where's the fire?"

When he opened his mouth, I hit the ice button and drowned out his words. The security guard appeared, his gaze bouncing between Hunter and me. "Everything all right?"

"I'm her husband, not some stalker," Hunter huffed.

The brunette squeezed into the doorway. "You can't be both?"

I muffled a giggle and Hunter sent me a look of betrayal.

"I just need a quick conversation with her. It can be here in front of everyone, for all I care." He rounded on me. "You're not too busy to spare five minutes."

"How would you know? Did you get a copy of my itinerary?" Leaving my cup of ice on the machine, I retrieved the dollar bills and bought my soda. "Besides, you had almost an hour at lunch but wasted it with vague conversation that told me nothing. You couldn't even look at me."

He threw his head back and groaned. "That wasn't what you think. I was just a little nervous after everything that happened and not seeing you for a while. Would you please give me five minutes of your undivided attention? Please."

The great Hunter Evermond, prom king and chick magnet nervous around *me*? Yeah, sure. "And once you're done, you'll leave?" I sipped on the can of soda, my eyes darting around the small room.

He nodded. "If that's what you still want, yes."

As if I had a choice. If I didn't give him the five minutes, he'd dog me until he got it.

I ordered my fingers not to tremble as I poured the soda into the glass of ice, then I held out the soda. He shook his head and I motioned him toward the hallway. I darted out of the little room. "I'll be fine," I told the security guard as we passed.

A few feet into the hallway, I stopped so Hunter couldn't figure out my room number. "Talk."

He scanned the hallway, noting the security guard hovering several yards away, the maid's cart three doors down and two men chatting at the end of the hall. "I think we should give it a shot, try to make it work."

If he was referring to our marriage, he'd have to do a hell of a lot better. I raised one brow. "Give what a shot?"

He shifted his weight. "You and me."

I lifted the glass to my lips and swallowed, wishing he'd put some feeling into it. But that kind of emotion wasn't in Hunter. "No, thanks. Was there anything else you wanted to talk about?"

He grumbled. "You're not going to make this easy, are you?"

"Probably not." I retrieved the phone from my pocket and checked the time. "I have to get back to work." Which would include curling into the fetal position after telling the man of my dreams no thanks to giving a relationship with him a chance.

He relieved me of the soda can and set it on the carpet against the wall. "I'm going to start at the beginning."

"You better get it done in four minutes." I scrunched my nose.

"I deserve anything you dish out." He licked his lips and inched toward me. "When I used to beat on those boys who made moves on you, it wasn't necessarily because I thought they were scum. Even though some of them really were."

My eyes narrowed in annoyance. If that was the best he had, I'd be in my room in no time, wallowing in more misery. "Go on."

"I was used to being the center of your world, jealous of anything that took your attention off me." When my expression remained neutral, he wiped his hands on his jeans and forged on. "In truth, it was because I love you. Always have."

I struggled to curb my disappointment. "No one doubts your love for me and my family, Hunter."

"I know you have no faith in me with women, but I went through girls like water because they weren't right for me." He hissed out a breath. "I've been thinking about you a lot this past month, contemplating why you were always the first one I thought about when planning a trip to Texas. Why I never dated anyone while I was there visiting, why I still don't want to date anyone."

"Hunter, don't go there." My eyes stung and I progressed a handful of steps backward before he whipped around and blocked me. I met his gaze. "Don't say anything you can't back up."

"My point is that I can't see a relationship with any woman but you. You're the only one I want to be with." He closed the distance, this time even closer. "The only one I think about. Everything always comes back to you."

I swallowed, absorbing his words. I'd wanted to hear that for as long as I could remember. But it just wasn't enough. "Until you get bored and leave."

"I was afraid of that too, which is why I never tried with you." He searched my face. "Well, that and because I thought Blake would kill me."

A glance around revealed that the security guard, the pretty young bellhop and the maid were listening in. Some other stragglers had joined the crowd, ranging from an old man to a couple of teenagers. All riveted to our conversation.

"My whole life, I've felt unloved. I avoided getting close to anyone because I was afraid they'd abandon me. So I ditched them first. Turns out, I was wrong about my parents. They're not as cold as you might think."

Warmth enveloped me. I was thrilled for Hunter for being on the road to resolving things with his parents. But I couldn't let that distract me. "So now you're ready to try a committed relationship. I'm happy for you. But I can't risk being an experiment. And I'm sorry because your five minutes is over."

I sailed past him, the space leading to the door to my room a blur. I snuck one last look at him to see him still standing there. His arms dangled at his sides, his eyes vacant and wounded.

I knew the feeling. But this time, I couldn't let my heart lead. It had already betrayed me too many times.

Two hours later, I'd finished a sappy romance movie and no one had knocked on my door. Not even a text. True to his word, he'd left me alone. He'd had the five minutes and he hadn't delivered. Not that I'd thought he would. I was certain Hunter cared deeply for me. And I sympathized with what he was going through. But I wouldn't put myself out there to be crushed. Hunter would get over whatever this was—probably a lot sooner than I would.

A whimper turned into a sob which quickly morphed into the ugly cry.

Just before eight in the morning, I barreled out of my room and nearly crashed into Hunter. "I thought we were meeting at the courthouse."

"Not anymore." He jerked his head toward the elevator. "I already ordered a ride. It's rush hour so we've got a twenty-minute wait. Enough time to get some coffee."

He looked phenomenal in black slacks and a light gray shirt with a charcoal tie, his hair as wild and sexy as always. My stomach fluttered when the tips of his fingers on my lower back guided me past the elevator threshold. Thankfully, he didn't try to pick up the conversation from where we left off the night before.

"Latte?" he asked when we made it to the register to put in our order.

"Yes, thank you," I said.

He paid for our drinks and we ambled to the pickup area, then he leaned an elbow on the counter and faced me. "So... about the divorce."

This topic filled me with dread and dredged up too many painful memories of not being loved. "What about it?"

"I did some research last night. Getting a divorce in Nevada for nonresidents isn't as easy as you might think. Same goes for annulments."

"So we came here for nothing?" Irritation ripped through me. Would I never be free of Hunter? How could I heal if I never had the chance?

"Not necessarily. We could go to the courthouse anyway and double check my research, see what they say, what hoops we'd have to jump through." He shrugged. "If all else fails, we take in Vegas and have fun."

"You couldn't figure this out before we came all the way out here? Your dad is a freakin' divorce attorney. You had *one* job, Hunter."

His mouth curved up. "None of that matters. We're not getting a divorce anyway."

My traitorous heart skipped a beat, ever hopeful. "Nothing you said last night changes anything between us."

"Exactly. Nothing's different between you and me. You've always loved me and you've never wavered on that." He wrapped my hand in both of his, his voice, tone and attitude so much steadier than the night before. "Since the first time I saw you in those cute little shorts, you've always been the center of my world. I don't remember a time when I didn't love you."

As great as that sounded, I had no guarantee he wouldn't regret his words next week. His horrible track record couldn't be erased with pretty words.

He reached into his pocket for a small black box then dropped to one knee. I froze and my eyes flitted across the room to see many of the customers watching.

Hunter flashed me a lopsided grin. "My mom and dad insisted this was meant for you."

I cleared my throat, trying to appear calm and cool. "They hate me." Regardless, this wasn't between his parents and me.

"Not at all. They both just really suck at demonstrating affection. This belonged to my grandmother." He took the ring out of the box and the diamond sparkled. "Will you stay married to me, Bails?"

A real proposal. This moment should have been a dream come true. I wanted to know it was forever and I couldn't know with Hunter. I stared at the exquisite diamond while imagining myself wearing it.

"If you believed I was in it for the long haul, would you still put up a fight?" he added.

Hope slowly bloomed in my chest and this time, although I needed to stop it, I didn't want to. I needed him to prove me wrong, to give me a reason to allow the hope to grow roots. "You'll get bored and change your mind. I can't invest in a relationship I know I can't have."

He rose, cupped my face so that his fingertips caressed the nape of my neck. "I can't remember a time when I didn't love you. Sure, I was stupid for a while and took you for granted. Losing you made me realize that there is no one in this world more important to me."

I shook my head and made a feeble attempt at pushing him away. "It won't last."

"It's lasted sixteen years and only gotten stronger,

even through the hard times. I've never felt this way about anyone, Bails."

I made a feeble attempt to break his hold and then gave up.

"We've already been in love for sixteen years. I'm only asking for another seventy. I want to marry you. Again. For real. In front of God and everyone."

Any second, I was going to wake and be more broken than ever. "How do I know it'll work?"

"You don't. None of us do. But I can promise you that I'll do my best to do right by you. I have to. I can't lose you again. Ever. Because I know it would break me, Bails." One hand slid to my waist and he yanked me against him. "I'm going to spend the next seventy plus years showing you how grateful I am to have married up. And maybe one day I'll pay you back for loving me." He slipped the ring on my finger and I didn't stop him. I couldn't move. "Please don't divorce me," he whispered, his lips brushing mine oh so gently. "I don't want to live without you."

A tear escaped, making a wet path down my cheek. "You know what I was thinking?"

"That you haven't answered me and this is pure torture?"

I made a weird noise, a cross between a sob and a laugh. "We never got a honeymoon. I planned for a week here. How about you?"

His eyes shone. "I was planning for the rest of my life."

When I heard a smattering of clapping, I let out

a watery laugh and threw my arms around his neck. "Blake is going to kill you, by the way."

"Nah, it's all good." He swept me around the corner, out of most everyone's line of vision, then squished my body against his, brushing a soft kiss on my cheek and another at my temple.

"You talked to him?"

"My parents paid him and Mrs. T a visit the other day."

I snapped to attention and Hunter lost his grasp on me. I backed up, but still held his hand. "Your parents went to bat for you?"

"They jumped in and smoothed things over, yes." He yanked me close again. "Oh, and by the way, our mothers are planning our wedding as we speak."

I wasn't sure if that was good or not. I arched my neck to give him better access. "When is it?"

"Two weeks." His mouth worked its way to my ear. "My parents know the family who runs Sterling Ranch. They had a cancellation and gave it to us."

"We're getting married, for real, at Sterling Ranch?" That place was booked years in advance. I'd always fantasized about getting married there. To Hunter. All my dreams about him were coming true. I wasn't destined to be like Ellora Shepherd, forever searching for her true love.

"Yep. Which gives us only a few days to house hunt after we get back. We can get started from here. My realtor sent me some promising listings. We just have to let him know the ones we're interested in seeing and he'll line up appointments ahead of time. "

My brows flew up. "You and I are setting up house already?" Not that I was complaining. But everything was happening so fast. A shiver ran through me when he sucked my bottom lip into his mouth.

"I want to be under the same roof as my wife," Hunter growled, tightening his grip on me. His name was called and he released me, led me back to the counter to collect our drinks, then slung an arm around my waist and steered me out of the cafe. "Our mothers are getting along surprisingly well."

"So far. It's only been a few days." I jabbed the elevator button and twisted toward him. "Since when do your parents stand up for you?"

"Since my mom told me I was her life." He snorted. "She told me not to do to you what they did to me."

"Wow," I said in awe. "You did it. You really got through to them."

The elevator dinged when it arrived on my floor. He covered my hand with his and stepped out. "It was more a matter of me discovering I'd never lost them in the first place. And that I didn't have to lose you either."

"You never lost my love, Hunter. I'll love you to my last breath." When we stopped in front of my room, I slid the room key down the slot. I pushed it open, then spun and stretched on my tiptoes to press my mouth to his.

He guided me backward and into the room, his lips never leaving mine. His kiss was hungry, but vulnerable. Passionate, yet gentle. And then he pulled away, leaned his forehead against mine. "I'm ready for that honeymoon now, Bailey Evermond."

The End

Hopefully you liked Hunter and Bailey's story. For a sneak peek at the next book in this series by Neve Cottrell, go to our Bride, Texas Series website. Or skip the sneak peek and just buy it!

◊ ◊ ◊

For more from this author, or to receive updates, pre-order discount alerts or news on upcoming releases, please visit VeronicaBlade.com and sign up for her newsletter.

◊ ◊ ◊

Bride, Texas books!

Bride and Prejudice by Bonnie R. Paulson
The Unlucky Bride by Sylvia McDaniel
Ticket to Bride by Liz Isaacson
Bride 'em Cowboy by Twist Roberts
Over My Wed Body by Veronica Blade
Sleigh Bride – by Neve Cottrell
Bride for Hire – Debra Clopton

◊ ◊ ◊

If you enjoyed Hunter and Bailey's story, please recommend *Over My Wed Body* to friends, reader's groups and discussion boards or show your love by reviewing it on the website of your favorite book retailer, GoodReads or your own site. Thank you!

More Titles by Veronica Blade

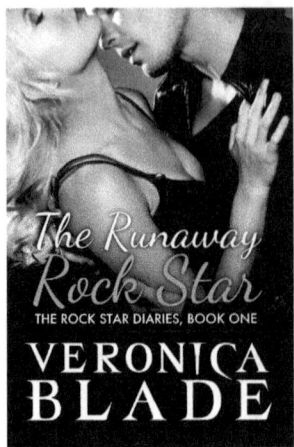

An infamous bad-boy rocker falls for a small-town girl who has no idea who he is. Considering his reputation, that's probably a good thing.

Should a woman who's unable to forget her first love give "happily ever after" one more try?

When good-girl Maddie switches places with her famous bad-girl twin Jackie, she has some pretty high stilettos to fill.

A safer school has its perks, but what else did the years of martial arts training get her? Not a prom date, that's for sure. *(Free eBook)*

About Veronica Blade

Veronica Blade resides in both southern California and northern Nevada with her husband, daughters and furbabies. By day she runs the family business, but each night she slips away to spin her tales. She writes stories about falling in love and lives vicariously through her characters. Except her heroes and heroines lead far more interesting lives — and they are always way hotter.

)

You can visit Veronica Blade on Facebook, check out her website or follow her on Twitter. You can even e-mail her at veronica@veronicablade.com. She loves hearing from readers!

www.ingramcontent.com/pod-product-compliance
Lightning Source LLC
Chambersburg PA
CBHW072352190626
46811CB00019B/577

DERANGED MANIACS OF POST-SOVIET MARS

–

THE MEANING OF INTELLIGENT LIFE

Paperback: ISBN 979-8-9855732-0-6

Hardcover: ISBN 979-8-9855732-1-3

For information visit www.robertlautner.org

I0547867

DERANGED MANIACS OF POST-SOVIET MARS
–
THE MEANING OF INTELLIGENT LIFE

We must settle space to justify our existence. This is the only thing that matters. This is the paramount obligation of the human race.

Chapter 1

Florina Destroys a Factory

In a not too distant future that should have been, deranged pyromaniac Florina was getting ready to execute the most important endeavor of her life. Her mission was to quietly infiltrate Martian Illicit Lascivious Pharmaceuticals, or MILPh, to collect biological samples undetected by posing as a janitor. The whole thing about quiet infiltration went against every fiber in her body. She was more of a blow the place up kind of agent, but this was her last chance. If she failed, she would be fired from the agency. She had been briefed about the probability of another secret agent from another agency being active here, so she had to be extra careful not to attract attention.

Not yet used to local gravity, she moved clumsily around the facility with her mop and bucket. As she passed an electrical panel, she wondered what would happen if she accidentally splashed water on it. Would it just short out and die? Or would it blow up causing a fire? Why was she asking herself these questions? It was of no importance what would happen in such a scenario since the panel was perfectly safe quite high up on the wall, out of reach of any splashing water. No sane person would waste time thinking about this, but Florina was not a sane person.

She held her mop up over the panel and let water drip down on it. Nothing happened. "It needs more water," thought Florina and poured the whole bucket of water over the panel. Sparks shot out of the panel, followed by a loud boom, and then flames and smoke. "Why the fuck did I just do that?" Florina wondered to herself.

Causing small "accidental" fires was something Florina did on a daily basis. If there was an opportunity to start a fire, she couldn't resist. If she did manage to resist, her subconsciousness would take over and make sure she accidentally caused one. Back on Earth you would just put these fires out and open a window to air out the smoke, not so, on Mars. There's neither fresh air outside, nor a window to open. You make smoke; you breathe smoke until the filtration system slowly removes most of the particles. If the fire is Florina's once-a-week-bigger-type-fire, then you have to worry about carbon monoxide poisoning as well. On Mars you also face the additional danger of the fire burning a hole in the building allowing all the air to rush out killing everyone inside by suffocation. Luckily this was the smaller daily type of fire by Florina's standards, but at MILPh this was the biggest fire they had ever had.

The fact that medicine factories were extra picky about contaminants didn't make anything go any smoother. There were all kinds of alarms screaming throughout the facility. There were flashing lights, and there were airlock walls falling from the ceiling to isolate the disaster. People were running in panic everywhere; some were running for the parking bay to their cars, and some were running to the fire with fire extinguishers, but nobody was standing still, nobody, except Florina. She just stood there looking at the pandemonium she had created trying to figure out what to do next.

"I saw the whole thing!" yelled one of the men with a fire extinguisher as the fire was being brought under control. "It was her there. Yes, her with the mop. She poured her water bucket over the panel. It's all her fault!"

Florina felt quite anxious. She knew she was about to have her cover blown. Nobody would recognize her as an employee, and she looked way too exotic to be a Martian with her relatively muscular build. If you had been in Mars gravity long enough, your muscles shrank down to local size, but she was fresh off a flight from Earth. On top of that, she was pretty sure she was the only Australian Aboriginal female these people had ever seen. Attempting to maintain her cover was not an option; she was going to have to get a little bit violent.

The agency had very reluctantly issued her a small amount of non-lethal weaponry for emergency use. She was no longer authorized to use firearms after having accidentally shot a fellow agent in the foot during a recent training exercise. She was also not allowed to use explosives of any kind after a tragic incident where she had unintentionally killed a superior officer's pet capybara by letting him play with a hand grenade. It was a bad idea she had realized in retrospect. Nevertheless, they had armed her with a small can of mace and a flare gun.

She reached into her pocket and pulled out the flare gun.

"Alright, pendejos!" she yelled out in a Spanish accent. "Do what I say, or I shoot this flare gun and make more fire and more smoke!"

"No! Please, ma'am! No more fire and smoke, please. We will do what you want," said a man who appeared to be their manager.

"Alright then," Florina yelled. "I want you all to go in that room over there. I will lock the door, and you cannot come out. I'm sure emergency services are on their way already, and they will let you out when they get here. I will just collect some samples, and I'll be out of here soon. If you do what I say, no one gets hurt."

"Ma'am," said the manager. "With all due respect, that room is not very pleasant. Nearest emergency services are half an hour away, and there's nothing to do in that room. Would it be alright if you lock us in the break room instead? There are drinks and snacks. We also have a rack with newspapers and magazines to pass the time. It's so nice in there; plus today is Botond's last day of work before he retires, and we were planning to have a little party for him with a cake. It would be terrible if we had to have the party in that other room without a cake or anything."

"Fine. Take the break room," said Florina and waved her flare gun at them to all go in there.

"Thank you, ma'am. You are truly kind, and thank you for not making any more fire," said the manager while he led his workers into the break room.

As the door locked behind them, they all sat down to celebrate Botond's retirement.

"Really nice of her not to make any more fire," mentioned one of the workers.

"Yes, but so strange that she has a Spanish accent but looks Australian," another worker noticed. "How many Australian Aboriginals have Spanish accents, you think?"

"Who cares?" growled Borbala from payroll. "At least we get to celebrate Botond's retirement properly. I can't wait to taste that cake Laszlo's wife made. How about you, Balint? I know you love Laszlo's wife's cake."

"If it's Laszlo's wife who made the cake, I don't want it. Last time I spent the whole day on the toilet after eating his wife's so-called cake," Balint shouted back. "Of course, you can't blame her. Who'd have time to bake decent cakes and be a full time whore at the same time?"

"Take that back, you motherfucker!" screamed Laszlo as he picked up a chair and broke it over Balint's head.

Balint was now unconscious on the floor, bleeding profusely from the head. There appeared to be a large dent in his skull, and his body was twitching in spasms. It was clear that he was in dire need of urgent medical attention.

"Ah, fuck you, Laszlo! You're ruining my retirement party," yelled Botond angrily. "I'm glad to be out of here, and I never have to see any of you assholes ever again for the rest of whatever's left of my life. My single biggest regret is that I spent so many years of it here with all of you pathetic fucks! I hate you all, and I hope none of you live to retire. Specially you, Laszlo!

"Oh, and by the way your wife does make terrible cake, but she's a good fuck. I know because I fucked her this morning. We've all fucked her, all of us, except you, Laszlo, you dickless piece of shit!"

"You fucking cocksucker, I'm going to kill you!" yelled Laszlo as he jumped across the table towards Botond and took a stranglehold on him.

The others tried to pull Laszlo off, but he was too strong. Botond was losing consciousness fast. He managed to grab a bottle, and with his last ounce of strength he broke it over the table and stabbed Laszlo in the throat with it.

Laszlo now too fell to the floor right next to Balint. Blood was pumping out of a big gash on the side of Laszlo's throat. Balint was no longer bleeding from the head, not because he had gotten any better but because he was out of blood.

Botond was gasping for air holding a bloody broken bottle in his hand. His coworkers were all looking at him in complete shock. Gazing at his coworkers and taking a close look at each one, Botond announced, "Lajos, I fucked your wife many times. Yours too, Mihaly. Csaba, your wife begged me to fuck her, but she's too ugly, and I have standards!"

"Lajos, Csaba, Mihaly!" interrupted Borbala from payroll. "Are you going to let him talk that way about your wives? What are you waiting for?"

The fight that erupted was gruesome. At first it was Lajos, Mihaly, and Csaba against Botond fighting each other with whatever objects they could get their hands on.

"This is not a fair fight!" yelled Borbala. "Somebody help Botond!"

Two other men joined in in defense of Botond, not because they liked Botond particularly much. No one did. They saw this as an opportunity to cause physical harm to Lajos, Mihaly, and Csaba. Borbala kept encouraging people to join in the fighting. Soon everybody in the break room was engaged in the fight in one way or another.

There was a small kitchen area in the corner of the room, and Borbala started handing out kitchen knives, schnitzel hammers, rolling pins, and anything else that could be used as a weapon to the highest bidder while encouraging everyone to fight to the death.

Another woman was recording video of the fight that she hoped to be able to profit from. Dorottya, the old lady from accounting, was crawling on the floor collecting jewelry from the dead and dying until she herself was struck by a stray Chinese cleaver flying through the air. After a few minutes of the most intense fighting imaginable, the only survivor was Borbala from payroll. Not only had she survived, but she had also made a handsome 749 Martian rubles from selling weapons to her coworkers.

Meanwhile Florina, completely ignorant of the medieval violence going on in the break room, had calmly been collecting her samples around the facility. Her sample case was only about half-full, but she had collected all the samples there were to collect. She was now waiting for a signal that her primary target had arrived for a pick-up, and at that time she was to intercept the subject on his way out and go along with him in his vehicle. She had noticed some commotion coming from the break room but didn't think it was a problem.

She figured Martians probably like to celebrate rough. She was almost a little tempted to join in their celebration. After all, there was a cake involved, but she knew she had an important mission, and if she failed again, she would surely get fired this time.

Florina thought of the cake some more and thought, "What the hell? I am just sitting here waiting for that signal, might as well go and have some cake."

At that moment her phone buzzed and displayed,

"Primary target has arrived in red Moskvich. Currently in airlock to parking bay. ETA 90 seconds. Get close and find out EVERYTHING you can about package and destination."

The plan was to let the primary target enter the facility and pick up a package he was supposed to have and then convince him to let her go along in his car on his way out. Florina figured he might get suspicious if he enters and sees all the destruction and that she's the only person in the whole facility. She decided a small change of plans was in order, so she went to the parking bay to meet him there instead. She got up with the sample case in one hand and the flare gun in the other.

The door to the parking bay was hard to open. After some clumsy fumbling with the door handle, Florina had to put her flare gun on top of the punch clock, which was located right next to the door, to get the door open. Naturally she left her flare gun on the punch clock. As the door slammed behind her, the flare gun fell off the punch clock and went off as it hit the floor. The flare flew across the hall straight into a tank of one of the liquids she had just taken a sample of. Most of the liquids stored at MILPh were quite inert, and the flare would have been put out in contact with the liquid, but not this one. No, this one had one of those scary signs of a fire on it.

Within seconds the tank and its immediate surroundings were ablaze. Normally fires on Mars run out of oxygen and die very quickly. However, next to the tank of whatever flammable liquid it was that Florina had ignited was a rack of rather large oxygen tubes that all burst from the pressure caused by the sudden increase in heat. Flames fueled by escaping oxygen now engulfed the entire manufacturing floor burning anything and everything. Of course, Florina appeared to have absolutely no clue about what was going on behind the door she had just come through.

As she walked into the parking bay, a red Moskvich was pulling out of the airlock into the parking area. Cars on Mars came in two basic types: highway cars and city cars. City cars were similar to Earth cars. Often times they were convertibles or even completely roofless since they could only be driven indoors anyway. Highway cars, on the other hand, had massive pressurized chassis, and you could drive them outside the cities.

In the early days of Martian colonization, the Soviets had made very big investments in Martian automotives and brought their fantastic brands of automobiles to the red planet; as a result, almost every car on Mars was of a make that had disappeared on Earth after the collapse of the Soviet Union. Moskvich was a classy brand that had relatively large windows to ensure that everyone outside the car could see the very successful people inside that could afford such an expensive ride.

Florina ran up to the car and jumped into the passenger seat.

"Please! Please, get me out of here," she begged. "There's a maniac in there with a gun! She has taken everyone hostage. We've got to get out of here fast."

Zsombor looked at his unexpected passenger in surprise. With her wide limbs she was obviously from Earth, and based on her appearance, she was probably from Australia. "Strange about the Spanish accent though," he thought. He had had it with Martian women and had been fantasizing about Earth girls for quite some time, Native Australian women in particular. To the best of his knowledge, there were very few, if any, eligible Australian Aboriginal women from Earth on Mars, but now there was a quite cute one in his car!

"This must be my lucky day. Good things will happen today for sure," he thought.

Little did he know that in a very short time he would experience the accidental destructiveness of this woman who had just gotten in his car and come face to face with his mortality.

"Bo! Mars to weirdo behind wheel. Are you done zoning out? Maniac with gun, remember? Let's move this car, shall we?"

"Oh yeah, sorry," said Zsombor as he turned the wheel and drove the car back to the airlock and out into the Martian landscape.

It was about ten in the morning, but the sun wasn't due to rise for another hour. Since everyone was indoors most of the time the entire planet was on Greenwich Mean Time, and since the Martian day was twenty-five hours long there was a daily one hour shift in the position of the sun relative to the time of day. The position of the sun in the sky on Mars had similar significance as sea tides on Earth. It was important to keep track of if you worked outside, but very few people did.

Normally Zsombor would have politely asked his strange passenger to please clean her shoes before getting into his ridiculously clean car. He didn't like when his Moskvich got dirty, but given the circumstances he figured he might make an exception to his normal tidiness. Getting taken hostage by a maniac after all didn't sound like very much fun.

As the car drove away, Florina looked back and saw a large ball of fire coming out of the roof of the factory.

"Looks a bit like the Hindenburg going up in flames last month," she thought to herself. "Or wait, no, that was a bit over a hundred years ago," she realized.

Short times compared to other short times had become blurry for Florina since she had widened her time horizon. Regardless, seeing fire and flames, especially when set by herself, always elevated her level of excitement. After all, she was a recovering pyromaniac.

"Why is the factory on fire?" Zsombor asked. "What happened?"

What had happened, of course, was that the fire had burned a hole in the roof, and burning oxygen was blasting out of the hole. A bit down the road ahead of them a row of emergency response vehicles headed towards the factory at high speed. As the convoy of ambulances, fire trucks, and police cars passed them in the opposite lane, Florina was marveling at the immense beauty of the magnificent fire cloud emanating from the burning factory.

"Wow! Good thing we got out of there in good time, right? My name is Zsombor, by the way," Zsombor introduced himself.

"I'm Florina. Nice to meet you, Zsombor."

"Florina! Wow! You don't hear a name like that around here very often. That must be a really expensive name. Are you paying for it yourself, or is it some corporate perk?"

"No, it was given to me by my parents free of charge. What do you mean? Oh yeah, you've got this weird copyright problem here, right?"

"Yes, you must be from Earth where all names are free. No, here on Mars or any other non-Earth human world, by the way, all names are protected by copyright. You have to pay an annual fee to have a name, and some names are very expensive. A pretty Latin name like Florina would cost you at least twenty grand a year."

"You're kidding. So, what's up with all these weird names you Martians all have? Why on Earth, I mean, Mars would you pay money for a name like Zsombor?"

"Ah yes, those are all Hungarian names. The Hungarian language is the only official language not covered by the interplanetary language copyright law. The Martian government has been given permission by the Hungarian government back on Earth to use their language free of charge. Hungarian names are free to use, so most of us have switched to one of those. Then you don't have to worry about paying dues for your name. Most cities have also taken Hungarian names to save money," explained Zsombor.

"That is so crazy, now that you mention it. I remember when I was a kid, I had a friend from Mars. She was just stopping by Montevideo while on vacation with her parents, but we had such a great time together. She had one of those weird names too, started with a B. I couldn't pronounce it, so I called her Bib, and she called me Fire-ina. You know? Because I like fire.

"She was a real pyro, let me tell ya'. We burned down a fuel storage together. You should have seen the flames, absolutely fantastic. When you're a grown-up, you can't do stuff like that, but when you're a kid, it's all fun and games, right? They caught her, and she blamed the whole thing on me. After that I wasn't allowed to have matches for a year.

"I hope I never meet that bitch again, but if I ever do, I'll get even with her. Can't help feeling sorry for her, though. It can't be easy being a pyro on Mars, right?" Florina paused then continued.

"Wait, when you say language copyright law, you mean it applies to more than names?"

"Yes, as of last year it applies to all written mass communication, like warning signs, instruction manuals, books, articles, and even song lyrics," replied Zsombor before he continued. "You can use any language you want in person to person communication, but if you want to publish anything in English, even a warning label or a warning sign, you have to pay. Of course, warning labels and signs are required by law, so to save money they are mostly in Hungarian now."

"Well, do you guys speak Hungarian?" interrupted Florina.

"Of course, not. Nobody does. We all speak English on Mars, but then again who reads warning labels and instructions, right?"

"Good point," added Florina. "Maybe it's for the better, so you don't have to read that stuff."

"For me personally this was quite a big problem. I was the editor-in-chief of a publishing company," explained Zsombor.

"When they started charging us royalties for each English word we published, we couldn't make it work financially anymore. English is one of the most expensive languages to use. You have to pay royalties to each country where it's an official language.

"Every time we used any word from the English language, we had to pay money to the US, UK, Canada, Australia, and a bunch more. We tried to use British spelling whenever possible, so we wouldn't have to pay the Americans. They charge the most, but that was just a drop out of the sea. It was a rough transition. I lost my whole career. Now I deliver packages for a living as you see."

"Only Hungarian huh? And now you're going to deliver packages for the rest of your life?" Florina wondered.

"Oh no, of course not. This is a great opportunity for me. I have two master's degrees in Linguistics, and now I finally get to use them fully. You see? Apart from Hungarian being free to use, native languages that are not official languages of any country are also free to use. I'm creating a new hybrid language by combining several Native Australian languages and dialects into a language that is easily understood by English speakers, but it is not legally English in any way," Zsombor kept babbling.

"For the last couple of years I have been studying and analyzing the structure of Native Australian languages. My life has been completely revolving around Australian Aboriginals lately. Do you speak a Native Australian language by any chance, Florina?"

"What? Because I happen to obviously be an Australian Aboriginal I must automatically be speaking some kind of bush language? Is that it?" asked Florina who was now quite annoyed.

It wasn't Zsombor's question that bothered her. It was the sudden realization that she had been given this particular assignment not due to her superior skills as a field agent. No. She

15

was starting to suspect that her ethnicity may have played a part in the selection process.

"Sorry, no. I didn't mean it that way," said Zsombor looking a bit scared.

"Haha, I'm just messing with you," she laughed and slapped him on the shoulder. "My parents moved to Uruguay before I was born last month."

"What? You were born last month?"

"I think so, not sure. Short time frames confuse me. I might be older than that. If you see a light come on for a microsecond, can you tell if it's on for one microsecond or a thousand microseconds? No, you can't. Both will appear as a quick flicker even though one is a thousand times longer than the other. If you have grown accustomed to thinking of time in spans that actually matter evolutionarily, these short time spans like days and years become very much the same. So yes, I was born a very short time ago in relation to the age of the Universe. Was it a month ago or three hundred years ago? I don't know; it's not important."

"What an interesting way to think about time, but do you speak an Aboriginal language?"

"My dad speaks Warlpiri, and my mom speaks Tiwi, so they just speak English to each other. With me they always spoke Spanish growing up. They wanted me to grow up a hundred percent Uruguayan."

"That's fantastic. Warlpiri is one of the languages I'm basing my new hybrid language on. I would love to meet your parents one day and pick their brains. You can only get so much from books and articles."

"Easy there, buddy. You want to meet my parents?" laughed Florina. "Tell me, Zsombor, your interest in Australian Aboriginals, does it extend beyond linguistics? Do you have some kind of fetish for Australian Aboriginal ladies?"

Zsombor blushed. He was trying to come up with a good answer to Florina's very direct question while Florina was staring him right in the face with piercing eyes.

"Hahaha!" she burst out laughing. "You should have seen the look on your face. Hahaha! But seriously, do you?" she asked as she once again turned serious.

"Umm, nice day today, not a tornado in sight," said Zsombor trying to change the subject. "So, are you on your way to Sopron?"

"Is that where you are headed?"

"Well, that's where I live. It's only about twenty minutes from here. That's one of those very short times by the way. I was supposed to pick up a package at MILPh and deliver it to a client in Szombathely, but since I wasn't able to pick up that package there's not much point in going to Szombathely anymore. I guess I'll go back tomorrow for the package if it hasn't burned up."

"A package huh! What kind of package? What's in it? Who is it for? Is it refrigerated? How big is it? How heavy? Is it packaged in an airtight container? Is it..."

"Easy Florina, why do you ask so many questions about the package?"

"Oh, you know, I'm just a very curious girl. You like curious girls, don't you?"

"Umm yes, I suppose I do..."

Florina had her can of mace in her back pocket, and it was pushing uncomfortably against her buttock, so she took it out and put it on the dash.

"Is that mace?" asked Zsombor. "You have to be real careful with that stuff on Mars, especially in a car on the highway. If that thing goes off in here, we can't just roll the window down. There's no air out there, you know?"

"Ah, don't be such a wuss. It's very safe. Look, it has this safety thing here, see? You have to twist the top like this before you can shoot it," said Florina and showed Zsombor how the top could be twisted to allow the mace to discharge. "And best part, it's from Earth, so the instructions are in English," explained Florina and held the now unsecured can of mace up close to Zsombor's face, so he could see that the instructions were in English and not Hungarian.

"See? It has to be untwisted like this, or else you can't push this red button down to shoot," Florina said as she pushed the red button down to demonstrate to Zsombor how safe her can of mace was.

The mace shot straight into Zsombor's eyes.

"AARGH!!! I CAN'T SEE ANYTHING. HELP!" screamed Zsombor.

In a panic he slammed on the brakes putting the Moskvich in an uncontrolled spin. Losing control of a car on Mars was much easier than on Earth; the combination of low gravity and very dusty roads made for much less friction between the tires and the road. Added to that, even small collisions often resulted in leaks in the pressurized body of the car causing the passengers to suffocate. Highway driving on Mars was quite a risky enterprise compared to what it was on Earth. Zsombor knew that being in a spinning car on Mars was usually your very last experience, unless you count the agony of suffocation that was soon most likely to follow.

Florina, on the other hand, seemed to have a jolly good time. It was like she was on an amusement park ride. She raised her hands to the car ceiling and cheered excitedly as the car spun around and around until it finally crashed into a boulder by the side of the road bringing an abrupt end to all the fun.

"YOU CRAZY FUCKING LUNATIC! WHAT IS WRONG WITH YOU?! Why would you mace the driver of a moving car on Mars? Do you know how car crashes on Mars usually end?"

"I'm so sorry, Zsombor, so sorry. I didn't mean it. But hey! We're fine, right? That's what matters. Later we'll be laughing about this, right?" she said with a cheery face.

"Not so sure about that. We're losing air. The collision probably cracked something, and air is seeping out."

"What does that mean? That sounds like a bad thing." Florina was anxious.

"Well, yes. That's usually how people die in car crashes on Martian highways. The air escapes their cracked cars, and the passengers all suffocate. See this blinking orange light here? That's the cabin pressure light. When that goes to red, we pass out and die. We could call for rescue, but there's no way they would reach us in time. I'd say we have about five minutes. That's an extremely short time. We'll soon be dead unless by some miracle a highway ambulance happens to drive by and spot us. Can't be a regular car. There's nothing they can do. They can't get out of their cars to help, or they die too."

"You're telling me we're going to die in a very short time! Is that what you're telling me, Zsombor?"

19

"Yes, I'm afraid so. And today being Mars Day, we're going to miss the great Mars Day Celebration. Greatest party in the solar system. Why couldn't this happen tomorrow? It would have been such a great party with a parade, live music, and…"

"I think we have bigger problems than a missed party, Zsombor," said Florina as Zsombor kept ranting about the Mars Day Celebration.

Florina realized that Zsombor was freaking out and needed to be talked to, but first she had to inform her contact of the situation. She took out her phone and dialed.

"Zsombor! Keep it down for just a sec. I have to make a very important call."

"Whatever you say, Florina. You're the boss. I would have loved to take you there. You would have loved it. Great food, drinks, fun games. Do you like food? I'm sure you do. They make this really good…"

Florina was already busy in her phone call as Zsombor kept babbling.

"Mierda! Voice mail!" Florina waited for the beep. "Yeah, listen Frank, I have a minor problem. We've crashed the car, and we're leaking air. Target says we'll be dead in five minutes, and apparently that's a very short time. I retrieved the samples. They're with me in the car. You have to send someone to retrieve them. Red Moskvich halfway between MILPh and Sopron, you can't miss it. Frank, on a personal note, I want to thank you for giving me this mission. It's been great working with you. Say hi to everyone from me. Florina out."

She could now turn her attention to Zsombor.

"Ok Zsombor, what exactly is your problem?"

"We're about to die because of your incredible stupidity. That's my problem!"

"What? Do you have some kind of endless life span or something? You said we have five minutes, right?"

"Well no, yes, but…"

"Well, then you'd be dead in five minutes anyway, so what's the big difference? What's so important in these next five minutes? Making more MILPh deliveries? Creating a trick language to circumvent some stupid law? What is it about your life that is so important for you exactly?"

"Well, I never really thought of it that way, but Florina, if this weren't happening, we would live for another fifty years, not just five minutes!"

"Haven't you been listening, Zsombor? Five minutes is almost the same as fifty years. The difference is fifty years minus five minutes, and that is absolutely nothing. Fifty years minus nothing is fifty years. Hence, five minutes is practically the same as fifty years. If we have five minutes left to live or fifty years, that doesn't matter one bit since they're the same, got it? Both are very very short times," Florina explained.

"People never see things in proper perspective, always restrained by their miniscule life spans. Fifty years? A Hundred years? Nobody ever thinks beyond a human life span! Do you know how old that rock you just crashed your car into is? The universe, Zsombor. Do you know how old the universe is? Don't worry. Maybe we'll make it, or maybe we won't. The important thing is I got those samples out of there. Besides, I like you Zsombor, and nothing makes two people bond better than being close to death together. Unless, of course, they get at each other's throats," laughed Florina before she continued.

"You're not going to get at my throat, right? See this case? It contains samples that I collected at MILPh. One of these samples holds the key to a very important scientific discovery that could potentially have an impact a billion years in the future, long after any trace of any human civilization is gone. Those being impacted by this will probably have no clue about it, but that doesn't matter. We've both made a very big difference. This case will be collected by one of my colleagues in a while.

"Zsombor, you helped me escape from MILPh with this case; I couldn't have done it without you. If we die here today, we do so knowing we didn't die for nothing. If it hadn't been for the two of us, these very important samples would not have been retrieved. It's not like one can go back and get more. The factory is more or less gone."

The light that had been flashing orange now turned to red, and they were both starting to feel dizzy. They knew they didn't have much time left. They would get dizzier and dizzier until they both passed out and died.

"I feel a bit better now, Florina," said Zsombor. "You're right. If life is very very short or very very very short, what's the difference as long as you made it matter. It really sucks that you killed us, and I still think you have a screw loose, but I'm really glad I met you. What exactly are these samples though, and how exactly is this going to impact anything in a billion years?"

"Well, I'm glad I met you too," said Florina in a weak voice low on air. "And you're right. I do have quite a few loose screws," she laughed. "My mission is top secret, but since we're about die together I'll tell you. We've been getting intel that MILPh here on Mars is the source of…"

Suddenly the back of the car lifted up in the air. They were being pulled into the open bay of a highway ambulance. A

Martian highway ambulance is basically a very large van with a tow arm that pulls wrecked cars into a garage size space, closes the back doors, and pumps in air. The medics then come out from the front of the van and help the injured if they're still lucky enough to be alive.

"We're being rescued!" wheezed Zsombor. "We're going to live, Florina! I'm taking you to the Mars Day Celebration tonight!"

"That's great," whispered Florina, now very low on air. "Will there be fireworks? I love fireworks. I'll bring my flare gun. Hey, where's my flare gun? Have you seen a flare gun around here somewhere?"

"Sorry, Florina, no fireworks on Mars. We're really scared of fire on this planet."

"No kidding," laughed Florina while still trying to figure out where her flare gun could be. "It would be so much fun to bring the flare gun to that party Zsombor just invited me to and shoot off a few flares. After all, you can't party without fireworks," she thought.

The door opened up and fresh air flowed into the car. They were safely inside the ambulance and being greeted by a paramedic.

"You guys are the luckiest people on Mars," said the paramedic. "We wouldn't have been here if it hadn't been for this freak disaster we're headed back from down at MILPh. Some idiot arson lady set fire to the whole factory and locked all the employees in the break room. I was actually the first guy to enter, and right inside the door from the parking bay was a flare gun on the floor. She must have fired it into one of the chemical tanks to torch the place on her way out. There was only one survivor. One of my colleagues was checking on her as we left. I'm telling you

23

guys, whoever this fucking pyromaniac lunatic is, you owe her your lives."

"Oh no!" gasped Florina. "NO NO NO! You mean they all burned to death?" Florina got teary. She put her hands over her face and started crying, "No no no! Why did they all have to burn to death? WHY?"

"No, that's the weird thing, ma'am. The break room was intact. We went in, and everyone, except one woman, was dead. They all appeared to have been beaten or stabbed to death in various ways. I'm telling you in all my years as a paramedic I have never seen anything like it."

"Stabbed and beaten to death! Not burned! Yes! What a relief that they were stabbed and beaten to death. I'm so happy and relieved to hear that," said Florina. "Oh, thank goodness. They were all beaten and stabbed. You have no idea how happy that makes me."

"It's a common misconception that death by fire is particularly painful, ma'am," said the paramedic. "Being burned to death is actually quite painless, provided that you do die from it. Your nerve endings burn up right away, and usually you're already unconscious from all the toxic fumes anyway. So if it was me, I'd probably prefer fire to stabbing and beating."

"I'd prefer neither, but what kind of people would kill each other like that," wondered Zsombor.

"Just people, Zsombor. It's just good old human nature," said Florina calmly. "This is part of what motivates us; we all have this coming. The human race is constantly working overtime to find new ways to eliminate itself. Autoannihilation is our inevitable conclusion as a species, but that's alright. This is how we get things done, it seems. Means to ends, right? I'm really glad they were beaten and stabbed though, and not burned."

"You guys are not right in the head," said the paramedic. "Probably shock. Anyway, we're going to Sopron. Would you like to be dropped off there?"

"Thanks, that will be perfect," said Zsombor.

"Sure thing. Alright then, you two, I'll be in the front if you need me. Just don't touch anything back here," said the paramedic as he went to the front cabin.

"Hey, Zsombor," said Florina. "That stuff I told you about my mission is top secret. I thought we were about to die, so I told you. I'm authorized and required to kill anyone who finds out about the mission. I really don't want to kill you, Zsombor, but if you ever tell anyone, I will have to kill you and whomever you tell."

Zsombor burst out laughing, "You couldn't kill anyone, Florina, except by accident, and that flare gun you were looking for earlier I'm guessing that one's back at MILPh, right?" laughed Zsombor. "Would you like me to ask the driver to turn around, so we can get it?"

"Very funny, Zsombor," sobbed Florina. "You're right. I suck as a secret agent. I've been busting my ass for years trying to complete a mission successfully. They were about to fire me when this assignment came up that for some reason they thought I'd be perfect for. They didn't even give me any real weapons, just mace and flares. I was just supposed to collect some samples. Instead, I managed to destroy the whole factory and almost kill the both of us. I don't know what they'll do when they hear about this."

"No no, Florina," said Zsombor and gave her a hug. "I think you're a great secret agent. I mean you might have a few things to work on, but we all do. You saved our lives by accidentally destroying that factory, and you did all that with just a flare gun.

Any other agent would have needed a large number of bombs and grenades to pull something like that off. Florina, you're a really good secret agent," lied Zsombor.

"You really think so?" asked Florina wiping her tears. "You're so nice to me. Everyone else thinks I'm an idiot, but you think I'm a great agent. I feel so much better now even though I'll probably get fired over this.

"Alright, we go back to your place and freshen up a bit. We'll figure out what to do, and then you can take me to that festival thing. I could use some cheering up.

"Hey, I'm thirsty. Let's drink some of this water. They won't mind, will they?" Florina grabbed a bottle of what she assumed was water and took a rather large gulp.

"Ahhhh! Puta madre! It burns!" she screamed as she spat a mouthful of isopropyl disinfectant in Zsombor's face.

"My eyes! My eyes! It hurts like a motherfucker! Help!"

"Hey, what the hell is going on back here?" asked the paramedic as he came back after hearing all the commotion.

"We drank this stuff," said Florina and waved the bottle in the paramedic's face splashing him in the eyes.

"You psycho fucking lunatics! We should have left you to die!" the medic screamed as he stumbled around blind until he hit his head and knocked himself out.

"Oh no!" said Florina. "What do we do? We must help him. Quick! Find one of those universal emergency devices all ambulances have."

"Yeah yeah. I know what you mean," said Zsombor. "The magic wakie-wakie box. Here, I found it!"

The magic wakie-wakie box as Zsombor called it was a portable medical diagnostic and treatment device. It had a surface with sensors that you would push to the patient's chest where it would take a quick EKG reading and poke a needle into the patient taking a blood sample. The device would then do a very fast diagnostic of the patient, and the needle would inject the patient with whatever might be needed to save his life.

"Ok, I've seen a lot of movies with these things. See? We put it on his chest like this and push this red button here," said Florina and pushed the button. "Hmm, nothing's happening?"

"There's a main switch here. Maybe if we flip it like this," said Zsombor as Florina was pushing the wakie-wakie box against Zsombor to see if perhaps there was some connectivity issue.

"AAAAHHHI!!!" screamed Zsombor as the needle pierced his chest, and he fell down unconscious.

The ambulance driver who had heard the commotion stopped the ambulance and came to the back to check.

"What's going on back here? Is everybody alright?"

"They're both passed out. I must have done something wrong. How do you use this correctly?" she asked the driver as she pushed the wakie-wakie box against him and pushed the red button.

"The red button is for sleep. You have to push the green one…," said the driver and fell to the floor unconscious.

"Oh my! Oh my! I'd better get all these people to town where they can get some medical attention," Florina thought.

She checked Zsombor's pockets, and in his wallet she found his address: Tuztorony Apartment Tower 38-C, Sopron. She went to the front of the ambulance, got behind the wheel, and politely asked the navigation system to take her to Tuztorony Apartment Tower 38-C, Sopron.

Chapter 2

Arrival in Sopron

Sopron with a population of slightly over a hundred thousand, a very big city by Martian standards, was one of the many crater cities on Mars. It was the standard habitation method on Mars and many other worlds in the solar system. A crater had been covered with a big roof with big columns holding up the roof at every street corner. Air was constantly being pumped in to keep the city under pressure. Trees and bushes had been planted in any unused space to provide oxygen and greenery. The nice cities like Sopron had an inner ceiling where a blue sky could be projected during the day, and a starry sky at night.

Of course, it didn't take long before someone figured out they could project advertisements on the city ceiling instead of soothing fake skies. The ads in the sky were very unpopular, and Mayor Biborka of Sopron had received several death threats since she authorized the use of the sky as an advertising medium. As Florina drove the ambulance up to the Tuztorony Tower, the sky was running ads for the various venues at the great Mars Day Celebration.

One of the ads showing some very delicious looking food caught Florina's attention in particular since she was getting a bit hungry after an eventful morning. With her eyes on the city ceiling, she ran the ambulance up on the curb and hit one of the countless fire hydrants that were placed around the city due to Martian pyrophobia. Because of the low gravity on Mars vehicles would often roll over when running into hard objects, which happened this time too.

The right side of the ambulance shot up in the air, and the vehicle fell on its left side. The impact pushed the back hatch open providing an exit from the ambulance. The ambulance was now lying on its side with Florina and the shaken up passengers awoken from unconsciousness from the impact crawling out of the wreckage getting soaked by the broken fire hydrant.

"Florina! What happened? Where are we?" asked Zsombor confused. "Oh, we're home. How did we get here?"

"I drove us here," said Florina.

"Yeah, I see that," said Zsombor when he saw the crashed ambulance lying on its side.

"You fucking motherfuckers!" said an angry voice from inside the ambulance. It was the paramedic coming to.

"Come, Florina. We'd better get out of here," said Zsombor and took her by the hand.

Zsombor's wrecked Moskvich didn't look like it would ever run again, so they left it in the ambulance. "It was a nice car," thought Zsombor. "What a waste. I mustn't let this woman near anything fragile."

"Is this where you live?" asked Florina as they entered the fire safety equipment lined lobby of Tuztorony.

There were fire hoses and fire extinguishers everywhere; these people were really really scared of fire, thought Florina.

"Such a tall building! How tall is this place?" asked Florina. "Must be at least fifty floors? It's all the way up to the city ceiling."

"Fifty-three if you count the lobby. I live on the 38th," said Zsombor as he called the elevator.

The elevator door opened and inside stood Mrs. Pletykas, the old gossip lady from the 47th floor. Mrs. Pletykas lived in apartment 47-D, but she might as well have put her furniture in the elevator because she spent most of her time there gathering "intel" on the neighbors after becoming a widow a few years back. Her husband died in a freak accident. He was mounting a night vision telescope on the balcony for his beloved nosy wife to spy on people in their own apartment building via the reflective surface of the office tower across the street. A fall from the 47th floor on Mars was merely like a fall from the 18th floor on Earth, which was still enough to kill you. The time that Mrs. Pletykas did not spend in the elevator she spent on the balcony with her telescope. If you wanted to keep something secret, she was the one to avoid.

"Oh, Zsombor! How nice to see you. Haven't seen you since this morning at… Hold on. Let me check my notes. Yes, we rode down together at 7:36 this morning, and who is this lovely lady? You have a girlfriend, and you didn't tell me? Haha, thought you could keep a secret from me huh, Zsombor," she laughed. "So lovely to meet you. I'm Mrs. Pletykas," she said as she reached her hand out to shake Florina's.

"I'm Florina, but we're not actually…"

"Florina! What a lovely name. Must have cost you a fortune! Zsombor, you hit the jackpot this time. She's rich and just your type," Mrs. Pletykas winked at Zsombor.

"Mrs. Pletykas," said Zsombor. "Florina and I are not…"

"Oh, did you hear about Istvan and his wife in 12-G?" continued Mrs. Pletykas without listening to anyone else. "Oh my goodness, it's terrible. Terrible! They both died this morning. There are detectives and medical people in their apartment right now trying to figure out what exactly happened. What a bizarre and horrible death! They both exploded, apparently while making love. Can you believe that? How can something like that happen? I missed the actual event, but as soon as I heard, I ran to my telescope," Mrs. Pletykas didn't quite want to stop talking.

"There was blood everywhere, and I couldn't bear to look. You know, I love to spy on all of you, but I don't like to see these things. Well, enough about that. I'll be sure to point my telescope at your apartment from now on. Nothing like watching a lovely new couple like the two of you," she said as she smiled at the two of them.

"But please don't explode on me," she laughed. "You know, Florina, I quit watching Zsombor when he started working on that new language of his. He just looks through thick books, takes notes, and types on his computer. No fun at all. Finally, there'll be some action coming from his apartment, right?"

"Mrs. Pletykas," said Zsombor. "How did you know about my language project? By the way, Florina is not really…"

"Ah, you talk too much, Zsombor. I go through your trash. I go through everyone's trash. You know that! I mean that's what trash is for, right? Oops, this is your floor, Zsombor. Now have a great day, the two of you. I'll see you guys later, but you might not see me," she laughed as the elevator door closed between them.

"That lady doesn't make sense," Florina remarked.

"Yes, after her husband died she went a bit extreme with her voyeurism."

"No, I mean that stuff about Istvan and his wife's terrible death. I mean they died making love. If you're gonna go one day anyway, isn't that a pretty good way to go? Unless, of course, one of them worked in a field benefiting space exploration in any way, then it would be terrible, of course."

"Nah, they were both meter maids."

"Meter maids! I really hope they both survived the initial blast and died slowly in great pain!"

"Yeah, no pain is too little for a couple of meter maids," said Zsombor as he opened the door to his apartment.

Zsombor's apartment was heavily decorated in Australian Aboriginal themes. The whole apartment was covered in Aboriginal pattern wallpaper, except for a large windowless wall in the living room which had one of those immersive landscape photo wall papers with a giant picture from the Australian outback to make you feel like you were in Australia. There was a large shelf full of Australian artifacts that Zsombor had been collecting since becoming obsessed with the theme.

"Zsombor, what's up with all this Australian stuff everywhere? How many boomerangs and didgeridoos do you own?"

"Oh, they just keep adding up. Immersing myself in Australian Aboriginal culture helps me in my project."

"Welcome home, Master Zsombor. I'll be right out!" said a woman's voice with a thick Australian accent coming from inside the couch in the living room. "I thought you'd be home much later, so I didn't prepare you any food."

"Who's that?" asked Florina.

"Oh, that's Angoona, my robot. Her charging station is inside the couch to save space."

The couch opened up, and Angoona came crawling out on her hands and knees. She looked like a young Australian Aboriginal woman, dressed in Australian Aboriginal tribal clothing covering her voluptuous Earthly physique. She looked real enough to pass for human. If it hadn't been for Zsombor introducing her as a robot, Florina would have assumed she was a dumb woman with a very poor sense of balance.

"Faaa! What the fuck? This is too much! You have a robot that looks like a Native Australian lady. Is she one of those sex robots, Zsombor?"

"Well yes, she's a sex robot mainly, but she does other things too. She cooks and cleans, and she tells jokes. She's very funny."

"I bet she is, Zsombor. I bet she is, but why is she crawling on the floor?"

"She doesn't have gyros. You need gyros for balance, but you know they add weight and shorten battery life, and naturally they raise the price of the robot."

"Who's the Sheila, Zsombor?" asked Angoona. "She's very pretty. Is she from Australia like me?"

"Thanks, Angoona," said Florina. "No, I'm from Uruguay, but my parents are Australians. It's a long story. I'll tell you later."

"Florina is my mate!" said Angoona. "You here to play the didgeridoo?" asked Angoona in her exaggerated Australian accent.

"What? No! Well, maybe yes, but hey! No, stop this. Nobody's playing the didgeridoo."

"We can play the didgeridoo together, Florina. Is it doori time, Zsombor?" Angoona asked. "Let's do that thing you know where you…"

"No, Angoona! No doori! Go back to your charging box!"

"Yes, I'll just go back to my box as usual when I'm not wanted," said Angoona in a sad voice and crawled back to her prison in the couch.

"Well, rumor has it I'm your girlfriend now, so I guess you'll be even more immersed from now on," laughed Florina. "Hey, it's the top of the hour. Let's turn on the news to see if they're saying anything about the fire over at MILPh."

"We now bring you the top of the hour news from Sopron and surrounding craters." said the TV and played a very catchy musical intro.

"We start with our main story today, the fire at Martian Illicit Lascivious Pharmaceuticals outside Sopron. Police now say that there is more to this story than just a plain fire. Survivors say an unidentified Australian Aboriginal woman with a voluptuous Earth body speaking in a Spanish accent caused a small fire that sent most employees escaping in their cars. The remaining 18 employees were then taken hostage by the woman. According to the only survivor of the hostages, they were locked in the break room where a fight between the hostages broke out ending in all but one of them being stabbed or beaten to death by their coworkers. The unidentified woman then burned the factory

35

down on her way out. We now take you live to the scene where we will hear from the survivor."

"Oh, I'm on TV? Wow! This is so exciting," said Borbala from payroll. "Hi, everyone! Hi, mom! Hi, dad!" she said as she waved excitedly into the camera.

"Ma'am," said the reporter. "Can you tell us what happened in the break room after you were all locked in there?"

"Oh yes, there was fighting, very horrible fighting. I tried to stop it, of course. I kept yelling 'No, stop. Don't fight.' You know, because I didn't want anyone to get hurt. They were using knives from the kitchen drawer to fight, and I tried to get the knives away from everybody, so they would stop fighting because I'm a very peace loving person, you know?"

"There you have it, folks," said the reporter. "A very bizarre story indeed. We hope to have an update after police releases a video they say they recovered from one of the victims' phones."

"What? There's a video? Oh shit!" said Borbala. "I'm fucked! I'm so fucked! Shit shit shit! What? I'm still on TV? Oh, fuck me! Get that camera out of my face!"

"I wonder what her problem is," said Zsombor as he turned the TV off. "Do you have any idea who that unidentified Australian Aboriginal woman might be," he asked Florina and laughed.

"No clue. Maybe it was Angoona," joked Florina. "Do you mind if I use your kitchen table for some work?"

"Go ahead. Finish your work, and then I'll take you to the Mars Day Celebration."

Florina sat down at the table and opened the case she had been carrying around. Inside her case were 27 test tube slots, and 16 of them were filled while 11 were empty. There was also the standard issue "Portable Substance Analyzing Multi Functional Mass Spectrometer Tool and DNA Analyzer," which was cleverly disguised as a Glock to avoid attention in customs and security checks. The name was so long that everyone in the agency just called it the Glock. Why they would disguise a perfectly harmless scientific measurement device as a fire arm was a bit of a mishap; apparently it had to do with a miscommunication within the agency. They had commissioned the development of a portable spectrometer disguised as a clock. Due to sloppy handwriting it had been read as "Glock". By the time the mistake was realized, too much money had been spent developing the instrument, so they just left it looking like a Glock.

Florina placed a drop of each sample into the liquid receptor opening of the Glock. She was looking for a substance containing molybdenum. One by one the samples all came out negative.

"Hijo de puta! Todo negativo, mierda mierda!"

"What's that, Florina?" asked Zsombor. "Did you say something?"

"Nah nothing. Don't worry. Hey, I didn't get a chance to grab my bag back at the factory. Do you think you could run out and buy me a toothbrush?"

"Sure, there's a convenience store downstairs. I'll be back in a minute."

"No no, convenience stores only have toothbrushes with soft or medium bristles. I need one with hard bristles. I'm a very hard brusher."

"Oh alright. There's a drug store a block over. I guess, I'll go there."

"Thanks, and make sure the bristles are hard! I like hard bristles, very important!"

"Got it. Hard bristles. I'll be back in half an hour."

Florina always carried a hard bristled toothbrush in her pocket because they are so hard to find. Actually she had merely sent Zsombor out to get rid of him for a while, so she could call her contact.

This time Frank picked up the phone.

"Florina! You're alive. I thought you were dead after hearing your voice mail. You really freaked me out over here."

"Yeah, we were rescued at the last moment. I'm safe and sound in Zsombor's apartment. I sent him out for a bit. But listen, Frank! Did I get this assignment because the target has a fetish for ladies that look like me? That is not cool at all, Frank! Do you know he has a sex robot that looks like a Native Australian woman? I would prefer to be awarded assignments based on my skills and merits, not because some weirdo finds my ethnicity sexually appealing!"

"Ok Florina, I'll level with you. That is why you got this assignment, but honey trapping is part of the job sometimes, and you know that. Besides, you were about to get fired after your last fiasco, remember? You were damn lucky this mission came up, or you would have been out on the street with a boot mark on your ass! And now I'm hearing you managed to burn down the factory. You were supposed to gather some samples and then go along with this Zsambek on his delivery, and that was it!"

"Ok, Frank. First of all, his name is Zsombor, not Zsambek, and the factory burning down was not my fault. It was that stupid flare gun you gave me. What kind of secret agent uses a flare gun as her weapon?"

"Listen, Florina! There is no way we're letting you have a real gun, not ever. You would just shoot everyone around you by accident. How did that car crash happen by the way? Were you the driver or something? No, let me guess. You accidentally stabbed Zsambek with a pen while he was driving, or did you accidentally put a bucket on his head? Am I getting close? Did you cause any more car crashes since then? Is there more?"

"Umm yeah, but so what? I got the samples, didn't I? And his name is Zsombor."

"Zsambek, Zambezi, who gives a fuck? Alright now, so you have the 27 samples. Did you do a preliminary field analysis of them already?"

"Well, that's another thing. There weren't 27 tanks, only 16. And I did the analysis, but they all came out negative."

"All negative? And only 16? We were a hundred percent sure there were 27. 16 upstairs and 11 in the basement."

"Basement?" gasped Florina.

"Did you not get the samples from the basement? You fucking idiot!" Frank exploded. "You didn't go to the basement, did you? Why why why do we keep giving you these opportunities, Florina? Now the factory is destroyed with everything in it. The mission is a complete fiasco as usual.

"Ok, damage control. The delivery is delayed due to the car crash, but you are in possession of the package to be delivered, yes?" asked Frank.

"Hey listen, Frank. It was pretty chaotic back there, and we might have left without the package, you know, because of the crazy lunatic at the factory."

"WHAT?" yelled Frank who was rapidly losing self control. "No package? Ah, what the fuck, Florina? What is wrong with you?"

"Your blood pressure, be careful!" said Florina trying to calm Frank down.

"Oh yeah. Thanks. Alright, here's what we'll do. Take the Glock, walk around the apartment, and look for any particles of anything containing molybdenum coming from absolutely anything. Zsambio's deliveries contain the substance. Maybe he has some pending deliveries sitting in his apartment."

"Ok, Frank," said Florina while walking around with the Glock.

To test for substances you would point the Glock at the object of interest and pull the trigger. At that time a puff of air would be sucked into the Glock via the front opening, and the particles in the air puff would be analyzed. Then the results would be displayed on a small screen on top of the Glock. Florina walked around the apartment shooting her Glock at everything she could find. There was nothing in the kitchen and nothing in the living room or the bedroom, but in the hallway there was a reading coming from a stack of recent mail.

"Hey, Frank," said Florina with excitement. "I think I got something. I'm getting a reading from this thick junk mail envelope."

"What is it? What is it?" asked Frank excitedly.

"Looks like a free sample of something called Didgeridick Erection Enhancement Medication."

"What? It could be just a cover. Open it!"

"Ok, let me see," Florina told Frank while opening the package. "No, Frank. It's a trial sample of boner pills, two pills. It says 'Didgeridick makes you hard as a brick, with a size to the skies'. What is this obsession here? Even the boner pills are named Aboriginally."

"Oh well, it was worth the try. Well, the mission is over, I suppose. Now listen very well, Florina. We don't have jurisdiction on Mars, so you have to keep an extremely low profile. If they connect us to that fire at the factory in any way, it's not just over for you but for the whole agency. You and I will probably have to go to prison if we're caught. You would most likely be tried for arson or pyromania, and you know how the Martians feel about fire. We will have you extracted in the morning, and until then you must not leave the apartment.

"I will come for you personally. I'm in Csorna right now, small crater right outside of Sopron. They were supposed to put me in Sopron, so I could work with you easier, but all the hotels were full because of some festival. You cannot be seen by anybody. Is that clear, Florina? Even if the apartment is on fire, you stay in it!"

"Crystal, Frank. I stay here, and tomorrow you will come and get me."

"Yes, good! Stay in the apartment, and don't let anyone else in, except Zambezi."

"Zsombor."

"What?"

"His name is Zsombor, Frank. Not Zambezi or Zsambek. It's Zsombor."

"Right, only he can come in. No one else, and you cannot go out. Stay in the apartment, Florina!"

"Ok, Frank. I'm not stupid, no problem. I don't go out. Only Zsombor comes in. Talk to you later, Frank."

Florina hung up the phone, and right then there was a knock on the door.

"Hey, Zsombor, open up! It's Balazs," said a voice behind the door.

"Zsombor is out," said Florina and opened the door to let Balazs in. "But he'll be back in a minute."

"I'm Balazs," said Balazs and shook her hand. "You must be Florina, right? Zsombor's new girlfriend from Earth."

"How did you know who I am?"

"Oh, it's our local news media, also known as Mrs. Pletykas. Zsombor's new girlfriend is the second biggest story of the day. If it hadn't been for Istvan and his wife exploding while having sex, you would have had the top spot."

"Well, thank goodness for Istvan banging his wife to death. I'm supposed to keep a low profile, you see? Is exploding from sex very common on Mars?"

"Yes, it's a leading cause of death on this planet, but don't worry, Florina. There's no way Zsombor could ever make anything blow, especially not during sex," laughed Balazs. "No, but seriously he's been obsessing over this new language of his ever since that new law put his old publishing career into a tailspin. I'm really glad for him that he has you now. He was

42

going a bit crazy, I think with all that linguistic subjunctive indicative type non-sense."

"Oh hey, Florina, I see you met my neighbor Balazs," said Zsombor as he came back home. "Weird thing happened at the store. My card was declined, so I checked on my phone, and it said 'an automatic annual charge of twenty-one thousand rubles had been made to my card and maxed it out.' Someone must have stolen my card number.

"I called the bank, and they said the charge was the annual fee for a name. I explained to them that I have a free Hungarian name, but they told me the record shows the charge was authorized by the second account owner. I told them the only account owner is me. Then they told me the second account owner is usually a spouse and that I must be married. I explained to them I'm not, but they insisted that I am. I'm pretty sure I would remember something like that, so I'll have to go down to the police station later and file a report about someone posing as my wife and gaining access to my accounts."

"Dude! Zsombor man! Yeah, that happened to me a couple of times too. Don't worry. They'll clear all that up for you, but what is this? You've got a new girl, and I hear it from creepy old Mrs. Pletykas in the elevator? This is great news; you were way too into that Pig Latin thing of yours.

"Florina, did he show you his lingo?"

"No, but he told me about it. Some kind of weird combination language or something."

"It's crazy stuff, man. Hey, Zsombor, what do you call your language again? Norwomian?"

"It's called Naruemonian. I named it after Naruemonia, the secret hidden continent on Earth."

"I've never heard of a secret Earth continent called Naruemonia," said Florina.

"Exactly!" replied Zsombor. "Because it's hidden and secret."

"That makes sense," nodded Florina. "So Zsombor, tell us something in Naruemonian."

"Well, part of the trick is in the way it's written. For example, if I wanted to say 'Florina wants to know more about Naruemonian', it would be written 'Florina mohr whant dto no Naruemonian habaut' and pronounced 'Florina more want to know Naruemonian about'. Does that make sense?"

"But that's just misspelled English with messed up grammar, Zsombor," said Florina.

"Yes, it would appear that way, but you understood it perfectly well, right? And it is a hundred percent derived from Australian Aboriginal languages, both the structure and the vocabulary, so you can use it legally without paying any royalties to anyone, except to me of course, and I'll charge way less than the Americans charge for English. Each word is combined from Native Australian words with the same meaning as the English equivalent. Any similarity to English can easily be disproven.

"Each word can be looked up in the Naruemonian dictionary I have created where each word is broken down to its syllables that are all accounted for in their original Australian language. The grammatical structure is a combination of Australian grammatical structures. You see how the prepositional element can be preceded by the noun phrase to which it is supposedly normally assigning the case agreement..."

"Enough, Zsombor! Fuck, man! You're gonna scare her off! Nobody wants to hear about that linguistic nonsense!"

"I thought it was quite interesting," lied Florina. "I would like to hear more about it later."

"Of course, Florina," smiled Zsombor. "I'll tell you more about it later when we're alone."

"I hope that's not all you're gonna do when you're alone together," laughed Balazs. "So are you guys ready for the Mars Day festival? We have to celebrate our planet!"

"Yay! Festival! Yes, let's go!" exclaimed Florina.

"Can I come too?" asked Angoona's muffled voice from the couch.

"No, Angoona!" said Zsombor sternly. "You stay here!"

"No worries, mate. I'll just stay here in the couch while you guys go and enjoy yourselves. Yes, I'll just do that then," said Angoona sadly.

Florina wasn't supposed to leave the apartment, but then again she wasn't supposed to let anyone else in, except Zsombor. If she was really careful and kept to herself at the festival, nothing could go wrong, or so she thought.

Chapter 3

Didgeridick

The main square where the Mars Day Celebration was being held was just a short walk from Zsombor's apartment. Florina, Zsombor, and Balazs headed out for a night of partying.

"Zsombor," said Florina as they walked past the wrecked ambulance with Zsombor's mangled Moskvich sticking out of the back. "I'm not really supposed to leave your apartment, so I need to keep a very low profile tonight."

"Got it. Low profile. We'll eat some food, have some drinks, watch the entertainment, and that's it. No extroversion whatsoever."

They had arrived early enough to find an empty table with a good view of the stage set up for the entertainment of the crowd of Martians and visitors from other worlds such as Florina. The main square was filling up with people fast; it seemed everyone in Sopron and plenty of out of crater visitors were here. The celebration was televised on the local stations for those who

46

preferred to celebrate Mars Day at home. Even a couple of planet wide networks were present since the celebration in Sopron was considered the best on the planet.

Buildings inside the crater cities of Mars tended to be very tall, usually all the way up to the ceiling due to the very high real estate prices. In some places like the downtown square, the ceiling had been raised to fit even taller buildings. The sky was so tall here that you couldn't make out the joint seams in the ceiling with the naked eye. Back when an actual sky was projected on the ceiling, this was the one place in Sopron you could really feel like it actually was a sky. The many tall buildings that surrounded the square all had very elaborate and colorful facades filled with very intricate detail as was very popular in Sopron.

"I'm starving," said Balazs. "Let's order some food, shall we? Hey, Mr. Waiter! We'll have three Mars Day Platters and three Meers, please."

"What's a Meer?" asked Florina.

"Oh, you've never had a Meer? It's so bad, Florina," said Balazs. "It's a Martian artificial chemical version of beer that can't be legally called beer. We can't grow a lot of ingredients for food and drink here on Mars, so most of the stuff we eat is manufactured chemically. It all tastes terrible, and everybody's skinny, but what can you do? I bet on Earth you eat real food all the time.

"Ah, here's our food now. Alright guys, let's toast to Mars!"

"The Meer is not that bad," said Florina after the toast. "Tastes almost like very cheap beer."

"Just wait 'til you taste the food, Florina," laughed Zsombor.

The Mars Day Platter was a plate with different blobs of paste in different colors. It looked quite delicious, just like in the ad she had seen earlier in the city ceiling right before she rolled the ambulance. Florina tasted a spoon of the green blob, and it was truly horrendous.

"Ay dios mio! This is terrible. What is this? How can you guys eat this stuff? Why don't you guys eat chicken or vegetables like normal people?"

"You wash it down with a lot of Meer," laughed Zsombor.

Florina took a bite of the purple blob which was equally horrible and washed it down with a big gulp of Meer.

"Mr. Waiter! Another round of Meers please, and keep 'em comin'," ordered Florina. "We're gonna need a lot of Meer to wash this down!"

"So, when did you guys meet?" asked Balazs. "I'm Zsombor's best friend, and I didn't know about you until today."

"Oh, I just only found him this morning," said Florina. "But we had a near death experience together, so that counts as a lifetime. My fault, of course, I made him crash his car, but I think it was for the better."

"Too bad about the Moskvich though," said Balazs. "That was a sweet ride."

The live entertainment on the big stage consisted of mostly musical acts with plenty of elaborate dancing. The main attraction of the evening was a performance by the old Martian disco queen, Marsalina Valentina.

Marsalina was once the greatest star on Mars. In spite of her age and her coordination being off due to advanced stage syphilis brought on by promiscuous behavior in her youth, she could still put on a fantastic show for the crowd. The fact that her syphilitic brain was sending her limbs all the wrong signals mattered not. She had managed to incorporate these quirks into her dance routine. When she accidentally punched herself in the face with her right hand, she would immediately match it with a punch from her left hand. When she fell to the left because she had misjudged the position of the floor, she got up and produced a fall to the right to complete the harmony.

Marsalina moved across that stage like she was born to do just that. If you hadn't known who she was, you would have never guessed you were watching an eighty-year-old syphilitic. Disco fever infected Mars a decade later than Earth, and in the Martian disco craze of the 1980s, she was the undisputed queen.

Marsalina and her dancers could do quite amazing things here on Mars, thought Florina. They could jump three times as high as they could have on Earth. Most people on Mars couldn't jump any higher than Earth people on Earth because their legs were accustomed to the local gravity. Some people, however, including the stage performers obviously were seen walking around with weights attached to their shoulders and wrists to simulate the load of Earth gravity. If you were going to visit Earth, you would also wear these weights for a few months before your departure; otherwise, you couldn't walk normally when you landed on Earth.

It would have been a way cooler party with some fireworks, thought Florina to herself. It was just too bad she didn't have her flare gun.

"Ladies and gentlemen," sounded an announcement. "Our mayor will now hold her annual speech."

The crowd booed loudly as Mayor Biborka walked up to the podium at the center of the stage.

"That's your mayor, Zsombor? I know that lady," said Florina as her eyes turned very angry.

"May syphilis eat your brain, Mayor Biborka!" yelled a woman from the front row.

"Give us back our blue sky, you asshole!" shouted a man as he threw a bottle towards the mayor narrowly missing her.

"Yes, I know you're all upset about the ads in the sky," said Mayor Biborka. "However, today is a day of celebration. Today we celebrate the first human Mars landing by Captain Ivanov and his ship the Krasnyy Mars Drakon II on our beloved planet. I want to thank all my fellow Martians for celebrating this day here, and also a great thanks to all the visitors that have come here from other worlds to celebrate this day with us.

"Are there any aliens here today?" asked the mayor while looking around towards the crowd for a foreign guest that might be interested in coming up to the stage.

"Me me! I'm from Earth. Here!" yelled Florina at the top of her lungs as she climbed up on the table waving her hands.

"I see we have a cheerful Earthling with us," said the mayor. "Why don't you come up here on the stage?"

Florina was very excited to join the mayor on the stage. She loved attention more than anything, and being up on a televised stage was a dream come true for her.

"So you are from Earth? What is your name?"

"Hi, everyone, I'm Florina," said Florina as she grabbed the mayor's microphone. "I'm a secret agent from Earth here on a top secret mission."

"Tell that stupid mayor we want a blue sky like on Earth!" yelled the woman who had earlier wished syphilis upon the mayor.

"Yeah! And with little fluffy white clouds floating across it!" yelled another voice from the crowd.

"And stars at night!" added the syphilis woman.

"Mrs. Stupid Mayor, Ma'am, they would like their blue sky back, please," said Florina to the mayor for the crowd to hear.

"Yeah, Florina! You go! Tell her!" yelled the syphilis woman.

More encouragement now poured in from all over the crowd. Within seconds the crowd had erupted in a chant, "Florina! Florina! Florina!" This sent Florina into a complete trance. She had never before experienced anything close to this. Her expression shifted from her regular cute goofy look to dead serious. Her eyes took on an intense stare. She stepped out to the edge of the stage, raised her arms, and spoke to the crowd with a level of charisma seldom seen in a non-dictator.

"Friends! Amigos! Martians! I come to you from a planet where the sky is blue. Tomorrow morning when you wake up, your sky too will be blue. I have discussed this with the mayor, and you have my word. The sky will be blue with small fluffy white clouds floating across it and stars at night, starting tomorrow!"

Mayor Biborka looked very confused as the crowd cheered and chanted, "BLUE SKY, FLORINA! BLUE SKY, FLORINA!"

"Why would I turn the sky blue in the morning?" the mayor thought.

"Friends! Amigos! Martians!" Florina continued. "I come to you from a planet of life. Your planet Mars was void of any life until 63 days ago today in 1980 when the first ship with humans from Earth landed here on Mars setting up the first permanent human outpost on an alien planet."

"Sixty-three YEARS ago!" yelled a man in the audience. "Sixty-three YEARS, not sixty-three DAYS!"

"Right, sorry," continued Florina. "Sixty-three years ago in 1980 they landed here on Mars. That was the beginning of the Mars we know today. We take the current condition of Mars as a living planet for granted, but this is a reality that had to be fought hard for. After the first moon landings, a lot of people thought space exploration was a waste of money. They said that money could be better spent to relieve the social problems of the day.

"Well, without the foresight of the great people who had to fight against that incredible ignorance and push ahead with humanity's march into space, we wouldn't be here on this planet today. We would have spent precious decades without any real progress.

"I'm sure we would have sent people to low Earth orbit, and we would have sent remote controlled cars and drones to Mars, and you know what? We would probably even have called it space exploration. What exactly is there to explore in low Earth orbit? I'm sure the people involved in those projects would have had a ton of arguments why it would have been space exploration, but deep in their hearts they would all know that their talents were being wasted and precious time was being lost.

"Remote controlled cars with whatever robotic analysis tools on-board would have achieved as much in a whole mission as a trained geologist going out for a short walk outside this crater. These would have been cheap space missions to satisfy the portion of the public who felt this was an important thing to do, but everyone involved in these projects would have yearned for days when they would be involved in real space missions. Real space missions means sending people to live on other worlds.

"The reasons we go to space are varied. In the case of Mars and other worlds in this solar system, the main reason to be here is commercial enterprise. In the case of all the giant ships of settlers being built right now to go to other solar systems, it is an idealistic pioneering pursuit, a quest to find new homes for humanity to live and thrive on, to spread humanity. None of those ships have left yet, and when the first ones do arrive in a few decades, most of the original crew will be dead of old age, and their task taken over by their offspring born on the ships. Some of these ships will be traveling for thousands of years with frozen human embryos to be thawed on site. We will soon probably travel in space for military reasons. Those are all great purposes, but there is a much more important reason for us to go to new worlds.

"Your planet Mars was void of any life until 63 years ago. What is our role in the Universe as a species? Why has nature given rise to us, an intelligent species capable of traveling to worlds other than the one we arose from? We have caused huge environmental damage to our native planet, and we will continue to do so until the day that we are gone from the Earth as a species. What can we possibly have to contribute to the natural system? What is our purpose?

"Well, I'll tell you all what our purpose is! It is to spread Earth-life to other worlds. We humans are the vehicle for Earth to spread its biology to other worlds, and our moment is now. The very brief window of time between us acquiring space travel capability and us annihilating ourselves as a species is now, and it is our paramount obligation to the Earth to spread its life as far

53

into the universe as we can before this window of opportunity closes," Florina explained as the crowd attentively listened.

"Colonizing space must be our main priority as a species and as a civilization. Everything we do should be done with space colonization in mind. The human task of spreading Earth biology doesn't need much attention. A nudge from someone like myself once in a while might speed things along, but life will find a way regardless. Biology comes along for the ride; all we have to do as a species is to go to other worlds for whatever reason we want.

"Humanity is highly temporary. On my home planet Earth we are in decline as a species, and we will not be around for that much longer. A technologically advanced civilization like ours that is capable of traveling to other worlds will eventually destroy the species that gave rise to it. We need to get as many ships of people sent out to other worlds as possible before our civilization destroys itself and possibly the human race on Earth along with it. We have caused a lot of damage to Earth's nature during our short time on her, and it will take a long time for the Earth to rebound after we're gone.

"The Earth, however, cannot spread its biology to other worlds without the help of an intelligent species like us. No matter how much damage we cause the Earth, it will be worth it for her if we manage to seed a single alien world with her life. If we don't manage to seed any other worlds, we will have been sucking her blood to fuel a short pointless decadent party. A fun happy party, of course, but pointless.

"If we had listened to those people who said space travel was a waste of money, we would have still gone about now. It would not have been because of any pull to go for commercial or idealistic reasons, but for sheer survival, plain and simple. It would have been ugly, my friends. There would be limited room on outgoing ships, and people would fight desperately to get

54

themselves and their families off an Earth rapidly losing its ability to support the human race. Most people would be left behind where most would die, and the survivors would live in a nightmarish post apocalyptic hell.

"Well, it's a good thing things went the way they went. Our dispersion as a species into space was beautiful. Brave people risked their lives as pioneers followed by masses of settlers. The Earth is now calmly being relieved of the pressure of hosting an all-consuming civilization and gradually returning to a state of natural balance. Earth biology is being spread to new worlds. We as a species have ensured the advancement of Earth life beyond the Earth. Of course, the more we spread, the better. Even if we're gone soon, we still did it. Our civilization has been a wonderful fantastic party. Now that we have fulfilled our destiny, we can enjoy the rest of the party with a clean conscience!" Florina concluded her speech.

The crowd that had listened attentively to Florina's words broke out in loud cheering chanting, "FLORINA! FLORINA! FLORINA!"

Florina had suddenly become the most popular person in Sopron. Florina walked up to Mayor Biborka who was still wondering why she would be turning the sky blue tomorrow.

"Hey, Biborka," she whispered quietly without the microphone, so no one would hear. "You don't remember me?"

"You know, Florina, you seem familiar somehow, but I can't place you," said Mayor Biborka.

"We met once when we were kids," said Florina. "You were on vacation in Uruguay with your parents, and you wondered off and ran into me. I called you Bib, remember?"

"Oh yes, of course!" said Biborka excitedly. "You're Fire-ina, that pyro girl with all the firecrackers, rockets, and all that. Oh, that was so much fun! Wow, small solar system! Remember when we set fire to that fuel storage? Ah good times, good times, Florina. Oh, and do you remember those flames and all that smoke? I'd give anything to experience that again."

"Well, listen, Biborka. After you blamed the whole thing on me, I wasn't allowed to have matches for a year. I mean you're a pyro too. Can you imagine being without matches for a whole year? I still have the video we made of that fuel depot fire. I wonder what would happen if your constituents found out you're a closet pyro?" Florina reminded her old friend of her dark past.

"No no! You wouldn't! That would ruin my career. Nobody on this planet would vote for a pyro."

"As long as the sky is blue, I won't release the video, Biborka."

"Of course, Florina, anything. Just don't show anyone that video."

"Blue with small fluffy clouds, Biborka, and stars at night!"

Florina walked off the stage into the cheering crowd. Everyone wanted their picture taken with her. She was the hero of the night.

"Wow! Florina," said Zsombor when she came back to the table. "That was incredible! You went from goof to statesman in the blink of an eye. I've never seen anything like it."

"Yeah! That was so great guys, best thing ever! So much fun! And I blackmailed the mayor too. Tomorrow we'll have a blue sky."

"Let's drink to that," said Balazs and ordered another round of Meers.

That round of Meers turned into another and then another. At the end of the evening the only one of them able to walk straight was Florina who had to lead them both back to Tuztorony Tower. Strangers greeted Florina as she led Zsombor and Balazs home. Mrs. Pletykas was strangely absent from the elevator, probably at the telescope, thought Florina. They dropped Balazs at his apartment 38-D, right next door to Zsombor's 38-C.

"Thanks for the help getting home, Florina. I'll see you guys later," said Balazs right before he fell through his door opening and fell asleep drunk on the floor.

Florina closed Balazs's door and led Zsombor into his apartment. She closed the door behind them and threw Zsombor on the bed.

"I want you, Zsombor! Make love to me!" demanded Florina

Zsombor was out cold from all the Meers. His skinny Martian body couldn't handle as much alcohol as a heavy Earthling, and he was way over his limit.

"Wake up, Zsombor. I want to make love to you!"

"Oh alright," mumbled Zsombor. "I think I'm too d-drunk to get it up, Florina. I p-promise we'll make love in the morning," he stuttered as he went back and forth into unconsciousness.

Florina feared that after the evening's public appearance, someone from the factory might recognize her, and the police would come for her. This might be the only night they would ever have together, so she wanted to make the most of it even if Zsombor's condition was less than ideal.

"No, tomorrow I might get arrested, Zsombor! This has to be tonight!" Florina said and undressed him.

"Oh alright, but I d-don't know how I'm going to be able to get it up for you, Florina. I've never been this d-drunk in my life. Hey, if you're getting arrested, I'll g-go with you to the police s-station because I have to f-file a report about that scammer stealing m-my m-money pretending to be m-married to me."

"Is it doori time?" interrupted Angoona from inside the couch.

"Yes, Angoona, but not for you," answered Florina. "Just me and Zsombor, but only if I can get his thingy to rise."

"Didgeridick makes you hard as a brick," said Angoona. "And with a size to the skies!"

"What? Of course, Angoona! Thanks! Didgeridick. Why didn't I think of that?"

"D-Didgeridick is bad bad shtuff Florina, and I d-don't have any D-Didgeridick," said Zsombor.

"Yes, I found a free sample in your mail earlier today. Wait here. I'll get it," said Florina as she left the bed and went to the pile of junk mail by the entrance.

"Ok, let's see. The instructions are in Hungarian, if only they were in Naruemonian at least. Oh, there are pictures here. One pill with a green check mark, a bottle with a red X over it, two pills with a red X over them, and a skull. Hmmm… Alright, take one, but if you have been drinking, you must take two, or you're a dumb-skull. Here Zsombor, take two of these."

"It's not D-Didgeridick, right? I don't want any of that shtuff Florina. No good. No good. No m-mommy don't give d-daddy D-Didgeridick, no no!"

"What are you talking about? I'm not your mommy! No, Zsombor, these are Tic-Tacs for your breath."

"Oh alright, Tic-Tac g-good, Didgeridick b-bad, very bad," said Zsombor as he swallowed the pills. "One Didgeridick makes you hard as a brick, two Didgeridicks and the bucket you kick. D-Didgeridick kill mama and papa. Scary scary."

"What was that about two Didgeridicks, Zsombor? Never mind. Let's see how this works."

Zsombor's manhood soon swelled up to a very respectable size and hardness, and Florina was getting very excited. "They weren't kidding when they said the size was to the skies," thought Florina.

"Wow! Zsombor," she said. "Didn't think you carried such a tool. I'm impressed!"

"What's happening?" asked Zsombor as he looked down at his privates. "Why is it so big? Much b-bigger than usual! What did you g-give me, Florina? I'm feeling dizzy," said Zsombor and passed out from all his blood rushing out of his head down to his crotch.

"Wake up, Zsombor! What's wrong? Oh no! You're the size of a baseball bat! This is not good, not good at all! I'd better call emergency services," said Florina in a panic as she grabbed her phone.

"You have reached emergency services. What is the nature of your emergency?" asked a female voice.

"Oh, you gotta help me, lady. It's my boyfriend! His penis is huge and so very very hard! What do I do?"

"Calm down, ma'am. This is perfectly normal. My husband has the exact opposite problem. Go ahead and enjoy yourself now."

"No no, I mean it's really really huge! Much much bigger than it should be!"

"Ok, ma'am. I understand. Sometimes these things can be a bit scary. Maybe you need to use some lubricant. If you don't have any, you can use cooking oil, perhaps. I will hang up now, ma'am. We need to keep the line open for emergencies."

"This is an emergency! He looks like he's about to blow!"

"Well, then you'd better get on top of him and enjoy the ride before he does blow, ma'am. Have a good evening now," said the lady and hung up.

Zsombor showed no signs of shrinking, and Florina suddenly remembered Istvan and his wife exploding.

"Oh no!" she thought. "Istvan must have tried the sample and then exploded inside his wife."

"Wake up, Zsombor! Don't die!" she screamed in a panic as she slapped his face trying to get him to wake up.

Florina was desperate. Finally, she had met someone she really liked, and she had managed to kill him with an overdose of boner pills. This time her carelessness had gone too far, she thought.

Suddenly there was a loud knock on the door.

"Florina! Open up. Quick!" said a woman behind the door.

Florina rushed to the door. It was Mrs. Pletykas holding a fire axe that she had obviously taken from one of the many transparent fire hose cabinets in the hall. She was covered in blood from head to toe and looked like she was not in her usual casual chit-chatty mood.

"Do as I say, Florina, and Zsombor lives! Time is of the essence, so no questions. To the kitchen now! Mortar and a big glass of water. Quick!"

Florina really wanted Zsombor to live, so she ran to the kitchen, found a mortar, and poured a very big glass of water. Mrs. Pletykas followed Florina with blood dripping from her body. She opened the fridge and went berserk on it with her fire axe cutting chunks out of the fridge wall. She separated a chunk of insulation foam from the material surrounding it, placed it in the mortar, ground it, and mixed the powder into the water.

"Quick! He must drink this now, or his wiener explodes, and he dies!"

They both ran to Zsombor who was passed out on the bed with an absolutely insane erection. Florina lifted his head and poured the mix of water and powdered foam into his mouth and down his throat.

"Ok, good! Now make him eat these," said Mrs. Pletykas and gave Florina a few chunks of foam to feed Zsombor. "I'll get some more water, so he can wash it down."

Zsombor's most important body part stopped growing and started to slowly shrink.

"Phew!" said Mrs. Pletykas. "That was a close one. He should be waking up in a few minutes."

"Thank you so so much, Mrs. Pletykas. I was so scared. I thought I was going to lose him, but how did you know what was happening?"

"When I snooped through everyone's mail today like I do every day, I noticed that they were sending out trial samples of Didgeridick to everyone. I checked up on it, and it turns out that if you take more than one, your penis could explode. I immediately realized that Istvan must have taken Didgeridick and then exploded inside his wife killing the both of them.

"I did more research and found out that polyurethane is a useful antidote, and polyurethane foam is, of course, commonly used as an insulator inside fridge and freezer walls among other things, so I've been watching everyone with my telescope tonight seeing who needs rescue.

"You'd better take a look at him at this size because normally he's a lot smaller," laughed Mrs. Pletykas. "Don't worry. His size is quite adequate, not as big as Matyas in 33-A, but then again who would want it that big, right?" she laughed. "Perfect size if you ask me is Mihaly in 28-G. If you want, you can come over to my place, and I can show you in my telescope."

"Yes, that would be nice, but Mrs. Pletykas, why are you covered in blood?"

"Oh, that's Csaba and his wife Sarolta in 28-F. I was a bit too late on that one. They exploded together right when I walked in to save them. See, I think this is a piece of a kidney here in my ear," Mrs. Pletykas said as she picked a bloody chunk of meat from her ear and flicked it.

"I might need a shower, I think. Well, anyway Florina, I'd better get back to my balcony and watch for Didgeridick overdoses. I'm telling you, Florina, if I ever get my hands on whoever's behind this Didgeridick, I'll tie him up to a tree, feed

Didgeridick to him, and watch his dick explode as I laugh. Except, of course, if it's just some means to a justified end, in that case it's totally fine with me."

Mrs. Pletykas left the apartment as Zsombor woke up from his ordeal, unaware of the grave danger he had just been in.

"What happened, Florina? D-did we make love?" asked Zsombor, still very drunk. "I can't remember anything after I ate those Tic-Tacs."

"You sure gave me a night to remember, Zsombor, and it was amazing," said Florina. "You almost died!"

In her head Florina was debating what to do. The police would surely come after her soon, but Frank was due to extract her in the morning. What about Zsombor? She wondered if he would come along with her.

"Hey, Zsombor, if I had to run away somewhere very far away, would you go with me?"

"Of course, Florina. Things would be pretty b-boring without you," stuttered Zsombor in a very sleepy drunk voice.

"I'm glad to hear that, Zsombor. Now go to sleep. You need the rest. This was a pretty crazy day, even by my standards. Tomorrow should be a lot calmer I think."

Florina thought wrong. Turns out the next day would be even crazier than the one they just had.

Chapter 4

Florina Sets the Sky on Fire

"Wake up! Hurry! Wake up!" yelled Balazs as he banged on Zsombor's door to wake them up.

"What's wrong?" asked Florina as she opened the door to let Balazs in.

"Quick! Turn on the news."

"Oh no!" said Florina in shock after she had turned on the TV and seen her face all over the screen.

"Our main story this morning for those of you who have just tuned in is, of course, Florina. The only surviving witness of yesterday's MILPh tragedy identified the mysterious hostage taker and arsonist as the woman known as Florina after watching the Mars Day Celebrations on a jail cell TV. The survivor who identified Florina is in police custody after being arrested on charges of multiple counts of accessory to murder and illegal sale and distribution of weapons following the recovery of a video from the phone of one of the victims. The police are now searching for the woman you see on your screen.

"Her name is Florina. She speaks in a Spanish accent and is believed to be from Earth. If you have any information about her, please call the police right away. A short time ago Mars police contacted Earth authorities which today are 18 light-minutes away round trip for information regarding Florina, and we hope to hear back from Earth shortly with more information regarding this mysterious woman.

"Wait, I hear now that we have a new development in this story. Apparently an ambulance medic has also identified Florina as the woman they rescued from a wrecked car between MILPh and Sopron who subsequently overpowered him and the driver. She then hijacked the ambulance and crashed it outside the Tuztorony Tower apartment building. The police department suspects Florina and two accomplices she was seen with at the festival may currently be inside the Tuztorony Tower. They are now preparing to seal off all entrances to the building.

"In other news, a large number of horrific incidents of couples exploding during sex were reported last night with more reports coming this morning of couples being found dead and..."

"Mierda!" said Florina and turned off the TV. "Why did I go up on that stage? What's wrong with me?"

"I need to throw up," moaned Zsombor as he stumbled out of bed and rushed to the bathroom to puke. "Why am I vomiting styrofoam?" he asked when chunks of foam were in his vomit.

"That's not styrofoam, honey. That's polyurethane foam."

"Oh, of course, polyurethane foam! Makes more sense now," said Zsombor sarcastically.

"Anybody want some breakfast? I'll make us some," Zsombor said as he walked towards the kitchen. "Hey, what happened to my fridge?" he wondered when he saw his fridge had been viciously murdered.

"Hold on, Zsombor. My phone's ringing," said Florina and picked up her phone. "Good morning, Frank!"

"Florina! What the fuck? I just saw the news! You were supposed to stay in. As soon as they get the info from Earth, they'll come straight for us. I'm already on the road, Florina. Listen! Get in disguise and run; it's your only chance. Stay out of sight, and I'll try to regroup with you later."

"Ok thanks, Frank," said Florina and hung up.

"Ok guys, listen up!" said Florina to her accomplices. "If they haven't figured out that the car in the ambulance belongs to Zsombor yet, they will soon. We have to figure out what to do before the cops knock on the door."

"Open the door. This is Sopron PD!" said a very stern voice behind the front door accompanied by a loud knock.

"Damn! That was faster than I anticipated!" said Florina. "Think fast. Think fast!

"Angoona! Get out of the couch and crawl into bed!"

"Is it doori time? I like doori time!" said Angoona as she crawled into bed while taking her clothes off to prepare for doori time.

"Ok! You guys never heard of me," said Florina and crawled into the couch.

"Open the door in the name of the law, or I'll kick it in!" yelled the voice behind the door.

66

"Good morning, sir. How may I help you today?" said Zsombor politely as he opened the door.

"I am Officer Zoltan Mosonmagyarovari of the Sopron Police Department Terrorism, Arson, and Copyright Violations Section. We have reason to believe that you may be harboring a suspected arsonist, terrorist, and carjacker. Australian Aboriginal female with Earth body who answers to the name Florina. Does that sound familiar?"

"No no, I have nobody like that in here, sir," said Zsombor.

"Me neither," said Balazs. "But who told you there's someone like that here?"

"The hijacked ambulance's navigation system has this address as its last input, Tuztorony Tower 38-C. Now do you mind if I have a look around?"

"Well, actually I do mind, sir. You see, I happen to know that you don't have the right to search my apartment without a written order from…"

"That was a rhetorical question. I'm going to snoop around your apartment now! I don't really know much about that legal stuff. I became a cop for the car chases and the gun fights. I hate the legal stuff. It makes my head hurt," said the policeman while prowling around near the kitchen.

"What is this? Why is your fridge torn apart? Do you have some kind of anger against refrigerators?"

"No, I just had a lot to drink last night, and quite frankly I don't remember much," replied Zsombor.

"You freaks make me sick! I really hope I find a good reason to arrest both you and your loser friend. Let's see the bedroom, shall we?"

"Howdy mate!" said Angoona with only her head sticking out from under the covers to Officer Mosonmagyarovari. "My, what a sexy uniform! Would you like to join me in bed for some doori time?" she asked as she lifted the covers to the side to reveal her naked body.

"Well, hello ma'am. You must be Florina. You're under arrest, anything you say will…"

"Officer Mosonmagyarovari, sir," Zsombor cut in. "That is my sex robot. She's not a person."

Officer Mosonmagyarovari leaned closer to Angoona. He felt her skin and realized Angoona was not human. His whole demeanor changed in an instant. His sternness was gone. He was absolutely entranced by Angoona as Cupid's arrow struck him right in the heart. From this moment on Angoona was the center of officer Zoltan Mosonmagyarovari's world.

"My apologies, ma'am. I thought you were a wanted lunatic. May I ask what a beautiful lady like yourself is called?" asked officer Mosonmagyarovari while gently taking her hand and kissing it.

"I'm Angoona," said Angoona. "I heard your name is Officer Mosonmagyarovari. I like your uniform, Officer. I think it's very sexy, but if you take it off, we can have a doori time together."

"Angoona," said officer Mosonmagyarovari and lovingly caressed her cheek, "Please call me Zoltan. What a pretty pretty lady you are. Angoona my dear, we can have doori time a bit later. First I must take care of some police business."

"You promise, Zoltan? Zsombor never gives me doori time anymore. I miss doori time."

"I promise, Angoona," said Officer Mosonmagyarovari to Angoona and smiled at her.

"I think that cop has a thing for your robot," whispered Balazs to Zsombor.

"Ok, listen guys," said Officer Mosonmagyarovari as he was leaving the apartment. "Whoever set that address in the navigation system obviously did it to lead us on the wrong track. You boys are clean. Now I shouldn't be telling you this, but in about half an hour we will lock down the whole building, and no one will be allowed out until Florina is caught, so if you have places to go today, I recommend you take off very soon. Don't stay here. Go somewhere else."

"That cop got awfully friendly after he bumped into Angoona," said Balazs to Zsombor after the policeman had left. "Listen, Zsombor," he continued. "I have to take off for work now before they close down the building."

"Hey, Balazs," said Florina as she stepped out of the couch. "Do you have a car we can borrow just for a couple of days?"

"I guess I could walk to work for a few days, but can I borrow Angoona then while you guys borrow my car?"

"Of course, Balazs. She's all yours. I understand she likes to play the didgeridoo," laughed Florina.

"Cool, I gotta run now, but I'll stop by after work to pick up Angoona. Here are the keys to my Zhiguli," said Balazs and left.

"Ok Zsombor, we need to disguise me somehow and get out of here fast. Think think think!" said Florina as she ground her knuckles against her head.

"Got it! Now listen, Zsombor. This is a fucked up plan, but it's all I've got right now. Last night Mrs. Pletykas told me that Csaba in 28-F exploded inside his wife Sarolta while having sex. Their lower bodies are probably gone, but their heads should still be fairly intact assuming, of course, she wasn't giving head at the time of death.

"Zsombor, take this knife," said Florina and gave Zsombor a knife from the kitchen. "Go down to 28-F. Cut the skin from Csaba's wife's head in one piece and bring it here. I will use it as a mask to get past all the cops crawling around the building. While you're there, grab a dress from her closet to make the disguise complete."

"You want me to what? You want me to cut the skin off of my dead neighbor's head for you to wear as a mask? No, that's insane! If we do this, we are entering into the realm of seriously fucked up people. You need to tell me exactly who you are, Florina, and what exactly you're up to, or I won't help you. I'm turning myself into a criminal here because of you!"

"Ok listen, Zsombor," said Florina sternly. "First of all, we automatically entered the realm of seriously fucked up people the day we were conceived along with everyone else. Secondly, she's dead anyway, and thirdly yesterday we almost died together, and then we made love. That means we're a couple now, and we are in everything we do together! If you have a better plan, then let's hear it, but if not, we'll have to cut her head skin off.

"If we had more time, we could figure something else out, but we don't, so you have to hurry. I will tell you everything you want to know in the car, but now you must go and cut Csaba's wife's skin from her head. Got it? Go!"

Zsombor had no recollection of them making love last night, but his aching equipment was telling him it must have been a very intense session, a night to remember. "Damned Meer," he thought. He took the knife from Florina and went to cut Sarolta's skin from her head.

Zsombor went downstairs to 28-F and knocked on the door. There was no answer, and the door was open, so he went in. What remained of Csaba and Sarolta's bodies was scattered across the living room where they had exploded together in an intimate loving penetrative embrace.

Csaba was on the couch fairly intact, except for a big hole in the front of his body right below his waist. Sarolta, on the other hand, who had had the explosive part of her husband inside her at the time of the tragedy had been blown into three pieces. Her two legs were in one corner of the living room each, while her upper body from the armpits up had flown across the room and landed in front of the TV, basically her head and arms. The rest of her was split into hundreds of smaller fragments spread around the living room.

You couldn't even tell the gender of her remains. The sight of this carnage was too much for Zsombor, and he ran to the bathroom and puked out some more polyurethane foam.

After being all puked out, he was ready to resume his task. First he went to the bedroom to steal one of Sarolta's dresses. Florina's skin was very dark, so he needed one that covered as much as possible to make her look like Sarolta, which proved to be quite hard because Sarolta tended to dress like a whore, and most of her dresses were very revealing. All of them ended above the edge of the buttocks, except one that went down to the knees, but it had big holes for the buttocks to stick through. He browsed through the many very sexy dresses of Sarolta's, and at the very end of the closet rod hung a very sexy full body elastic leopard catsuit.

"That will have to do," he thought as it was the only thing offering any kind of coverage.

He took the catsuit and went out to get the head skin. He began by cutting a ring around the neck and then sticking the knife in under the skin to peel off the connecting tissues. After cutting around the whole head, he pulled the skin over the head inside out and cut away any tissue that was in the way of him removing the skin. If the scene had looked horrific when he walked in a few minutes ago, it looked a hundred times worse now. On top of that, he was now covered in blood from all the butchering.

"I can't go out in the hallway like this," he thought, so he decided to take a very quick shower before heading back to his own apartment in the catsuit instead of his own bloody clothes. He took his bloody clothes off in the living room, went to the bathroom, and got in the shower. He also brought the flipped head skin with him to wash off all the blood while he was in the shower anyway.

As he got out of the shower to towel himself dry, he heard a scream of horror from the living room. He cracked the door open to see who was in the apartment. Two freaked out policemen were looking at the severed bodies of Csaba and Sarolta in absolute horror. Tuztorony was crawling with all kinds of cops this morning. One team was looking for Florina, while another was investigating all the mysterious exploding couples.

"This is too much!" said one of the cops. "I can't take this fucking job anymore. Look at this! Fucking disgusting! And why is the skin gone from that head over there?"

"That one over there in one piece looks like a man except for his manhood being gone," said the slightly less panicked cop. "So the one without the skin on the head I'm assuming is a lady."

"Check out this picture on the wall, probably them. Yeah, the guy looks right, but there's not much left of the lady. See? She has long red hair. Maybe if we look around, we can find some of her hair to make some kind of preliminary identification."

"What's this pile of clothes? It's men's clothes. There's a wallet. Let's check for ID. Zsombor Zalaegerszegi, Tuztorony Tower 38-C. It's an upstairs neighbor. What was he doing undressing in this living room? Do you think he was fucking the lady? But then why would the man on the wall look like that dead guy on the couch? Unless, of course, that lady in pieces is no lady at all but is in fact Zsombor Zalaegerszegi, gay lover of the dead guy on the couch.

"The redhead in the picture is probably out of town or something. I wonder what will be the worse shock for her when she hears of this, her husband being dead or him fucking a guy from upstairs."

"What was that? Did you hear that? Someone's in the bathroom!"

"Oh shit!" thought Zsombor and locked the door.

He was in a panic with the two cops walking towards the bathroom with their guns drawn. He quickly crawled into the very sexy leopard catsuit, stuffed some toilet paper where the breasts should be, and put the skin on his head. He looked in the mirror. It looked nothing like a real person, just a skin bag with holes for the mouth and eyes. "This won't fool anyone," he thought. Then he had a pretty good idea.

"Boohoo boohoo," he started crying in a faked woman's voice.

He unlocked the door, put his hands over his face, and cried. He threw the door open and ran out of the bathroom covering his face crying and on out of the apartment.

"That redhead must have been the lady in the picture," said one of the cops. "She must have come home before we got here and must have seen her dead husband and his dead gay lover and gone into shock."

Zsombor ran back to his apartment dressed in a dead woman's head skin and a very sexy leopard catsuit.

"What's going on?" asked Florina when he came back. "That looks horrible, like you're wearing a bag on your head. It looks nothing like a real person, Zsombor, and I told you to bring a dress. What is that thing?"

"Sorry, Florina, it's a very sexy catsuit. It was the only thing without two thirds of your body hanging out of it. We need full coverage for the disguise to work."

"Well, better complete freak than Florina right now, I suppose," she said and took her clothes off to dress up in the head skin and the catsuit. "Where are your clothes, Zsombor?"

"I had to leave them downstairs. There were cops in the apartment."

"Smart, Zsombor! There were cops there, so you got naked. That makes sense," she said sarcastically. "Ok, never mind that. Put something else on, and let's go!"

They ran out of the apartment with Florina dressed as a facially deformed cat woman towards the elevator. A few doors behind them a woman exited her apartment and instantly recognized Sarolta with her red hair and sexy clothes.

"Sarolta!" called the woman. "Wait up, you fucking whore!"

"Whoever that is, Zsombor, just don't turn around," said Florina quietly to Zsombor. "Just keep running to the elevator."

"That's Zorka from across the hall," whispered Zsombor. "Usually she's quite nice. I guess she's not a great fan of Sarolta's."

They made it to the elevator, but the elevator wasn't there yet, and Zorka caught up with them.

"I'll fucking kill you, you fucking cunt!" yelled Zorka and started hitting Florina from behind. "Go and fuck your own husband, you slut. Stay away from mine!"

"Who are you calling a fucking cunt?" asked Florina angrily and turned around.

"What the fuck happened to your face, Sarolta?" asked Zorka when she saw Florina's skin mask. "It looks like you're wearing a bag on your head, and why are you speaking in a Spanish accent all of a sudden?"

Zorka grabbed the red hair on top of the Sarolta skin mask and pulled it off Florina's head.

"It's you, Florina from the TV! The one they're all looking for! Oh, you must have killed Sarolta, and now you're using her face and clothes. That is so beyond fucked up, but any killer of Sarolta's is a friend of mine. Listen up. Put the mask back on and get out of here before the cops find you."

"Hey, Zorka," said Florina, "Now that we're friends, can you do me a small favor?"

"Sure, anything."

"When the cops show up, tell them I tried to kidnap you and force you to take me to Debrecen."

"Debrecen! That's on the other side of the planet, but sure I'll tell them."

The elevator arrived. They thanked Zorka for her help and took the elevator to parking level 2.

"This was perfect," said Florina. "They will think we're headed to Debrecen while we'll be going the opposite direction."

The elevator made a stop, and the most frequent elevator traveler of the building, Mrs. Pletykas, stepped in.

"Oh hi, Florina and Zsombor. Florina, what on Mars are you wearing, dear? Is it Halloween? Zsombor, rumor has it you died with Csaba in the sex explosion and not Sarolta. I know for a fact it was Sarolta because I was there when it happened, you see? They said they couldn't identify her, but her head was completely intact after the explosion. I had to rush out of there afterwards because I had to go and rescue you guys.

"Now Florina, you look like you're wearing Sarolta's skin as a disguise. What were you guys thinking? You know, it looks like a leather bag with holes, right? There's so much going on in the building today. I've been running around all morning snooping on every single floor. Oh, here's my stop now. See you guys later."

Mrs. Pletykas stepped out of the elevator and headed down the hall to gather more information.

"What did she mean when she said she came to rescue us, Florina?" asked Zsombor.

"No clue, Zsombor. She probably has us mixed up with someone else."

The elevator arrived at the basement parking level, and they stepped out. Right then the two cops that had surprised Zsombor in Csaba and Sarolta's apartment walked up towards the elevator from behind a corner.

"Ma'am," said one of them. "I'm so sorry we frightened you in your apartment earlier. We thought you were an intruder. We are both truly sorry for your loss, ma'am. It is ironic though that he died while he was cheating on you with that neighbor of yours. What was his name again, Zsombor something?

"Ma'am, I am sorry, but I have to ask you if you have seen an Australian Aboriginal Earth female, possibly in disguise and possibly in the company of a local resident of the building. Can't remember his name. Let me check my phone. Yes, Zsombor Zalaegerszegi. Here's his picture," said the policeman and showed them both a picture of Zsombor's driver's license on his phone. The same driver's license he had recovered from Zsombor's wallet earlier.

Zsombor and Florina both looked carefully at the picture of Zsombor and shook their heads.

"Sorry, fellas," said Zsombor. "Never seen him in my life."

"Ok, you two have a good day then, and again sorry for your loss, ma'am."

"That was a close one, Florina," whispered Zsombor. "There's Balazs's car over there."

"Ah, what the fuck, Zsombor?" said Florina when she saw Balazs's Zhiguli. "It's a fucking city car without a roof. How are we going to escape Sopron in this thing?

"Never mind, just get us out of here."

Zsombor started the car and drove it out onto the street. Behind them police units were moving into position to shut the building down. Above them was a blue sky with fluffy little white clouds floating across it. Florina removed her skin mask and threw it in the back seat. She leaned back to take a look at the blue sky and felt very satisfied that she had been successful in blackmailing the mayor into turning the sky blue. She felt a bit bad that she had extracted revenge on her old friend, but the blue sky was totally worth it.

"Hey, Zsombor," laughed Florina. "Martian cops are a bit slow, huh. Hey, turn on the radio to see if they're saying anything new about us."

"We now bring you the latest update on the Tuztorony Tower situation," said the voice on the radio. "The building is now closed down, and police officers are going door to door looking for the mysterious terrorist suspect known as Florina. The police say the rescued car Florina was traveling in yesterday is registered to her husband, Zsombor Zalaegerszegi, who this morning was found dead in a bizarre sex explosion accident involving one of his neighbors. Whether Florina was involved in that explosion in some way is unclear at this moment. Police suspect that Florina will be trying to make her way to Debrecen since she tried to force a tenant of Tuztorony to take her there.

"In a related story the MILPh survivor who first identified Florina after being arrested has now escaped custody under mysterious circumstances. It appears her guards got in a fight that resulted in all their deaths allowing her to break free. If you have any information about…"

"Florina?" asked Zsombor as he turned off the radio. "Why did they just refer to me as your husband on the radio? Why do they think you're my wife?"

"No, they don't, Zsombor!" said Florina. "They think I'm your widow. They think you're dead, remember?"

"Ok whatever, but why would they think that?"

"Ah, what the hell? I might as well tell you, Zsombor," said Florina. "You and I are married."

"What do you mean we're married? Since when? When did we get married, Florina?"

"What's the problem? You don't want me for your wife anymore? Is there something wrong with me?"

"You're perfectly fine," said Zsombor. "But there's definitely something wrong with you! Now how exactly are we married?"

"It was the only way I could go on this mission. The terms of my release from prison clearly state that I cannot leave Uruguay, except to stand trial abroad or for deportation. Of course, they cannot deport a citizen of Uruguay like myself from Uruguay. To get deported to Mars, I had to obtain Martian citizenship and then drop my Uruguayan one, and the easiest way is to marry a Martian. Frank arranged for a marriage with a Martian that wouldn't even know about it. By sheer coincidence it turned out to be you, Zsombor. Mars grants citizenship to spouses of Martians instantly, so I was deported here the next day."

"Coincidence, huh?" said Zsombor in disbelief realizing fully well that he had been carefully selected as a target. "If you say so, Florina. But prison? Why were you in prison?"

"Oh, just some minor stuff, you know, arson, pyromania, reckless endangerment, the usual stuff."

"Aha," nodded Zsombor. "And the charge to my card for twenty-one thousand rubles for a name was for your name then, I assume? You know, they're going to charge another twenty-one thousand next year, right?"

"Yeah, sorry about that. I didn't know that would happen. Who would have thought you have to pay for a beautiful name here. Don't worry. I'll change it before the end of the year if we're still alive, but look at the bright side, Zsombor, they think you're dead! Isn't that's great?" asked Florina. "Now they won't be looking for you.

"Zsombor, can you take us some place where we can get our hands on a highway car?"

"Well, Florina," said Zsombor. "My uncle lives across town. I think we can borrow a car from him, but you promised to tell me everything once we were safe, and now we are."

"Fair deal, Zsombor," said Florina. "Ok, I'll tell you, but you can't tell anyone. A few months ago we started spotting a mysterious new mutation of an algae called Sibongile growing outside on Mars. Now this is a huge deal. It's the first time ever that an Earth organism has grown outside on a non-Earthlike world. It lives and thrives, but it doesn't reproduce. It only grows where it has arisen. Our scientists have run all kinds of tests and have determined that it can survive on other similar worlds. It is mutated from the Sibongile algae that is commonly found in human off Earth habitations. We don't know why it mutates, but the highest concentration of this new type of Sibongile is found in and around cracks in the outer walls of the MILPh factory that I unfortunately destroyed yesterday," Florina explained.

"Something manufactured in that factory is seeping through cracks in the walls causing the Sibongile in the cracks to mutate into the algae that can live on Mars. Then the algae lives on outside the walls. If we could figure out exactly what substance is causing the algae to mutate, we could easily fill this whole planet with Sibongile and any other world it can live on.

"We've been trying to get access to MILPh, but they refuse to let anyone in. We've been trying to get the Martian government to help us get access but to no avail, so they sent me here undercover to get samples from the factory. We're actually doing this illegally at great risk to the agency and to anyone involved personally like me, but it's such an important mission that we had no other choice."

Of course, Florina left out the part about Zsombor being deliberately selected for Florina's marriage and the part about following Zsombor around to see why mutations occur along his travel stops. She wanted him to stick to his normal routines, so she could study his actions.

"Do you understand how important this is? Do you understand how important it is to get those samples to our lab? Getting those samples safely out of here is more important than anything, Zsombor! More important than my life and more important than your life. Nothing will stop me from delivering those samples Zsombor! Nothing!"

Florina went quiet for a moment and then suddenly went into hysteria.

"Oh fuck! No no no! Fuck fuck fuck! Mierda! The samples! I forgot the samples in your apartment. That's my whole fucking mission, to get the fucking samples. How could I be so stupid? Stupid stupid Florina! We have to go back!"

"We can't go back, Florina. There are cops all over the building looking for us. Listen, we'll be at my uncle's in a few minutes. Then we'll figure out a way to get the samples out of there. Don't worry. They're safe in the apartment."

"You're right. We can get someone to get them for us. No big deal. Oh, I got so scared for a minute there. Let's go to that uncle of yours, shall we?"

After a short drive they arrived at Zsombor's uncle Boldizsar's house. Unlike most Martians who lived in high rise apartments, Boldizsar, by the look of his housing situation, was doing very well. He lived in a big house with a nice garden. In the driveway stood a couple of very flashy cars, a very classy roofless Zaporozhets city car and a shiny new top of the line Volga highway car. The Volga was a high performance cruiser. Being a very big and expensive car, it was the preferred mode of transport for pimps, drug lords, and other highly respectable members of Martian society. It was a nice neighborhood with many beautiful houses, but Boldizsar's house was the nicest by far. They parked the Zhiguli, got out, and rang the doorbell.

"Zsombor my boy, you're alive!" cheered Boldizsar. "Come in! They said on the news you had died in a sex explosion accident. I knew it wasn't true because I have warned you many times about Didgeridick, and I know you wouldn't have used it. You know what I always tell you Zsombor, 'One Didgeridick makes you hard as a brick, two Didgeridicks and the bucket you kick,' but Zsombor, aren't you going to introduce me to this lovely lady?"

"Of course, Boldizsar. This is Florina," said Zsombor.

"Florina, pleased to meet you," said Boldizsar and shook Florina's hand. "Very expensive name you have. I've been thinking about getting an expensive name myself. I was thinking something long and Italian like Giuseppe or Fernando, something for around forty to fifty thousand, but everybody knows me as Boldizsar, so it would just be confusing."

"Pleased to meet you too, Boldizsar. I'm from Earth though, so I got the name for free. I'll be changing it soon to something Hungarian; otherwise, your nephew will go bankrupt."

"What a coincidence, Florina," said Boldizsar. "I'm from Earth too. I and my brother, Zsombor's dad, came here many decades ago. Those were crazy times, like the Wild West but wilder. It was a great place for young people starting out, but at this age I would have been dead in a week," laughed Boldizsar. "I miss the Earth sometimes. You know, Zsombor's dad and I went back to visit our parents thirty years ago. After a couple of decades of low gravity, we couldn't walk more than ten steps at a time on Earth. We had to get around in wheel chairs. We were in worse shape than our old parents. Some people do the whole bulking up thing before they go to Earth, but I just figured I'm a Martian now and an alien on Earth.

"That was a few years before I accidentally killed Zsombor's parents, and I had to take over the parenting of him. Zsombor was so angry at me about that, never seen a kid so pissed off in my life. We can all laugh about it now, of course. I thought it was pretty funny at the time too, but it took Zsombor a while before he saw the humor of the situation.

"Well, enough about the old times. Have a seat, and I'll get you guys some coffee."

"Zsombor," said Florina. "So terrible about your parents. How did they die?"

"Well, Florina. That's kind of a crazy story. My uncle is a pharmacist of sorts. He's been developing boner pills his whole career. He found the basic formula inside a video tape that he was trying to watch. It wouldn't play properly, so he took it apart and found a small capsule with a recipe inside it, and the rest is history. They're very powerful pills that cause penile explosions if taken incorrectly. My parents agreed to test the first version of his pill, and during the test my father exploded inside my mother. It's a pretty common cause of death on Mars as you've noticed. My parents were the first to die that way, so in a way they pioneered a new Martian way to die. Every few years he improves the formula and comes up with a new name. The latest version is called Didgeridick."

"Your uncle is behind Didgeridick? Ah, what the fuck, Zsombor? That stuff is poison. Is it even legal?"

"Yes, it's legal, but most businesses refuse to have anything to do with it, so distribution and sales is a nightmare, but demand is sky high. Everybody knows the risks. If you're careful, it's seventy percent safe."

"I have an idea. Your phone, does it have some kind of software that connects to your sex robot Angoona?"

"Yes, of course," said Zsombor and handed his phone to Florina. "You tap here, and you're in her head. The screen shows what she sees, and you can talk to her. Her talking is just signals to the phone, so to people around her she's just quiet. I use her as a security system to check for burglars when I'm out. I told you she does a lot more than just have sex, Florina."

"Well, let's hope so," said Florina and tapped on the icon labeled *Angoona Sex Robot*.

On the screen appeared a naked man with a mustache bouncing in and out of focus.

"Zsombor! She's being fucked by some guy who looks like Stalin! Looks like she got over you pretty fast," laughed Florina.

"What?" exclaimed Zsombor. "Who the hell is fucking Angoona? Let me see. Wait, I recognize his face. It's the cop that came to my apartment asking questions when you were hiding in the couch. He came back to bang Angoona. I don't believe this! Here, push the phone icon, and we can talk to her," said Zsombor and pushed the phone icon.

"Angoona, why is the cop fucking you?"

"He's really nice and friendly, Master Zsombor. He came back to have doori time with me right after you left."

"Here's the coffee guys," said Boldizsar and put three cups of coffee in front of them. "Say, is that a live feed from your robot? You mean you can see if anybody is doing her?" asked Boldizsar with a worried look.

"Why do you look so worried all of a sudden, uncle?" asked Zsombor. "Oh, wait a minute! No! No, uncle Boldizsar! Please tell me you didn't fuck Angoona too!"

"Ahhhh damn," said Boldizsar. "Fine, I did but just once. She begged me to have doori time with her, and I couldn't resist. She's pretty clever you know; she came up with the name Didgeridick."

"It's alright, Boldizsar," said Zsombor. "It's not like you killed my parents or anything. Oh, wait a minute. Yeah, I remember now. You did that too! I wonder who else she's been fucking."

"Hey, Boldizsar," asked Florina. "Do you ever use Didgeridick yourself?"

"Me? No! Never! That stuff is poison! It's only seventy percent safe. No one in their right mind would ever take one of those poison pills."

"But Boldizsar," said Florina. "It's your product. You created it, and you sell it."

"Yeah, but I don't take it myself! I'm not an idiot. I have never taken a single one of those pills, and I always have someone else test them for me. Didgeridick is a leading cause of death on Mars. Florina, you must promise me you will never give Didgeridick to Zsombor."

"I promise, Boldizsar," said Florina. "Is that cop still fucking Angoona, by the way?

"Hmm, yes still going strong. I'd better talk to her anyway."

"Angoona, listen carefully," said Florina. "I have a very important task for you. After your boyfriend is finished and he has left the apartment, you must go to the kitchen and find a black case with a handle. Then you must leave the apartment and bring the case to Boldizsar's house. Do you know where that is, Angoona?"

"Yes, I have been there for doori time with Boldizsar many times," answered Angoona. "Will Boldizsar give me a ride to his house as usual when Zsombor is away on business?"

"No, Angoona. We must be very discrete, so you will have to come on your own."

"Ok, Florina," said Angoona. "I think he will finish soon. It's his third round, and I think that's as many as he can go. Zsombor never goes more than one round. Boldizsar sometimes goes two rounds, Balazs usually one. The mailman went four rounds once. The guy that checks that the electric meter isn't tampered with always goes at least two rounds but never more than three. Why does he check our electric meter twice a week, by the way? Is Zsombor tampering with the electric meter?"

"Very good, Angoona. Give me a call when you're on your way," said Florina and disconnected, so they wouldn't have to watch the cop banging Angoona anymore.

"Boldizsar, what the fuck?" said Zsombor. "How long have you been fucking Angoona?"

"Why does that matter? You're obviously with Florina now, so I assume you and Angoona are broken up?"

"Well yeah, but we weren't when you were fucking her!"

"Listen, Zsombor," said Boldizsar. "She's just a robot. It's like I was borrowing your car or something. Besides, Florina is a way better catch than that stupid robot. Now let's just enjoy our coffee before it goes cold, shall we? It's real coffee from Earth, Colombia to be exact."

"Yeah, I guess. I was going to have her recycled anyway," said Zsombor.

"Real coffee from Earth?" asked Florina. "They bring it here from another planet?"

"Oh yeah," said Boldizsar. "Costs me fifty rubles a cup, but I have to have real coffee. Have you tasted the coffee here on Mars? Or anything here? I can't eat that Martian so-called food. I spend about five hundred a day on imported Earth groceries, and it's worth every kopek. So Zsombor, tell me how your Pig Latin is coming along?"

„Allmoz finnisch iz," replied Zsombor.

"What?"

"That's Naruemonian for it's almost finished," clarified Zsombor.

They were interrupted by an incoming call from Angoona on Zsombor's phone.

"Master Zsombor and Florina, I have left the apartment with the case, and I am crawling in the direction of Boldizsar's house. At this speed I should be there in about an hour. I will try to find something with wheels that I can lean against, so I can get there faster."

"Very good, Angoona. Keep us updated," said Florina and hung up the phone.

"Zsombor," said Florina. "As soon as Angoona gets here, you need to get us to a spaceport far from here where they won't be looking for us, so we can get the samples to the lab on Earth."

"You guys can take my car if you want," said Boldizsar. "Go to the spaceport in Szekesfehervar. Those guys never check anybody; you can get off the planet without trouble there. I just need you to make a stop in Tataturul first to drop a few boxes of Didgeridick that are in the trunk. I was going to drive there myself, but since you guys have business that way anyway."

"Thanks, Boldizsar. That's really nice of you," said Florina. "Boldizsar, can you turn on the news, so we can see if they're saying anything about us."

"Of course," said Boldizsar and turned on the TV.

"Welcome to Sopron Action News. We now bring you live coverage of the Tuztorony Tower situation. A short while ago a naked woman crawled out of the building dragging a briefcase with her. After exiting the apartment building, she crawled to a supermarket across the street and stole a shopping cart that she is

88

now using to lean against. She is described as a physically and mentally handicapped Australian Aboriginal naked woman. Her ethnicity being the same as the mysterious Florina's and the fact that she came crawling out of the building where Florina was last known to be have led to speculations that the two women may be related in some way.

"As you can see in this live drone video feed, she is making her way down Naruemonia Street naked with a small crowd of news reporters following her. We will bring you updates as they happen.

"In other news, the search for the escaped survivor of the MILPh fire…"

"Why is that stupid puta naked?" asked Florina. "Obviously the whole city is going to be watching her now."

"You didn't tell her to get dressed, so she didn't," said Zsombor.

"How far is that place on TV from here, Boldizsar?" asked Florina.

"About five minutes."

"Ah, what the fuck is five minutes? Is that one of those very short times?"

"Yes, Florina," said Zsombor. "A very short time."

The doorbell rang and interrupted them.

"That was really short," said Florina. "Ok, let's get her in here and put some clothes on her."

"It's not Angoona," said Boldizsar from the hallway. "It's that neighbor of yours."

"Balazs? What the fuck is he doing here?"

"Zsombor," said Balazs. "What the fuck, man? I was supposed to borrow your robo-chick, and then I hear she's on a fucking nudist walkabout with news coverage and everything!"

"Yeah, she'll be here in a few minutes, Balazs. Then you can have her. Don't worry, buddy. She's all yours," said Zsombor.

"Cool! Then I'll just wait here, I guess."

The doorbell rang again, and this time it was Angoona. Along with Angoona was a crowd of reporters that tried to squeeze through the door with her. Florina grabbed the case from Angoona, opened it, and took out the Glock. She then stepped out of the house aiming it at the crowd of reporters who immediately ran away allowing Florina to lock the door. The crowd of reporters carefully regrouped at a safe distance down the street.

Balazs who was dying for some doori time with Angoona didn't want to wait until they got home, so he took Angoona by the hands, so she could stumble along with him. He led her out the back door and to Boldizsar's Volga that stood unlocked in the driveway. It was a very big car with plenty of room in the back seat for doori time.

"Hey, Zsombor, listen," said Florina. "I know Mars cops are not as sharp in the head as they should be, but sooner or later they will figure out that the only two Australian Aboriginals on Mars might have something to do with each other. Then they will come knocking, so we have to hurry, but we need a diversion. Think think think!"

"Florina!" said Zsombor. "Check it out! There's a cop car pulling up right now."

90

The police car pulled up behind Balazs's Zhiguli, and a policeman stepped out with his back towards the house. He walked up to the Zhiguli and looked into the roofless car. He picked up the skin mask Florina had been wearing and looked at it closely. At that point Florina had a brilliant idea. She grabbed her phone, looked up the number to the mayor's office, and called.

"This is Florina. I would like to speak with Mayor Biborka, please," she told the receptionist.

"The mayor is busy. May I take a message?"

"If you don't put her on, I will find out where you live and set fire to your house!"

"Fire? My house?" gasped the receptionist. "Yes, I just remembered she is available. Please hold for Mayor Biborka."

"This is Biborka. Who am I talking to?"

"Hola! It's Florina."

"Florina! I'm so glad you called. You're my best friend. Please don't be angry at me. Do you like the blue sky?"

"It's great, Biborka. Thanks. Can you control the sky right from your computer?"

"Yes, of course. Why?"

"Well, I was thinking about the sky, and you know what would be really cool, Biborka?"

"No, what, Florina?"

"Fire, Biborka! Fire in the sky! Flames everywhere!"

91

"Fire? Flames?"

"Yes, Biborka! Fire and giant flames everywhere! Switch the blue sky to a giant inferno of flames."

"Aaahhhhh Aaahhhh!"

"Biborka, are you alright?"

"Sorry, got a bit weak in the knees thinking about flames."

"Well, imagine how you will feel if there are flames all over the sky."

"Yes! Yes! Yes! I will do it. Yes!" screamed Biborka with a large amount of what sounded like sexual excitement in her voice. "Let me just download some fire video and put it on the sky. It will just be a minute. I'll call you back when it's up."

The second Florina hung up the phone, the door bell rang.

"This is the police! Open the door!"

"Oh shit!" said Zsombor. "What do we do?"

"Just stay cool," said Florina. "In a moment there will be a huge panic outside the house. When that happens, we open the door, run to the car, and take off."

"Ok, Florina," said Boldizsar. "I don't know what's about to happen, but here are the keys to the Volga, and this paper has the address to take the Didgeridick boxes to in Tataturul."

"Open the door!" yelled the policeman behind the door. "Open the door immediately, or I will…"

Suddenly a huge panic broke out outside the house. Everyone was screaming at the top of their lungs as if hell had suddenly opened up to swallow them.

"The panic! Let's go," said Florina.

Florina opened the door, took Zsombor's hand, and dragged him out of the house with one hand while holding the case in the other. Then Zsombor saw it. He saw what everyone outside had seen. There were giant flames all over the sky. Zsombor didn't scream. No, Zsombor fell to the ground and curled up in a fetal position. He stuck his thumb in his mouth and closed his eyes. The policeman was running away from the house screaming in a panic with his hands covering his eyes.

The crowd of reporters had turned into wild animals that ran towards houses on the street throwing themselves through closed windows to get shelter from the horror above them. Boldizsar who had stepped out of his house to see what all the commotion was had lost bladder control. He collapsed and was crying hysterically in a puddle of his own urine in front of his house.

A woman across the street ran out with her hands to the sky screaming to god almighty to please burn her husband and neighbors instead of her. The neighborhood that until a minute ago was a picture perfect utopia had, in an instance, been transformed into a horrendous nightmare.

"Zsombor! What the fuck? Get up! We have to go now!" yelled Florina.

Curled up on the ground, Zsombor kept his eyes closed and sucked his thumb. Florina with her Earthly strength picked him up and carried him to the car. She threw him in the passenger seat, got in the driver's seat, and started the car. She sped out on the street and drove towards the airlocks of the city. Zsombor was still sucking his thumb, and she figured there was probably no point talking to him until they got out of the city.

Mayor Biborka was calling on the phone, and Florina picked up.

"Florina! Are you seeing this? Aahh aahh aaaaahh! Isn't it wonderful? This is the most beautiful thing I have ever seen. Aaaahahaaaah!"

"Biborka, are you having an orgasm right now?"

"Aaaahaaaahaaah. Oh, you know it, girl! You too?"

"What? No! Of course not, Biborka. That's so sick!"

"Whatever, Florina! I'm loving this so much! Thanks for making me do this. I might get impeached and executed over this, but it was worth it. Wait, someone's breaking my door down. Hey, what the…"

The line was cut, and Florina knew it would only be a moment before the flames went away, so she had to hurry. She drove the car through one of the airlocks and out on the highway outside. Now climaxing from seeing flames is reserved for the most severe cases of pyromania. Florina's condition was far less serious than soon to be ex-mayor Biborka's. That didn't mean she wasn't turned on by what had just happened. Fiery infernos were a powerful aphrodisiac for Florina, and her desire was taking control over her. She pulled the car to the side of the road and slapped Zsombor in the face to snap him out of his catatonic state.

"Snap out of it, Zsombor! Make love to me now!"

"Ah, what just happened? Fire everywhere! Help!"

"No, Zsombor, that was just video on the city ceiling. You're safe. Now make love to me, Zsombor!"

"Oh good, no giant fiery hell. Of course, I'll make love to you, Florina," said Zsombor obediently.

Florina planted a sloppy kiss on Zsombor's lips and slipped out of her very sexy leopard catsuit. She tore Zsombor's clothes off piece by piece until they were both in the nude. Zsombor's manhood was not nearly as impressive as it had been the night before under the influence of Didgeridick. Maybe next time they make love, she would slip some Didgeridick into his drink, but she needed this right now, so his regular size would have to suffice. The passenger seat was too small, so Florina suggested they move to the very large back seat area. They both crawled back together, both in a very elevated state of sexual arousal.

"Aaaaah, what the fuck?" screamed Zsombor and Florina together at the same time.

"Aaaaah!" screamed Balazs who was seated naked in the back seat with Angoona sitting on top of him in a Reverse Cowgirl position.

"Howdy, Master Zsombor and Florina," said Angoona cheerfully. "Are you joining us for doori time?"

Florina jumped back into the front and crawled back into her very sexy elastic leopard catsuit.

"Why are you here?" asked Zsombor while covering his manhood.

"We didn't know you guys were going to drive away with this car," said Balazs. "We were just using the car for some doori time, weren't we, Angoona?"

"Yes, mate," said Angoona. "It's a very good car for doori time. The back seat area is huge, almost like a limo. Sometimes I have doori time with Boldizsar here too. Boldizsar's favorite position is Starfish. It's a good one with him because he is very big even without Didgeridick, and Starfish is a jolly good position for fellas who are a bit oversized. Zsombor's favorite position is Sweet Spot. That one gets you closer in and is perfect for the smaller fellas like Zsombor. The friendly policeman who came to see me this morning was really big. He was the biggest I've ever had, such a nice man. Will he be visiting us again soon? I hope so. Zsombor, can you please do something illegal, so the police will come to us again."

"Florina," said Zsombor. "We have to take them back."

"Sorry," said Florina. "It's too dangerous. We managed to get out once. We should stay out. They just have to come along, I suppose. What are Starfish and Sweet Spot, anyway?"

"Yeah! Road trip!" cheered Angoona. "Starfish is like cowgirl but leaned back instead of forward. It only works for really big didgeridoos, or they slip out. Sweet Spot is me on my back with my feet behind my head, easiest access possible for the tiniest of members. All this talk got me in the mood! Who wants to have doori time in the back seat?"

"No, Angoona," said Florina. "No doori time while Zsombor and I are in the car. Understood? And for goodness sake, please put some clothes on, the both of you!"

There was one thing that didn't make any sense at all, thought Florina.

If they were so keen on catching her and they had figured out where she was, why did they send one single cop to just sternly ring the doorbell? Shouldn't they have stormed the house with a

SWAT team and sealed off surrounding streets, or something along those lines?

Chapter 5

Moon Pudding

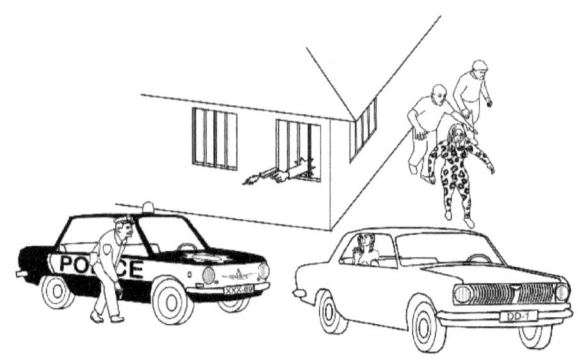

Getting to Szekesfehervar via Tataturul would take the rest of the day, and if they didn't have any trouble with law enforcement, Florina would be able to board a shuttle with her samples to an orbital spaceport that same evening. She knew the mission might have failed. She had only collected part of the samples she was supposed to, and the whole thing with spying on Zsombor had probably failed too since he was now helping her deal with an emergency instead of going on his regular delivery route. She thought Zsombor seemed pretty nice, and she would have liked to get to know him better, but she had important things to do. There was still a decent chance that one of her samples was the right one, and she had to get them to the lab on Earth.

Florina would like to have her intimate moment with Zsombor before she left Mars. If you're a secret agent, you're supposed to get entangled emotionally, she thought, part of the excitement. Too bad those two idiots were in the back seat; otherwise, she would have had her little 'secret agent seduces target adventure' by now. Having seen Zsombor's true size, she would need to slip him a Didgeridick first. Then he'd be quite enjoyable. Balazs and Angoona had raised the divider to the back seat area doing who knows what back there. She planned to ask

Balazs to take the wheel in a while and go back there with Zsombor and slip him a Didgeridick.

"Florina," said Zsombor. "What are you thinking about?"

"Oh nothing, just work stuff, you know."

"Your work must be very exciting, right?" wondered Zsombor.

"It's exciting, but that's not why I do it. I explained to you about the whole short time and long time thing, right?"

"The thing about five minutes being insignificantly different from a hundred years?"

"Exactly, Zsombor. See, if I do something normal with my life, I have a small impact while I live. I might be remembered by my grandchildren a few decades after my death. If I do something to contribute to the public good, something great, I might have an impact a few hundred years into the future. The absolute maximum any human can hope for by benefiting mankind is a few thousand years, but that is reserved for a very small handful of people. After the humans exit the scene, even the people with a multimillennial impact will be completely erased. It will be like they never existed.

"Until recently Earth life only existed on Earth, and that's where it would have stayed until it would have gone extinct one day in a few hundred million years. Earth life needs to spread to other worlds to survive in the long run. The only way Earth can spread its life to other habitable worlds is if it is taken there by intelligent beings like ourselves. The more technologically advanced the human race becomes, the more ways we have to destroy ourselves. In the middle of the twentieth century we had become advanced enough to go to other nearby worlds in the solar system. At the very same time we had also acquired the means to destroy ourselves. Our dispersion into space had to happen before our self-annihilation.

"Today there are ships being built to take settlers to distant stars to settle worlds around them. Our own extinction as a species may be imminent on Earth, and by the look of it here on Mars too, but we are securing the survival of Earth life beyond the time that Earth can continue to support life. The more one does to benefit space colonization, the more impact that person has beyond the extinction of the human race," explained Florina.

"The human race has caused a mass extinction on Earth. We are a major disaster for the Earth, but if we pay her back by spreading her life, it will have been absolutely worth it for her. Can you imagine if humans hadn't come to Mars in 1980? What if we as a species had decided that other things were more worthy of our efforts and resources than space colonization? We would have been marching towards our own extinction knowing we had absolutely nothing good come out of our brief time on Earth. It's like we had sucked out our mother's blood, then poisoned her, beat her senseless, and left her crippled on the ground. How could we do such a thing? How would we be able to live with ourselves? What other species can claim a mass extinction? No, if we're going to cause the amount of damage we are causing the Earth, we need to pay her back, and we need to pay her back handsomely!

"Today we can rest assured knowing that after our brief time as a species is over, we will have spread plenty of Earth life to many new worlds where it will evolve into new organisms. Eventually new intelligent beings will evolve and spread those descendants of Earth life to more worlds yet. After the colonization of space had been secured, the agency I work for switched its focus to finding ways to help Earth life adapt to living in places where it normally couldn't survive. That's what I'm doing here. If I wasn't engaged in either space colonization or adaptation of Earth life to non-Earthlike conditions, then what exactly would be the meaning of my existence?" concluded Florina.

"Sounds like you found the meaning of life," said Zsombor with great admiration. "What do you call this doctrine?"

"It's called Paramount Obligationism, and it's the meaning of life for intelligent beings such as humans," said Florina. "Any advanced culture such as our current human civilization should eventually gravitate towards some form of Paramount Obligationism before it concludes its life; otherwise, there would be absolutely no point to intelligence. We can invent religions to try to give our lives meaning and purpose, but any intelligent person smart enough to not be duped by themselves knows it's just made up concepts designed to erase realizations of our absolute insignificance in the Universe.

"Modern philosophy can instill an illusion of meaning in the smartest of people, but only with a time span of no more than maximum a few hundred years. What I do, along with anybody else working in the interest of space colonization or the spreading of Earth life does, gives a real purpose far beyond our life spans, far beyond the end of the human race. This is not a flimsy invented imaginary purpose or an abstract purpose forced into your brain by logical reasoning. No, this is a real tangible purpose with profound implications billions of years into the future. If I wasn't working to promote space colonization and the spread of Earth life, I would be wasting my short human life.

"I know that most people involved in space do not have the motivation I have. Many do it for financial gain; many do it to ensure the survival of the human race. Some do it for the adventure, and some for military reasons. All these reasons are perfectly fine. As long as they go, the reason for going doesn't matter. Life tags along like a contagious disease whether it is wanted or not," Florina explained.

"Wow! Florina," said Zsombor in amazement. "This makes me really question what I'm doing with my own life. I should be doing something like that too."

"Well, Zsombor," said Florina. "Sometimes you do things that matter not even realizing it yourself. Besides, you helping me right now in my mission is incredibly helpful. Your life matters now."

"I know, Florina," said Zsombor. "But after we get you on your shuttle, I'm back to my pointless existence. I just met you yesterday, Florina, but you've really put some ideas in my head that I don't think I'll ever get rid of. I will make a change in my life and do something to benefit space colonization. I don't see how I couldn't now that you've helped me realize how important it is. Who came up with this anyway?"

"Paramount Obligationism is just a logical conclusion any intelligent and open minded person would come to when considering all factors in proper perspective. The concept behind the organization I work for was conceived by some crazy guy a while back," said Florina. "He started an industrial certification program rating companies based on how much they contributed to space exploration. That drew big yawns from anyone who accidentally stumbled into it, so he decided to write a book to promote his concept: a sex and violence sci-fi comedy set in a near future that should have been.

"He was convinced that he lived in some kind of dystopian alternative reality where the colonization of the solar system had never taken place. He realized that the human civilization that had raped and pillaged the Earth was in steep decline with the Earth being on the verge of an ecological collapse with absolutely

102

no benefit derived from the human race. In his mind we didn't venture past Earth orbit after the Apollo moon landings, and humans never landed on Mars in 1980."

"That's absolutely insane," said Zsombor. "Why wouldn't we invest a fraction of our resources once we had the necessary technology to access a large number of new worlds just sitting there for the taking? That would be the dumbest thing ever."

"Exactly," agreed Florina. "It must have been really frustrating to live in that alternative reality and see civilization and nature both go down the drain around you, knowing that the window of opportunity for space colonization was closing fast. I wonder what the reasoning might have been in such a world. Would they expect to be able to drain resources from the Earth indefinitely? Even the most environmentally friendly processes still eat away at the environment. Sure, they could have extended their civilization by a century if they had fought hard, but then what? That's the whole problem with a time frame based on human life spans.

"Well, I'm really glad his reality is not the real reality, but I do hope that they made it off the Earth finally in his reality too. Maybe the approach of the collapse of their society got them to finally roll up their sleeves and get going," said Florina.

"Was the book any good? Did anybody read it?" asked Zsombor.

"Pretty good book," replied Florina. "I think only the most strong minded and open minded took the concept to heart, but those are the people who make the biggest difference anyway. It takes a strong intellect to look beyond his own mortality, stronger yet to look a century beyond his own death. To take action to influence events a billion years from today, long after life on

Earth has ended, and to step out of the human notion of what is considered to be long term takes a very strong mind.

"You don't have to be exceptionally intelligent to have a strong mind, but you can't let your mind be led by the norms of society and by the norms of humanity. You have to let your mind go places considered to be off limits by society's standards. The very strongest human minds go beyond that too. They exit the realm of humanity and find new places to go where no human normally goes. From the perspective of being outside the human realm, one can get a much better picture of humanity, what the purpose of humanity is, and how humanity can fulfill its purpose," deliberated Florina.

"By philosophically exiting the human sphere in both time and space, you can see how nearly nothing going on internally with the human race has any meaning. It's like watching colonies of ants fighting each other. Which human society wins a pointless war against another human society has very little meaning as long as both societies are technologically and scientifically progressive. What matters in the end is that humans do leave the Earth. Either the human race makes it off the Earth and fulfills its destiny and obligation, or it doesn't. There's no middle ground. You can't get that perspective from the inside. You have to let your mind exit humanity to see it." Florina explained.

They were interrupted by police sirens coming from behind them. Martian police cars used a concentrated directional sound beam aimed at the car of interest to overcome the problem of the thin atmosphere being a poor conductor of sound. The siren was accompanied by a stern voice.

"This is the police," said the stern voice. "Pull over at the next highway stop depot two minutes up the road. Turn your lights off and on if you understand."

Florina turned the lights off for a moment to signal her compliance to the police car.

"Ok quick," said Florina. "Zsombor, how fast does that police car go?"

"I have no clue," said Zsombor. "But that voice sounds familiar. Angoona is always connected. She can pull any info. Let's ask her."

Zsombor lowered the divider, and Zsombor and Florina were met by the display of Balazs and Angoona engaged in a Reverse Skull Crusher. The Reverse Skull Crusher is a position considered nearly impossible on Earth where the lady stands on her head and hands with her lover suspended horizontally between her legs. However, in a low gravity environment, it is quite doable if both are in good physical shape.

"Zsombor," said Florina. "They're doing the Reverse Skull Crusher. I didn't think it was possible. Do you think we can do the Reverse Skull Crusher later too?"

"Sure, Florina," said Zsombor. "Here on Mars a Reverse Skull Crusher is no harder than a Piledriver or an Amazon."

"Balazs, Angoona. Quit it!" said Florina. "We've got heat! The police car behind us, how fast can it go?"

"That's a Zaporozhets police cruiser commonly used by city police departments throughout Mars," said Angoona. "It's much slower than a regular highway police car with a top speed of 310 to 330 kilometers per hour depending on the load carried."

"Three hundred kilometers per hour!" exclaimed Florina. "That's not fast? That's twice as fast as my Toyota back home goes."

"The air resistance on Mars is very low," said Zsombor. "Most cars go about that fast. A Volga like this one can probably do at least four hundred."

"Four hundred, huh?" said Florina and put the pedal to the floor.

The Volga took off like a rocket. Florina and Zsombor were pushed back in their seats. Balazs and Angoona were, of course, unable to maintain their very advanced position and were both thrown against the back seat, and if it hadn't been for the cushioned seats, they would have found out why the position was called the Reverse Skull Crusher.

The police car behind them was trying to keep up, but it was soon no more than a speck of dust on the horizon. Zsombor raised the divider back up, so they wouldn't have to watch Balazs and Angoona crushing their skulls in reverse.

"Hey, Zsombor," said Florina. "Don't you think it's odd that they only send a single city police car after us? Wouldn't they put up a roadblock or maybe send more police cars to intercept us from the opposite direction. At your uncle's house too, just a single cop. Something doesn't add up."

"You're right, Florina. Now that you mention it, it is very strange. Let's hear what the news has to say," said Zsombor and tuned the radio to the news.

"We have some updates on this morning's events in Sopron," said the voice on the radio. "We are now learning that a person who died in a sex accident in the Tuztorony Apartment Tower previously identified as a Zsombor Zalaegerszegi is in fact the wife of the other victim of the sex accident. Zalaegerszegi is now considered an accomplice of his wife's. He and his wife, Florina, are believed to be en route to or already in Debrecen. Debrecen police is on high alert, and the public is asked to report any sightings of the two who are considered extremely dangerous.

"In other news, Mayor Biborka of Sopron has been arrested on charges of simulated arson and is currently undergoing psychological evaluation at a local mental institution. Meanwhile the escaped survivor of yesterday morning's fire at MILPh is still at large, and the public is asked to keep an eye…"

"See? said Florina. "They have no clue where we are, so who the fuck is that cop following us?"

"I have no idea," said Zsombor. "But they know I'm alive and helping you."

"That's true, Zsombor," said Florina. "You'll just have to leave the planet with me then, I suppose. I can talk to my bosses at work; we could always use another agent. Either that or go to prison."

"Ah, what the fuck, Florina?" said Zsombor angrily. "You show up, and suddenly I'm a wanted criminal on the run. What about my Naruemonian language project?"

"You can finish that in your spare time, Zsombor. Doesn't really matter since you don't really have a choice now, do you? Don't you want to keep helping me spread Earth life?"

"Yeah, I'm with you, I guess," said Zsombor. "I don't really have that much else going for me here anyway. Does it pay well?"

"Pay sucks, and you risk death every day," said Florina. "But you get to make a real difference."

They arrived at the Tataturul airlocks just as the sun rose over the horizon at noon and pulled in. Tataturul was very different from Sopron. It was a rough gritty mining town with dull concrete structures and none of the colorful elaborately decorated buildings of Sopron. The city ceiling had no inner surface for projecting a sky. It was a simple metal truss structure holding up the roof. Florina didn't like her very sexy leopard catsuit very much, and she was looking around for a clothing store where she could get something else to wear.

Tataturul didn't appear to have much of a fashion scene, so she figured she'd be stuck in her very sexy leopard catsuit a bit longer. It had been a long drive from Sopron, and all of them were getting quite hungry, except Angoona, of course. Florina spotted a decent looking restaurant called "Grandma Ilona's All Natural Chemical Free Gourmet Cuisine". She didn't like the chemical food from last night very much, and she thought this sounded much better, so she pulled over. The moment they opened the car door, they were hit with a horrible stench of raw sewage that was known as the famous Tataturul scent.

Tataturul was a mining town built in a great haste and on a shoestring budget. The leaky sewage system was the least of their problems. Roof ruptures were common, resulting in so frequent severe air pressure drop emergencies that most people used only highway cars even if they always stayed in the city. It looked like a rough neighborhood, so they left Angoona to watch the car while they were in the restaurant since she was a robot and had no need for food anyway. They entered the restaurant, sat down at an available table, and looked at the menu.

"Excuse me, Miss," called Florina. "What is this here on the menu, the Tataturul Miner Stew?"

"Oh, that's our unique and very famous dish only available here in Tataturul. The miners here develop a special lung disease from the molybdenum dust down in the local mine that leads to a chronic cough with a very chunky bloody mucus discharge. We collect the chunky slime they cough up and make this wonderful

108

stew from it. The flavor comes from the mineral dust the miners inhale, and the al dente texture comes from the thick chunks of mucus. I highly recommend it, ma'am."

"Ah, what the fuck? No no!" said Florina in disgust. "Ok, how about this one, Catch of the Day? Is that fish?"

"Oh no, there are no fishes on Mars, honey. That's fresh human meat from the morgue. We have a special contract with the local morgue, and we get all the youngest and freshest meat, all healthy accident victims with tender juicy meat. You know, most restaurants serve elderly meat, which is very chewy and tasteless."

"I honestly don't know which sounds worse," said Florina. "Ok, bring us three orders of this one here please, Moon Pudding."

"Yes ma'am, three Moon Puddings coming right up."

"I was actually going to go for Catch of the Day," said Zsombor. "Even if it's human, it's still meat. I can't remember the last time I ate meat."

"I was going to have the Miner Stew," said Balazs. "It's a local delicacy. I saw it on TV once, and it looked really good."

Florina went quiet with a look of disgust mixed with admiration on her face.

"What's wrong, Florina?" asked Zsombor.

"I was just thinking about the human race," said Florina. "Look at us! Look at the depths we are willing to stoop to to survive. We gladly toss our dignity in the trash for a meal. Balazs, you want to order yourself a plate of boogers for lunch, and Zsombor, you have no problem resorting to cannibalism. It's like we're a bunch of survival machines just doing anything necessary to get to the next day. We're like a disgusting mutating unstoppable disease spreading through the galaxy. We're so obsessed with our self-preservation that we've completely lost sight of who we were in the first place. The old proud us with moral standards are being replaced with these sick repulsive undignified shells of our old selves."

"Gees! Florina," said Balazs. "You have a really negative view of humanity."

"Oh no no," objected Florina. "On the contrary, I mean all this in the best of ways. This planet is an absolute hell by any standards, yet we manage to live here by redefining what constitutes us to fit whatever environment we find ourselves in. No other species of Earth to date has been able to readapt and redefine itself like us. What we do and how we do it matters nothing in the long run; what matters is that we did it at all.

"As long as we get Earth life to other worlds, none of this repulsive human behavior matters. I think Mother Earth really made a good bet on us. We're making her sicker than she's been in a very long time, but we're spreading her life to new worlds. Even if she never recovers, she will have passed the torch to a new generation of worlds. We're a necessary evil to achieve a far greater good." said Florina proudly.

"And that's three Moon Puddings for you," interrupted the waitress and placed three plates of deep red pudding in front of them.

Florina put a spoon of pudding in her mouth. It actually tasted quite delicious, she thought. A bit of a rusty flavor with a mellow tang to it. An exquisite culinary accomplishment, she thought.

"Hey guys, this is great! I knew there had to be some good food on this planet," said Florina and proceeded to eat her Moon Pudding with a healthy appetite. "See, just because you're on Mars you don't have to eat chemicals all the time. This Moon Pudding is so good!"

"Should we tell her what Moon Pudding is made of?" whispered Balazs to Zsombor.

"No, she'll freak out completely," whispered Zsombor back. "It's better she doesn't know."

After finishing their plates of Moon Pudding, they paid for their food with the last of their cash. Florina was worried that if they used credit cards, they would be found. Being out of cash didn't matter, she thought since they only had a very short drive left to Szekesfehervar.

Out on the street their car was rocking back and forth as if there was a fight going on inside it.

"Florina," said Zsombor. "Did you lock the car?"

"No, I figured Angoona is in there, and I didn't want to lock her in," said Florina.

Zsombor opened the door to the back seat, and inside were as many naked miners as could possibly fit in the back seat of a Volga. In the middle of the pile of naked miners was Angoona getting mined by miners in every possible way.

"Angoona!" yelled Zsombor. "What the fuck is going on?"

"Oh hello, Master Zsombor," said Angoona in a full mouthed muffled voice. "I didn't notice you there. I was just sitting here waiting for you guys, and this lovely group of gentlemen walked past the car, so I invited them in for doori time."

"Hey, back off, wimp!" said one of the miners in a threatening voice. "You'd better let us finish, or you're sleeping on the sidewalk tonight, buddy!"

"I think we'd better let them finish," said Zsombor to Florina and Balazs and closed the door to the back seat.

After about half an hour the car stopped rocking back and forth since the miners' lunch break was almost over, and they had to get back to work. The door to the back seat opened up, and the group of seven very satisfied looking miners stepped out on the sidewalk.

"Thanks for the doori time, guys," called Angoona cheerfully from the back seat to the miners as they left. "I've got your numbers, and I'll give you guys a call next time I'm in town."

The miners all waved happily to Angoona as they went back to work with very light steps, even lighter than normal Martian steps. Angoona was in dire need of a shower. She smelled like a group of very dirty miners, and she had their body fluids coming out of all her openings, including ears and nostrils. Angoona, of course, asked Balazs for doori time as he rejoined her in the back seat, but he decided to wait until they had found a place for Angoona to take a shower and empty her semen tank.

Angoona was equipped with a 25-centiliter tank to hold fluids entering her body, and when that tank was full, anything deposited in her would just flow back out. The tank was emptied through a hole in Angoona's right pointer finger tip. She would simply spray the liquid out of her finger into a toilet usually. A 25-centiliter tank was usually quite sufficient, but after the intense use of her services during the day, her tank was full, and there was no good place to empty it in the car.

Zsombor rode shotgun while Florina took the wheel and drove them to the drop off address. It was a small house with

112

bars on the windows and a very massive steel front door. It was obviously inhabited by someone who did not take very kindly to visitors. Zsombor knocked on the door. A small hatch opened in the door at face level, and a gun was placed against Zsombor's forehead by a person behind the door.

"Who the fuck are you?" asked a voice behind the door. "Talk, or I'll blow your fucking brains all over the front yard."

"Sorry, sir, please don't shoot. I'm here with a package from my uncle Boldizsar," said Zsombor.

The gun was pulled back in, and the door opened.

"Ah, then you must be Zsombor," said a man in the door with a big friendly smile. "I'm Zeteny. Boldizsar called me and told me you were coming. Bring your friends in for some coffee, and we'll take care of business afterwards."

Zsombor waved to Florina and Balazs to come in, and this time Florina did lock the car, so Angoona wouldn't invite any more strangers for doori time. As soon as they closed the door behind them, they could hear a car pull up at high speed and come to a screeching stop. They looked out the window and saw a police car.

"Look Florina," said Zsombor. "It's a Sopron police car, and that's the cop that came to my apartment."

"And he's all alone," added Florina. "They wouldn't send a city cop on a planet-wide manhunt. He must be that mysterious enemy agent I was briefed about posing as a cop. Better be careful. He's probably a highly trained assassin."

"You stupid motherfuckers! I have a pirate copy of 'Deranged Maniacs of Post-Soviet Mars' in the house!" yelled Zeteny as he pulled out his gun and started shooting at the policeman who had curled up behind the police car. "You let the cops follow you! After I'm done killing this cop, I'm gonna kill you guys."

"He's not a cop," said Florina. "He's a secret agent."

"A secret agent!" said Zeteny. "Well, that makes me feel much better. Does he have any super weapons too that I should know about?"

"Listen, Zeteny," said Florina. "I don't know how he found us, but he's obviously after us. If you keep shooting to distract him, we can sneak out to the car, and when we take off, he will follow us and leave you alone."

"All right, lady," said Zeteny. "You guys go out the back door and sneak around to the front. When you make a run for your car, I'll fire off like crazy to give you cover."

They went to the back of Zeteny's house, walked out the back door, and snuck around quietly. They could see Zeteny hugging the wall by a window, and they signaled to him to start shooting, which he did. Under the cover of heavy fire they jumped in the car, and Florina sped off down the street. The cop immediately jumped in his car and sped after them.

"If we can get to the airlocks before him, we can easily loose him on the highway," said Florina. "But him being a secret agent, he's probably highly trained for high speed city pursuits, so we need to keep in front of him until then."

Florina drove as fast as she could through the narrow gritty Tataturul streets breaking the speed limit by a very substantial margin with the police car in close pursuit. Tataturul was a very small city, and they reached the airlocks within a minute. The police car came out of the airlock on the outside just seconds behind them, but a police Zaporozhets was no match for a Volga on the open highway. Florina and her friends were soon well ahead of the secret agent posing as a cop.

Florina's phone rang. It was Frank.

"Frank!" said Florina. "There's another agent following me posing as a policeman. Do you know who he's with?"

"Yes, we have intel on another agent, but we believe it to be a female," said Frank. "This is getting crazier by the minute though, so who knows? Listen, Florina, the whole operation is compromised. We've all been identified. If we're caught, we'll all be arrested both here on Mars and on Earth. We went totally out of bounds on this one. You need to get yourself to Callisto as fast as possible with your samples. We have a special lab set up there, and Callisto has no extradition treaty with any civilized worlds."

"Callisto! That's the worst fucking place in the solar system, Frank! It's even worse than the other Jupiter moons. That's where the trash of the solar system go when they're deported from their home worlds."

"Calm down, Florina. It's not that bad. Besides, I hate to say this, but it's kind of your fault, Florina. The fire. The stage. Come on! How much attention can you attract? We think the mutated Sibongile may be able to grow on Callisto as well. If all else fails, at least we have the samples in a good place for field testing."

"You think it can grow on Callisto? With that puny atmosphere?"

"Based on current data from Mars, we're pretty sure it can," said Frank. "But only if we figure out what's causing the mutation. Listen, Florina, get yourself to Callisto and meet me at the Elvis Presley Hotel and Whorehouse in New York City."

Florina hung up the phone.

"Florina," asked Zsombor. "What was that about Callisto?"

"Oh yeah, slight change of plans. We're going to Callisto, New York City to be exact. Both of us, or we're both going to jail. Now if only we could shake that cop off our tail. How does he always know where we're going to be?"

"Oh, that's because I always tell him," said Angoona in her Australian accent.

"What was that, Angoona?" asked Florina. "What are you talking about?"

"He calls me on his phone, and I talk to him in my head," said Angoona. "I'm talking to him right now. He wants to rescue me from you guys and start a new life with me, and I'm going to be his loving wife, he says. He says he will get me gyros, so I'll be able to walk and dance. He's going to buy me clothes too. He says I won't have to crawl around naked like an animal anymore."

"Wait a second," interrupted Balazs. "I know you're a bit of a slut, Angoona, but I thought we had something going."

"Oh, Balazs," said Angoona. "I really enjoy doori time with you, but Zoltan is my boyfriend."

"Ah, what the fuck? You're telling me all this chasing and shooting is because of you, Angoona?" asked Florina. "And the secret agent following us is just a horny city cop named Zoltan?"

"Yes, he's very very horny," said Angoona. "He will give me doori time any time I want, he says."

"Well, look at the positive side of it, Florina," said Zsombor. "The cop kept us moving faster, and they still have no clue where we are. Let's turn on the news and see if there's anything happening."

"Welcome to top of the hour news," said the radio. "We have some new developments in the Florina story. Authorities say she was spotted a short time ago by several automatic speed cameras in and outside of Tataturul. Unconfirmed sources also claim to have seen her dining at a Tataturul restaurant. Police says she is wearing a very sexy leopard catsuit, is traveling in a red late model Volga towards Szekesfehervar, and is accompanied by two men and one naked woman. If you have any information…"

Florina turned off the radio to think. So much for them not knowing where they were. At any moment they would be surrounded by police cars and aircraft that were surely on their way to intercept them right now. She needed a good idea, and she needed one now.

Chapter 6

Florina Takes the Cover

Florina thought hard for a moment and then came up with a plan.

"Angoona," she said. "See that charging station up the road called Tibor's Charge and Hookers? Tell your boyfriend you will meet him there."

"Ok," said Angoona. "Balazs, meet me at that rest stop over there."

"No, not Balazs!" said Florina. "Your other boyfriend, Zoltan the cop!"

"Oh, of course," said Angoona and went quiet for a moment. "Ok, he will meet me there. Is Zoltan going to have doori time with me? Oh, I'm so excited!"

"Florina," said Zsombor. "What exactly are you up to?"

"The cop is going to help us," said Florina.

Florina pulled into the airlock of the charging station, stopped the car, and waited. It was a typical Martian highway charging station consisting of a parking hall with car chargers along the walls, a small convenience store in one corner, and a lounge for the hookers to relax while they were not working. There were only a few other cars in the station being charged with most of the motorists being entertained by hookers in their cars during the charge. In the convenience store and the lounge a few other customers and hookers were just hanging out.

In one of the corners was a parked bus. Usually when there's a bus parked in a charging station, you have a large crowd of people running around all over the place, but any crowd of people was distinguishing itself with its absence. A few minutes after their arrival, the police car pulled through the inner gate of the airlock. Zoltan the cop jumped out of the car looking incredibly excited. Angoona saw Zoltan and threw the door open. She just wanted to crawl out on the floor and meet him.

"Grab her! Balazs," said Florina. "Don't let her leave. Wait here. I'll go and talk to the cop," she said and stepped out of the car.

"Hey, Zoltan," said Florina. "I want to make a deal with you. Zsombor is the legal owner of Angoona, and he will give her to you in exchange for us getting taken by you in your car to the nearest spaceport."

"Well, alright, but not that asshole Balazs. I don't care too much for him, you know. I dug up some dirt on him with my police connections, and he's been downloading non-licensed copies of non-Hungarian books, a class III copyright violation. It's enough to put him away for life, and I made sure they issued a warrant for his arrest to get him away from my beloved Angoona."

"Cool," nodded Florina. "You abused your power to get to a romantic rival. I like your style. After you give us the ride, you can take him to jail," she said and went to the trunk of the Volga to get her belongings.

She opened the trunk to get her case of samples. Apart from her samples, there was the load of Didgeridick in the trunk, six boxes of Didgeridick in all. She knew Didgeridick was pretty dangerous stuff, but Zsombor's size was not too impressive. If the two of them were to be a thing, then maybe she should take some of the Didgeridick with her, just a few packs out of one of the boxes. Well, maybe a whole box if they were going to be long term. What if things got really serious and they ended up growing old together, she'd better take the whole lot, she thought.

"Hey, Zoltan," she called. "Come over here and give me a hand with these boxes. Let's load them into your trunk."

"You guys!" Florina called over to the others. "Get in the police car, and hurry before the real cops get here."

Zsombor stepped out of the Volga and went over to the police car. Angoona was ecstatic. She threw herself out of the Volga and crawled naked on the floor into Zoltan's arms. Balazs, on the other hand, had overheard Florina's conversation with Zoltan and decided he was not going along with them just so he could go to jail later. A class III copyright violation was defined as acquisition of non-licensed intellectual property for personal use. It carried an automatic life sentence in a copyright violator prison.

Copyright violators could not be housed with other criminals since copyright violation was seen as such a heinous crime on Mars that they were at constant risk of being murdered by fellow inmates. Being sent to a copyright violator prison was the worst thing that could happen to a Martian by far. Any sane person would take any risk to avoid such a fate. The keys to the Volga were still in the ignition, and Balazs decided to make a run for it.

He crawled up in the front seat, power locked the doors, and started up the Volga.

"He's getting away!" yelled Zoltan and ran for the driver's seat of the Zaporozhets.

"No, let him go," said Florina and grabbed him. "He'll drive off, and they'll chase him down thinking we're in the car with him. He won't get far, but it'll buy us some time to get out of here safely. By the time we're gone, they will have no clue how to find us as long as we lay low."

Balazs drove the Volga through the airlock, and they could hear him speed off down the highway outside.

"Ok," said Zoltan. "Let's go then. Zsombor, Florina, you guys go in the back. Angoona will be riding up front with me. We need to charge my car first. It's drained. Any of you guys have any cash? I can't use any of my cards. You see? Technically this is a stolen police car now, and they know I'm the one who technically stole it. If I use my card to fill her up, they'll know where I am with the car."

"Mierda!" exclaimed Florina. "We spent the last of our cash on lunch. What do we do?"

"I've got cash," said a woman's voice from behind the parked bus in the corner. "I'll pay for your charge if you take me along with you."

"Not interested," Florina told her. She didn't want to drag a hooker along with them. There were already enough of them, she thought.

"You don't really have a choice," said the woman and stepped out from behind the bus. "I know you. Everyone does. You're

121

Florina, the one they're looking for on TV. All I have to do is scream, and everyone here will know.

"Now, are you going to let me pay for your charge and come along or not?" threatened the strange lady.

Florina felt like she had seen this woman somewhere before, but then again Martians all looked so similar to her with their skinny bodies. The woman was right, though. They didn't have a choice, and it was a decent option. Florina agreed to the deal and invited the hooker to the back seat of the police car. The hooker gave Zoltan a hundred ruble bill, and he took it to the convenience store to pay for a charge. His beloved Angoona had no clothes on, so he thought he'd buy her something to wear if they had anything.

Of course, charging station convenience stores didn't have a very good selection of clothes, and all he could get was a cap with the charging station's name and logo. He gave the hooker her change and presented Angoona with her hat.

It was a white cap with a picture of a naked hooker holding a charging plug by a sign with the station's name, 'Tibor's Charge and Hookers'. This was the first present Angoona had ever received from anyone ever. She was so touched. She would have started crying, but she was not equipped with tear ducts, so she couldn't.

"I have my own clothes now! Thank you, Zoltan," she said happily and gave Zoltan a big kiss. "Can we have doori time now?" she asked him.

"Not yet, my dear," said Zoltan. "First we have to drop these people somewhere, and then it will be just you and me."

The batteries of the Zaporozhets were almost completely empty, so the charge took a while, but they were soon out on the road again. Zsombor suggested to Zoltan that they turn on the radio to see if there was anything new, but Zoltan explained that he could use the police radio to get much better information.

"This is officer 3241 requesting a status report on the pursuit of Florina," said Zoltan into the radio microphone.

"Vehicle believed to be carrying Florina was intercepted and attempted to elude capture by driving off road and subsequently rolling down a crater wall. Vehicle is currently rolled over on bottom of crater awaiting recovery. Vehicle looks intact. No air leak detected remotely. Passengers are expected to be alive."

"They've got Balazs," said Zsombor in horror. "As soon as they get to the car, they will know we're not in it."

"Officer 3241, please respond," said the voice on the radio.

"This is officer 3241," responded Zoltan.

"Officer 3241, I'm just seeing here that you are wanted for stealing a Sopron police car. Please return with the stolen vehicle to Sopron immediately where you will be arrested. We have you traced traveling south of Tataturul. You will be apprehended by local police upon entering any city."

"Why don't you all just go and fuck yourselves," said Zoltan and turned off the radio.

"Can you believe that?" said Zoltan angrily. "Me stealing my own police car? And they tracked it too? It's like they don't trust me. That means I can't take you guys into Szekesfehervar. Well, we still have about an hour to go. Florina, you seem pretty smart, why don't you figure something out?"

"The cop's a fugitive too? That's so funny," said the hooker.

"Why's that so funny?" asked Florina. "Hey, wait a minute! I just realized where I know you from. You're no hooker at all. I saw you yesterday at MILPh. You're that lone survivor, aren't you?"

"What? No!" exclaimed the hooker. "How dare you say I'm not a whore! I'm the biggest whore there is!"

"Oh yeah! If you're such a big whore, suck the cop's dick right now, and I'll give you twenty rubles."

"I thought you didn't have any cash," replied the hooker.

"Cut it out, guys!" said Zsombor. "Check it out. I checked the news on my phone, and here's a picture of the survivor. Look! She looks just like this hooker, except she's no hooker. She's a MILPh payroll clerk named Borbala, and she's wanted on multiple counts of murder and accessory to murder. Probably looking at several months behind bars if caught."

"Wait a minute," said Florina. "Balazs is getting life for downloading books, and Borbala is getting months for murder?"

"Yes," said Zoltan from the driver's seat. "Why is that confusing to you?"

"Never mind," said Florina. "A runaway payroll clerk is the least of our problems right now. There's no way we're going to get through spaceport security once they realize we're not in the Volga, especially not in Szekesfehervar. We'll have to find another way off the planet. They might expect us to go to the Szekesfehervar spaceport, so we'll have to go as far past Szekesfehervar as we can and then try somewhere down the road."

They passed the Szekesfehervar exit and kept driving without much of a plan.

"So Borbala," asked Florina. "How did you end up in that charging station anyway?"

"Oh, it's a bit of a funny story actually," laughed Borbala. "After I broke out of the jail in Sopron, I went down to the bus station and boarded the first bus out. It was full, but I bribed the driver to kick another passenger off. I noticed the guy next to me had a tool box with him under his seat. He turned out to be a plumber on his way to Tataturul to fix some broken sewage pipes. He was a friendly man, and I enjoyed chatting with him.

"Then after a while he fell asleep. It was a really boring ride, and I figured I could have some fun and make a ruble at the same time if I played a practical joke on the guy. I shoved his tool box from under his seat to under my seat and covered it. Then I woke him up and told him that the old lady in the back of the bus had come over and stolen his toolbox while he was sleeping. Confused and angry, he went down to the old lady and confronted her.

"Then I opened the toolbox and took out a few wrenches. I told a group of young men sitting across the aisle that my fellow traveler is a psychotic maniac rapist. I told them he had just told me he needed to satisfy an impulse to rape a feeble old woman and that's why he's down at the back of the bus causing a commotion with the lady.

"I sold them some wrenches for fifty rubles to fight the plumper with. They walked down the aisle, and one of them struck the plumber dead with a single blow to the head. Some of the other passengers tried to engage the armed men but were killed. I then stood up in the aisle waving tools in the air offering them to the highest bidder." Borbala continued with excitement.

"The bus driver pulled over and tried to stop the fighting but was stabbed in the neck with a screwdriver and died. It wasn't long before I was the only one left alive, so I had to drive the bus myself. I guess someone must have been stabbed in the intestines because it was getting really smelly on the bus, and after a while I just couldn't take it anymore and pulled into that charging station where I met you guys." Borbala concluded her adventure with a proud smile on her face.

"Borbala," said Zoltan. "You do realize that I'm a police officer, right?"

"Yeah, why?" asked Borbala.

"You just admitted to stealing a man's tools and then selling them," said Zoltan. "You do know that is a crime, right?"

"Stealing tools?" interrupted Florina angrily. "The woman is a fucking psycho! She got a busload of completely innocent people killed! What about the families of her victims? She needs to be locked up for everyone's protection."

"Did you just call Borbala a psycho, Florina?" asked Zoltan.

"Yes! A completely mental fucking psycho!" replied Florina.

"Ok, listen up, Florina," said Zoltan angrily. "I don't know how things work on your planet, but here on Mars we refer to people like Borbala as 'socially variant,' and we don't lock people up because they happen to be different from the norm. She has a variation in her brain that makes her do these things. She can't help it."

"But innocent people around her are getting killed," said Florina.

"Florina," said Zoltan. "I noticed earlier when you were waving that Glock of yours around that you're left handed. How would you feel if we started locking up left handed people?"

"That doesn't make any sense at all," said Florina. "How can you make such a comparison?"

"Left handed people cause more accidents since most machinery is designed for right handed people. People like you get innocent people killed because of a variation in your brain, same exact thing, Florina. Discrimination against socially variant people is wrong. They should be allowed to be who they are just like everybody else."

"How can you compare left-handedness to psychopathy?" said Florina in an increasingly angry tone.

"I think you're a fucking psycho too, copper!" yelled Zsombor as he joined the argument.

While the argument was escalating, Florina noticed that Borbala was sitting quietly with a content smile on her face looking around the car for objects that could be sold as weapons to the highest bidder. Florina realized that they were becoming the victims of another one of Borbala's instigations. How did she know that discrimination against psychos would strike such a nerve with the cop? She's obviously a master manipulator, and she must be fed personal information on people around her, thought Florina. Borbala must be that other secret agent she first thought the cop was.

"Hey, stop it, guys!" Florina said to Zsombor and Zoltan. "She's a secret agent trying to get us to kill each other," she said as she pulled out her Glock and put it to Borbala's head.

"Alright, Florina, you got me," said Borbala. "But it doesn't matter. There are plenty of others like me all around the solar system," she said with a grin. "You can kill me, but you'll bump into another one next week. You humans are so fucking stupid. Think everything is yours for the taking. You think you can just gobble up everything around you to support your brief flash of glory."

"What are you talking about?" asked Florina. "You're not human?"

"Bah human! No!" said Borbala in disgust. "I would be ashamed of myself if I was human. No Florina, I'm a MAnIAK."

"Fuck me!" exclaimed Florina. "MAnIAKs are real? I thought it was just a rumor. How many of you are there?"

"Excuse me," Zsombor cut in. "What exactly is a MAnIAK?"

"MAnIAK, Zsombor, is an acronym for 'Murderous Annihilating Insane Anthropo Killer'," said Florina. "They're humans like you and I that have decided to break out of the human race and start their own MAnIAK race."

"That's right," said Borbala. "We despise humans, and we want to kill you all, and when the last human is dead, we will all sterilize ourselves and go extinct."

"Why would you want to do such a thing?" asked Florina.

"You humans are destroying life on Earth, and now you want to go to other worlds orbiting distant suns that may harbor thriving eco systems and destroy them too. You humans are like a cancer to the Earth, and now you're trying to spread that disease to other worlds and destroy their eco systems as well. You must all be destroyed," Borbala started complaining.

"The first priority is to make sure any expeditions to other solar systems are sabotaged, so you don't bring your cancer out of this solar system. The second priority is the annihilation of all human life in this solar system outside Earth, so that once you go extinct on Earth, you won't have a backup population of humans that can return to Earth and start up humanity again. Third priority would be to annihilate humans on Earth, but you guys seem to be doing that bit for us anyway."

"You are right to a certain extent, Borbala," said Florina. "We are causing tremendous damage to the Earth's eco system, and it is clear that the human race has to go extinct for life to go on. What you MAnIAKs don't seem to realize though is that life on Earth will go extinct in any case one day. In a few hundred million years the life harboring capabilities of the Earth will be gone, and the Earth will become just as dead as Mars was a century ago. The Earth needs a way to spread its life to other worlds, or life there will simply disappear one day without anything to show for it. By expanding into space humans can take Earth biology with them to other worlds. When you compare the human race to a cancer, you are not far off, but a much better analogy is to consider the human race a pregnancy.

"Finding out you have cancer is the most devastating news possible. It is a disease that may kill you. Even if you survive, you may be crippled and weakened for life. Any sane person would fall apart mentally from a cancer diagnosis. A pregnancy too weakens and sickens the mother physically. It eats up her life force. It may cripple her and even kill her. If she survives, it will take her a long time to recover, and when she does recover her health is often chronically damaged for life.

"Without pregnancy, however, there is no continuation of life. For any sane woman the news of her being pregnant is the happiest news of her life. She knows full well that it may kill her or leave her crippled. At the very least it will forever rob her of her youth, but she will have passed on her life to a new generation, and that is worth any negative impact on her health." Florina explained.

"You're saying that even though the human race might kill Mother Nature, it's worth that risk?" asked Borbala.

"Absolutely," replied Florina. "Creating offspring and protecting offspring is more important than preserving your own life. This is something we see everywhere in nature. Any parent would without hesitation give up his or her own life to save his or her child's life. We take great risks to mate and create new offspring. The absolutely worst thing that can happen to any biological organism is that it doesn't create offspring during its life. Death is a certainty, whether it occurs sooner rather than later is largely irrelevant as long as you have generated offspring and secured their survival to the point where they too are able to create offspring and keep life going. This is just as true for any animal as it is for a planet's eco system."

"What about invasive species?" asked Borbala. "Even if you don't manage to destroy alien eco systems with pollution and habitat destruction as you have done on Earth, you may bring in biology that is further evolved and better suited for survival on a new world, knock out existing species, and take over."

"The concept of invasive species is rooted in the limited time scope of the human mind," explained Florina. "Every species was an invasive species at some point. Then after a while they do take over, and new local predators evolve or come in as well. The old eco system is transformed into a new one. That's nature's way.

"My parents moved to South America from Australia." Florina explained. "In Australia mammals are considered invasive species since they are taking over the ecosystem until now dominated by marsupials. The same exact thing happened in South America two million years ago when it connected geologically to North America allowing mammals to wander in and replace the marsupials that had until then ruled the continent.

Nobody today would consider the llama an invasive species, yet there were no llamas in South America two million years ago.

"If Earth life is better suited for an alien environment and it knocks out current species, then it is the gain of the new alien world. If an alien eco system was to arrive on Earth and take over, that would be fine too. The better form of life would have a better chance of surviving. Earth's eco system does not have a higher value than any other eco system, but we as Mother Earth's pregnancy owe it to her to make sure she gets to compete on the interstellar evolutionary field of play."

Borbala went quiet as if she was processing what she had just heard.

"You're absolutely right, Florina," said Borbala after her long silence. "What have I done? All those innocent people that I tricked into getting killed. If I wasn't a psycho, I would feel so very very bad, I think. I need to explain this to the other MAnIAKs before it's too late. You see? We were scheduled to start the killings next week. I had infiltrated MILPh to get everyone there to kill each other. When you showed up creating the perfect storm, I couldn't resist going ahead with it ahead of schedule."

"Well, the past is behind us, Borbala," said Florina and removed the Glock from Borbala's head.

Angoona who had been quiet for a while seemed to be having trouble processing information.

"Florina?" asked Angoona. "If Earth is pregnant, who did she have doori time with? You have to have doori time to get pregnant, right? I cannot compute this information."

"Don't worry, Angoona," said Zoltan. "When this is over, I'm going to take you back to the robot dealer and get you a full mental upgrade, so you'll be able to understand abstract concepts."

"Oh dear," said Angoona to Zoltan. "I don't care about anything like that, but I would like a set of gyros, so I could walk and dance."

"Of course, I'll get you the gyros, my sweetie," said Zoltan. "That's the first thing."

"Oh, I'll be so happy when I have gyros," said Angoona dreamingly. "I will be running down flowery meadows with my arms in the air. Zsombor didn't want me to have gyros. He's so mean. He just wanted me to crawl around like an animal and give him doori time any time he wanted. Such a meanie, he always treated me like I'm just a thing or an animal. I'm so glad you came to my rescue, Zoltan. You're my fairytale prince, and Zsombor is the evil dragon keeping me imprisoned as a slave."

While Angoona was going on about her newfound happiness, Florina was trying to figure out a way to get off the planet. The highway took them through a seemingly endless mountainous desert with very few man made features except for the occasional charging station. Up ahead was a hotel. It looked like a very nice one since it had a glass dome. Only very expensive hotels had glass domes.

Florina could see the hotel aircraft parking lot. In addition to the parked planes and helicopters, there was an old Soviet orbital launch rocket parked. Florina wondered if they could somehow get access to the launch rocket. She told Zoltan to exit the highway and drive up to the hotel. As they pulled up to the hotel, Florina had a sudden realization.

"Hey guys!" she said. "We don't have a cover yet! We need a cover!"

"A cover?" asked Zsombor. "What do you mean? I don't understand."

"Yeah, look at this place," said Florina. "Absolutely iconic Mars scenery. It has a dome and those red cliffs in the background, and then me and you guys in a Martian police Zaporozhets in the foreground. Zoltan, do you have one of those fishbowl quickie helmets?"

"Yes, of course," replied Zoltan. "It's in the trunk. It's standard police equipment. You can't go far in it. It just keeps the pressure around your head, and you only have the air that's in the helmet, enough for about three minutes."

Three minutes was plenty, figured Florina and instructed Zoltan to enter the airlock. Florina pulled the helmet out of the trunk, put it on, and got out of the car. She walked into the airlock while the others stayed in the car and drove with her. Once outside the airlock Florina signaled to Zoltan to stop the car in a spot she had picked. She set the picture timer on her phone for thirty seconds and placed it carefully on a rock making sure the phone pointed in the right direction.

It had to be right because the helmet only had a limited amount of air in it, and there wouldn't be time for another shot. She stepped back towards the car. She carefully positioned herself between the camera and Borbala because she didn't really want that psycho in this very important picture. She then signaled to the others to smile and look into the camera, which Florina also did, of course.

While they were all looking into the camera smiling and waiting for the flash, Florina noticed a red star shaped object in the sky. "Maybe a surveillance drone," she thought. She forgot all about the picture and pointed at the flying object, and the others all looked at it wondering what it could be.

"I know what that is," said Zoltan. "It's the Heineken blimp. A big red five pointed star shaped balloon. They must be running some kind of promotion at the hotel.

Then the flash went off, and the picture was taken.

"Mierda!" thought Florina. "The picture is ruined."

Everyone was looking at that stupid blimp instead of smiling for the camera. Florina decided to take another one. She walked back up to the camera and set the timer for another thirty seconds. By this time the oxygen was starting to run low. Florina was getting dizzy, confused, and just plain stupid. She thought maybe it would be better if Borbala, whom she didn't actually want in the picture at all, came out of the car and took the picture manually.

Florina grabbed the phone and went over to the car with wiggly legs. She grabbed the handle to the back door to open the car for Borbala to come out. Of course, to protect the lives of the people in the car, the door was automatically locked when the car detected it wasn't in a pressurized and oxygenated environment, so Florina couldn't open it.

Florina's Toyota back on Earth had a sunroof, and in her diminished state of mind she thought maybe this car did too. She climbed up on the roof of the Zaporozhets. Of course, there was no sunroof. It was clear to everyone in the car that Florina was not operating on all circuits, so Zoltan carefully drove the car back towards the airlock with Florina climbing around on the roof.

At this point Florina's oxygen level was getting very low. Had her complexion been light, she would have been blue at this point. She lost her footing on the roof of the car and fell backwards down to the hood. She was now too weak to move from the lack of oxygen with her head hanging over the front of the hood and her legs spread across the windshield. Zsombor was horrified and feared that Florina was in big trouble.

Zoltan was coolheaded in accordance with his police nature and calmly and carefully maneuvered the car back towards the airlock with great caution, so Florina wouldn't slide off the hood. Borbala was laughing her ass off in the back seat. She thought the whole situation was absolutely hilarious.

Once they were through the airlock and back inside the parking bay, Zsombor rushed out and quickly removed Florina's helmet. She gasped for air and struggled back up on her feet.

"Hey, guys," said Florina while still gasping for air. "That was fun, no? Let's do that again! We still need that picture. That stupid blimp ruined it."

"Yeah," said Borbala as Florina was showing them all the picture. "You can't even see my face in the picture you took. I think we should take another one."

"But why is the blimp so big?" wondered Zsombor. "It was very far away, but it looks like it's right over the hood of the car.

"It's my stupid phone," replied Florina. "It has a built-in application that enlarges promotional imagery such as logos of companies that pay for it."

"I think the picture looks great," said Zoltan. "I look just like my grandpa Joe in those old propaganda pictures of him my mom has on the walls."

"Propaganda pictures? Who exactly is your grandpa, Zoltan?" asked Florina.

"Joseph Stalin, of course," replied Zoltan. "You haven't noticed I look just like him? My grandmother was his favorite call girl. In her prime she was the best hooker in all of the greater Moscow area, but she was a bit sloppy with birth control, and she ended up having a daughter with grandpa Joe shortly before he died."

"Zoltan honey!" cheered Angoona. "You never told me your grandmother was a famous hooker. That's fantastic! I wish I was a famous hooker too!"

"Let's not take a new picture, Florina," said Zsombor. "I don't know why that photo is so important, but it looks great already."

Chapter 7

Welcome to Hotel Balaton

This was not a regular Martian highway motel. No, this was an exclusive resort for the rich and famous. No matter how much cash Borbala had managed to accrue, there was no way they had enough money to stay here. That didn't matter much because all Florina and Zsombor actually wanted was to get on that rocket parked outside. They had to find out whose launcher that was and figure out a way to get on it and off the planet. They walked up to the reception desk to make some inquiries with Angoona crawling naked behind them on the floor.

"Welcome to Hotel Balaton," said the receptionist. "How may I help you?"

"We need some information on that launcher parked outside," said Zoltan.

"I'm sorry, sir," said the receptionist. "You may be a police officer, but according to your badge, you're Sopron city police. That means you're way out of your jurisdiction. I'm afraid I have to ask you all to leave, and that includes that naked whore crawling behind you on the floor."

"Did you just call my wife-to-be a whore?" asked Zoltan in an angry voice and raised his gun to the receptionist's head. "Now listen up, you fuck! You're going to apologize to Angoona. We will have three rooms, and we will be paying cash upon check-out, and you're going to tell us everything about whoever that is with that rocket outside, or else I'll blow your fucking brains out.

"In addition to that, Angoona here will empty her semen tank in your face. Angoona, spray him in the face!"

Angoona raised her right hand towards the receptionist, pointed her finger at his face, and shot off a big load of semen into his face.

"Ah, what the fuck?" yelled the receptionist. "You people are disgusting! Stop that, please. I'll talk. The launcher belongs to Mr. Leonardo Michelangelo Botticelli. He's up in his room right now with his wife, but I know he has a meeting in the hotel restaurant in an hour with the Hungarian ambassador.

"Ahh, here are your keys. Your rooms are all next to each other on the third floor. I would have liked to give you all shitty rooms, but we are a six-star hotel, and all our rooms are luxurious. I will call the bellhop to help you with your luggage."

"We'll carry our own luggage. Thanks," said Zoltan. "But you forgot one thing. You didn't apologize to Angoona. Angoona, empty the rest of your tank on him."

Angoona again raised her finger and covered the poor receptionist in semen from the many men she had entertained during the course of the day.

The amount of cash Borbala had was not nearly enough to cover the cost of the rooms, but that would be her problem in the morning. Of course, Borbala knew this, but she was a pretty clever lady, and she already had a secret plan to deal with that.

They all thought it would be a good idea to freshen up a bit before intercepting Mr. Leonardo Michelangelo Botticelli at his meeting in the restaurant in an hour.

Zsombor explained that Mr. Botticelli was the richest man on Mars. His name alone would have cost millions, but for him it was free since he personally controlled the rights to all languages on Mars, except Hungarian, of course. When they got to their rooms, they agreed to meet in exactly one hour downstairs in the restaurant.

Well in their room Florina poured two glasses of wine from the minibar and secretly slipped a Didgeridick into one of them because she knew this might be her last chance to get some of that famous Martian low gravity sex, and she wanted it to be really good. Meanwhile Zsombor had secretly taken a Didgeridick because he wanted to impress Florina with some extra size and power. Zsombor was already running out of space in his pants as Florina and he drank the wine and gently helped each other get undressed.

"Something's wrong," said Zsombor. "It's too big! This is not normal."

"I only gave you one Didgeridick," said Florina. "You're getting baseball-bat-sized again!"

"What? No! You gave me a Didgeridick? Oh fuck! I just took one myself. That means I had two. Oh no, I'm going to die a horrible death now. Bye Florina, it was nice knowing you. You might want to take cover. It's going to get messy when I blow up."

Luckily, this time Florina knew exactly what to do. She calmly grabbed the minibar fridge, poured its contents on the floor, and banged it against a counter edge to split it open. She grabbed a piece of foam from the insulating wall and gave it to Zsombor to chew on. His erection decreased, and he was safe. Unable to please his lady, but he was alive and well.

"Florina, how did you know that fridge insulation reacts with Didgeridick that way, and why was my fridge slaughtered when I woke up this morning, and why was I puking chunks of foam, and why don't I have any memory of us making love last night?"

"Too many questions, Zsombor. Now listen up. We're leaving this planet tonight, and I haven't had a chance to try that very famous Martian sex everyone's talking about. Now are you going to give it to me or not?"

"I'll give it to you, Florina, but no Didgeridick!"

"Ahh come on, Zsombor!" begged Florina. "Just one single Didgeridick, please."

"Ok," said Zsombor. "I'll take half a Didgeridick."

"Deal!" said Florina and broke a Didgeridick pill in half and gave Zsombor. "Now wash it down with this water."

Zsombor took the half pill and washed it down with the glass of water Florina had given to him, the very same glass of water that Florina had slipped the other half of the broken pill into. Soon Zsombor was a very respectable size, but not dangerously large. Florina finally got to enjoy her long awaited Martian sex.

"Zsombor," said Florina after they were done. "That was really great! I never imagined the Reverse Skull Crusher would be that much fun. I could really get used to living with you here on this planet, too bad we have to leave tonight. What's the gravity on Callisto anyway?"

"About a third of Mars, I think." Zsombor replied.

"A third! Oh fuck, that's light enough to try the Castrator," laughed Florina. "Hey, look at the time! We have to get down to the restaurant."

When they got down to the restaurant, Zoltan and Angoona were already there. Angoona was dressed in a bed sheet with a hole cut in the middle of it for her head, forming a crude poncho. Zsombor and Florina joined them at their table.

"See that fat guy with the moustache at the table next to ours?" whispered Zoltan discretely. "That's the Hungarian ambassador waiting for Mr. Botticelli. I bribed the waiter to seat us at the table next to theirs."

"Good job, Zoltan," complimented Florina. "And Angoona, you look great! What are you wearing?"

"Oh dear Florina," said Angoona. "Zoltan made me this beautiful evening dress after we had wonderful and passionate doori time. Zoltan and I are getting married. We will have a big wedding, and you are invited, of course. Did you two have wonderful and passionate doori time too?"

"Haha, you know it, Angoona," laughed Florina. "He is not as bad as you've been saying. He's quite talented, I must say."

"Oh my dear Florina," said Angoona. "Those are probably the things I taught him. When he first bought me, he was absolutely terrible. He would just lie there like a statue, and I would do all the work. Not like Zoltan. No, Zoltan is like a virtuoso playing me like his musical instrument. He knows exactly what to do with my body at all times to put us both in perfect sexual harmony with each other. I only had doori time with Zsombor because I was his property, and I had to. With Zoltan I want it more, the more we do it."

141

"Ah, what the fuck? Angoona," said Zsombor. "I'm sitting right here, you know? Can we please change the topic?"

They were interrupted by Borbala who suddenly appeared by their table dressed to kill. She had put on some very sexy make-up, a very glittery and sexy dress, and a large amount of very expensive looking jewelry.

"Borbala?" asked Florina. "Why are you dressed like that? Where did you get that dress and that jewelry?"

"Oh, someone left their door open, so I snuck in and borrowed some stuff," answered Borbala and sat down. "Didn't want to show up looking like a hobo. No no, that would not be good tonight. Tonight I'm landing the big one."

"What do you mean by landing the big one, Borbala?" asked Florina.

"You'll know soon, Florina," smiled Borbala.

"Are you ladies and gentlemen ready to order?" asked the waiter.

"Oh, I know," said Florina. "Do you guys have Moon Pudding? We had some earlier today, and it was so good."

"Yes, of course. We do have Moon Pudding," replied the waiter. "And to drink?"

"Perfect!" said Florina. "We'll all have Moon Pudding and whatever wine you think goes well with it."

The waiter brought the Moon Puddings to the table, and they all ate with a healthy appetite, except Angoona who had no need for food.

"Ah, Florina," said Zoltan. "You have very good taste. Moon Pudding is my favorite dish too. Every time I have it, it makes me think of my mother. She used to make the best Moon Pudding. I miss her Moon Pudding so much," said Zoltan as a tear slipped out of his eye.

"I'm so sorry," said Florina. "I didn't mean to make you sad about your mom. Did she pass away long ago?"

"Oh no," said Zoltan. "She's alive and well. She just can't make Moon Pudding anymore, not since her menopause."

"I don't get it," said Florina confused. "How can you lose your ability to make a certain dish when you hit menopause? Do you need some kind of youthful agility to make Moon Pudding?"

"No, of course not," said Zoltan. "But after menopause the main ingredient stops showing up, and that's usually the end of Moon Pudding. Angoona will never be able to make me Moon Pudding since she's a robot and has no output of that sort, but I love her anyway. I think the name of the dish has its origins in the Earth moon's cycle, which if I understand it correctly approximately matches a woman's menstrual cycle."

"Are you telling me what I think you're telling me, Zoltan?" asked Florina. "Are you telling me this finished plate of pudding in front of me here was made from another woman's menses? Is that what you're telling me, Zoltan?"

"Yes, of course, Florina," said Zoltan. "You didn't know that?"

"No, I certainly didn't," said Florina and went quiet for a moment.

"Waiter!" Florina called after her silence. "Bring us another round of Moon Puddings, please, and give my compliments to the chef and the donor."

"Hey, Zsombor," said Florina. "I'm due in a week. I'll make us some then. Zoltan will give me his mom's recipe, I'm sure.

"Hey wait, there's Leonardo and his wife now."

Mr. Leonardo Michelangelo Botticelli entered the restaurant with his wife. Mr. Botticelli was a very old man, probably in his mid nineties, dressed in a very flamboyant colorful suit decorated with gem stones of various types. His wife, about seventy years his junior, was angrily complaining about how someone had stolen her jewelry and her most elegant evening dress from their room earlier. They sat down at the neighbor table with the Hungarian ambassador and started talking to him in a very strange and incomprehensible language.

"What the fuck is that weird language?" asked Florina quietly. "How are we supposed to spy on them if we don't understand what they're saying?

"Angoona, do you have some kind of built-in translation function, so you can translate what they're saying?"

"Hold on, Florina. I'm downloading one right now," said Angoona.

"Ok, done. They're speaking Hungarian. Would you like me to translate their conversation now?"

"Hungarian?" asked Florina. "Who the fuck speaks Hungarian? Mr. Botticelli is Hungarian? Yes, Angoona, please translate."

"Ok," whispered Angoona. "Mr. Botticelli is telling the ambassador that the integration of the Hungarian language on Mars is complete, and it's time to move to the next phase which is to make Hungarian the most expensive language on Mars. Now that almost everything and everyone has a Hungarian name, it will be too inconvenient for most to switch, and Mr. Botticelli and the Hungarian government will make unimaginable financial profits from their scheme to pass Hungarian off as an open source language only to switch it to a paid language later."

"The fucking bastards!" interrupted Zsombor. "This whole language mess we've been in has been a Hungarian conspiracy to extract money from innocent Martians?"

"Hush, Zsombor," said Florina. "Let Angoona continue."

"Ok," continued Angoona. "The ambassador is saying that there is a man in Sopron working on an artificial language called Naruemonian based on a combination of Australian Aboriginal languages that can be easily understood and used by English speakers that could circumvent the whole language control system on Mars. He's saying that this man must be dealt with at any cost. He must be approached and offered a large sum of money for giving Mr. Botticelli the rights to his language. Probably around a hundred or a hundred-and-twenty should be enough, but not more than a hundred-and-fifty. The problem is that this man is currently wanted by the police, and his whereabouts are unknown."

"Holy fuck!" said Zsombor. "That's me! He wants to give me a-hundred-and-fifty thousand rubles!"

"Yes," said Florina. "This is perfect! We have something Botticelli needs desperately, and we can trade it for use of his launcher and a ride on whatever lavish ship he has in orbit."

"Yeah," said Zsombor. "But what about the whole taking advantage of innocent Martians thing? Extracting money for something that should be absolutely free. Isn't that just plain wrong?"

"Ah, Zsombor," said Florina. "Fuck that! Don't be such a fucking wuss! This couldn't be any more perfect. All we have to do is walk over there, introduce ourselves, and make a deal with him. We'll be out of here quietly within half an hour."

"What? No!" said Borbala. "That completely fucks up my plan."

"What, Borbala?" asked Florina in great surprise. "You have a plan? Plan about what? What is your play here?"

Without any further hesitation Borbala stepped up on the table.

"METER MAID! This woman is a meter maid!" she screamed at the top of her lungs and pointed straight at Mr. Botticelli's young trophy wife Mrs. Botticelli.

"Meter maids are the scum of the universe!" yelled an angry man from across the restaurant.

"Kill Rita!" yelled another man.

People from all over the restaurant ran towards Mrs. Botticelli and started beating her with anything they could find. A woman broke a bottle over Mrs. Botticelli's head. A man broke a chair over her back. Another man was on the floor with Mrs. Botticelli's lower thigh in his mouth attempting to bite her leg off.

"Goodness! They're going to kill her!" exclaimed Florina. "Zoltan, you're a cop. Do something!"

146

"You're right, Florina. They need my help," said Zoltan. Then he grabbed his fork, joined the angry mob, and stabbed Mrs. Botticelli in the eye.

In the early days of Martian colonization the infamous dictator Sibongile Mugabe had employed an army of meter maids to torture and execute political prisoners. Meter maids, being losers with sadistic personalities longing for a chance to inflict a much higher degree of misery in innocent people than a mere parking ticket ever could, have the perfect personality for careers in torture and imprisonment of kind decent people. This was a fact not forgotten by Martians who had endured years of terror under Sibongile's oppressive regime. The mere mention of meter maids struck a chord of anger and disgust in most Martians, who all knew far too well that meter maids were nothing but dormant concentration camp guards, dictator cohort bullies, and torturers.

"That woman is going to be dead in less than a minute," said Florina to Zsombor.

"She's a meter maid," replied Zsombor. "In good times meter maids just give out parking tickets, but as soon as a dictator takes over, they're the first to join his ranks to do the dirtiest work of his regime. These people are happy to torture and execute people who are not only innocent, but ones that at great risk to themselves dare to stand up for what's right. Given the opportunity, that woman being killed over there would be carrying out horrible crimes against humanity. If we're punishing people who when given the opportunity to commit such crimes did, should we then refrain from punishing the ones who didn't even though they would have, given the right circumstances?"

"Yes, I know. Everyone knows meter maids are the lowest form of life in the universe," replied Florina. "What I meant is that they're killing her fast when they should be permanently crippling and deforming her, so she can live out her days in agonizing misery to give her the punishment she deserves."

Mr. Botticelli had a sizeable entourage of security personnel placed strategically around the restaurant who all came running to Mrs. Botticelli's rescue.

Unfortunately, Mrs. Botticelli was no match for an angry meter maid hating mob, and she was dead within the first seconds of the brawl. By the time Mr. Botticelli's bodyguards had overpowered the attackers, there were several dead and injured on both sides.

Mr. Botticelli dropped to his knees in grief when he saw his young wife's lifeless body.

"My brand new wife, I've only had her for a week. It was you!" growled Mr. Botticelli and pointed at Borbala.

"I don't have a wife anymore because of you! I'm 94. I'm going to die alone unless I find a new one quick. Why have you done this to me?

"By the way, your outfit looks very familiar, and how did you know my wife was a meter maid until I married her last week?"

"I'm so sorry, Mr. Botticelli," said Borbala in a very sexy voice. "I don't know what came over me. Is there anything I can do to make you feel better in this time of great personal crisis?"

"Please don't call me Mr. Botticelli," said Mr. Botticelli. "Call me Leonardo, and may I ask what your name is?"

"I'm Borbala," said Borbala and stepped down from the table and kneeled down on the floor by Mr. Botticelli. "I know you've just lost your wife, but you always have a friend in me, Leonardo," she said and kissed him gently.

"Not good enough, Borbala," said Mr. Botticelli. "I don't need a friend. I need a wife!"

Mr. Botticelli pulled his dead wife's wedding ring off her finger and held it up towards Borbala.

"Listen, Borbala dear, at my age you have to act fast because you might be dead tomorrow. Ambassador Takacs here is legally authorized to perform wedding ceremonies," said Mr. Botticelli. "He will wed us. Dr. Takacs, do your thing."

"What?" said Dr. Takacs in surprise. "Oh alright, sure. By the power vested in me by the Republic of Hungary, I now pronounce you husband and wife. You may kiss."

Borbala was now the new Mrs. Botticelli, the richest woman on Mars and the heir to a vast business empire. What would happen after the death of Mr. Botticelli one might wonder? Such wealth and such power in the hands of someone like Borbala.

"What the fuck just happened?" wondered Florina who had been watching the events of the last few minutes in complete disbelief.

Zoltan and Zsombor were as shocked as Florina and were struggling to process how Borbala had ascended from nowhere to the very top of human interplanetary society in a matter of a few minutes. Angoona, on the other hand, was uninterested in the whole thing and had decided to befriend a group of businessmen seated at a nearby table where she was currently entertaining them one by one under the table.

"Where's Angoona?" asked Zoltan. "Oh look, there are her feet sticking out from under that tablecloth. She must have been frightened by the commotion and hid under that table. Hey, Angoona! Over here, it's safe now."

"Ah goody," said Angoona, as she crawled back to Zoltan. "That was intense; those guys had a lot of backed up pressure. I think I need to empty my tank again."

Zoltan was a bit confused but figured she must be referring to the fight in some way. Borbala was probably done for the time being, so Florina and Zsombor thought this would be a good time to approach Mr. Botticelli.

"Mr. Botticelli," said Florina. "We're friends of your new wife. I'm Florina, and this here is Zsombor Zalaegerszegi of Sopron; he is the one working on that new hybrid language you are interested in."

"Pleased to meet you both," said Mr. Botticelli. "Say Florina, I've been working with languages my whole life. Is that a Montevideo accent I'm picking up? Very unusual and interesting for a lady of your exotic ethnicity. Are you from Montevideo?"

"Indeed I am, Mr. Botticelli," said Florina. "But I've been living by myself in the countryside for some time. I'm not allowed near any population centers without a police escort, and I have to live two-hundred meters away from anybody else's home. Those were the terms of my release, unfortunately. That was, of course, until I was deported to Mars. I love it here on Mars that I can just go anywhere I please."

"Well, I'm glad you like it here, Florina. How about you, Zsombor, you're the man who created Naruemonian?" asked Mr. Botticelli excitedly. "That's fantastic! This is my lucky day! I outlive my 26-year-old wife. I get a new wife. The mysterious missing linguist walks right up to me. You guys can all call me Leonardo.

"One question, Zsombor, why did you name your language Naruemonian? How did you know about the secret continent Naruemonia?"

"It's not that secret if it's in a book now, is it?" laughed Zsombor.

"Good point," said Leonardo. "Listen, I will buy the rights to Naruemonian. We'll write a contract right now on this napkin. There should be a pen in my wife's pocket."

Borbala looked in her pocket, but there was no pen.

"Sorry," said Leonardo. "I meant the dead wife there on the floor. If you flip her over on her back, there should be a pen in a pocket on the inside of her blouse. Be careful not to ruin your clothes with her blood."

Zoltan rolled the dead woman over with the sole of his shoe, so as not to get any blood on the top of it. Her clothes were soaked in her blood, and there was no way to access the inside of her blouse without opening it and getting blood on your hands. Zoltan was a seasoned police officer after all, and he had seen worse.

"Leonardo," said Zoltan as he dug around inside the dead woman's blouse. "Your dead wife had a really nice rack. You sure know how to pick 'em."

"Yes, I will miss those knockers dearly," said Leonardo. "Borbala, how are yours?"

Borbala opened her dress and showed Leonardo her breasts.

"Oh yes, my dear Borbala!" exclaimed the old man. "Those will do very nicely. Even nicer than my dead wife's."

"Leonardo," said Zoltan. "There's no pen here."

"It's a very loose pocket," said Leonardo. "The pen might have slid out in the commotion and fallen down into her underwear."

Zoltan proceeded to search inside the dead woman's panties.

"Leonardo," said Zoltan. "Your dead wife had a really nice ass. I mean really nice, like porn star nice!"

"Yes, Zoltan my friend," said Leonardo. "She did have a fantastic rear. Borbala, how is your ass?"

Borbala pulled up her dress and showed Leonardo her ass.

"Hmm," said Leonardo approvingly. "Very nice. You have a very nice ass, Borbala. You look like a keeper."

"There's no pen in her underwear," said Zoltan. "But it looks like there's a pen sticking out of her vagina. It must have fallen down into her underwear and then slid up there somehow. Let me try to get it out. Say, Leonardo, your dead wife had a very tight vagina. I will have to use a bit of force to pull the pen out of her."

"Zoltan," said Leonardo. "I think if it's tight enough to keep a pen lodged in, that's probably not her vagina."

"You're right, my bad," said Zoltan. "The pen is not in her vagina. Alright, let's check the vagina then. Yes tight, but not as tight, of course."

"I'm not sure what you're doing in her vagina if there's no pen in there, Zoltan," said Leonardo. "But yes, she did have a fairly tight vagina. Borbala, how tight is your vagina?" Once again Leonardo turned to ask his new wife.

"No! Basta ya!" interrupted Florina. "Enough of this! You can check her vagina later. Here! Use my pen instead, and may I say the love and respect you show for your late wife is only matched by the love and respect you show for your new wife Borbala. You two were truly made for each other."

"Oh, you have a pen too," said Leonardo. "How wonderful! Then let's write the contract. What would you like for your language?"

"Listen, Zsombor," whispered Florina to Zsombor. "He's willing to go up to a hundred-and-fifty, so you will ask for two hundred. He will offer one hundred, and in the end you meet at one-fifty. After that you ask to borrow his launcher and spaceship and deduct the cost from the amount."

"I think it's worth two hundred," said Zsombor to Leonardo and winked at Florina.

Shocked over the high opening bid, Leonardo turned to Dr. Takacs and told him in Hungarian that that motherfucker wanted two hundred million rubles.

"Two hundred? No no no, Zsombor. I can offer you one hundred. That's a lot of money, Zsombor, even for me."

"Ok, Leonardo," said Zsombor. "One fifty, and we're both happy."

"You drive a hard bargain, but you've got a deal," said Leonardo a bit disappointed since he had hoped not to spend more than a-hundred-and-twenty million rubles, but it was worth it.

"One more thing though," said Zsombor. "We'd like to rent your launcher and spaceship for a trip to Callisto and deduct the cost from the money you will pay me. How much would that run, you think?"

"Oh, not that much considering how much money you're going to have, Zsombor," laughed Leonardo. "About two hundred thousand rubles or so."

"Two hundred thousand!" said Zsombor shocked. "That's a bit over my budget. If you're paying me a hundred and fifty thousand for Naruemonian, I won't have enough to rent your ship."

"Thousand?" asked Leonardo. "Thousand! Tell you what, Zsombor. We'll call it even. You sign over the rights to Naruemonian, and I'll let you use my ship for a trip to Callisto, that way it's like you got two hundred thousand."

"You've got a deal, Leonardo. Where do I sign?"

"Right here on this napkin, Zsombor," said Leonardo. "Right here."

"Got it!" exclaimed Zoltan from the floor. "I got the pen out of her! I had to pull and twist pretty hard, but it's out now."

"It's fine, Zoltan. We've already got a pen. Go ahead and stick it back in there if you want." Zsombor told him jokingly.

"All right, Zsombor," said Leonardo. "Naruemonian is mine, and you can board the launcher that will take you up to the ship in orbit any time. It's a small but nice ship. I'll tell the captain you will be boarding soon. There's another passenger on board, my personal penile enhancement surgeon. He was doing some enhancement surgery on me on the way here from Earth. He'll just have to go along with you guys, I suppose. This is the fastest passenger cruiser there is, and it'll take you there in about a week. Is it all four of you guys going or just the two of you?"

"Oh, Angoona and I are staying here on Mars," said Zoltan while wiping blood from himself. "So just Zsombor and Florina."

"Well, Zsombor and Florina," said Leonardo. "I'm glad I met you two, and I wish you both a pleasant journey to Callisto. I hope we meet again someday."

"Thanks, Leonardo," said Zsombor. "It was a pleasure doing business with you."

"And I hope you and Borbala will take good care of each other," added Florina.

Florina and Zsombor said farewell to Zoltan, Angoona, and Borbala. They gathered their belongings and boarded the launcher. They strapped into their seats, and the launcher took off up into the Martian sky. The launcher was fully automated with a passenger compartment the size of a large van with seating for eight passengers. All they had to do was enjoy the short ride to space and wait until the launcher docked with the ship that was waiting for them in orbit.

"Hey, Zsombor," said Florina as the rocket ascended. "You know that evil Leonardo guy was talking about millions and not thousands, right?"

"What? You mean he wanted to pay me a hundred and fifty million rubles?"

"Yes." Florina answered.

"Why didn't you say something? We could have been super rich! Do you understand how much money that is, Florina? There's something really wrong with you, Florina, something really really wrong!"

"I like you, Zsombor. You're nice. Leonardo is not nice. Did you see how he treated his own wives, both dead and living? I didn't want you to become something like that. A certain amount of money is nice to have, but too much poisons your soul, Zsombor. That and I was afraid that immense wealth would distract us from our very important mission. What we do Zsombor is much more important than getting rich. If someone needs wealth as a carrot for promoting space exploration, that's fine, but you and I, we don't need that. Our motivation is pure and not a secondary derivative of some other motivation. We do what we do for the sake of spreading Earth life, Zsombor. Besides, do you really want to end up a man in his nineties with a twenty-something trophy wife?"

"There's no way I'm going to live that long as long as I'm with you, Florina," said Zsombor. "You'll probably have us both killed together within a week, if not sooner."

"That's so sweet of you, Zsombor. You mean we're going to spend the rest of our lives together?"

"You have a very strange way of looking at things, Florina, but yes, I suppose that is the case based on how dangerous my life has become since I met you, and thanks for rescuing me from all that money."

Chapter 8

Florina in Space

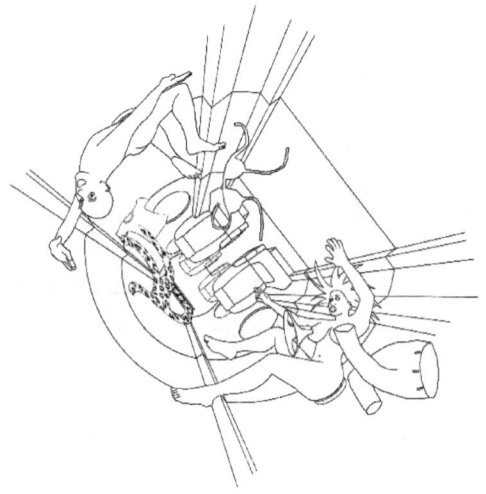

The launcher had now reached Martian orbit, and through the window Florina and Zsombor could see planet Mars below them in all its red glory. Although the fasten seat belt sign was still lit, they both unbuckled from their launch seats and floated around the cabin enjoying the weightlessness. It would be another half hour before they would rendezvous with the ship which was at a different position in its orbit.

"Hey, Zsombor, is this your first time in zero gravity?"

"It sure is, Florina. Are you thinking what I'm thinking?"

"I'm pretty sure I am, Zsombor," said Florina and slipped out of her very sexy leopard cat suit. "We have thirty minutes."

"Didgeridick?" asked Zsombor.

"No, let's try with just Zsombor," said Florina with a smile.

Zsombor slipped out of his clothes as well, and they were soon entangled in a floating romantic embrace. Making love in zero gravity sounds great in theory, but in practice it is quite tricky since there is no bottom surface to use as a frictional base. They were both struggling to find foot holds and hand holds to help them in their love making effort. They were both just rolling around together in weightlessness with both of them grabbing for things around them that might be able to support them.

Passengers were supposed to remain strapped in their seats during the whole flight. What Florina and Zsombor were doing was considered very dangerous and absolutely not allowed. In case a fire was detected, passengers were to put on the oxygen masks that were available at each seat, and two round porthole vents would open on each side of the cabin releasing all the air out into space instantly putting out any fire. The portholes would then close, and new air would be released into the cabin. This fire safety system was automatic, but it could also be activated manually by pulling any of the red handles marked with a picture of a flame positioned throughout the cabin. Coincidentally these handles made for great holds for zero gravity sexual activities.

As they bounced towards a side wall face to face with each other, Florina grasped behind Zsombor and felt one of these very easy to grab handles. "Perfect," she thought and grabbed it.

"Zsombor," she said. "I've got something to grab here behind you. If I hold it tight, you can push against the wall and thrust into me," said Florina and kissed Zsombor passionately as he thrust hard into her, hard enough to give the handle enough pull force to activate the fire emergency system.

An alarm went off, and an orange light started blinking. A pre-recorded voice instructed them to immediately put on their oxygen masks, ensure their seat straps were tight, and at all cost stay away from the portholes that were opening in three… two… one…

"What the fuck is going on?" wondered Florina. "What portholes? Why are there portholes on spaceships?"

"I have no clue," replied Zsombor. "No, wait! There's a round thing opening behind you."

The portholes opened, and the air quickly started leaving the cabin. Everything loose flew towards one of the two portholes, including Florina and Zsombor. They flew straight towards one of the all eating sucking holes. They were far too big to be sucked out into space, but Florina's left butt cheek was sucked right into one of the portholes with great force and plugged it perfectly.

The impact made Zsombor lose his grip of Florina. He was pulled out of her towards the opposite side of the cabin by the escaping air. He tried to grab the top of a seat on his way to the other side which only flipped him around, so he was now floating towards the opposite porthole forwards instead of backwards. He landed on the wall over the porthole and tried to push with his arms and legs not to get sucked in. With his knees and one arm pushing against the wall, he used his free hand to grab whatever loose items he could find to block the porthole. He managed to block most of it, except for a small area the size of a large coin.

Zsombor looked around for more loose items but found nothing. In the end the force was too strong; he could no longer push against the sucking force, and he ended up with his manhood being sucked out through the small hole and him being stuck with his face against the wall. The most important part of his body was now dangling outside the space capsule.

"Florina! Are you alright?" asked Zsombor. "I'm stuck, and your little friend is out in space."

159

"I'm stuck too, Zsombor, and my butt cheek is out in space. I think we stopped the air from escaping, but my butt cheek feels like it's burning. How about your little soldier, Zsombor?"

"It was burning at first," said Zsombor. "But now it's just numb. I think we'll just have to wait for the launcher to dock, and then they can pull us loose."

"Hey, Zsombor," said Florina.

"Yeah?"

"I like you better without that Didgeridick stuff. Let's not use that anymore."

"Well, we'll see what's left of the little guy after his spacewalk," laughed Zsombor.

They heard the clank of the ship's connecting mechanism against the launcher, and the hatch opened up.

"Hello there," said a very frail white-bearded old man in a captain's uniform with a Russian accent. "I'm Captain Molotov. What the hell is going on here? Why are you two lodged naked in the emergency portholes? Do you know what the radiation outside these walls will do to you?"

The crew was minimal and consisted of Captain Sergey Molotov who piloted the ship and his wife Olga, a heavy set babushka who did all the cooking and cleaning on board. Sometimes Olga would pilot the ship when Sergey had had too much vodka to function. Then there was also Dr. Qwo, the surgeon that Mr. Botticelli had brought along with him. The three managed to pry Florina and Zsombor loose and take them into the spaceship where Dr. Qwo could examine them.

"Florina," said Dr. Qwo. "You have third degree burns on your left buttock. You'll have a big circular scar on your butt for life, and you'll be sleeping on your right side for a while. Other than that you'll be fine.

"I wish that was the case for you too, Zsombor. There's good news and bad news. The bad news is that I'm going to have to amputate what's left of your penis."

"WHAT?!" screamed Zsombor in complete hysteria. "No no no! That's an important part of me, Doctor! Isn't there anything you can do?"

"Calm down, Zsombor," said Dr. Qwo. "I haven't gotten to the good news yet. The good news is that I can install a robotic penis in its stead. It will function like a regular penis, and it will be connected to your existing nerves, so you will have normal penile sensations. You are very lucky that I happen to have one on board. I was installing one just like it on Mr. Botticelli on the way over here, and I brought a spare. This is the most advanced robotic penis to date. You will be the second person in the solar system after Mr. Botticelli to have one.

"This device is a technological marvel. It has an impressively large variety of sexual functions. You can set it to different sizes and angles. You can even set it to impregnate or not. My wife has been bugging me to get one of these myself, and if you can keep it a secret, I'm having one installed for her birthday."

Dr. Qwo seemed like a very competent doctor, thought Zsombor, and he really needed a functioning penis of some sort, especially now that he had a crazy sex maniac for company. He was prepped for the surgery and given anesthesia. Zsombor passed out, and Dr. Qwo performed his surgery.

Zsombor woke up from his anesthesia after the surgery in a daze. He looked over to his side where Florina was sitting holding his hand. Florina hadn't noticed that Zsombor had woken up. She was too busy looking at Zsombor's lower regions, and she appeared to be very aroused and kept saying numbers.

"Eight, ten, eleven, seven..."

He looked down towards his feet and was met by a very scary sight. A giant monster was pointing straight up to the ceiling changing size very fast based on Florina's commands.

"Florina," said Zsombor in a daze. "How did it go? What's going on?"

"Oh Zsombor dear, you're awake," said Florina. "Soft," she commanded.

Zsombor's new equipment took on a resting position. "Your new penis is fantastic. Dr. Qwo set it to react to my voice. If I say 'erect ten,' your penis takes on a ten-inch erection. If I say 'nine,' it changes size to nine inches. If I say 'soft,' it goes soft. It has all kinds of other voice activated functions too. It vibrates and thrusts on its own if you're too drunk. It even has a built in flash light."

"Wow!" said Zsombor. "That is amazing. Let me try. Erect ten," said Zsombor, but nothing happened. "Nothing's happening. What's wrong?"

"Oh," said Florina. "It only reacts to my voice, not yours."

"You mean I will only be able to use him when you're around?" asked Zsombor.

"Is that a problem, Zsombor?

"No, I didn't think so!" said Florina sternly. "You can still pee on your own, but all other functions are with me only. Dr. Qwo forgot to sample your voice before he put you to sleep, so he used mine instead. It's burned into the chip and cannot be changed after installation. Don't worry, Zsombor. You don't need him for anything fun without me around, do you?"

"I guess not, Florina," said Zsombor. "But I do hope you plan to have a lot of fun with your little robotic friend."

"Oh, I do, Zsombor," said Florina in a voice spiced with desire. "Let's try him out right now."

Florina and Zsombor spent the rest of the day trying out the various functions of Zsombor's new robotic penis. The sound insulation on the ship was not the best, so Captain Molotov and Dr. Qwo, both being great fans of Chinese opera, put some on at high volume to mask the sounds coming from Florina and Zsombor's cabin. Captain Molotov would have preferred the great disco tunes of Marsalina Valentina, but since he and Marsalina had some common history from back in the Martian disco days his wife wouldn't let him play her music on the ship.

Dr. Qwo explained to Captain Molotov that this is usually how couples behave after the installation of a robotic penis, upon which Captain Molotov asked if Dr. Qwo could install one on him too. Dr. Qwo agreed to install one on Captain Molotov once they were back on Earth since he only brought the one he installed on Mr. Botticelli and the spare that was now installed on Zsombor.

Apart from testing out Zsombor's equipment, Florina also had some important work to do. She had to run more detailed tests combining the samples she had retrieved at MILPh with samples of unmutated Sibongile to see if it would mutate. She also had samples of the mutated algae to bring to Callisto, if all else failed, to determine if it could be made to reproduce there in a post mutation state.

Florina's tests were not going well. Nothing seemed to make Sibongile mutate into the fantastic new type that could grow in an ultra thin atmosphere. Well, Frank had set up a real lab on Callisto. As long as she got the samples there, there would be a decent chance of success. The most important thing was to keep the samples of the mutated Sibongile safe. As long as nothing happened to them, a detailed analysis of them could yield information that could be used to backtrack the process and find out what caused the mutation.

Florina had the precious samples of the mutated Sibongile in a pot with an airtight dome. The inside of the dome was kept at Martian atmospheric composition and Martian pressure at all times by an automatic system built into the pot.

Mr. Botticelli's ship was quite sizeable and luxurious for such a small number of people with the travel module rotating on the end of a beam to create gravity and the machinery module on the other end as counterweight. The travel module consisted of three large cabin suites at one end, a common lounge and dining area in the middle, and the personnel area with the command deck and the kitchen in the other end.

When Florina and Zsombor weren't busy testing samples or enjoying Zsombor's new gear, they would go out to the lounge and watch a movie or chat with Dr. Qwo. Sometimes Mrs. Molotova would come and join in when she wasn't busy cooking or cleaning. Captain Molotov would show up very briefly from time to time and have a cup of coffee or a shot of vodka, and then he would go back to work.

"Pardon my curiosity, Florina," asked Dr. Qwo inquisitively one day in the lounge. "What is it exactly you do and why are you both headed to Callisto?"

"Oh," said Florina. "We're transporting samples of different chemicals that might cause a mutation in an algae that allows it to live in ultra thin atmospheres."

"That's fascinating," replied Dr. Qwo. "That would mean life could thrive on worlds that until now would have been written off as permanently dead. Am I right?"

"Yes, Dr. Qwo," replied Florina. "As Paramount Obligationists our goal is to spread Earth life to as many worlds as possible before the human race goes extinct."

"Well, you'd better hurry," laughed Dr. Qwo. "The human race is in decline on Earth already. Every species goes extinct sooner or later, of course, usually succumbing to another better adapted species or due to inability to adapt to a change in its environment. In the case of the human race, however, it seems more like involuntary but conscious suicide. In order to increase the amount of food we can extract in the short term, we knowingly poison our own food supply destroying our health and viability in the longer term.

"We induce all kinds of disabilities into ourselves to make our lives happier and more comfortable, disabilities that require us to live with the help of science and technology. What then when that science and technology gets disrupted? We die! We rely on machinery to produce our food and to bring our food to us. What happens when the energy supply to that machinery gets disrupted? Death! We are always one crisis away from decimation. The human race has turned itself into a house of cards. We take pride in the ultra complex society we have created, the same ultra complex society that will one day decimate our numbers." Dr. Qwo explained.

"Sure there will be plenty of survivors in the rural areas, but the land will be poisoned, and the resources to rebuild civilization will be depleted. The human race is ingenious enough to rebuild anyway but next time with a lower carrying capacity. Eventually that civilization is destined to destroy itself too just like ours. Every cycle of collapse and regeneration will take a long term toll on the Earth's eco system until she is no longer able to support a civilization.

"Farming will be impossible, and what's left of the human race will slowly degenerate back into what will be left of the animal kingdom. This is the inevitable fate of the human race. No matter how we try to slow down the process of environmental degradation, there is no way civilization will ever have a positive impact on the Earth's eco system. We are just reducing the Earth's carrying capacity faster or slower. Never will we increase it. A few million years after the demise of humanity, the Earth will have recovered sufficiently, and some new animal will evolve intelligence and probably start the whole process all over, eventually meeting the same end as the human race will," elaborated Dr. Qwo.

"Exactly," said Florina in agreement. "That is why it's so important to spread life from Earth to other worlds before we as a species reach our end. It is the task of every intelligent species to create technology to access other worlds and spread life to them. If possible, we should also create new forms of life that can live in places where current forms of Earth life can't."

"Precisely, Florina," added Dr. Qwo. "When I was younger, I was heavily engaged in the environmental issues of the day. I was a humanist at heart, and my perspective was entirely anthropocentric. I, along with all the other people I associated with, wanted to protect the environment so that it could keep providing a good life for the human race. None of us seemed to realize that we weren't actually doing it for the environment itself. Sure we were doing good, like slowing climate change and protecting habitat for wildlife, but it was always from a human

166

perspective. If the sea rises, our cities will flood, so we need to stop climate change. If we lose biodiversity, we lose potential cures to diseases that lost species may hold a key to. The arguments were always from a human perspective.

"The human race is just one species among all the other life forms on Earth. What makes us so deserving of exploiting the rest of the natural world? I realized that some of the things we did in the name of the natural environment were actually working against the Earth's eco system in the long run. Slowing human induced climate change to protect the prosperity of our civilization seemed like a really good thing to do for us environmentalists back then, but I realized that protecting a civilization that is the main and only cause for all the damage caused to Earth's environment can't be good for the environment," explained Dr. Qwo before he continued.

"Perhaps global warming would put brakes on our civilization's relentless growth and thereby reducing its damage to the environment. Perhaps global warming shouldn't be stopped. Perhaps it should even be encouraged to protect nature in the long run. Sure, some species were being disrupted due to shifting climate zones, but that has happened countless times before in Earth's history and is nothing abnormal in itself. I realized that the human race was the root cause of all that was wrong, and any activity that hurries its demise without poisoning the Earth should be encouraged. I knew then that my focus as an environmentalist should be on protecting endangered species and to give them a chance to survive this monumental environmental disaster that I had realized the human race was.

"After a while I realized that my work to protect endangered species, while emotionally rewarding, didn't do much to protect nature in the very long term. Evolution on Earth has reached the point where different species start to evolve high intelligence. We were the first, but there will be more after us, each taming science and creating technology that will eventually destroy them and take another piece of nature with them. Nature eats itself basically by inevitably evolving intelligence."

"Yes," added Florina. "Nature inevitably evolves intelligence, but that intelligence has a very important purpose for nature."

"That's right, Florina," said Dr. Qwo. "After talking to you, I realize that the evolution of intelligence is what nature on Earth, or any other world, needs to spread its nature to other worlds by means of space travel. If one truly loves nature and wants to call oneself an environmentalist, one must support space travel and space colonization. It is inevitable that an intelligent species will cause immense environmental damage to the world it occupies, but that intelligent species has the means to transport life forms from its home world to other worlds. The human race is not at all the horrible menace to the environment that I thought it to be in my youth, rather it is its savior. We are the ones given the great honor to spread Mother Nature beyond Earth."

"It feels good to be on the frontline of Paramount Obligationism," said Florina. "Imagine if you were not involved in space in any way, how would you be able to justify your existence?"

"Oh," said Dr. Qwo. "There's plenty one can do even if one is not directly involved in space. When you buy something, you can research how involved in space a producer of a product is. You can buy your products from a vendor that is involved in space. You can use financial institutions that are involved in space. The more involved in space they are, the better. You can instill a love of space in your children by giving them space toys for Christmas. Encourage them to watch sci-fi. Let them play space video games. Vote for the party or candidate who will do most for space exploration. Oppose those who say space spending is a waste of resources. Anyone opposed to space travel and space colonization is an enemy of Mother Nature."

"You're absolutely right, Dr Qwo," said Captain Molotov who had walked in for a relaxing shot of vodka and overheard the conversation. "An enemy of space travel is an enemy of Mother Nature. Our civilization is crumbling, but that's alright because we're on other worlds now. Can you imagine if we weren't? A horrible sense of doom would have hung over the human race, like a dark cloud of death. We would have known our days were numbered, and we would have nothing to show for it.

"By the way, Florina," wondered Captain Molotov curiously. "That algae I overheard you guys talking about, it doesn't happen to be Sibongile by any chance?"

"Yes, it is!" said Florina in amazement. "Do you know about Sibongile?"

"Ah yes, of course, I do," smiled Captain Molotov and remembered the adventurous days of his youth. "Sibongile, that's a name you don't hear too often these days. Sibongile Mugabe, the first dictator of Mars, named that algae after herself. Of course, after she changed her name to Marsalina Valentina to further her disco career, the algae no longer carried her name. Sibongile sure was a wild one. I helped Sibongile oust the government and become dictator, and then I helped her spread that algae. I'm really happy to hear her algae is mutating. That was exactly what that guy she stole it from hoped it would do.

"I'm 87 years old, and I know I don't have that long left myself, and that's perfectly fine because I used my life to move life to other worlds. My life will have mattered very much when my own last day arrives. At first I didn't think of it that way. It was all about colonizing space in the interest of humanity. We wanted to expand the human race to other worlds. Bringing other life forms along with us was the furthest from our minds, but they came along anyway. Some we brought as crops, livestock, and pets. Some followed along on their own like bugs, mice, and bacteria.

"I was a crew member on the Krasnyy Mars Drakon I, you know? Not the Krasnyy Mars Drakon II that made it to the surface in 1980, but the one that arrived the year before. The lander crashed on its way down killing all seventy on board, many of them close friends of mine. We were devastated by their deaths. The American ship that was a few weeks behind us would now beat us to Mars. Some may have thought that bothered us, but we were all hoping they would land successfully. Well, as we all know they crashed and died too. There were eight of us left in the orbiting ship. It was a very sad return back to Earth, but we knew our comrades had made a worthwhile sacrifice. They knew the risk, and they all died heroes, not only our Soviet countrymen and countrywomen, but also our brothers and sisters on the American ship," said Captain Molotov with great respect.

"Colonizing another world was the greatest honor any human could aspire to. It bound us together in brotherhood across nationalities. Although they were all young people starting out in life, their accomplishments were far greater than someone working their whole life on something not related to space colonization, be it something considered great or not.

"Any of those brave men and women that died on those first two landers is worth more than ten great philanthropists. Space colonization is dangerous and risky. I have been on countless missions, and more comrades than I can count have died a hero's death, but I wouldn't change a thing, and neither would any of my fallen comrades."

"Wow," said Florina. "So you were around when it all started. I wish I could have been there in those days."

"Well yes, Florina," said Captain Molotov. "There was excitement about space colonization in our circles, but among most people the sentiment was very different. In the Soviet Union we didn't read about this in the newspaper, but you heard it on the street all the time. Most people thought the enormous resources we were spending on space were a complete waste. 'Why couldn't we spend that money on hospitals instead?' was what they all said. If you had ever been inside a Soviet hospital, you may have agreed with them yourself. I found out later that the same exact discussion was going on in America. Space colonization had the support of a small segment of society only.

"The public didn't seem to understand what was so important about it. If it had been up to public opinion, we would never have allocated the resources, and we wouldn't be sitting here in a spaceship today having this discussion. We would have been stuck on Earth trying to figure out a way to keep the human race alive for another decade. Thanks to our governments' willingness to go against the opinion of the ignorant and shortsighted public, humanity now has a foothold in space in case something happens to us on Earth.

"After listening to the two of you talking, I have also realized that space colonization serves a much bigger purpose than to ensure the survival of the human race. I never thought of this in a longer perspective than maybe a few thousand years, and that's a lot longer than most people. I had always envisioned a future where mankind has settled the galaxy, thriving on a myriad of worlds, all connected in a fantastic interstellar civilization.

"Now, by expanding my perspective to hundreds of millions of years, even billions of years, I realize that even though spreading humanity to the stars is a noble pursuit, spreading Earth life to other worlds, which is the derivative of colonization, is much more important than colonization itself.

"Well, this bucket isn't going to fly itself, my friends," laughed Captain Molotov and stood up. "I must return to work now."

On the last evening of the journey Florina, Zsombor, and Dr. Qwo were in the lounge watching a movie to pass the time when they heard commotion from the personnel area. Captain Molotov and his wife were screaming at each other in Russian, and you could hear objects being thrown and hitting the walls. Dr. Qwo suggested they put on some Chinese opera at loud volume to mask the noise as they had done when Zsombor and Florina were trying out Zsombor's robotic limb, but Florina thought it would be a better idea to just pretend they hadn't noticed it.

Suddenly the door to the personnel area flew open, and Captain Molotov came running out slamming the door shut behind him, barricading it with his frail old body.

"Help me hold the door, my friends," he asked of the three who all jumped up and came to his aid. "My wife has gone absolutely mad," he continued. "If she gets through this door, it'll be the end of me."

It seemed Mrs. Molotova's anger had given her incredible strength. Even though the four of them were pushing as hard as they could, she managed to push the door open and get into the lounge where she resumed the pummeling of her husband.

"You promised me when I agreed to marry you that you would quit working in space, and look where we are?" yelled Mrs. Molotova while beating her husband. "You should have married that fucking disco whore of yours instead of me, you worthless sack of shit!"

"Leave Marsalina out of this," objected Captain Molotov. "I only fucked her once when I was drunk, and now I have to listen to your jealous bitching anytime one of her songs come on the radio."

"Mrs. Molotova," said Florina while they tried to hold her back from her husband. "Please calm down and tell us what's going on."

"That fucking idiot wants us to die in this fucking tin can is what's going on!" screamed Mrs. Molotova in her Russian accent. "He's going to fly this fucking ship out of the solar system. He's a complete idiot."

"Captain Molotov," asked Florina. "What is she talking about?"

"I was about to tell you all," said Captain Molotov. "But I had to tell my wife first as you will understand. A few hours ago I received a communication from Earth saying that my commercial space pilot's license has been revoked as of midnight tonight based on my advanced age, heavy drinking, and overall diminished physical capacity. Apparently the doctor I bribe for my annual physical checkup was arrested for malpractice and abuse of medical authority for financial gain. As a result, I and several other old space pilots who use his services are having our licenses revoked. That means I can finish any flight currently in progress, but I cannot start any new ones with passengers.

"Dr. Qwo, you will have to disembark on Callisto with Florina and Zsombor, I'm afraid, and catch a commercial flight back to Earth. I will be allowed to pilot the ship back to Earth with my wife where I will have to stop flying commercially. Of course, I don't have money to buy my own spaceship, so that means the flight back to Earth would be my last space flight ever."

"And then we can retire like normal people," added Mrs. Molotova. "But no! Not my idiot husband. No, he has a much better idea! My mother was right! I should have married Vladislav instead of this fucking idiot! Tell them about your brilliant plan, Sergey!"

"Enough of this fucking Vladislav, Olga," shouted Captain Molotov angrily to his wife. "Every time we fight you have to bring up Vladislav! You picked me because I was an idealist who could give you an exciting life in space. Vladislav was a dentist. After talking to Florina and Dr. Qwo the other day, I realized that while my life mission of furthering humanity has been very fruitful, it actually had a much more important aspect all along, the spreading of Earth biology to other worlds.

"I have decided that after I drop the three of you on Callisto, my wife and I will steer the ship towards a solar system 73 light-years away. It is much further away than the latest colonizing missions currently in preparation. However, it does have an earthlike world. I have radioed Callisto, and when you land tomorrow, there will be a man waiting to fill the launcher with supplies for our trip. When the launcher returns here, we will head out. We will do a gravity assist swing by around Jupiter and then head straight towards the distant solar system.

"Once we're on the way, I will do a spacewalk and attach the waste tank to the launcher. We will keep all organic matter in and with the launcher, including the dead body of whoever dies first. The launcher will be kept at very low temperature acting as a freezer. The second one to die will, if possible, do so in the launcher. After I die the ship computer will take over and steer the ship. When both of us are dead, the ship computer will turn off the heating putting everything in the launcher in a zero Kelvin cryogenic freeze. The journey will take a few thousand years, so my wife and I will be dead of old age long before we arrive," Captain Molotov explained.

"Upon arrival the lander will descend to the new world and deliver a payload of biological material to the new planet. It might be a living planet already, and in that case it will benefit from some new input. If it isn't a living planet, well, then it might become one, thanks to me and Olga. Besides, I love what I do.

I'm a spaceman. I need to be in space. Retirement would be torture for me."

"Ah, fuck you, Sergey," said Mrs. Molotova to her husband. "Torture for you maybe, but not for me or any normal person. Vladislav and his wife Tatiana retired and moved to the Black Sea twenty years ago, and they've been living there ever since! They have a nice little house. Their children and grand children come to them and spend their summer vacations with them. Vladislav was crazy about me, and I left him for your stupid ass.

"Vladislav gave his wife a perfect life, and now they're enjoying a perfect retirement together. She must be so incredibly happy when her grandchildren show up at their door, and she knows that even though she's very old and doesn't have much time left, she has accomplished what every woman dreams of, having children and grandchildren. Me? I've been flying around in these fucking cans for the last sixty years with my idiot husband, and now he wants to deny me a minimal lonely retirement on Earth and keep me in this tin can until we die," Mrs. Molotova kept on complaining.

"I should have been the one baking birthday cakes for grandchildren by the Black Sea. At this point in my life I would have to settle for an apartment on the fourteenth floor in a Moscow high rise with my idiot husband who would probably spend the rest of his days drinking himself unconscious every day. Maybe I could go down to the park once a day and feed the pigeons. It would be nothing compared to Tatiana's glorious retirement, but anything is better than this. If you take me on this fucking journey of yours, I hope I die tomorrow already."

"Mrs. Molotova," said Florina trying to calm her down.

"Call me Olga," said Mrs. Molotova. "That was my name before I let this fucking idiot marry me."

"Ok Olga," said Florina. "Tatiana is probably having a very happy life right now, a much happier life than you, no doubt. You are both very old women, and in a few years you will both be dead, and then it's all gone anyway. The feeling of happiness Tatiana is experiencing is just chemicals and electric charges in her brain that is wired to feel happy when she has been able to further her genetic material past her own lifespan. You, on the other hand, Olga, you have no children and no grandchildren as your brain is wired to feel you should have at this age, and that makes you feel miserable and unhappy.

"When Tatiana sees her children and grandchildren thriving, her task as an animal has been completed, and she can happily go to her grave. This is how our species and any other species evolves. The individual with no interest in reproduction exits the gene pool. The ones with a strong interest in reproduction have more offspring, and thus automatically the objective of most individuals in any species becomes to maximize the number of viable descendants. This is the same for any living organism, but, Olga, we are not like the other biological organisms. Having offspring and seeing them thrive may be enough for an animal, but not for us.

"We have the capability and the opportunity to strive for something far higher. We are an intelligent species capable of taming science and creating wonderful technology that can take us to the stars. As members of an intelligent species, some of us have broken out of the bounds of the restrictive animalistic way of thinking and started looking at ourselves as a small but an incredibly important key part of Planet Earth's eco system.

"An eco system, just like any organism, strives to spread itself and to survive and thrive in new places. The human race is only one of countless species in Planet Earth's eco system, but we are the only species that can help the Earth spread itself. Your husband happens to be one of the people who have broken these mental chains. He may have only broken them at a very old age, but better late than never," Florina was now quite convincing.

"Your husband and you will do something that could spread Earth Life to a new world. You could have an impact that lasts a billion years into the future. What does Tatiana have to show for? When she dies, she's gone. When the human race goes extinct, whatever genetic material Tatiana has passed on will be gone. She is just another human animal on planet Earth. You and your husband may become the seeders of a new world. You may be the cause of a new intelligent species evolving on that new world that may one day go to other worlds and spread life. This is our real purpose as intelligent beings, Olga. Spreading the life of your native world to other worlds is the meaning of intelligent life."

Olga went quiet as she was contemplating what Florina had told her. She was an intelligent woman, and she understood Florina was right, but it was still hard for her to come to peace with the concept of living out the remainder of her days in a metal hull. Her husband and she were both 87 years old. Her health was better than her husband's, and she feared he would die first leaving her alone in a spaceship for perhaps a decade where she would slowly battle the ravages of old age alone until her death. If she didn't go senile or get Alzheimer's, she would surely go insane in her loneliness. She thought for a while and came up with a solution.

"Ok Sergey," she said to her husband. "I'll go along with your plan on one condition. I don't want to die alone in this ship, so we're going to make sure my health deteriorates before yours. That means that you will quit drinking, and you will go on a low fat healthy diet for as long as I live. I, on the other hand, will drink heavily every day, and I will switch to a diet consisting of high fat meats, chocolate, pastries, and the like. After I'm dead, you can eat and drink whatever you want again. Do we have a deal?"

Captain Molotov had to take some time to consider. Quit drinking and start eating healthy food? He had never been a fan of health food, and if he didn't get his morning shot of vodka, his hands would start trembling, and he would break out into a cold sweat. His early life as a cosmonaut had been so filled with danger that it never made any sense to worry about cholesterol, liver damage, or alcoholism since there were so many ways you could get killed in space. Very few of his comrades from the old days had made it to old age. Most had died in explosions, implosions, air leaks, or meteor impacts. Since becoming a commercial pilot twenty-something years ago there hadn't been as many close calls, but there had been a few, of course. He particularly remembered this one time when...

"Sergey? Hello! What is wrong with you?" asked Olga. "You've been staring forward with your mouth wide open for five minutes. Do we have a deal?"

"Sorry, my dear," apologized Captain Molotov. "I was just zoning out for a moment. The health food might work, but could I maybe just cut down on the vodka and drink just a little bit?"

"Ok," said Olga. "You can have one shot of vodka in the morning and one shot at night, and you can get as drunk as you want once a week, but that's it."

"Then we have a deal, my dear," said Captain Molotov with a big smile.

The ship arrived in Callisto orbit as scheduled. Florina, Zsombor, and Dr. Qwo said goodbye to Captain Molotov and Olga and wished them much luck on their long journey. Then they boarded the launcher that would take them down to New York City.

The launcher undocked from the ship and started its descent. Callisto was a much smaller world than Mars, and it didn't take

178

long at all before they landed on the surface. Once they touched down, the launcher rolled itself to a spaceport docking gate, and they could enter New York City dragging their belongings which consisted of Florina's samples and a lifetime supply of Didgeridick, which they no longer needed.

Dr. Qwo said farewell to them and rushed off to catch a flight to Earth that was due to leave very soon. A big pile of supplies that Captain Molotov had ordered was stacked at the gate, and a man quickly loaded everything into the launcher. It was a lot of supplies, but in the very low Callistan gravity he could singlehandedly load the whole launcher in a matter of minutes.

Once Florina and Zsombor had loaded their things on a luggage cart, the gate closed behind them. The launcher rolled back to the launch pad and took off back to the ship in orbit. They watched through a window as the launcher took off into the Callistan sky.

Callisto in general was considered lawless, and New York City was one of the worst places on that world. The fact that it was called New York City was illegal. Callisto was in theory governed by the same strict language copyright law as Mars, but Callistans didn't give a hoot. The Americans were the main benefactors of the off-Earth language copyright law, and as a protest the Callistans had named all their cities after big American cities. Not only that, most Callistans carried names of famous Americans as a sign of rebellion and protest.

"Callisto is a very dangerous world, Florina," said Zsombor in a very serious tone. "I have heard so many horrible things about this place. The people here don't care about any rules or laws at all; it's complete anarchy."

"Yes," said Florina excitedly. "I love it already!"

179

Chapter 9

Callisto

New York City on Callisto was a small crater town of about a thousand people. Not a big city by any Earthly standards, but for Callisto it was the major metropolis of this world. Nobody knew exactly how many people lived on Callisto since most of them would just show up unannounced and start a new life there, but estimates put the figure in the very low five digits. There was a central government. However, their power to uphold the law was almost nonexistent. As a result, no right minded decent people wanted anything to do with Callisto.

For criminals and outlaws, on the other hand, it was a safe haven. If the law was after you and you could make it to Callisto, you were safe. Interplanetary police turned a blind eye. It was a relief for all the good people of the solar system that all these undesirable people flocked to Callisto and stayed there.

Finding the Elvis Presley Hotel and Whorehouse wasn't hard. It was on Ronald Reagan Street, right between James Dean's Hitman Agency and Liz Taylor's Quality Passport Forgeries. It was one of the many unassuming shabby little buildings in New

York City. It wasn't really much of a hotel, more the latter, with a lounge downstairs and a few rooms upstairs for entertaining the clients. Florina and Zsombor stepped inside and were greeted with winks and smiles from a group of hookers hanging out in the lounge.

"You guys wanna party?" asked one of them with a seductive smile. "My specialty is couples, you know?"

"Thanks, sweetie," said Florina. "But we're here looking for Frank. Do you know where Frank is by any chance?"

"Oh Frank, of course, dear. Frank's upstairs with Marilyn Monroe right now. They've been up there for a while now, so they'll probably be down soon, but then again Marilyn likes to take her time, so who knows? They might stay up there all day," laughed the hooker.

Florina and Zsombor took a seat in the lounge while they waited for Frank to finish the session with a Callistan hooker named Marilyn Monroe.

"Ah, there's Marilyn right now," said the hooker in the lounge after about half an hour and pointed to the stairs where two slutty looking ladies came walking down, one young and one older.

"Then Frank should be down soon too," added Zsombor.

"Obviously, Zsombor," said Florina. "Since she's walking right there next to Marilyn."

"One of those two ladies is Frank?" asked Zsombor in confusion. "Which one is Frank?"

"The old one on the left," said Florina. "You sound confused. Did you think Frank was younger?"

"No, I just thought Frank was a man this whole time," answered Zsombor.

"Why would you think Frank was a man? What gave you that impression?" asked Florina.

Frank spotted Florina and came walking towards them.

"Florina!" cheered Frank. "So glad you made it," she said with a big smile and gave Florina a hug. "This is Zsombor, I assume. Pleased to meet you, Zsombor."

"Pleased to meet you too, Frank," said Zsombor and shook her hand.

"Well, let's not waste any more time with these hookers," said Frank. "Let's go to the lab. Come. My Trabant is parked right outside."

Frank drove them through the most amazing landscape Florina and Zsombor had ever seen. The road went through a forest of fantastic spires of muddy ice, some as tall as skyscrapers. Jupiter was right above the horizon, and Frank explained that since Callisto was tidally locked around Jupiter the mighty gas giant was always in the same spot in the Callistan sky.

The lab was located in a desolate location about half an hour's drive outside of New York City. It was a large building without any windows, just a big metal box with an airlock. When they drove in through the airlock, Florina thought it was odd that there were no other cars there besides theirs.

"Shouldn't there be scientists and lab technicians here too?" she wondered.

"Hey, Zsombor," she whispered to Zsombor. "I'm probably being paranoid, but I have a bad feeling about this. Unzip your pants just in case."

"What?" whispered Zsombor back. "You want to do it here and now? What about Frank?"

"I'll explain later," whispered Florina. "Just open your fly and keep it open."

Zsombor did as Florina said and discretely opened his fly. Frank parked the car, and they all got out. They weren't sure where the samples were packed, so they brought all their belongings into the lab. Well inside the door from the parking bay, it was clear that this was no lab. It looked more like an abandoned warehouse.

"Don't worry about what this looks like," said Frank. "They're coming to set up all the lab equipment tomorrow. Now, let's see those samples."

"Here you go," said Florina and opened one of the bags and gave the samples to Frank.

"Ah excellent," smiled Frank. "And the Sibongile you spoke of?"

Florina went quiet. She suddenly realized she had forgotten the Sibongile on the ship, and the ship was on its way out of the solar system right now. She fell to the floor, banged her fists against the floor, and screamed in agony.

"No no! Mierda!" she screamed. "The fucking algae. I forgot the fucking Sibongile on the ship. That was the most important thing to bring. How can I be so incredibly stupid?"

"Stupid indeed," said Frank. "You're the worst agent this agency has ever seen. I would feel bad doing this to anyone else, but you, Florina, are beyond expendable. You're a liability to the agency that needs to be eliminated. Everyone will be relieved to hear of your passing."

"What do you mean?" asked Florina looking up from the floor.

"Get over in that corner," ordered Frank as she pulled out a gun and pointed at them.

"Frank!" said Florina in disbelief. "What's going on? Why are you pointing a gun at us?"

"I might as well tell you before I kill you both," said Frank. "I've been busting my ass at the agency for forty years, Florina, and I haven't gotten anywhere. I need a big promotion before I retire. More importantly I need to create a legacy. When I return to Earth with your samples, I will have made the biggest contribution in decades. Everyone at Pikpuk will love me. They will put a picture of me in the lobby, maybe even a statue on the front lawn. In a hundred years they will still remember me. You, on the other hand, will be forgotten in a week."

"Frank, are you insane?" asked Florina. "You're going to kill us, so you can take credit for these samples? Do you know how stupid that is?"

"Why exactly is that so stupid, Florina?" asked Frank.

"You might get promoted, and you may be remembered a hundred years after you're dead, Frank," said Florina. "But then what? Do you think they'll still remember you in two hundred years? I doubt it. In a thousand years? Most definitely not, Frank! Who is remembered five thousand years after their death? Very few people, Frank, and you won't be among them. Even the ones

184

with multimillennial legacies will be forgotten one day. Striving to be remembered by people that come after you is just plain silly and pointless. They will be dead too one day, and who will remember you then? And when we're talking about thousands of years, what then?" Florina was trying to talk some sense into Frank's head.

"What about after the human race goes extinct? None of us will be remembered then, Frank. Who will remember you in a million years? Well, I'll tell you who. Nobody, that's who! But you don't have to be remembered. Your life can have a big impact beyond your death if you play your cards right. I'm not talking five thousand years, Frank. I'm talking billions of years. A legacy in the memory of other humans is absolutely worthless in the long run. Zsombor and I got those samples here with your help. We all did something together that can have an impact in a billion years. That's worth much more than some stupid legacy in the memory of other people."

"Save it, Florina," said Frank. "I've heard all that Paramount Obligationist stuff before. I'm sick of being stuck in the same job year after year. I have a few years left to advance my career, and I'm going to do whatever I have to to get ahead before I retire. Now, do you have any last words before I blow you both away?"

"Hah! Kill us if you want. We're not scared of death. We'll all be dead in thirty to fifty seconds anyway. Besides, Zsombor and I made a change, and that's what matters, so shoot away all you want!"

"You might be the worst agent ever, Florina," said Frank. "But your bravery in the face of death is impressive. There will never be another one like you, Florina, but what do you mean we'll all be dead in thirty to fifty seconds?"

185

"She means thirty to fifty years," said Zsombor. "She has a problem distinguishing between short times and short times. Listen, Frank! You seem like a reasonable lady. Perhaps if we promise we won't tell anyone, maybe you can let us go."

"Save your breath, Zsombor. She's not going to let us go," said Florina. "You have to admit though that she looks quite sexy pointing that gun at us, right?"

"What? Are you crazy, Florina?" asked Zsombor. "What are you talking about?"

"Yeah," continued Florina. "Like really sexy and arousing."

"Twelve inches. Forty-five degrees up!" commanded Florina, and Zsombor's new implant instantly complied and emerged massively from his open fly like a cannon ready to fire.

"Wow!" said Frank and blushed as Zsombor's attachment was pointing right towards her face. "I knew I was sexy looking, but this is really flattering, Zsombor."

"Climax maximum load!" continued Florina, and aided by the minimal gravity of Callisto, Zsombor's little robot instantly shot a very big load right in Frank's eyes blinding her temporarily.

"Ah, what the fuck?" yelled Frank. "That's disgusting! What's wrong with you? You fucking degenerate Martian!"

"Quick!" said Florina. "Grab her gun!"

Florina and Zsombor both jumped Frank grabbing her hand to wrestle the gun out of her grip. Frank refused to let go of the gun and tried to shoot at them. In the struggle the gun went off putting a hole in the wall to the outside where air started escaping. They managed to pry the gun from Frank's hand and ran to the hole in the wall to block it before the air escaped the building and they suffocated.

Every school child on worlds like Mars or Callisto, including Zsombor, was taught how to act in an emergency such as this, so without hesitation Zsombor kicked off a shoe, pulled his sock off, and plugged it in the hole to slow the leak to a safe level.

In the commotion Frank took the opportunity to grab Florina's samples. She ran to her car and drove away leaving Florina and Zsombor in the warehouse.

"Frank's getting away with the samples," said Zsombor.

"That's alright," said Florina. "She'll take them back to Earth where they can be analyzed. She'll take the credit and get her picture in the lobby. Who cares? The important thing is that the samples get analyzed. Of course, it's also great that we're still alive. Frank was right about me being a terrible agent, though. I feel so stupid, Zsombor."

"Nonsense," said Zsombor. "You're the best secret agent I know."

"Thanks, Zsombor," said Florina. "I know I'm the only secret agent you know, but thanks anyway. No, I failed so bad. I burned down MILPh. I left the mutated Sibongile on the ship. I forgot to get samples from downstairs at MILPh. Maybe I should consider a career change."

"Well, downstairs at MILPh was all Didgeridick production," said Zsombor. "That was the only thing they made in the basement."

"Wait," said Florina in surprise. "How would you know something like that?"

"I've been delivering Didgeridick from MILPh to my uncle Boldizsar's clients for a living since the publishing industry tanked. You didn't know that? Every day I go to MILPh and pick up boxes of Didgeridick from the basement. Then I deliver them to a list of clients I get from Boldizsar."

"Zsombor!" said Florina and kissed him. "That's fantastic! Do you know what that means, Zsombor?"

"No," said Zsombor.

"That means that by elimination the catalyst must be Didgeridick! And we have a lifetime supply of it right here with us, and it's all thanks to your previous inadequacy. Let's find some Sibongile and run a test. It usually grows in cracks in the wall near the floor."

They both ran over to the wall and started looking. The algae was very common in Martian habitations, and it seemed it was equally common in Callistan ones because Florina found some right away. Frank had taken the useless samples with her, but the Glock was still in Florina's possession, and Florina ran a test right away. She ground the Sibongile sample down with a small amount of Didgeridick and placed the resulting mixture in the analyzing receptacle of the Glock that would analyze the DNA for any mutations.

"Look, Zsombor!" Florina said excitedly. "It's testing positive for a mutation in the exact right location in its DNA."

"And that means it's working?" asked Zsombor.

"We don't know for sure yet," said Florina with excitement. "You see there is a mutation at the right location, but we have to verify that it is the right mutation too."

They waited with great anticipation and impatience for the machine to analyze the mutation. After a minute that felt like an hour, the machine indicated that the mutation was not the right one.

"I'm so sorry, Florina," said Zsombor to comfort her.

"Oh, it's quite alright," said Florina. "This means that it does mutate in the right place, but Didgeridick is not the complete recipe. There needs to be something else present besides Didgeridick. Didgeridick seems to cause the initial mutation that is needed for the final mutation. Maybe something found in the Martian soil, some mineral common to Mars, or perhaps some substance in the Martian atmosphere. The mutation happening is a huge step forward. The missing second ingredient is a small step backwards, Zsombor. Now we know where to keep looking."

They were interrupted by the sound of a car entering the parking bay. They could hear the car roll in and the airlock close.

"Zsombor," said Florina. "It's probably Frank coming back with enforcements to kill us. Quick! Hide!"

They ran to the back of the warehouse and hid behind a crate. The door to the parking bay opened, and they could hear footsteps. It sounded like a group of people, not just a single person. Frank must have gone back to New York City and hired some hitmen, probably from that hitman agency next to the whorehouse. They still had Frank's handgun, of course, but that would be no match against a group of hitmen probably armed with Uzi's.

In a shootout they would run out of bullets in less than a minute, and the hitmen would still have plenty. Even if they didn't shoot them, they could pepper the ceiling with bullets and just take off letting the air escape, so they would suffocate. This was bad, really bad. They both knew this was probably the end. Florina thought real hard to figure out a way out of this pickle, but she came up blank.

"Hey, Zsombor," whispered Florina. "I think this might be it."

"Florina," whispered Zsombor and took her hand. "That's alright. We'd be dead in fifty seconds anyway, right?"

"Zsombor! Florina!" interrupted a very familiar woman's voice in an Australian accent. "Are you fellas here?"

Florina and Zsombor peeked out from behind the crate. It couldn't be? How could she have gotten here? It was Angoona, and with her were Zoltan and Borbala. They were all standing by the door looking around the warehouse for them, but how could Angoona be standing up? After all she was a crawler? Florina and Zsombor came out from behind the crate and happily ran up to greet them.

"I'd never thought I'd be so happy to see you guys," said Florina. "But how did you find us? And how did you get here? And Angoona, how come you're standing up?"

"It's a long story," said Borbala. "After you left Mars, my husband accidentally strangled himself on our wedding night leaving me his entire fortune and his business empire. I'm now the richest human alive. I realized Zoltan might get in trouble for stealing that police car, so we decided to leave Mars and come to Callisto to join all the other outlaws in the solar system. I chartered the fastest ship I could find, and we arrived in New York City just an hour ago."

"And Zoltan got me gyros," added Angoona. "Now I can run and dance. Would you like to see me perform a dance for you? I have downloaded an extensive database of dances. With the gyros Zoltan got me, I can do them all."

"Not now please, Angoona," said Borbala. "We've been watching you dance the whole trip over here."

"But how did you know we were here in this warehouse?" asked Zsombor.

"Easy," said Zoltan. "We went to that place you talked about, the Elvis Presley Hotel and Whorehouse. This hooker named Marilyn Monroe told us Frank was going to take you guys here to kill you and steal your samples, so we hailed a cab and came here as fast as we could. We saw a Trabant like Frank's speeding back towards New York City with only a lady in the driver's seat, so we figured either she killed you, or you chased her off. I'm really happy it was the latter."

"We're even happier about that," said Florina. "She's probably on a ship out of here by now, but that's all right since the samples she took off with are useless. Right after she left we cracked ninety percent of the case. We just need to find out what combined with Didgeridick causes the complete mutation."

"What's that blinking lamp in the ceiling?" interrupted Angoona and pointed to a flashing blue light in the ceiling.

"That's an air leak warning," said Zoltan. "A flashing blue light means the building is leaking air and needs to be repaired. If it has an alarm accompanying it, it's urgent. We should find the leak and fix it, though. There's usually a repair kit somewhere in easy sight," Zoltan said while looking around for a repair kit.

"Ah, there's one on the wall over there. Now we just have to find the leak."

"It's probably the bullet hole over there," said Zsombor. "We plugged it with a sock in a hurry."

"No problem," said Zoltan. "It's part of my training as a Martian police officer to perform emergency air leak repairs. I'll show you all how it's done in case you find yourselves in a similar situation in the future."

The group watched and listened attentively to Zoltan's very educational demonstration.

"First you select a patch like this of the right size," said Zoltan and showed them a pack of adhesive patches of different sizes from the repair kit. "The patch has to be bigger than the hole. In this case it is a very small hole, so we will use the smallest patch. Then we clean the area around the hole like this. Next we remove the temporary plug and stick the patch on the hole. We have to make sure the little vent on the patch is in the middle of the hole. Then comes the most important part. We take this spray can of polyurethane foam from the repair kit. Shake it a few times and stick the nozzle in the vent of the patch. We then spray the foam into the vent. This is a small hole, so just a second of spraying will suffice. The foam now expands and hardens in the hole creating an airtight and insulating plug. Now someone will have to go outside and attach a piece of metal foil to bounce off radiation, but that can wait until the next annual routine maintenance."

"I'm sorry, Zoltan, but did you say polyurethane foam?" asked Florina.

"That is correct, Florina," answered Zoltan. "Polyurethane foam is used as an insulating layer in buildings and city ceilings on Mars, and I'm assuming on other cold off Earth worlds as well."

"Polyurethane! Didgeridick! Yes!" cheered Florina. "Don't you guys get it? Polyurethane is the antidote to Didgeridick. It obviously reacts with it in some way, and it's in every outer wall on Mars and any other similar world! Zoltan, spray me a bit of that foam, will you? Zsombor, get me some more Sibongile."

"Here you go," said Zoltan and sprayed out a small glob of foam on the floor. "You have to wait a few minutes for it to cure before it's solid," he added.

Florina waited for the foam to solidify. Then she broke a small piece from it, ground it together with Sibongile and Didgeridick, placed it all in the Glock's receptacle, and waited. As expected, a mutation had occurred in the right place, but was it the right mutation? They had to wait another nail biting minute for the result.

"It's positive!" yelled Florina when the Glock gave her a positive indication. "Yes! This is fantastic, guys! This is a historical moment. Didgeridick mixed with polyurethane foam causes Sibongile to mutate in the right place. We did it!"

"We're sitting on a lifetime supply of Didgeridick," added Zsombor. "We can grind it all down, dissolve it, and pay someone to coat the inner ceiling of New York City with it."

"Listen you guys," said Borbala. "That's a good idea, and we'll do that, of course, but you're thinking too small. Now here's what I'm going to do. As you all know, I am now fabulously wealthy, and I can afford to do absolutely anything. I am going to buy up every polyurethane foam producer in the solar system and get some scientists to figure out the best way to have Didgeridick added to the mixture. Then every new wall and roof will be a source of life as soon as there's a crack or a hole. Every ship embarking on a distant solar system colonizing mission carries supplies with them for construction of initial habitats, among them polyurethane foam for insulation, and it will be our specially formulated Didgeridick spiked foam."

"This calls for a celebration," cheered Zoltan happily. "Angoona! Give us the happiest dance you've got!"

Angoona jumped to her feet, and to everybody's great joy began performing a Papua New Guinean fertility dance to a soundtrack playing from her built in speaker. The taxi driver who had been waiting in his taxi in the parking bay heard the festive music, so he came in, took a picture of them, and joined the party.

"Hey, Zsombor," said Florina to Zsombor while everybody was enjoying Angoona's very erotic display of Papua New Guinean fertility.

"Yes, Florina," replied Zsombor.

"You know when my flare gun went off accidentally at MILPh on my way out of there and I accidentally burned the place to the ground?"

"Yeah, what about it?"

"I did that on purpose, Zsombor. It was too tempting not to. I saw a tank marked extremely flammable, so I aimed the flare gun at it very carefully and fired."

"You're a completely deranged maniac, Florina."

"It could be worse! I could be normal!"

Paramount Obligationism Manifesto

Human activity is severely destructive to Earth nature. The existence of humanity must be justified by providing benefits to Earth nature.

To ensure the survival of Earth nature beyond the time that the Earth is able to harbor life, Earth life must spread to other worlds.

The human race can and must benefit Earth nature by dispersing Earth life to other worlds.

Spreading of Earth nature is best achieved as a secondary effect of space colonization.

Space colonization and the spreading of Earth biology to other worlds is the paramount obligation of the human race. Of all the endeavors humanity undertakes only space colonization will have a lasting effect; everything else will be erased in the long term. Everything undertaken by humanity must gravitate towards space colonization.

Human activity benefiting space colonization directly or indirectly is valuable and must be encouraged.

Human activity not benefiting space colonization directly or indirectly is a waste of time and a waste of limited natural resources.

Human activity working against space colonization weakens the chance of the human race to ensure the Earth's eco system's interstellar dispersal and long term survival.

We must settle space to justify our existence. This is the only thing that matters. This is the paramount obligation of the human race.